Servant of Fear

Song of the Dark Series

Book Two

BRYN SUDDARTH

Neena
BOOKS

For everyone who ever thought being scared made them weak.

Chapter One

York

It was the first day of the rest of eternity.

It was not going well.

Dark gray clouds brought the windy omen of a storm as Thomas and his crew prepared their ship. They were to depart for Brenton that morning, but the approaching storm would mean tricky navigation through the shallow waters leading to the open sea. Even Fiona, a native of Dufonn, had remarked on the unusual weather.

Fiona had accompanied Thomas to the market that morning for supplies, and Thomas had enough cabills for the five of them to live comfortably during the month-long journey. Now that they had returned to the ship, they hurried preparations to get out of town before they were recognized as a crew of magi aboard a lost Hambleton ship.

Fiona retrieved the self-sailing enchantment from the mast. The tobacco in it was more like fuel than a part of the enchantment, so it needed to be replaced regularly. Faya, Fyavine, and Ametta were below deck, securing loose articles. Thomas was in the captain's cabin at the map table, trying to determine the safest route back to Tinera.

The thought of returning to his hometown of Brenton hung as heavy as the dark clouds outside. Now that Thomas knew his own family, the Hambletons, were infamous for capturing magi and taking their magic away, he had to stop them. As a member of the Hambleton family, he was possibly the only person in the world who *could* do something.

The magi depended on him.

Thomas smoothed out the crinkled map with his hands, eyeing the dotted lines marking each trade route. Before Mariana had rerouted this ship into a school of sirens and killed its crew to give Thomas a working ship, it had been on a course from Chratan to Tinera. Now they were in Dufonn. The route back to Tinera from here was shorter, but the waters were choppier. Thomas had to choose between a long and safe journey or a short and dangerous one. The choice seemed obvious—they had plenty of food and fuel.

Wind whistled around the cabin as Thomas notated the date in the travel journal and calculated the number of days it would take to return home. The ship rocked and creaked against the high winds, and the flame of the cabin's lone lantern flickered from the gusts sneaking into the small room through the crack beneath the door.

A heavy knock pounded against the wooden portal. Thomas expected Fiona to walk in, but it was not Fiona on the other side.

A peacekeeping officer, tall and wide, stood in the doorway, decorated with all the silly ribbons and leather belts that accompanied the uniform of a military man. In his hands he held a magic meter.

"Can I help you?" Thomas asked, glancing past the man's shoulder, trying to determine whether the officer was alone. He could only hope this was a minor matter of forgetting to pay the dock fee, but the magic meter was not a good sign.

"Sir, are you aware that your crew consists of three wanted magi and one unregistered mythical creature?" the officer said.

Thomas raised his eyebrows, peering past the officer's shoulder once again. Thick gray clouds churned in the sky beyond. The man was too tall. He obscured the view of the deck. "Who gave you permission to come aboard this ship?" Thomas asked. "The origin of my crew is no business of yours."

"This ship was reported stolen by Chratanian military, and it is known to be harboring magi, as well as the Hambletons' missing son using the alias *Felix Warren*. Is that you, sir?"

Thomas's mouth fell open as he tried to form a response. "I'm headed back to Tinera, officer. There's no reason for military intervention."

"Is that *you*, sir?" the officer asked again.

Thomas clenched his jaw. "Yes."

The man gave a curt nod. "Were you aware you were traveling with magi, Mr. Hambleton?"

"What difference does it make? They are good people," Thomas said.

"You know as well as I do that unrefined magi are not welcome aboard a Hambleton ship," the officer said.

"Unrefined?" Thomas asked before he could stop himself.

The officer narrowed his eyes. "Since you are a Hambleton, you won't mind if I scan you for magic." It was presented as a question, but Thomas knew it was not.

Thomas stepped back. "That's not necessary," he said. The last time he had been scanned, the light flashed yellow, and the officer assumed Thomas was from a Hambleton ship. A yellow reading meant his magic had been removed.

But Thomas had recently gotten his magic back.

Without waiting for Thomas to comply, the officer pointed

the device at him and pressed a button. The bulb lit up, lighting every surface in the room in brilliant red.

Thomas stared wide-eyed at the officer, not sure what to do. "Um—that thing must be broken," he said, shaking his head. "That can't be right."

"You're not Thomas Hambleton. You've got to be a shapeshifter or something," the officer said.

A shapeshifter. They might not have known to look out for shapeshifters wearing his face if it weren't for the deal he had made with Felix before he left Brenton. Felix, a shapeshifter himself, had traded lives with Thomas and had been caught. Thomas never would have agreed to it if he had known the danger Felix was in.

The man stepped fully into the room, finally revealing the deck behind him was swarming with peacekeeping officers. Thomas's heart sank. His friends had been caught, and he was about to be too. "Wait," Thomas said, taking another step back. "I *am* Thomas Hambleton. You can't arrest me."

"You are not a Hambleton. You're a filthy, lying magus."

"I am *not* a liar," Thomas said.

The officer pulled a hefty pair of shackles from his belt and moved across the cabin toward Thomas. Thomas waited for the officer to round the side of the map table before he darted around the other side and ran for the door.

Thomas emerged into the icy morning air, hoping to slip past the other officers unnoticed. If he could find someone who believed him, he could get his friends out of this. Ivan York knew who he was. If he could get back to the peacekeeping station and speak to Ivan, he could make this right.

A firm grip around his arm stopped him in his tracks and yanked him to the middle of the deck. Another officer had caught him easily, holding him in place while the big man lumbered out of the cabin, shackles dangling in one large hand.

Thomas struggled to get away, but these officers were much stronger than him. "Release me!" he demanded, to no avail.

Cold metal clamped tightly around his wrists, the shackles locking his hands together behind his back. The officer pushed him across the deck and down the gangplank, where an angry Fiona stood shackled by her own peacekeeping officer.

"Fiona!" Thomas said. "Are you okay?" The large officer kept Thomas in place.

Fiona smiled sympathetically. "I'm all right, thanks. Are you?"

Thomas nodded. "I'm so sorry."

"Quiet!" the large officer said.

Thomas flinched. Fiona glared at the officer.

"I was afraid for a second—" Fiona started quietly, then let out a shrill laugh and looked away.

Thomas hesitated. "You thought I reported you."

Fiona's smile was gone. When his friends had first learned he was a Hambleton, they seemed okay with it. Now that the night had passed, he could sense their increasing wariness. If any good came of being captured, he hoped it would at least get them to trust him again.

"I'm sorry," Fiona finally said.

"You're right to be cautious," Thomas said.

Fiona smiled at him again, but it didn't last long. "What's going to happen to us?"

"I wish I knew."

"No talking!" Fiona's officer yelled.

Fiona ignored him. "Are they going to take your magic away again?" she whispered.

Thomas shook his head. "I don't know."

"Can't you do something to stop this?" Fiona asked.

"I tried, but they think I'm a shapeshifter. I'm powerless. Can *you* do something?" Thomas asked.

Fiona shook her head. "These shackles suppress our magic."

"No talking!" Thomas's guard said. A sharp pain across his face sent him stumbling to the side, a powerful ache spreading through his jawbone. The officer had struck him.

Fiona struggled against her officer's hold, throwing colorful profanities at the large guard and promising to curse his entire family when she got out of the restraints.

"Fiona, I'm okay," Thomas said. "Don't get yourself into more trouble than you already are." His vision was blurry from the blow. If he weren't immortal, it could have seriously hurt him.

Fiona continued swearing at the officer until two more came down the gangplank with a snarling Faya, an irritated Fyavine, and Faya's frightened daughter, Ametta. Ametta's eyes were wide as they darted around the hectic docks. Thomas's heart ached for the young girl, who at only six years old had already been imprisoned for being a magus twice.

"Faya, Fyavine, Ametta . . ." he said in a strained tone. "Are you all right?"

"Haven't you learned your lesson, shapeshifter?" the large guard boomed. "No more talking or you won't make it to Brenton."

Thomas's jaw dropped. He could not believe keepers of the law spoke to human beings this way simply because they were magical. Faya's expression burned with the fire her shackles stifled. Fyavine's usual cheerful attitude was replaced by a flat, angry glare. Fiona was livid. Thomas was simply glad the hateful remarks were directed at him and not his friends.

The guards moved the prisoners through the piercing cold city in silence. The dark clouds that had threatened their departure were now dispersing, but it didn't matter. They probably wouldn't be planning a voyage any time soon.

The townspeople shamelessly watched the spectacle of five captured magi like they were animals on parade. It was as if all their humanity was gone now that they were known as magi.

Eventually they reached the peacekeeping office, where just the day before, Thomas, Fiona, and Faya had found the file on Fiona's brother and discovered he had been captured and taken to have his magic removed.

The guards pushed the prisoners through the door at the back of the building. His friends moved through the hall while he trailed behind. One by one, Fiona, Faya, Fyavine, and Ametta were pushed through a heavy wooden door at the back of the hall into a dark room. Just as Thomas was brought to the door, someone called out his name.

"Thomas?!"

The voice was so familiar it made his skin crawl. It made him nauseous. It made him whip around desperately.

Standing at the end of the hall beside the door to Ivan York's office, watching him with surprisingly genuine shock on his pretty face, was Charles Southworth.

Tinera – Two Months Earlier

The horse-drawn coach rumbled along the muddy trail, noisy with the sound of hoofbeats and creaking wood. Felix sat alone inside, still wearing Thomas's fine clothing. He rested his head against the cool glass window, his unseeing eyes passing over the leafy green forest landscape.

He couldn't believe he had been so stupid.

Why had he agreed to trade lives with Thomas Hambleton? Why did he ever think he would get away with it?

And why did he think he could trust a Southworth? Thomas himself had warned Felix not to trust them. It was the only piece of advice Thomas had given him, and he didn't listen. He had taken Thomas's place and proceeded to fall for the same trap that caused Thomas to leave his life behind—he fell in love with a Southworth.

Rebecca Southworth had not responded well to learning Felix was a shapeshifter, and he could not blame her for being upset. She had fallen in love with Thomas's face, not Felix's.

She had promised not to tell the Hambletons about his true identity, yet here he was, on his way to the Hambleton magic rehabilitation camp.

It had taken her less than twenty-four hours to break her promise. When he woke up that morning, Edmund Hambleton asked to speak to him, which should have been warning enough. Felix had only spoken a handful of sentences to the man over the two months he lived as Thomas.

Edmund had carefully explained to Felix that the Southworths were claiming that he was not Thomas, that he was a shapeshifter. Felix denied the accusation. Edmund seemed eager to believe Felix. In an act that Edmund called a formality, he pulled out a magic meter and scanned Felix.

Edmund's reaction to the red light was odd. He looked at Felix as though he were still Thomas and said, "How did you do it?"

Felix believed he had been caught. He tried to reason with Edmund, explaining the deal he made with Thomas, that Thomas chose to leave. The hope on Edmund's face crumbled as Felix spoke.

"Tell me, son," Edmund had said, cringing at the last word. "Were you truly on the Southworth's *Exchange III*?"

Felix confirmed he was.

"That ship is missing. By trading places with Thomas, you sentenced him to death," Edmund said. His tone was accusatory, like Felix himself had planned for the ship to go missing.

Not long after, Felix was injected with a magic-suppressing serum and taken to this coach to be carted away. The guilt of

Thomas's death weighed on his conscience, but a selfish part of him couldn't help considering himself lucky for leaving when he did. If it hadn't been Thomas, it would have been him.

Although Felix tried to fight them, thoughts of Rebecca tormented him on the tiresome journey, until the ache in his body matched the ache in his heart. After several hours of travel, the morning sun had risen high in the midday sky. He didn't know where he was being taken, and he couldn't ask the coachman because both doors were locked and the windows did not open.

Finally, the coach rumbled to a slow stop. Felix pulled aside the dull pink curtains to get a look at his destination. Beyond the glass waited a low brick building with one plain wooden door and two wide, barred windows. A fence at least twenty feet tall stretched far into the forest on both sides. Felix could not see where it ended from inside the coach. Its planks were firmly set together—nothing inside was visible.

The coachman made Felix wait while he entered the building with a letter in hand and eventually returned with a pair of leather-clad mercenaries, who yanked Felix out of the coach and guided him toward the building. He stumbled through the mud in Thomas's expensive shoes.

The guards shoved him into the building and shut the door behind him without another word. The inside was just as plain as the outside. A simple wooden table sat at the center of the room with a set of plain linen clothing atop it. A middle-aged woman with graying hair and a smile too big for her face stood on the other side.

"Welcome!" she said in a tone that did not match the suffocating dread in Felix's chest. "We're happy to have you here."

Felix glanced at the door behind him, wishing for moments ago when he had been outside the limits of this strange place. In the short span of time he had spent taking in his new surroundings, a leather-clad guard had positioned himself at the door to ensure Felix did not try to leave.

He faced the smiling woman again but did not speak.

"We are here to make sure your journey to becoming the best version of yourself is as comfortable and smooth as possible," she said.

"The best version of myself?" Felix asked. He was almost offended at the implication there was anything wrong with this version of him, although he knew there was.

The woman lifted the pile of neatly folded clothing from the table and offered it to Felix. "Everyone should aspire to become the best they can be, don't you think?"

Felix couldn't argue, despite the urge to disagree. "Yes," he said. He took the clothes from her.

"What's your name, dear?" she asked.

"Felix," he admitted, but he suspected she already knew that.

"Lovely to meet you, Felix. My name is Helen." She gestured to the clothes in his hand. "This will be what you wear for the duration of your stay. Everyone here wears the same clothing so that we all recognize one another as equals," Helen said, eyeing his expensive attire.

Felix felt the undyed, scratchy linen in his hands. The outfit was a simple long-sleeved shirt and pants with a pair of thin leather slippers resting on top. "How long will my 'stay' be?" Felix squinted up at Helen.

"That's up to you," she answered. "Some people only stay for a few months, while some people have chosen to stay here for years."

"They *chose* to stay?" Felix asked.

"Yes. You can leave at any time, but I think you might like it here."

Felix turned to the door behind him again, which was still

guarded by the mercenary. "All right," he said. "I'd like to leave now."

Helen laughed like he had made a joke, and he wondered if maybe he had. He obviously would not get out of this so easily. "Give us a chance to show you around first," she said. "Please change into your clothes, and we can start the tour."

Out of options, Felix sighed and began to undress. When he was in his egalitarian uniform, a young man wearing the same dull outfit emerged from a door at the side of the room and took away the expensive attire he had arrived in.

"Are you ready for the first day of the rest of your life?" Helen asked, and then she led him through another door at the back of the room and out into the bright daylight. The tall fence had been shielding a muddy field of dying grass bordered by brick buildings. A large square building sat at the center. People in the same beige clothing milled about, staying close to the buildings to avoid the mud.

Helen shut the door behind them. "Welcome to your new home!" she said, gesturing to their glum surroundings. "These four long buildings are the residential halls, where you'll be staying with those who were most like you. You'll be in the Oleander hall," she said, pointing at the building closest to them on the left. "That's where those who had physical magic reside. Those who were elementalists are in Larkspur." She pointed to the building on their right across from Oleander. "Behind Larkspur is Hemlock, for those who had mental abilities. And across from them is Belladonna."

Felix was acutely aware that she talked about magic in past tense, and that the halls had been named after magic-suppressing flowers. "Who stays in Belladonna?"

"Everyone else," she said before leading him through the field toward the largest building at its center. "This is the dining hall.

You'll have all three meals in here with the other residential halls."

She pointed at a smaller square building hiding deeper within the camp, between Larkspur and Belladonna. A forest of tall trees served as a buffer between the large space that separated the buildings and the fence. It seemed the Hambletons didn't want people staying here to remember they couldn't leave. "That's the library. On the other side between Oleander and Hemlock is the crafting room. At the back of the camp is the temple, where our priestess will guide you through your weekly Pietanist service. She'll be, uh . . ." Helen suddenly seemed uncomfortable. "Absent for the next few weeks."

"I'm not a Pietanist," Felix said.

"Consider it a free lesson on morality, then," Helen said with a smile.

"I don't need a lesson on morality."

"Your day will be divided into parts," she continued. "You will have breakfast at dawn, and then you will go straight to your recreation time in one of those three buildings, or you will be sent to the dining hall to prepare ingredients for the next three meals. Each hall also has dedicated kitchen staff to work during mealtimes. If you stay with us long enough, you might be lucky enough to join them," she said with a wink like they were in on a secret.

Felix didn't say anything, so she continued, "After recreation time, you will have lunch. After lunch is free time, where you are free to walk around outside as you please."

"And we can come and go from the grounds?" Felix asked. It was the only way the term *free time* would make sense.

Helen laughed again. "Yes, soon you will. Dinner comes after, and then bedtime at sunset. Let's introduce you to your hall leader," she said, heading toward Oleander.

The exterior door led directly into a long room lined with

beds that sat perpendicular to each side wall. Beside each bed was a small wooden stand with two drawers. A set of wooden double doors waited at the back of the room.

Many people sat on beds, chatting with their neighbors. The beds closest to the entrance were well-loved, and their occupants hardly cared to look up. The ones toward the back were tidy and unused.

Only a few heads turned when Felix entered the room. Most people minded themselves.

"Hello!" a cheerful voice called as they walked in. It came from a young man with brown hair, brown eyes, and a smile that didn't match the room. He wore the same linen clothes as everyone else, but instead of undyed beige, they were a sickly gray. He approached Felix and Helen, extending his right hand toward Felix. "My name is Matthew. I'll be your hall leader. What's your name?"

Felix shook his hand. "Felix."

"It's nice to meet you, Felix!" He turned to Helen. "I've got it from here. Thanks, Helen."

She nodded. "Felix, if you ever need anything, don't be afraid to ask Matthew. He's here to help you. We're all friends here."

"All right."

Helen seemed satisfied with his answer, so she left Felix alone with his new hall leader and their many, many roommates.

"Isn't she great?" Matthew asked.

"Sure," Felix said. This camp made him uneasy, and the smiles Helen and Matthew refused to put away only worsened the feeling.

"Let me show you where you'll be sleeping," Matthew said, striding the length of the room.

Felix shambled along behind him until they stopped halfway down, where the empty beds began. "You'll take the first empty bed, which appears to be . . . this one!" he said, pointing to a neatly laundered bed on his left. "The communal bathroom is through the double doors in the back. I'll let you know when we're heading to dinner."

Felix gave a nod, feeling like he would be sick.

"Let me know if you need anything in the meantime, okay?" Matthew said, patting Felix on the shoulder before returning to his own messy bed.

Felix numbly sat down. The volleyed whispers around him seemed a lot sharper than they had been when he walked in. The residents' eyes followed his stiff movements.

A woman with black hair sat on the bed beside Felix's, fiddling with the hem of her shirt but refusing to look up at him.

"Hey," Felix greeted her. "I'm Felix, what's your name?"

"Jasmine," she said with a tight smile.

"Nice to meet you," he said. She gave a curt nod but said nothing, so Felix continued, "Everyone in here has physical base magic?"

Jasmine's brown eyes widened. She nodded again.

"I'm a shapeshifter. What kind of magic do you have?" Felix pried.

She swung her legs over the bed and stood up. "I'm sorry, Felix. I just remembered I have to, uh . . . go. I'll see you later."

Felix watched her leave, trying to figure out if he had said something wrong. As far as he was aware, it wasn't rude to ask about another person's magic. Everyone here was a magus, after all. But maybe Jasmine thought it was rude.

Felix met the eyes of another young woman in the bed next to Jasmine's, but she looked away the moment he caught her gaze.

Something was very off about this place.

Chapter Two

What was Charles doing here? Why would Charles need to speak to Ivan? He should have been on his way back to Brenton by now, comfortable in his private quarters on a Southworth ship. He should have been anywhere but the same Dei-damn hallway as Thomas.

"Excuse me, Officer!" Charles shouted, strolling confidently through the hall toward Thomas and his captor. "Do you have any idea who that is that you've got handcuffed like some common scoundrel?"

"I know who he claims to be," the officer said.

"And you've chosen to keep him in shackles." It was not a question; it was an accusation.

"Who are *you?*" the officer retorted. "Why should I listen to some skinny little rat tell me who I can arrest?"

Charles reached in his pocket and swiftly withdrew the silver cigarette case Thomas had returned to him the night before. He popped it open and pointed to his name engraved inside.

"Charles Southworth. I'm sure you recognize the name, officer, and I'm afraid *I* would recognize my own archrival on any continent."

The officer paled at the sight of Charles's name but recomposed himself quickly. "If he's your archrival, then why do you care if he's handcuffed?"

Charles placed the cigarette case back in his pocket. "I suppose I consider him something of a friend as well," he said with a careful smile, deliberately not looking at Thomas. It wasn't until that moment Thomas realized he hadn't looked away from Charles at all since spotting him. He forced himself to look at his feet instead.

"If you're so certain he's your *friend,* maybe you can explain why he scanned red on the magic meter," the officer argued.

"What are you saying, Officer? You think he's a shapeshifter?" Charles asked.

"That's exactly what I'm saying. He's a charlatan."

"*You're* a charlatan," Charles snapped, "masquerading as a peacekeeping officer, but you can't even use basic logic to understand that a shapeshifter would shift back into himself while wearing magic-suppressing shackles. Or did you use regular, unmagic shackles? Surely you wouldn't be so careless with a *magus.*"

Thomas looked up again, shocked Charles was defending him with such vehemence after Thomas had basically said he didn't want Charles in his life anymore.

The officer was stunned into silence. He stammered a few times before finally saying, "I'm so sorry, Mr. Hambleton. My meter must be broken, as you said. My apologies."

A metallic click and the relief of cool air against Thomas's wrists told him he was free. He rubbed his wrist. "Thank you, Officer. Now that you know your meter is simply broken, you can free my friends from the holding cell as well," Thomas said.

The officer's deference from being berated by Charles quickly disappeared. "Your 'friends' all have arrest warrants. It would be irresponsible of me to release them. Don't push your luck," he said, and he disappeared into the dark doorway.

"Damn it," Thomas muttered to himself, watching the heavy prison door separating him from the magi he promised to protect. He didn't know how to get them out without trying something similar to the jailbreak in Chratan.

"Are you all right?" Charles asked, placing a gentle hand on Thomas's arm.

Thomas turned to look first at Charles's hand, then his face. Thomas hated the way his heart beat a little faster at the sight of Charles. He hated Charles's golden hazel eyes and the dark brown hair that fell over his perfect face, which he also hated.

"Yes. Thank you for helping me. Can you convince them to let my friends go too?" Thomas asked.

Charles smiled, and Thomas had to look away. "I don't have much influence in that realm, but I think it's something *you* could easily achieve as a Hambleton."

Thomas shook his head and carefully removed Charles's hand from his arm like it was a dangerous creature that would strike if he moved too fast. "I don't know how to do that. I've never been good at using my social status to be shitty."

Charles furrowed his brow and laughed. "It wouldn't be shitty. You would be helping your friends. Do you think what I just did was shitty?"

Thomas shrugged. "A little."

Charles raised his eyebrows. "I think what you meant to say was, 'No, Charles, you're my hero. Thank you for rescuing me from that big scary man.'"

Thomas glared at him, but Charles's smile only widened. "Shut up, Charles," Thomas said, shaking his head.

"All I'm saying is that you have more power than you seem to realize, and you could do a lot of good if you learn how to wield it," Charles said.

"My name is a curse, and I don't want anything to do with it."

"Thomas, no—" Charles started, but he was cut off when Ivan York strolled up behind him.

Thomas had only seen Ivan yesterday, but his entire world had changed since then. Yesterday felt like years ago. Ivan folded his arms behind his back and scrutinized Thomas with his dark brown eyes. "Mr. Hambleton, did I hear Officer Clemens say that you scanned red?"

Thomas's mouth fell open, but no words came out. He shook his head until he found something to say. "No sir. Green—I mean, yellow. Or, uh . . ." Thomas wasn't sure how much Ivan knew about his situation, and he had forgotten to consider that before speaking.

From the corner of his vision, Thomas saw Charles turn away to grimace. Thomas ignored him. He did not need Charles to tell him what he already knew—he was a terrible liar.

Ivan narrowed his eyes. His gaze darted from Charles back to Thomas. "You got your magic back," Ivan said.

Thomas froze, unable to look away. "N-no. You heard the officer—Officer Clemens—his meter is broken."

"It's not broken," Ivan said. "How did you do it?"

"I'm not a magus. Don't be ridiculous." Thomas finally gained his bearings in the conversation. "I'm Thomas Hambleton."

Ivan kept his shrewd gaze on Thomas. "I won't tell your parents. Just tell me how you did it."

"Yes, you will—I mean—you *would*. If I were a magus," Thomas said. "You've imprisoned my friends for being magi. Why wouldn't you do the same to me? If—if I were the same. Just because of my name?"

"Relax, Hambleton," Ivan said.

Somehow, he did. The grip of anger around his chest

loosened. He took a deep breath and exhaled, mildly embarrassed at his anxious stammering.

Charles watched him with wide eyes and lowered eyebrows, his mouth agape.

"If you know something that could turn the tide, Thomas, that's quite serious," Ivan said.

"I don't know anything," Thomas said carefully.

"Right. But if you did, the entire world could change. You understand your place in this conflict, don't you?"

Thomas couldn't figure out why Ivan's phrasing didn't seem right. Ivan almost seemed like he *wanted* Thomas to stop his parents from taking magic away.

"Commissioner York," Charles said quietly. "Are *you* a magus?"

"I did not say that," Ivan said quickly, shooting a stern look at Charles. "I've no idea why you would accuse me of such a thing."

Charles shrugged. "I've *never* been able to tell Thomas to relax without him completely losing his temper. It could only be the workings of magic."

Thomas rolled his eyes. "Maybe because *you* choose to say it when I'm already pissed at you."

Charles raised his eyebrows. "Right, my mistake. Because moments ago when you were yelling at him, you were just having a calm, friendly conversation?"

Thomas had had enough of Charles's smug face, so he moved his attention to Ivan and suddenly remembered something from the day before. When he, Faya, and Fiona had snuck into Ivan's office, Ivan had somehow known Fiona was there even though she was invisible.

Charles was right.

"You *are* a magus," Thomas said quietly. "Why are you hurting your own people?"

"I am not a magus," Ivan said.

"Right. Me neither," Thomas answered. Charles snickered.

Ivan watched the two of them levelly. "Aren't you curious why your ex-boyfriend is here, Thomas?"

Thomas froze, and Charles stopped laughing. They exchanged a brief look, but Charles looked away first. "Yeah, actually . . . Why *are* you here?" Thomas asked.

Charles narrowed his eyes at Ivan before answering. "Negotiating passage home. My ship left without me."

"Why? What happened? Are you all right?" Thomas asked.

A shadow of a smile crossed Charles's face. "Yes. Thanks for the concern," he said with a wink. "None of the Southworth ships will let me on board. I suspect my father told them to leave me here."

"That's awful . . ." Thomas said. "Gods, your father is the worst."

"Yeah . . ." Charles rubbed his neck and looked at Ivan again. "What kind of magus are you, Commissioner York?"

Ivan's expression tightened as he narrowed his eyes at Charles. "Drop it, Southworth."

Charles shrugged. "Fine. I suppose you can let us go back to Brenton with our suspicions."

"Why would you bother mentioning it at all? You have no proof. Besides, I could do just as much damage to you, Thomas," Ivan said, directing his gaze at Thomas. "Surely, we can rely on each other's discretion regarding this sensitive matter."

Ivan was right, and Thomas was inclined to leave it at that. What good would it do to tell his parents that Ivan was a magus? It would simply be a bad thing to do to another magus.

Charles shot a pointed look at Thomas that he did not understand. Thomas stared stupidly back until Charles rolled his eyes and turned to Ivan again. "Do you really think Thomas's own parents would imprison him? He doesn't have much to lose, but you have a lot at stake. If you let his friends go, we won't tell anyone."

Thomas did not understand how Charles expected him to figure that out from just a look, but he was grateful Charles happened to be in this hallway. He was saving Thomas a lot of trouble.

Ivan's calm demeanor tensed. "I know for a fact that they would. I'm not letting the prisoners go. That would draw far more suspicion than a rumor from a couple of disreputable boys."

Thomas crossed his arms. "I'll see you at the camp, then."

Ivan's eyebrows shot up. Thomas did not expect this reaction, but he shouldn't have been surprised blackmail worked. It was Charles's idea, and Charles was a Southworth. The Southworths knew about blackmail.

"Fine," Ivan said briskly. "I'll tell the captain to let them on board as crew. You and Southworth will have to show them the ropes, so to speak."

Thomas whipped his head around to look at Charles. "What?!" he demanded.

Charles also seemed surprised by this. "Um—yeah, what?"

"I told you that you would be on a Hambleton crew, Southworth," Ivan said. "It's the only ship going back to Brenton that will take you. It's not a Southworth ship nor is it truly a Hambleton ship at the moment, since it's under command of peacekeeping forces until your captain takes over."

"Can't he wait for the next one?" Thomas asked.

"He might be here for a while," Ivan answered. "Every Southworth ship captain refuses to let him aboard, and I doubt a Hambleton captain would let a Southworth aboard."

"You can tell them *I* said it was okay," Thomas said.

"Oh, *now* you're fine with using your name to get what you want," Charles grumbled.

Thomas scowled at him. "You're a pain in the ass. Aren't there other merchants heading to Brenton? It doesn't have to be a Hambleton ship."

"Thomas," Ivan cut in. "Charles's help is much needed on your crew. There aren't enough people to make a skeleton crew as it is, but with Charles there will be. Not even your friends will be enough due to their inexperience."

"I will pay you to put him on a different crew," Thomas said. "Our ship had a self-sailing enchantment attached to it, anyway. Why can't we just use that?"

"Magic? On a Hambleton ship?" Ivan asked as if that were enough of an answer.

"Yes. Magic. On a Hambleton ship," Thomas said.

"Don't be ridiculous," Ivan said. "Besides, I suspect you don't have a single cabill on you."

Thomas patted his pockets before remembering he had spent his money that morning on supplies for the trip. "I'll send you money when I get back to Brenton."

Charles sighed from beside him. "You really want me off the crew that badly? I won't bother you."

"Yes you will," Thomas said.

"I promise I won't," Charles said. "I just want to go home."

"Why?" Thomas asked.

Charles was quiet as he held his steady gaze on Thomas. After a moment, he looked away.

"I'm sorry," Thomas said quietly. "It's fine."

"I have nowhere else to go," Charles said.

"I know."

"Perfect," Ivan said. "Your captain will meet you at the ship in an hour, Charles. Don't be late. Thomas, may I speak with you privately?"

"Okay," Thomas said.

Charles patted Thomas on the back twice, gave him a wink, and walked away. It was a complete flip of his attitude seconds ago, and it was suddenly clear Charles was just being manipulative during the conversation with Ivan. Thomas clenched his teeth as he watched Charles walk away, his fury growing with every step Charles took.

Ivan approached the door to his office and held it open for Thomas. The room was the same as it had been the day before—a wide mahogany desk and a high-backed chair. Two visitor seats sat in front of the desk.

"Have a seat," Ivan said, gesturing to the chairs as he took his own seat behind the desk.

"No thank you. I have to be somewhere in an hour," Thomas said.

Ivan smirked. "I won't keep you."

"How did you know I was a magus? Why didn't anyone tell me?" Thomas asked.

Ivan folded his hands together and watched Thomas carefully before speaking. "You deserve the truth. I would have shared it with you had your boyfriend not blackmailed me, but I suppose there's nothing I can do about that now."

"He's not—" Thomas shook his head and sighed. "You wouldn't have let my friends go if he hadn't."

"Fair enough," Ivan said, leaning forward again to place his elbows on his desk. He lowered his voice. "I want you to know that everything I have done for your family has been purely out of the necessity of self-preservation. I do not agree with many of their beliefs, but if I refused to help, I risked exposing myself."

Thomas nodded but said nothing.

"I have met many magi who have had their magic removed, and I have seen what it does to them, you included. I never imagined there was any hope. I need you to tell me how you got it back," Ivan said.

"You wouldn't believe me," Thomas said.

"Try."

Thomas thought back to the encounter with Tetra in her temple. He had to die to get his magic back. How could he explain that?

"A god fixed my soul," Thomas said.

Ivan narrowed his eyes. "Which god?"

"The god of the ocean. Mariana."

Ivan nodded and looked away, rubbing his chin. "Do you know where magi are being sent?"

"No," Thomas said, taking a step forward. This was it. He was about to learn what he had been dying to know.

"The other side of Mount Baine. If you can figure out how to share your cure with others, that's where they'll be," Ivan said.

"Mount Baine?" The mountain that loomed over Brenton. How could such a huge problem be so close to Thomas his entire life and he never knew about it?

"You have to help the magi, Thomas," Ivan said.

Thomas suddenly felt suffocated. How could someone as powerful as Ivan York be asking *him* for help? "Why can't you help them?"

"Why would I do that?" Ivan asked with a polite smile.

"You just asked for my help. You want them to be free," Thomas said.

"Maybe," Ivan admitted, "but I am not willing to risk my own life over it. Do you realize how often I communicate with your parents? Do you know how many magi I have sent over to Tinera?"

Nausea sat heavy in Thomas's stomach. This man was a magus in a position of power, but he was doing nothing to help. "Do you have any idea how much I've suffered? Do you have any idea how it *feels*?"

"I do."

"How could you possibly know?" Thomas's voice rose

alongside his anger. "You don't care at all! You're actively working against magi, and you *are*—"

"That's enough," Ivan interrupted.

The overwhelming anger inside Thomas cooled. He took a seat, ashamed once again he couldn't control his anger.

"Have you ever heard of empathic magic?" Ivan asked calmly.

Thomas shook his head. "What is that?"

"Empaths are magi who can feel and control other people's emotions. It's a very subtle form of magic, but it can be very effective if used properly."

"You're an empath?" Thomas asked.

Ivan frowned, once again glancing at the door behind him. "I did not say that."

Thomas crossed his arms and leaned back in his seat. Why couldn't anyone give him a straightforward answer? "So, you *do* know how it feels?"

Ivan examined his hands folded on the desk in front of him. "I'm not proud of the things I've done. I'm not a hero. I'm a survivor."

"I'm not a hero either," Thomas said, "but I'll be damned if I let another human being lose their soul. You should be ashamed."

Ivan looked into Thomas's eyes, and Thomas was overcome by guilt. He looked away, quickly realizing Ivan was using magic on him.

"Stop that," Thomas said.

Ivan's eyebrows rose, but Thomas felt the guilt ease away. "I'm aware of who I am. You don't need to scold me. However, I am tired of hiding and I would like this era to meet its end. If you ever need any help, you know where to find me," Ivan said. "You may go. I'll have your friends meet you out front."

Thomas left the room without another word.

When he made it outside, the storm had returned.

TINERA

Felix quickly learned that "recreation time" was anything but recreational. It was their nice name for unpaid labor and brainwashing. Recreation was the most tedious four-hour stretch of the day, and Felix dreaded it. So far, Felix had been to the library, the prep room, and the crafting room. They were nothing like he expected.

Talking was not permitted in the library. Everyone was required to read, but the only reading material in the entire camp was anti-magic propaganda. When Matthew caught him looking around the room instead of reading the offensive literature, he received a "demerit." When Felix asked what that meant, he was only told he didn't want to receive three.

Crafting was four hours of sewing or mending clothes, shoes, and bedsheets. He somehow did not receive a demerit in the craft room, despite his shoddy work.

The prep room was the furthest thing from recreational. It took place in the dining hall's kitchen. They spent their time chopping vegetables for the horrible stew they were forced to eat, which was just boiled vegetables in water. They also made dough and baked it inside a large brick opening over the massive fireplace. Felix received another demerit here for cutting his finger while chopping vegetables, which he argued was unfair. He hadn't cut himself on purpose. It fell on deaf ears, as did his question about what would happen when he received a third demerit.

Felix had not yet experienced the fourth recreational rotation —the temple. Two weeks passed, and still nothing. He was told it would happen every four days, but their priestess was unavailable.

Finally, Matthew announced they would begin their temple services again. Felix tried to mentally prepare himself, worried he would be tricked into receiving his third demerit. His hall leader pulled him aside after breakfast on the day they were to go to the temple. "Felix," Matthew said, "you have two demerits now, and it has only been two weeks. The priestess has asked me to talk to you and ask that you please not make a scene today. Can you be on your best behavior for her?"

"Make a scene? Why would I do that?" Felix asked.

Matthew shook his head. "Please don't argue. Just tell me that you can do this."

"I won't make a scene," Felix said with a shrug. He didn't think he had made a scene at all yet, and he was irritated some woman he had never met felt the need to request he be on his best behavior based on arbitrary demerits.

Matthew smiled. "Good. Let's get going, shall we?" He walked off without waiting for an answer.

Felix begrudgingly trailed behind the rest of the hall as they made their way to the small square building called the temple. It looked nothing like a temple from the outside, but upon seeing the interior, he understood.

Rows of pews sat before an elevated stage with a lectern at the center. As the residents of Oleander took their seats, Felix chose one at the very back of the room on the edge of the pew. More people filed into the room behind him and created a noticeable boundary of empty space around him.

He had found it difficult to make friends. Whenever he tried to make conversation, he received curt responses and little acknowledgment that he was speaking. He didn't understand how anyone else had done it. Everyone here was so closed off.

But this was suspicious. Nobody else in the temple had empty space around them. They disliked Felix, and he did not know why.

Matthew stepped up to the lectern, and Felix resisted the urge to roll his eyes. Matthew led all of their recreational activities. His enthusiasm about the camp was sickening.

"Good morning, Oleander!" Matthew said, as he did at every recreation. "Our priestess will be here momentarily. Questions are encouraged, but only those of a religious nature will be answered. All other inquiries will be handled punitively."

Felix searched the other faces in the room, wondering how they could all pretend this was a normal thing for someone to say in a temple, which was supposed to be a holy place of worship to a kind deity. Their expressions remained blank.

"Ah—good morning, Catherine!" Matthew said with a big smile.

Catherine?

A breeze blew past Felix as a woman walked between the pews wearing a flowing black dress with long sleeves. A tight swirl of pale blonde hair sat on her head, and she walked with haughty authority. Felix watched her with curiosity as she took Matthew's place at the lectern and turned around, wearing a pleasant smile. "Good morning, everyone," she said, loudly enough for the small room to hear her.

All the air was sucked from Felix's lungs at the sight of her. This wasn't just a priestess. It was Thomas's mother, Catherine Hambleton.

Felix stood up before he could stop himself, clutching the back of the pew in front of him tightly. He opened his mouth to speak, but he was at a loss for words.

Catherine's bright blue eyes immediately fixed on him and narrowed. "Sit down," she said. The adoration and charm in her voice from moments ago was gone.

Felix remained standing until he remembered Matthew's

warning. Now he understood. He wondered if these people knew who she was. Judging by the way they all called her "the priestess" or "Catherine," he suspected they didn't.

Felix lowered himself back down.

Catherine's fake smile returned to her mousey face. "Thank you."

Throughout the sermon, her eyes scanned her audience with love. When she met Felix's gaze, the love died. She hated him, and he couldn't blame her. He was the reason her son was dead.

Catherine's eyes met his more frequently as the service progressed. Her tone became stiff, and her movements jerky. Finally, she stopped and apologized to the hall, stepping aside to whisper something to Matthew. When she returned to the lectern, her nose was red, and her eyes were watery.

People turned in their pews to watch as Matthew approached Felix and leaned down to whisper, "Catherine has asked me to remove you from the temple."

Felix tried not to squirm in his empty pew. He hated that he was responsible for the loss of a life, even if it was a Hambleton. Thomas was a person. He had accepted Felix despite his magic, and they had helped each other. At least, Felix thought they had. If anyone bothered to ask, he would have dared to say that Thomas was his friend.

But no one cared. To them, Felix was just a murderer.

Felix nodded and stood, following Matthew out of the temple while his peers watched. They waited outside for the rest of recreation time. Matthew tried to make small talk, but Felix was not interested in speaking to someone who believed magic was immoral, even if it was a fellow magus.

"Felix." Matthew's lowered voice got Felix's attention. It wasn't a voice for small talk. "I tried to stop the rumors from spreading. I'm sorry."

"What rumors?" Felix asked.

Matthew tilted his head with a tentative smile. "The rumors that you killed Catherine's son. Everyone knows you were the reason she's been gone."

"I didn't kill him," Felix said with a tightness in his voice he did not expect.

Matthew sighed through his nose. "You were involved, though. And everyone knows. I know it hasn't been easy for you to adjust, but I truly am trying to make it easier. Please bear with me."

Felix didn't say anything. Matthew clearly knew Catherine well enough that he would side with her over a new prisoner. Catherine might have even instructed Matthew to make Felix's life *more* difficult. In fact, the only way that rumor would have started was if someone on the outside brought it in, and Felix hadn't said a word about Thomas.

Things were starting to make a little more sense.

Chapter Three

Hard drops of rain buffeted Thomas's skin and dampened his heavy overcoat as he waited outside the peacekeeping office for his friends to be released. It seemed the longer he waited, the harder the storm got. Thomas considered waiting inside, but his anger toward Ivan kept him standing in the cold.

After ten minutes, the door finally opened. A tall man stepped through and settled his searching gaze on Thomas. He had long black hair and dark eyes, and he was probably around the age of Thomas's parents. He had the weathered skin of a man who spent many years at sea, and he hardly seemed to notice the bruising rain.

"Hambleton," he said in a low, gravelly voice.

"Yes?" Thomas asked, not sure who this man was or why he was addressing Thomas.

"My name is Alastair Caldwell. I'll be your captain on the expedition back to Brenton." He extended a rough hand.

Thomas carefully reached his own hand forward and was immediately faced with the reality of his smaller size. Caldwell's large hand enveloped his in a firm grip. When Caldwell released him, Thomas resisted the urge to shake out the cramp in his hand.

"Nice to meet you," Thomas said.

"Likewise," Caldwell said with a nod. "I've worked for your parents for years, but I'm afraid you and I have never crossed paths."

Thomas nodded and glanced at the door, uncomfortable knowing Captain Caldwell had been associated with his family for so long. It could only mean he was prejudiced against magic too. "Has Commissioner York released my crew yet?" Thomas asked.

Caldwell crossed his arms and looked at Thomas over his large nose. The rain rolled off him as though making way for him. "York told me about your situation. They'll be waiting on the ship."

"No. I'm staying here until they come out," Thomas said.

"They've already been taken to the ship, Hambleton. We've got no time to waste," Caldwell said. "Don't get yourself worked up; we'll be sailing with an empty brig."

"As we should," Thomas remarked. "Thank you, Captain."

Caldwell nodded once. "We sail at the hour, Hambleton. Don't make me wait," he said, and then he took off into the rain-blurred city streets.

Thomas took a deep breath and exhaled slowly. He was inclined not to believe the captain, but why would he lie? Ivan had a lot at risk if he didn't let Thomas's friends go. Thomas had not been bluffing. He would not hesitate to turn Ivan in after learning he betrayed magi.

Thomas headed for the docks along a different route than the captain had taken. He did not want to risk running into him again. When Thomas had sailed on the Southworths' *Exchange III*, the captain was also a gruff older man, but he never looked down at Thomas the way Caldwell had. And they weren't even at sea yet.

Thomas pushed aside thoughts of his former captain. It would do him no good to compare the dead to the living, and it was not easy to think about his old crew.

He strolled alongside the cold, dark rocks this depressing country considered a beach. The inky sea churned in the distance, but the rain above slowed to a light drizzle.

A particularly large wave slid over the rocks, daring to approach Thomas's feet. As it retreated, it left a tall, translucent woman made of water in its path.

"Good morning, Thomas!" Mariana said with a smile. She was the same dark gray as the water on the horizon beneath the rain clouds. Her long hair tumbled down her back in white-capped waves.

"Hi, Mariana." Thomas stopped to speak to her. "Do you need something?"

"I need to talk to you about the deal you made with Tetra. I've been thinking about it a lot."

Thomas hadn't even begun to process his deal with Tetra. Promising to damn some poor soul to eternity with the god of evil, death, darkness, and fear was serious, but it was the price for saving the mermaids. "Okay . . ." Thomas said, waiting for her to continue.

"It worries me. If you find her a servant, you might die," Mariana said.

"I can't die," Thomas reminded her. "I'm immortal now."

"Yes, it seems that way." Mariana squinted down at him through the rain, but not the way Caldwell had. She seemed . . . nervous? "But there is something I didn't tell you."

Thomas got the feeling he didn't want to know what she had to say. "What is it?"

Mariana sighed and looked up at the sky as she spoke. "The Pantheon is a complicated organization of gods who frequently clash due to the entwined nature of our existence. Naturally, we often have territorial problems, similar to what I experienced with Tetra and the sirens. To make a very, very long story short, we've recently created a solution to the endless squabbling."

"Okay . . . ? What's the solution?" Thomas asked.

"Godservants," Mariana said.

Thomas didn't feel his question had been answered. "How?"

"We've been allowed one immortal servant to represent us in battle whenever we take issue with another god. This means that you will have to battle to the death if I ever have a conflict with a god who also has a servant."

"*What?!*" Thomas would not have agreed to immortality if he knew it meant he would have to kill people.

Mariana nodded. "If Tetra finds herself a servant, she'll use them to kill you. If you agree to help her, you are sentencing yourself to death."

"Why didn't you tell me this before I gave you my soul?!" Thomas asked.

"Why would I? There is no one for you to battle yet," Mariana said.

"That doesn't matter! There will be more people soon!"

"Yes, thanks to you!"

Thomas exhaled angrily. "That's not fair. You lied to me."

"I did not lie to you," Mariana said.

"A lie of omission is still a lie."

Mariana frowned and crossed her arms. "It's too late. You'll just have to deal with it."

"I won't kill anyone," Thomas said.

"You might have to."

"Or what?" Thomas demanded.

"I can make you do things my way if you don't obey me," Mariana said.

Thomas gritted his teeth as anger burned to the surface of his skin. "What does that mean?"

"It means I can control you if I have to, so don't disobey me, and don't find Tetra a servant."

Thomas threw his hands up and shrugged. "Fine. I'll just let Tetra create the sirens again, and your mermaids will suffer until Tetra has drowned enough humans to find the right person to serve her. So, nothing will change, and Tetra will still have her servant, and she'll kill me anyway." Thomas turned away to stumble across the salty rocks in a great effort to distance himself from Mariana.

"Thomas, wait!" Mariana shouted. "Come back here!"

Thomas continued to walk away. He was done speaking to her.

"Thomas Hambleton! Do not walk away from me!" Mariana yelled, much louder this time. Thomas stopped, but not of his own will. He couldn't move his feet. His body turned around and walked directly toward Mariana, stopping firmly in front of her.

Her narrowed eyes were glued to him. He had made her angry, but she had made him angry first.

"Did you *make me* walk over here?" Thomas asked.

"I'm not done talking to you."

"So my autonomy is completely gone?"

"Of course not. You just have to do what I say forever." Mariana crossed her arms. She obviously did not see the hypocrisy in her statement. "You're right. Clearly there is some good to your agreement with Tetra. This could be an advantage for us."

Thomas rolled his eyes. "Oh really?"

"Tetra has given us the ability to choose who will join you in the Pantheon forever. This is good."

"She's not going to accept just anyone I bring her. It has to be someone evil," Thomas said.

"Yes, but the influence we do have will make a big difference." Mariana extended a fist toward Thomas. "Here, I need to give this to you now."

"What is it?" Thomas asked, holding his hands beneath hers.

"Your sword." She dropped a rod-shaped aquamarine crystal into his hands.

Dim blue light sparkled along its geometric ridges as Thomas turned it over. "This doesn't look like a sword to me."

"It looks like that so that you can carry it around without drawing attention to yourself. That's the weapon you will use in duels between servants. It's unbreakable."

"Okay . . . so how do I get it to look like a sword?" Thomas asked.

"Use your intention. It may take a while to get the hang of it," Mariana said.

"My intention?" Thomas asked, staring at the handle. "What does that mean?"

"It's like using magic, but it's not magic. When you intend to use magic, you will. When you intend to produce the blade, you will," Mariana explained.

"I've never done magic before," Thomas said.

"Aren't you a magus?"

"I didn't know I was until you fixed my soul yesterday."

"Oh . . . You've got a lot to learn," Mariana said.

Thomas sighed. "Can I leave now, or are you going to possess me again?"

"You can go. Find someone good," Mariana said.

Thomas turned to leave without saying anything else. It would be impossible to find a good person who Tetra would approve of, and who would *want* to be her servant. And whoever Thomas found would have to agree to it.

He decided not to think about it. For now, he needed to get to his ship.

As he walked, he started to feel shaken by their conversation. Being possessed by Mariana had stripped him of control, and she didn't seem to feel any remorse. Mariana had never understood humans well, and her lack of care was a bad omen.

She could do whatever she wanted with him, and he could do nothing to stop her.

Tinera

The days passed slowly. Nobody in Oleander would speak to Felix because of what he had done to their beloved priestess's son. Nobody knew who Catherine really was, and nobody believed him when he tried to tell them she was a Hambleton. They thought he was a murderous lunatic.

At every temple service, Catherine would kick him out halfway through. Felix asked Matthew if he could skip, but Matthew refused. Catherine wanted the spectacle.

One afternoon, Felix strolled around Belladonna and through the long stretch of forest between Belladonna and Hemlock. He tilted his head back to look through the branches of the trees. Pale circular patches decorated the trunks where branch limbs had once swayed in the wind. The lowest branches had been sawed off to prevent residents from climbing to escape. He often wondered how difficult it would be to reach the higher branches.

He lowered his gaze back down when he detected another prisoner in his peripheral vision. No, not prisoner. *Resident.*

Felix froze at the sight of the young woman with pale silvery-blonde hair and gray eyes shiftily scanning her surroundings. He couldn't believe she was here.

He turned around and walked the other way.

"Hey!"

Felix winced and stopped walking. He pivoted to face her, knowing he had been caught.

"Felix?! It's so good to see you!"

He sighed and braced himself as she approached. "Hey, Aella. It's good to see you too."

"How are you?" she asked with the same big, fake smile everyone else in this place wore. Had she fallen victim to their lies?

"I've been better." Felix looked around the camp. "I had no idea you were a magus."

"Yeah, I hid it pretty well, huh?"

"I guess you did. Which hall are you in?" Felix asked.

"Larkspur. Are you in Oleander?" she asked with a narrow-eyed smile.

Felix nodded. "You're an elementalist?"

"Yep! Wind," she answered.

"I never knew that."

Aella crossed her arms and arched an eyebrow. "And I never knew you were a shapeshifter. I had to find out the same way as everyone else."

Felix averted his eyes. He didn't like to think about how his entire hometown learned he was a magus.

"How long have you been here?" Aella asked.

"About a month, but it feels like it's been longer. I—" He stopped himself from bringing up the situation with Catherine. "What about you?"

"A couple years. Ever since the raid."

"What raid?" Felix asked.

Aella's eyes widened. "Oh—um . . . Yeah, I guess you weren't there for that." She tucked a strand of hair behind her ear and examined the trunk of a nearby tree. "After your mother, uh . . . you know . . ."

"Yeah."

"The Hambletons raided New Brook for any other magi. They *saved* us from the brutality of the town."

Felix couldn't help noticing her careful wording. "That's awful. I'm so sorry. Who else was caught?"

"My dad. We were the only other magi in town."

"Your dad is here? That's lucky," Felix said.

Aella scoffed. "No, he converted."

"Oh . . . Sorry." When magi converted, they agreed to have their magic removed in exchange for their freedom, but that freedom was really just unpaid labor in a new setting.

Aella shook her head. "I'm not."

Felix wondered if she was genuinely happy for him or if that meant something else. He had never known how she felt about magi, and that didn't change now that he knew she was a magus herself. She might have been ready to convert too. "Well, it was nice catching up. I'm going to go now," he said, walking past her.

"Wait!" She followed him to walk in step beside him. "Don't you want to stick together?"

Felix tried to word it nicely. "Aella, you seem to think we were friends in New Brook."

Aella chewed her lip as she walked, taking a moment to think before she spoke again. "I know that I wasn't very nice to you back home, but I'm—" She shook her head with pursed lips. "I'm trying to change."

Felix stopped and turned to face her. He hadn't expected her to agree.

"I've always liked you, and this place is scary," she added.

"Aren't you lonely here? I know I am, and it would be nice to know I have a friend."

"You may be trying to change, but that doesn't mean we're friends. I don't trust you," he said.

"Why not?" She seemed surprised.

"Aside from the way you treated *me,* I don't like the way you treat animals when there are no people around," Felix said.

Aella squinted at him and smiled. "What?" she asked with a fake laugh. "How could you see the way I act without people around? You're a person too."

Felix held her gaze. "Not always."

Her eyes widened. "Oh, Dei. I have changed, I swear. Please give me a chance. I'm all alone here. You don't want to be alone too, do you?"

"I'm starting to think it's better not to trust anyone," Felix said.

Aella tilted her head. "You can't go your whole life without trusting *someone.*"

"I trusted someone, and it got me here," Felix said.

Aella's silvery brows furrowed in concentration. "Oh no . . . Was it a woman? Did you get your heart broken?" She stuck her lip out in a pitying pout. "What kind of horrible woman would ever think herself better than Felix Warren?"

Felix shot her a glare before shaking his head. It was amazing how quickly she reverted to taunting him. "You haven't changed." He continued walking through the small forest, wishing more than ever he could climb the trees around him.

"No, Felix, I mean it!" Aella said, following him through the speckled shadows of the canopy. She grabbed his hand to stop him. "I think you're great. I always have."

Felix pulled his hand away. "Don't touch me."

Aella lifted her hands in surrender. "I'm sorry. Please, just consider it."

Felix ignored her and looked up at the mangled tree trunks again. Maybe he *could* climb them.

"What are you looking at?" Aella asked.

"Just enjoying the view," Felix said.

Aella looked back and forth between Felix and the tree branches a few times before she gasped. "Oh, I see. You're looking for a way out, aren't you?"

"What? No." Felix looked around to make sure no guards were nearby. Despite the camp's attempts to appear welcoming and comfortable, guards were always patrolling the fence and blocking the door to the main entry building. "You can't say things like that out loud," he whispered urgently. "You'll lose your meal privileges."

"Oh no, not my stale bread," Aella said dryly.

Despite his attempts to fight it, Felix smiled.

"I can help you," Aella said, raising her eyebrows as her smile grew.

"There's nothing to help me with, because I'm not planning anything." Felix frowned at her.

"Right," Aella said with a wink.

"I'm serious."

"Oh, I know you are." Aella looked over her shoulder just as a guard came into view walking along the fence in the distance. The guard eyed them warily. Aella smiled and waved as he passed. When he was out of sight again, Aella leaned close to Felix. "Come with me to my residential hall. We can make a real plan."

"No," Felix said.

Aella pouted. "C'mon, Felix. Don't you want to be free?"

"Yes, but I don't trust you with my freedom."

Aella sighed heavily and muttered something under her breath.

"What was that?" Felix said, despite knowing she hadn't intended him to hear.

She shot him that catty smile he recognized from their youth. "Fine. We don't have to make plans, but it would be nice to have company, wouldn't it?"

As much as he didn't want to talk to Aella, he *had* been lonely. It was hard to spend every day with fifty people who hated him as much as Catherine Hambleton did. Maybe Aella was right. "Okay," he said, "but I'm not trying to escape, and I am not going to talk to you about it."

Aella grinned. "Yay!" She threw herself at him and squeezed tightly. "Thank you, Felix."

Felix grimaced and waited for the embrace to end.

Chapter Four

"Well, well, well . . . Look who finally decided to join us." Captain Caldwell's voice carried over the deck as Thomas scrambled aboard, nearly missing the hour mark. His conversation with Mariana had caused more of a delay than he realized.

The captain was holding some kind of briefing for the crew at the center of the top deck. Five men and Charles stood together, watching the captain and waiting for his command. Only Charles looked at Thomas, wearing an expression that made him wonder if Charles got seasick. The distraction of seeing him momentarily kept Thomas from the horrible realization that explained the look on Charles's face.

Fiona, Faya, Fyavine, and Ametta were missing.

"Captain," Thomas said suddenly, interrupting whatever the captain had been saying.

Caldwell looked at Thomas with that same condescending sneer. "Do not interrupt me while I'm speaking, Hambleton."

His surname sent a ripple of whispers through the small crew.

"We are missing a few hands," Thomas said anyway. "You told me they would be here."

"Are you questioning my integrity?" Caldwell asked.

Thomas stopped himself from saying "yes" and instead asked, "Where are they?"

"They're working the galley," Caldwell said. "I've already given them their instructions. They don't need to hear this. I hope you'll allow me to speak to my crew without interruption again."

The captain's explanation didn't sit well with Thomas. It didn't help that Charles was uneasy too.

Thomas gave a short nod. "Carry on, Captain."

"We've got a long journey ahead of us," the captain projected, drawing his crew's attention back to himself. "We'll be running this ship on a skeleton crew, as you can see. I will not tolerate any nonsense." Caldwell's eyes landed on Thomas and then darted over to Charles. Clearly, the captain was aware of their history.

Charles did not acknowledge the remark, keeping his eyes on Caldwell.

It was strange to see Charles at sea. He did not belong out here. Even beneath the ratty clothes and the messy hair hanging in his face, it was obvious. He stood up straight, keeping his chin high and his wits about him. No other sailor Thomas had met walked or talked with such carefully placed pride. Thomas wondered what it looked like when Charles actually worked instead of sitting around, smoking and gossiping. He couldn't even imagine it.

Thomas knew he should be focused on the captain, but how could he not look at Charles Southworth taking orders from the captain of a Hambleton ship? This was a rare moment in history, something nobody outside of this crew would ever witness.

"Dismissed," Caldwell said.

Thomas hadn't been listening. He had no idea what the captain's orders were. Charles took off to his post without another glance at Thomas. He watched Charles leave, then looked at the captain as if he could figure out orders by the look on the captain's face.

Caldwell gave him one last wary look before strutting into his cabin and slamming the door shut behind him. Thomas was surprised he refused to help his crew when they were shorthanded, but not as surprised as he wished he was.

Thomas didn't need the captain's commands to get a ship out of port. However, he had more important things to worry about. The crew could be down a pair of hands for a few minutes.

Thomas snuck to the hatchway, but before he could drop himself into the dark living quarters, the captain's door swung open.

"Hambleton!" Caldwell yelled.

Thomas jumped and swiveled around, his feet dangling from the edge of the hatchway into the lower deck. "Yes?" he asked, trying to sound innocent despite the damning poise of his body ready to push into the open hatch.

"What do you think you're doing? We need all hands right now."

"I just need to grab something from the living quarters," Thomas lied.

The captain strolled over and pulled Thomas up by the collar of his coat as easily as scruffing a cat. Thomas stumbled back a few steps and shot a bewildered look at Caldwell, alarmed at his strength.

"There is nothing left of yours down there. Get back to work," Caldwell said. "If I see you sneaking away again before the next watch, believe me, your friends will *not* be down there. Galley or otherwise."

"Are you threatening your own crew?" Thomas couldn't believe a merchant ship's captain could be so cruel.

Caldwell narrowed his eyes. "My crew? Never. But sometimes we lose cargo along the way."

It took Thomas a moment to understand what he meant. When he did, anger burned inside him like a fire. "They aren't cargo. They're people."

A heavy bout of rain fell upon the ship, thudding loudly against the wood planks beneath their feet.

Caldwell looked around the dock as it darkened with a heavy hiss of falling water. Any other captain would delay departure in this bad weather, but not Caldwell.

"Get back to work," Caldwell yelled over the percussive rain before retreating to his cabin again.

Thomas clenched his fists and closed his eyes, trying to fight back his anger before joining the rest of the crew. His soul was whole again thanks to Mariana, and now he could feel everything with an intensity he couldn't handle. This anger was too much.

Captain Caldwell was going to throw his friends overboard as punishment, as though they were not people but something that would simply inconvenience Thomas to lose. Was this how all people viewed magi? And because of *his own family?*

It was disgusting.

Thomas found an empty post and got to work prepping the ship for departure to the best of his ability in the awful weather, stuck in his own head. For all he knew, his friends were still at the peacekeeping station. He needed to see them with his own eyes, but he didn't want to risk getting them killed. He couldn't leave the ship to check with Ivan for the same reason. If this ship left without him, his friends would be in peril. Charles might take care of them, but that was not enough.

Thomas would see them in Brenton either way. All he could do was wait.

TINERA

Felix excused himself from his walk with Aella to spend the rest of his afternoon free time in bed, claiming he was going to nap until dinner. Aella reluctantly let him go.

Back in New Brook, Felix had a few friends, but he had never considered Aella one of them. As desperate as he was for companionship in this place, he didn't know if Aella was better than loneliness. She seemed fine during their conversation, but as he remembered more, he became less certain. If he couldn't trust her in a normal setting, he *definitely* couldn't trust her in a place like this.

But if she had been at the camp for two years and believed there was a way to escape, maybe there was.

When Matthew rang the dinner bell, Felix waited for the rest of the hall to clear out before he stood to join them. Outside, his fellow prisoners filed toward the dining hall. But instead of following them, Felix headed into the forest.

His feet carried him through the thick mud and sparse grass while he examined the empty spots on the trees where branches had once been. He had originally brushed off climbing the trees as impossible, but it seemed the most likely method of escape. If even his captors could acknowledge its potential, maybe there was a chance it would work.

He stopped under the shade of a tree, staring through the impossible pattern created by the stark black silhouette of leaves beneath the dimming sky. The tree's branches were too high to reach.

His fingers ran over the ridge of one of the bald patches where a branch had once been. As thorough as they may have tried to be, it would have been hard to saw every tree in this vast forest without becoming careless now and then.

He scanned the trees around him. If he could find just *one* with even a suggestion of a branch left behind, he could scale the trunk and make himself a path to the farthest tree at the edge of the camp. Then he would be free.

Felix began his search, moving carefully between each trunk. He scanned the area intermittently to make sure he was still alone. The forest was quiet, but he couldn't be too careful.

Time was running out. Dinner would end soon, and Felix had felt nearly every tree. Finally, his fingers caught on a small ridge. It didn't protrude even an inch from the trunk, but it was enough.

With the ridge under his fingertips, he pressed his foot against the base of the tree to support himself. In one quick motion, he pulled himself up just enough to graze the lowest branch but fell to the ground before he could grab it. There were no better access points on the tree. There were no lower branches. He would just have to keep trying.

Three more unsuccessful tries left him frustrated. He could only swipe the lowest branch with his fingertips before falling.

He paused and took a deep breath. If he was going to do this, he needed to stay calm and be smart. After his third deep breath, he jumped. He stepped up the trunk and grabbed the branch, swinging his other arm up to keep it in his grip. He pulled himself up until he could swing his leg over to straddle the large branch.

He had made it. He leaned back against the tree, taking a second to catch his breath. Now that he was among the sturdier limbs of the tree, it would be easy going. This was a moment to celebrate, but there was no time to waste.

He nimbly climbed higher into the tree, until he could reach the next tree. It would be difficult making the transition, but he could do it.

Every last branch and leaf rattled as he climbed from one tree to the other. He cringed with every deafening movement. Someone was bound to hear him.

He stilled, waiting for the sound to stop. There was no way he could make it across the sea of trees without someone noticing. His eyes scanned the ground around him, and he found he was no longer alone.

The noise had summoned a patrolling guard, who was searching the area for the source. Felix stayed still, praying to all the gods he wouldn't be seen. The gods must have been angry with him, because the guard looked up and made direct eye contact with Felix.

The guard's eyes widened. "Hey!"

Felix's instinct was to run, but to where?

Did he really need to?

He sat up on the tree limb he had been clinging to and smiled. "Hey," he said.

"What are you doing? Get down from there!"

Felix shrugged. "Why?"

The guard seemed surprised by the question. "Because—" The guard stopped and glanced at the fence, only four more trees away. Felix's plan was obvious, but the guard wouldn't say it out loud.

"Because?" Felix taunted.

"It's dangerous to be up there."

"You don't care about my safety."

The guard crossed his big arms. "Your safety is priority here."

Felix lowered his eyebrows but refused to respond.

"Come down from there," the guard said.

Felix ignored him. There was nothing they could do to stop him now. All of the lower limbs had been sawed off the trees, and they wouldn't dare bring out a ladder. Felix was free.

By the time he made it to a new tree, two more guards were yelling at him to get down, confirming how powerless they were.

Eventually, dinner ended. A small crowd of people formed to watch the spectacle. The guards tried to keep them away, but it only drew more attention. Felix was nearing the end of the tree line. Once he got over the fence, he would no longer be bound by magic suppressants. He could turn into a bird and fly as far as he wanted.

But the gods had other plans for him. In one moment, his fantasy of freedom became a dream as he stepped onto a sturdy-looking branch without taking care to test the full force of his weight against the pliant support. It curved under him, making way for him to fall directly into the arms of his captor. He grasped at branches as he fell, but it was too late.

He tumbled to the ground and fell on his back. The impact of the fall knocked the wind out of him, and the group of magi who had been watching let out a sympathetic groan in unison. The guards were on him in an instant, pulling him up while he struggled to breathe.

He finally took a deep breath while they threatened him. Fear was all they had. If they truly saw the absence of magic as a reward, they wouldn't dare punish him with it.

"Are you happy now?" the original guard asked Felix, hoisting him up from the muddy grass.

"No," Felix said. "I'm still here."

The guard answered him with a displeased grunt, then glanced at the crowd of curious onlookers before dragging Felix away.

One face in the crowd stood out to him. Aella watched him with a hard frown and crossed arms. When their gazes met, she shook her head and rolled her eyes before walking away.

Felix didn't trust her, but maybe he shouldn't have left her behind.

Chapter Five

The storm lasted throughout Thomas's first watch and into the second. Waves battered the ship, sending the crew stumbling across the deck as it rocked back and forth. The cold wind whipped stinging rain into their faces, but Thomas worked through the miserable conditions.

The first watch ended after four exhausting hours. The moment the bell rang, Thomas abandoned his post to head for the galley.

Before he could reach the hatchway, Captain Caldwell stopped him. "Hambleton!" he bellowed through the rain.

Thomas forced his feet to stop moving and whipped around to look at his captain. "What?!" he yelled.

The captain narrowed his eyes and strolled across the rainy deck. "You say, 'Yes, Captain?' Do you understand?"

Thomas shrugged. "What do you want, Captain?"

"Yes, Captain," Caldwell prompted.

"Yes, Captain?" Thomas parroted.

"You're working the second watch. Get back to your post." The captain turned around to return to his warm, dry cabin.

Thomas followed after him through the piercing rain. "But you said I was on first watch. I need to make sure my crew is okay."

"You're a strong sailor. You've been working tirelessly through this storm. I need you up here. Some of the other crew are losing energy and focus, and they need to rest. You don't want to let your crew down, do you?"

"No, Captain. I don't," Thomas said. Working through such a powerful squall would usually leave him just as exhausted as the rest of the crew, but today he did not feel the weight of lost energy. "Just let me have five minutes, and then I'll get back to work." Thomas would keep working to spare his crew from working themselves to death, but he needed to make sure his friends were okay.

"I'm afraid I can't lose you for even a moment, Hambleton. Get back to work, and don't even think about going below deck," the captain said, shutting himself inside his quarters before Thomas could argue again.

Thomas rubbed his dripping face futilely as the rain continued to douse the ship. He groaned and turned to get back to work, but a large wave crashed against the hull and sent him stumbling into another sailor. Together, they tumbled to the boards of the slippery deck.

Thomas groaned and lifted himself up. "Shit, I'm s—*Oh.*"

The sailor he had fallen into was Charles.

Charles grinned up at him. "Hey, Thomas."

Thomas pushed himself off the ground and scrambled back onto his feet. "Of everyone on the crew . . ." he muttered. He offered Charles his hand.

Charles took it, letting Thomas pull him up. When Charles

was on his feet again, he didn't let go. "Thanks," he said with a dreamy smile.

Thomas yanked his hand away. "I would have done the same for anyone."

Charles's dreamy smile turned smug. "Uh huh."

A fresh gust of rain washed over them. "I have to get back to work. Leave me alone."

"I'm not the one who pinned the other to the floor just now, but sure," Charles said.

Thomas rolled his eyes and began walking away, but he stopped and turned to face Charles again, whose eyes were wandering down Thomas's body. They snapped back up to his face with a tinge of guilt. Charles recovered quickly and flashed another smug smile. "Sorry, I wasn't expecting you to turn around."

"I need your help," Thomas said, ignoring his reluctant satisfaction from the attention he didn't want to want.

Charles raised his eyebrows. "Sure. Anything for you."

Thomas released a sigh that became a groan. "Can you stop being so . . ." He couldn't find the right adjective, so he moved on. "This is serious."

An amused smile lingered on Charles's lips, but he didn't say anything.

"Are you on second watch?" Thomas asked.

"No. The captain let me off so I could take a break. He said he'd have someone else take my place," Charles said.

Thomas squeezed his eyes shut and turned away for a moment, fighting the untamable frustration. "Gods . . . whatever. Can you check on my friends? Caldwell won't let me see them, and I'm not sure if they're even on the ship. He says they're in the galley, but I have my doubts."

"I thought you were off second watch," Charles said.

"I was, but the captain said another sailor needed a break."

Charles's smug smile broke into mild surprise. "Oh. Um . . . I can talk to him," he offered.

"Don't bother. It's fine," Thomas said. Charles *did* look tired. They had both been up the entire previous night for the confrontation with Tetra, but Charles was a mere mortal. Of course he was tired. "You should rest. I don't mind taking your place, but can you please check the galley for me?"

"Sure," Charles said soberly. "Um . . . thank you."

Thomas shook his head and walked away before he could acknowledge the pleasant feeling blossoming beneath the firestorm of his anger.

It was a struggle to return to his post. Every step he took was misplaced by the unsteady rocking of the ship. One tall wave forced him to hold all his weight against the railing of the steps to the quarterdeck to keep him from sliding to the other end of the ship. He didn't know how he would make it through four more hours of this.

Suddenly, he remembered his divine connection to the very entity currently making his life miserable. He didn't know why it had taken him so long to ask her for help.

When the ship became steady enough for him to stagger to the edge, he threw himself over the bulwark and peered into the dark, sloshing water.

"Mariana!" he yelled, but his voice got lost in the wind and the rain. He yelled again, and the next wave that hit the ship clung to the hull and slid upward, manifesting as the blurry form of Mariana, who was just as choppy as the water below.

"Thomas!" she said, splashing violently as she sat on the ship's railing. "What can I do for you?"

"Can you stop this storm? The waves are going to kill us!" Thomas shouted.

Mariana glanced around at the dark turbulent landscape for a minute before turning her attention back to Thomas. "Look over there," she said, pointing to the distant waters. The current beneath her translucent skin flowed fast through her.

Thomas squinted out at the spot in the water where Mariana pointed, noticing for the first time they were coming upon clearer waters. "Oh. We'll be out of this soon?"

"Probably not if you can't calm down," Mariana said, dropping her arm and facing him again.

"Calm down?!" he demanded. Another wave crashed against the hull, sending Thomas falling hard on his butt. "What the— Did you do that?" he yelled.

"No," Mariana said again. "You did."

He squinted up at her through the heavy rain. "What?"

"Haven't you noticed how much energy you have now? You haven't stopped moving since I immortalized you," Mariana said.

"Yes, I've noticed. What does that have to do with the weather?" Thomas asked.

"You have unlimited energy, which means that you have unlimited magical energy too. Your magic is coming out of you faster than you can handle, and when you feel a particularly strong emotion, it gets worse. Either learn to control your magic or learn to control your temper and it'll stop."

"*I'm* making it rain?" Thomas asked.

"Neat, right?" Mariana asked.

"No!" Thomas yelled. "It's awful. How do I stop it?"

Mariana shrugged. "I am not a magus. I can't help you." She let herself collapse back into an oncoming wave that sent the ship lurching again. Thomas fell hard onto his elbow and bit his lip in an attempt to stop the pain from stoking the roaring flame of anger, and apparently magic, inside him.

As Thomas pushed himself from the drenched boards of the deck, a gentle hand guided him up. Alarmed by the unexpected touch, he jerked away and stumbled back before realizing who it was.

Charles raised his hands in a gesture of surrender. "Sorry. I was only trying to help. Are you all right?"

Thomas sighed and looked out at the calmer atmosphere in the distance. "Please tell me you have good news for me. I don't think I can take any more bad news today."

When Charles didn't answer, Thomas forced himself to look at him. Charles's eyebrows were high and his eyes wide. His lips were pursed like he could barely contain his words.

Thomas violently swiped wet strands of hair out of his eyes, suspecting he knew what Charles wasn't saying. "They weren't in the galley?" he asked.

Charles shook his head.

"Living quarters?"

Charles shook his head again. "I checked everywhere, Thomas."

Thomas's chest tightened. The fire in his heart was suffocated by a void of cold fear. "They're not here?"

"Uh . . ." Charles pulled at the drawstring on the front of his shirt. "No, they are."

"Tell me. Where are they?" Thomas asked.

Charles met Thomas's eyes with a panicked look. "They're in the brig."

___

TINERA

Pitch darkness filled the room around Felix. After his escape attempt, the guard had dragged him to a muddy corner of camp and pushed him to a set of steps leading underground. The steps were carved from earth with wooden planks laid over them. The bottom of the steps led to a long, dark tunnel. Felix couldn't see down here, but based on the sound of a door slamming and the metallic clank of its lock, he knew he was in a cell.

The room was cool and humid and smelled like damp earth. The walls were firm and cold to the touch; probably brick like the rest of the camp. For the first day or so, he paced the room. It grew warmer as time passed, and Felix began to worry there was no ventilation. When this concern occurred to him, he spent his time lying in the tacky mud at the center of the room, saving as much oxygen as he could.

Nobody brought food or water. Nobody checked on him. It was just him and his thoughts for hours or days. It was impossible to know how long it had been. Had he been forgotten? Had they left him here to die?

Severe thirst brought him to his feet. He felt his way around the room until he touched wood. His hands ran up the length of the door until they stopped on an interesting feature. The door had a window, blocked by three metal bars. He pressed his face against the bars and took a deep breath. The air was much cooler outside.

"Hello?" he yelled into the darkness. He couldn't tell if it was day or night. The tunnel curved so that the stairs weren't visible, and no light reached the holding cell.

No answer. He called out a few more times but gave up when he realized no one was coming. He resigned himself to the floor again, only able to think about the dryness in his mouth and the rumble in his stomach.

His breathing became heavier from the pain of unbearable thirst, or maybe from the diminishing oxygen. His stomach had stopped rumbling a long time ago, giving up on asking for food. There was none. They had left him to die.

Just when he decided this was the end, the metallic latch echoed through the small chamber. Felix sat up, staring in the direction of the door with wide, unseeing eyes.

"Warren," a gruff man's voice called out.

"I'm still here," Felix croaked. He pushed himself up, feeling heavier than ever.

"Let's go," the voice said.

Felix ran for the door as fast as he could, which was not very fast at all. He was desperate not to be stuck here for a second longer. He followed the sound of footsteps until the tunnel curved and bright light stung his eyes.

"Can I have some water? I'm dying," Felix said.

The guard ignored him.

"Please?" Felix added.

Still, the guard ignored him.

"Hello?" Felix said.

"Mealtime is in an hour. You can have water then," the guard responded as he climbed the stairs.

Felix followed, squinting into the unbearable sunlight. "That's it? I can go?"

"That's right. You're free."

Felix tripped over himself as he stumbled away from the dark corner of the camp and into the central courtyard. It had rained during his time underground, the muddy lawn now slick with wet puddles of brown water.

Felix felt all sense of pride and dignity leave his body as he ran to a shallow pool and dropped to his knees, filling his hands with murky water and drinking it down faster than he could stop to consider whether he should.

When he finally looked up after swallowing as much dirt water as he could hold, people were watching. He stood, knowing that what he had just done was animalistic and disgusting. Sometimes it was hard for him to act human again if he spent too much time as an animal, but it had been far too long since his last transformation for that to excuse his behavior. This place had taken his humanity from him.

Still unfamiliar with this new environment, Felix decided to visit the vast forest again. The dirt water was working its way through his body, and he already felt much better. He was ready to relax alone under the shade of a tall elm tree. The last thing he wanted to do after a week in that hole was go indoors.

As he turned the corner around the edge of the camp, the forest came into view, and it was apparent why they had locked Felix up for so long.

Every tree within twenty feet of the fence had been cut down, and the remaining trees had lost their neighbors. It would be impossible to get from one tree to another if he ever managed to climb one again, and it would *really* be impossible to get over the fence via tree.

They had taken away his only escape route.

Felix sighed heavily and sat down on a ragged stump. It had been for nothing. There was no escape. It didn't matter how hard he fought. His opponent had the time and resources to fight back with ten times the power. He rested his elbows on his knees and held his head in his hands, taking a moment to grieve.

He should have listened to Aella. That was obvious now. How did he ever think he could do this alone? He was letting his memory of the person she used to be cloud his judgment. She had been nothing but friendly when they ran into each other here. That didn't mean he could trust her, but he shouldn't have abandoned her.

There was still an hour until mealtime. Enough time to find her and apologize.

Felix got up and headed for the corner of the camp where the Larkspur residential hall sat nestled in its own balding forest. As he walked into the hall, he took in as much as he could. The layout of Larkspur was identical to Oleander's, but almost all of the beds in this hall were filled.

Felix scanned the room but couldn't find Aella. He searched

again, then began walking through the room. He ignored the prying eyes of the hall's occupants as he made his way to the double doors at the back.

The bathroom was the same as in his hall. To the right was a row of stalls covered with cloth curtains. Across from the stalls was a long trough basin with taps spaced evenly over it. To the left were shower stalls with latching wooden doors.

Felix's eyes scanned the room and landed on a familiar head of silvery-blonde hair standing by the sink, facing away from him. Aella stood with her arm outstretched toward a stranger; a young man who was rubbing a chunky green paste on her skin.

The stranger stopped and looked up. His ginger hair fell in curls over his forehead, and his brown eyes locked onto Felix. He looked at Aella and whispered something.

Aella whipped around, eyes wide. She scanned Felix from head to toe, and when their gazes met again her face held an expression of mild disgust. "Felix!" she said. "What are you doing here? Go away."

Felix opened his mouth to say something, but he could not think of a response.

"Why are you so *filthy?*" Aella asked.

The man let go of Aella's arm and raised his eyebrows. "Are you the person who tried to escape?" He spoke with an accent Felix recognized from his brief time in Dufonn as a sailor. "What did they do to you?"

"They locked me in a cave. I just got out," Felix said.

The man's eyes widened. "Really? Did they feed you at all?"

Felix wondered how miserable he must look for a stranger to be asking that. He shook his head.

The man exchanged a look with Aella, but she only rolled her eyes. "I asked you if you were up to something, and you said no. Why did you lie to me?" Aella asked.

Felix stuffed his hands in his pockets and exhaled. "I didn't want you to turn me in."

"And look where it got you. Why did you try to escape in broad daylight? Are you crazy? Now nobody is getting out."

"Be nice, Aella. Look at the condition he's in," the man said.

"I know it was stupid. I came to apologize," Felix said.

"To *her?*" the man joked.

Felix laughed. Aella narrowed her eyes at the stranger, but a smile snuck its way onto her face when he only grinned in response.

"It's nice to see you made a friend, Aella. I didn't think it was possible," Felix said as he approached.

"Ha-ha. You're both very funny," Aella said. "Felix, this is Finnlay. Finnlay, Felix." She gestured to each of them.

Finnlay nodded at Felix, seemingly finding him trustworthy enough to get back to work on Aella's arm. He spread the sticky green goo onto her skin again. Finnlay's arms were covered in tattoos of sigils, and some peeked from the collar of his shirt as well. They were the markings of a witch, but his hair was too short. Witches usually had long hair.

"Are you a witch, Finnlay?" Felix blurted.

Finnlay stopped working again to point a look of awe up at Felix. It quickly brightened into a smile. "I am! Not many people catch on."

Felix instantly felt at ease. Nobody that dedicated to magic would ever give it up. "My mother was a witch. I've never met a male witch before," Felix said.

"I'm honored to be the first," Finnlay said with a short bow of his head. "What are you?"

Felix laughed at the blunt phrasing. "I'm a shapeshifter."

Finnlay raised his eyebrows. "That's amazing. I always wished I was a shapeshifter."

"Really? Why?"

He shrugged and looked away. "There's a lot to like about it, but I'm sure you know that."

"Sure. What are you doing to Aella's arm?"

Aella scoffed. "Some horrible little six-legged creature bit me. Finnlay made me a soothing salve."

"No," Finnlay said. "It's not a salve. I only crushed up some wild lavender into a paste for its soothing properties. It is *not* a salve, but please don't say anything. It's all witchcraft to these people."

"I won't," Felix said.

Finnlay gave a small smile and got back to work. Aella eyed Felix again. "All right. Go ahead," she said.

"What?" Felix asked.

"You were going to apologize to me," Aella said.

Felix suddenly did not feel sorry for trying to leave her behind. "I think I changed my mind, actually."

Aella pouted at him. "Fine. I won't let you in on our plan, then."

Finnlay shot Aella a warning look.

Aella shrugged at him. "What? I told you about Felix."

"Not so loud," he said, tugging the sleeve of her shirt down to cover the greenish stain on her arm.

"You have a plan?" Felix asked quietly.

"You would have known that if you hadn't made a run for it before I could have a real conversation with you," Aella said.

"Okay, yes. I'm sorry. I shouldn't have tried to run, and I shouldn't have left you behind," Felix begrudgingly said. "So, what's the plan?"

Aella eyed the covered stalls. "I'll tell you at dinner. Try not to get imprisoned before then, and clean yourself up before I have to eat with you for gods' sake. You're filthy," she said, turning away to head for the door.

"I was locked in a cave!" Felix called after her, but Aella pretended not to hear him as the door shut behind her.

Felix stood in silence with Finnlay for an uncomfortable moment.

"So . . . You knew her before you got here?" Finnlay asked.

"Yes," Felix said, his discontent accidentally sneaking into his tone.

Finnlay eyed the door and ran his fingers through his hair, his curls bouncing back into place as he pulled his hand away. "She's a bit, um . . ."

"It's okay. You can say it," Felix said. "She's mean."

Finnlay laughed. "She told me you two were friends."

"Yeah, she keeps saying that." Felix frowned at the door Aella had walked through. "She must have a strange definition of the word 'friendship.'"

"Hm . . ." Finnlay said, his easy-going smile now turned down at the corners of his mouth, and Felix feared he said something wrong. "Have you known her long?"

"Too long," Felix said.

Finnlay rubbed his chin and scrutinized Felix with narrowed eyes. Felix wondered why he couldn't stop himself from saying stupid things out loud.

"She said you're trustworthy. Are you?" Finnlay asked.

Felix did not know what to say. "Would you just believe me if I said yes?"

Finnlay shrugged. "Maybe. It depends how you say it. You're off to a good start, I have to say."

Felix considered this for a moment and then laughed. "Well, I *am* a shapeshifter, but yeah, I try to be honest."

Finnlay watched Felix carefully for a long time, like he was thinking hard about Felix's answer. Finally, he nodded. "That's not lying, you know."

"What isn't?" Felix asked.

"Shapeshifting. You're not lying when you shift into something or someone else, because you were born a shapeshifter. When you shift, that's part of who you are. All identities are yours if you take them."

Felix had not thought about it like that before, but he didn't entirely agree. "You wouldn't think so if I stole *your* face."

Finnlay grinned. "You can use my face if you need it. I'm already a twin, there might as well be three of us."

"Is he here too?" Felix asked.

"Who?"

"Your twin."

"Oh!" Finnlay said with a short laugh. "No, thankfully. She got away."

His answer confused Felix. He knew it was possible for twins to be different genders, but Finnlay had implied they were identical. "How did you get caught?" he asked, deciding it didn't matter and it was probably rude to ask anyway.

Finnlay walked to the basin and turned a tap, releasing a solid stream of water into the trough. He stuck his hands under it and began scrubbing the pungent paste from his fingers. "I made a salve for a friend, and she turned me in."

Felix watched Finnlay wash the lavender away. Did Finnlay really let himself make that mistake *twice*? And for Aella, of all people?

Finnlay followed Felix's gaze to his hands and gave a short laugh before turning off the tap. "I can see how this must look to you, but I don't regret my choices."

"Why not?" Felix asked.

"Because I will never apologize for helping another person. I did it out of compassion for a friend who was in a bad accident, and now she's better for it, even if I am not," Finnlay said.

"Why would she turn you in if you helped her?" Felix asked.

Finnlay shrugged. "Why are *any* of us here? People hate us, and nobody can seem to agree about why."

Felix nodded, but like the rest of the world, he did not have an explanation. "How long have you been here?"

"A couple of months, I think. The trip here was long," Finnlay said.

"Were you sent here from Dufonn?"

Finnlay shot him a wry smile. "How did you know I'm from Dufonn?"

Felix laughed. "I've been to Dufonn. I could hardly understand a word those people spoke, even though they claim to speak the same language, but I eventually got the hang of it. I can mostly understand you."

Finnlay threw his head back and laughed. When he was done, he asked, "How long have you been here?"

"One month," Felix said.

"Ah, so we're in the same boat. A lot of these people have been here for years, including Aella."

Felix shook his head. "I can't imagine being here that long."

Finnlay nodded. "Neither can I, but if we stick together, we might never have to know what it's like."

A light of hope Felix hadn't felt since arriving in this horrible place sparked deep within him. "I hope you're right."

Finnlay smiled. "If you knock on the door of the main building and ask nicely, they'll give you another set of clothes," he said, heading for the door to follow Aella into the main room. "See you later!"

Felix was left alone in the bathroom, but he was now indefinitely in the good company of a witch.

Chapter Six

Thomas's first instinct was to run to the brig, until he remembered Caldwell had threatened to throw his friends overboard if he ditched his work to see them.

Thomas let out a string of curse words, clutching his hair in both hands while Charles watched. With every word that left his mouth, the rain hit his skin harder. He forced himself to stop and breathe slowly, but the storm did not ease.

"Charles," Thomas said carefully. "I need your help with something, and I need you to please not be a dick about it."

"But I thought you liked—"

"*Stop.* Go away and do not talk to me until this storm has passed, do you understand?" Thomas squeezed his eyes shut, fighting the fresh wave of frustration Charles brought out of him.

"Whoa, sorry . . . It was just a joke," Charles said.

"You're not sorry. You must have some kind of sick fetish for making me mad because you're an expert at it!" Thomas yelled.

"What? I don't have . . ." Charles's smirk washed away in the rain. It flickered back to life for a moment with a nervous laugh, but it was gone again just as fast. "Sorry."

"Go away!"

Charles nodded feebly and ran off.

"*Asshole,*" Thomas muttered, turning to get back to work.

He tried to cool the white-hot anger inside him, but the storm raged on. His hands slipped on slick icy ropes, and his eyes and skin stung with frigid salt water from high, crashing waves. He couldn't do this much longer, and judging by the faces of his crewmates, they couldn't either.

If Fiona were here, she could help him. Fiona knew everything about magic, and he had no doubt in his mind she could pinpoint exactly what he was doing wrong and why, and then walk him through how to make it stop.

Unfortunately, Fiona was locked up and would get thrown to the vicious sea if Thomas visited her during his watch. Thinking about this only made the weather worse, so Thomas tried to clear his mind.

He tried to focus on his work, but the solitude of it forced him to face his thoughts. He fought to suppress his feelings like he had been so good at just one day ago, but his anger was too big to keep down. He considered making conversation with one of his new crewmates—then he remembered Charles had told him the people on Hambleton crews were former magi. These sailors had been through the Hambleton rehabilitation camp.

If Thomas took the effort to ask, they could help him. However, Thomas didn't want to risk the captain learning he was a magus. And if these people were truly brainwashed by the Hambletons, they might not be his allies.

He decided to wait until he could speak to Fiona. In the meantime, he focused on his breathing and redirected his thoughts to something happier. This proved to be a struggle.

Everything that made him happy before were his biggest problems now.

To his surprise, the storm eventually calmed to a drizzle, and the rocking of the ship settled to a disruptive sway. It was calm enough to work through the next two watches with only mild difficulty.

The moment the bell rang to signal the end of the third watch, Thomas scanned the deck for any sign of Caldwell. Finding none, he ran for the hatchway.

The living quarters were livelier than Thomas was used to. Although the crew was small, there were still more people aboard the ship than there had been for a long time. Two sailors sat in one corner playing a hand of cards. One sat against the port side wall, writing in a journal.

Thomas's eyes landed on Charles, who was lying back in his hammock. He had been looking at Thomas when their eyes met, but the eye contact didn't last long. A large wave crashed over the hull, scattering the playing cards and flipping Charles onto his face while Thomas stumbled backward into the wall.

"You all right?" the writing sailor asked Thomas, who was rubbing his aching shoulder with a grimace.

"Yeah. Thanks." The pain in Thomas's shoulder was already gone by the time he finished speaking.

"Weird. I thought the storm passed," the sailor said.

Thomas nodded and looked across the living quarters where Charles had pushed himself off the ground and was helping his crewmates gather their scattered cards.

"Sorry," Thomas muttered.

The sailor's face twisted with confusion. "Why? Not like you control the sea."

Thomas forced a short laugh and walked to the hatchway that led to the cargo hold. He kept his gaze on the ground as he passed Charles, feeling Charles's eyes on him the whole way.

When he reached the dim hold, he ran through the tight space and threw himself into the brig. One dim lantern hung from the far wall between the same two cells in which Thomas had first found Faya and Fiona.

Thomas stomped through the narrow aisle that divided the room. He let out a sigh of relief when he caught sight of Fyavine's frown in the flickering yellow light, and then he spotted Fiona and Faya in their original cells. Ametta sat beside her mother, looking as grim as the day he had met her in the Chratanian jail.

"Thank all the gods you guys are okay," Thomas said, looking back and forth between Fiona's and Faya's cells. "I was so worried you didn't make it on this ship. Charles blackmailed Ivan into letting you on as crew, but then the captain wouldn't let me down here to see you and I was afraid they had put you on a different ship or—or—thrown you overboard or something! But then Charles told me you were in the brig, and I've been so upset that it's been storming for hours and I can't make it stop because I don't know anything about magic, and I don't know what to do!" Thomas rambled, gripping the roots of his hair between his fingers. Being with his friends again undid the calm he had managed to find earlier as he relived his fear and felt his anger turn to sinking sadness that he had let them down.

The ship lurched violently, pinning Thomas to the bars of Fiona's cell as she tumbled into the back wall. She sat up to look at him with wide eyes. "*You're* doing this?" she asked.

"Yes," Thomas said miserably. "Please help me."

"How is that possible? You'd have to be incredibly powerful to control the weather and the sea for that long," Fiona said.

"Mariana says it's because of my immortality. I have unlimited magical energy, whatever that means," Thomas explained.

Fiona exchanged an astonished look with Faya across the aisle.

Thomas turned to look at Faya, who was watching him with a slack jaw. "Amazing," she whispered.

Thomas shook his head. "It's not amazing, I'm a disaster. I'm a magus who can't use his magic, and I'm a socially awkward aristocrat. I have no idea how to use any of my power and I'm ruining everything."

"I can help you with your magic, Thomas." Fiona stood, straightening herself out. "I may not be able to show you very much from in here, but I can at least explain it to you."

"Yes! Please!" Thomas said. "How do I make the storms stop? I managed to weaken them by focusing on my breathing, but beyond that I'm hopeless."

Fiona offered a sympathetic smile with a nod. "That was very intuitive of you. The magus instinct in you is alive and strong. There is a lot more to controlling your magic than breathing, but that's a good start."

"What else can I do?" Thomas asked.

Fiona grinned. "It's quite simple. When you—"

The door to the brig exploded open. Captain Caldwell stomped inside and aimed his menacing scowl at Thomas.

Thomas pushed himself away from Fiona's cell. "Captain!" Thomas yelled. "You told me my friends would be in the galley! Why are they in the brig?"

"Commissioner York told you they would be part of this crew, Hambleton, but *I* am the captain. These are unrefined magi, and you are not to talk to them while under my command, do you understand?"

"No, I don't," Thomas countered. "They are good people, and they are my friends. I am not on duty at the moment, so I will speak to whomever I please."

"What a shame," Caldwell said. "Your father will be so disappointed to receive a ship missing half its cargo. Too bad your *friends* fell ill on the journey, otherwise they might have made it."

Thomas clenched his fists tight, trying to fight the rage burning in his chest. He had been trying to avoid his anger by coming down here, but Caldwell followed him and the anger wasn't far behind. His friends were his only respite from the uncontrollable emotions, and now he wouldn't even have them to help. If he wasn't careful, he would lose them forever.

"Breathe, Thomas," Fiona whispered.

Thomas took a deep breath and exhaled heavily. "Don't hurt them. I'll leave," Thomas said.

As Thomas shouldered past him to get to the door, Caldwell stopped him. "If I see you down here one more time, you'll never see these *magi* again. Do you understand me?"

Thomas forced himself to breathe. "Yes, Captain."

TINERA

Felix was the first to arrive to the dining hall when it was finally time for lunch. His thoughts were no longer on Aella and Finnlay. He was ravenous.

The sunlit dining hall was nearly empty when he stepped inside. Dust motes fluttered down like daytime stars in the bright sunlight shining from the high windows. Tables filled the room in rows, seating about six people each. All of the tables were empty.

A long wooden table parallel to the right wall held crooked, towering stacks of pewter bowls. A dark-haired girl lugged a giant pot from the kitchen door toward the table. Felix made his way over to her.

She stood behind the table with a ladle, scooping the

contents of the pot into bowls and handing them off to whomever happened to be on the other side.

Felix accepted his bowl but did not move on. The girl raised her eyebrows at him as she ladled another sloppy serving into a bowl she pulled from the stack.

"Can I have a little more?" Felix asked.

The girl's eyes scanned him as she shoved the bowl into the next person's hands without looking at them, spilling some down the front of their shirt. "Is this your first day or something?"

"No, but I haven't eaten in days."

"Sorry. That's it," she said, looking away from him.

"Can I come back for more?" Felix asked.

The girl only furrowed her brow and grabbed another bowl from the precarious stack.

"Felix!"

A line had formed around the room, leading to the table. Aella waved at him from the middle of the line. Finnlay stood behind her and gave a small wave too when Felix spotted them.

Felix headed toward them, fighting the urge to immediately drink down the vegetable stew as his stomach ached with hunger.

"Do you see the table directly at the center of the room?" Aella asked as he came closer, pointing at the middle of the room as if it would help.

"Yeah, I think so," Felix said, searching the empty room for the exact center.

"That's where we sit. Meet us there," Aella said.

Felix looked from the empty tables back to Aella and Finnlay. "Does it have to be that one? They're all empty."

"Yes, it has to be that one," Finnlay said.

"Stop arguing and go sit down," Aella said.

Felix frowned, wondering why they were both being weird about which table he sat at. He turned and marched to the center of the room.

He stopped at the simple wooden table he believed to be at the center and turned to Aella and Finnlay, who were both watching him. Aella shook her head, and Finnlay subtly pointed one table to the left.

Felix took a step to his left and slowly began to sit down at the next table. When Finnlay gave him a thumbs up, he dropped himself onto the bench. At the moment, he was too hungry to think about why they were acting like their usual table was a secret. He shoveled the warm vegetable water into his mouth quickly. His stomach grumbled as he ate, barely chewing before swallowing. It was the most delicious thing he had ever eaten in his life, despite its watery consistency and unseasoned chunks of raw vegetables.

"Gods, Felix," Aella said a few minutes later, dropping herself onto the bench at the other side of the table. "Slow down."

Felix ignored her and lifted the bowl, emptying the rest of its contents into his mouth.

Finnlay sat down beside Aella with his own bowl and a large pewter flagon. He filled a matching pewter cup with water and slid it across the table to Felix while watching him with curiosity.

Felix downed the water. "Thank you," he gasped over the empty cup. Finnlay nodded and refilled it. Felix drank that down too. Aella ate her food in silence.

Felix sighed and eyed the food table again. He wondered what it would take to convince the kitchen worker to give him another bowl. "Do you think I could get more?" he asked.

Finnlay gave him a pitying frown. "No." He looked down at his own bowl and pushed it toward Felix. "You can have mine."

Felix's jaw dropped. "Finnlay, no. I'm not going to take your food from you."

"I ate this morning. You ate three days ago," Finnlay said, nudging his bowl toward Felix again.

Felix shook his head. "I won't eat your food."

"Why not? It's not contaminated." Finnlay squinted into the bowl. "Actually, I can't promise that," he added, "but I didn't contaminate it."

"No," Felix said again.

Finnlay picked up his bowl and tilted it over Felix's. The vegetable slop fell into it. "Oops," Finnlay said, sliding his empty bowl back to himself with a relaxed smile.

"Are you out of your mind?" Felix asked.

Finnlay shrugged and rested his elbows on the tabletop, folding his arms together. "Maybe."

"Thank you," Felix said with resignation.

"You're welcome," Finnlay said.

Aella watched Felix quietly as he continued to eat the stew. After a minute, she said, "Felix, do you feel any different?"

Felix stopped eating. "What?" he asked, looking into the bowl. "Why? What did you do?"

Finnlay laughed. "Nothing! It's not the stew."

Felix looked back and forth between Finnlay and Aella. "What is it?"

Aella rolled her eyes and shook her head at Finnlay, who only smiled back. "Use your brain, Felix. Don't you feel different?" she asked.

Felix tried to focus on something other than the pressing hunger that overtook every sense. He *did* feel different, but he couldn't place what it was. He looked at Finnlay for an answer.

Finnlay leaned forward and spoke in a lowered voice. "Watch this." Finnlay's eyes scanned the room before he clamped his left hand over his upper right arm and muttered a string of words Felix did not recognize. A pale light peeked between his fingers for a second, but it faded fast. He removed his hand from his arm and smiled at Felix. "Try it now," he said, pointing at the bowl of stew.

Felix was too stunned to process the command. Finnlay had just done magic. But how? "Was that—"

"Hush," Aella said.

Felix raised his eyebrows at Finnlay. Finnlay nodded with a wide grin and pointed at Felix's soup again. Felix cautiously lifted his spoon to his mouth, wary of whatever magic Finnlay had done. He took a small bite.

It was much more tolerable. In fact, it was tasty. Felix took another bite. And another. He forced himself to chew and swallow before speaking. "Why didn't you do that to my first bowl?" he joked.

"It was gone before I got here," Finnlay said with a laugh.

"This is amazing," Felix said, looking into his bowl as if he could see the magic in it.

Finnlay gave a small bow of his head.

"How is this possible?" Felix asked.

"I've figured out exactly how they are containing our magic, and consequently, where the weak spot in the containment is," Finnlay explained.

Now that Felix knew, he could feel his magic flowing through him. The familiar energy at his core was no longer stuck inside. It flowed through his body, as it did before he was put in shackles and brought here. His eyes scanned the bored faces of the other magi eating their watery lunches or waiting in line. Clearly, no one else knew about this or they would all be fighting to sit here.

"What can we do with this?" Felix asked.

Finnlay briefly scanned the room before looking at Felix again. "I can't say much now, but meet us here tonight at midnight. I have a plan."

Chapter Seven

When Charles had agreed to work on this ship, he suspected it would be hard not to think about Thomas with all the Hambleton symbols adorning the sails and equipment. He didn't realize *how* hard it would be. It was impossible to avoid any member of the crew, even when that crew member was trying to avoid him, too.

Charles often wondered if he should have stayed in Dufonn. Tetra's words played on repeat in his mind. *Your father will be so disappointed if you ever make it home.* She was an evil and mean-spirited god, but she was correct. His father didn't want him home. So why was he going back?

Part of him wanted to be available, just in case Thomas ever needed his help. There wasn't much Charles could do for Thomas's cause, but whatever it was, he would do it. For Thomas. He could not let go of Thomas in the aftermath of his grief. Every time he looked at Thomas was an unbelievable reminder he was still here.

"Southworth!" the captain shouted from the main deck.

Charles looked down from the ratlines, ignoring the panic tightening around his chest at the distance to the hard surface of the deck. Not even months working as a sailor could cure his fear of heights. "Captain," he called back.

The captain didn't answer, simply pointing at the space beside him. He climbed down with urgency, grateful for the relief of the deck against his boots.

"Yes, Captain?" Charles asked.

"I need you to go below deck and feed the cargo. One piece of hardtack each and a pail of water to share. Nothing more. If they complain, let me know."

"The cargo, Captain?"

Captain Caldwell narrowed his eyes at Charles as if insulted. "Yes, and if Hambleton tries to sneak in behind you, I'll throw you both overboard."

The threat was so surprising that Charles had no response. He nodded and turned to find the hatchway. He stopped by the galley to fetch the food and water, wondering all the way why he would get thrown overboard if Thomas tried to sneak into the brig.

Hushed voices hissed through the crack of the door to the brig as he walked through the cargo hold. The voices stopped when Charles pushed his way inside.

"Thomas?" a voice asked quietly.

"Unfortunately not. Sorry to disappoint," Charles said as he walked into the room.

He recognized two of the three women from York. Thomas had introduced him to Fiona and Faya. Faya now had a child with her who looked so similar to her that she had to be Faya's daughter. Charles had not yet met the last woman, but the ease in her posture told him she knew the other two well.

"Oh. It's you," Fiona said.

Charles had stopped by during the second watch at Thomas's request, not staying long enough to have a real conversation. He asked if they were okay and if he could get them anything, but what they had wanted most was for him to leave.

Charles nodded at Fiona as he approached the cell closest to him, the one that held the stranger. She was a beautiful woman with dark skin and long, curly hair. Charles handed her a serving of hardtack and offered a smile. "Hello. I don't think we've met. My name is Charles."

"Fyavine," she said, taking the food from him with a suspicious gaze. "You're Thomas's ex-boyfriend."

"Yes," Charles said. "I didn't realize Thomas had made so many magus friends."

"I'm not a magus," Fyavine said.

This surprised Charles. "Really? Why are you in a cell?"

Fyavine shrugged, biting into the hard biscuit. The corner snapped off in her mouth, and she grimaced around the loud crunching.

"She's a mermaid," Faya explained as Charles handed her two servings. She passed the second to her daughter, who gnawed at it right away.

"A mermaid?" Charles asked, eyeing Fyavine again. She sat in her cell, two long legs stretched in front of her while she crunched on the hardtack. "I've never seen a mermaid with feet before."

Fyavine arched an eyebrow and scanned him from head to toe. "I would believe you've never seen a mermaid at all."

"What's that supposed to mean?" Charles asked.

Fiona giggled behind him.

Charles sighed as he turned to give Fiona her serving. "What did she mean by that, Fiona?"

"Aw, you remembered my name," Fiona said, brushing a strand of ginger hair behind her ear with a big smile.

"Why wouldn't I? You remember mine, don't you?"

"I made her the enchantment she's wearing. Isn't it neat?" Fiona asked, ignoring his question. "It turns merpeople into humans and humans into merpeople."

Charles nodded as he examined Fyavine's legs again. Fyavine pulled them into herself and frowned. "Why does it work in there? Shouldn't these cells be magic-proofed?" Charles asked.

"They lined her cell with buffer panels, which suppress the magic suppressants. If you look closely, you can see them," Fiona said.

Charles inspected inside Fyavine's cell and noticed the walls and ceiling were a different color of wood than the planks in Faya's and Fiona's cells. "Wow. You know a lot about magic," he said.

Fiona's smile grew, but it fell just as fast. She exchanged a nervous look with Faya. "Yes, and speaking of magic . . . Thomas needs help, but I don't think we'll see him down here again anytime soon."

"Thomas needs help?" Charles asked. "With what? Is he okay?"

Fiona shook her head. "I don't know. He seems to think he's the cause of this storm. I was about to walk him through how to control his magic, but the captain interrupted us."

"*Thomas* is doing this?" Charles pointed to the ceiling as though they could see the storm through two decks. "How? Why?"

"He must be really upset about something," Faya said. When he turned around to look at her, she was frowning pointedly at him.

Charles faced Fiona again. "It's not all my fault. Learning you were all in the brig didn't help." he said, but he suddenly understood why Thomas asked to be left alone until the storm passed. Maybe it *was* all Charles's fault.

Fiona pursed her lips. "Well, whatever the cause, we need to help him. His parents generously taught him nothing about magic, so he is unwittingly letting his immense magical energy flow into the atmosphere and ocean currents. Can I count on you to relay my instructions to him?"

"Of course. I'll do whatever I can to help," Charles said.

Fiona smiled at him. "Thanks, Carl."

"It's Charles," he said.

Fiona only laughed.

TINERA

The rest of the afternoon dragged as Felix waited for night to descend. Dinner came and went with another bowl of bland stew and a slice of bread with cheese, which Felix was grateful for. It was nearly unbearable to sit at that table knowing he could do magic there, but he would get thrown right back in that cave if he tried.

Still, his mind buzzed with the possibility of doing magic again. He would have a chance to sit at the magic table late at night, without prying eyes on him.

When the time finally came, Felix was careful not to attract attention. He snuck to his residential hall's exit while his fellow occupants snoozed.

Felix slowly turned the doorknob and pushed open the door as quietly as possible. He emerged onto the first wooden step leading down to the grass. To his horror, the stair let out a shrill squeak. Felix froze, turning slowly to make sure he hadn't awoken anyone.

Nobody moved.

Felix let himself release his held breath. He quietly shut the door behind him, not bothering with the rest of the noisy stairs and instead taking one large step down onto the grass. He slipped through the obscuring darkness of the moonless night and made his way to the large building at the center of the camp.

As he reached for the doorhandle to the dining hall's entrance, he paused. Was it a good idea to put his faith in one person he didn't like and another he didn't know?

What if he turned around and went back to his residential hall? That was the safer option, and the path less likely to lead to Aella or Finnlay betraying him. He wouldn't have to worry about being thrown in the cave again. He wouldn't miss another meal.

But he wouldn't get to do magic again, either.

The thought of doing magic was enough to convince him to turn the knob and slip inside the dark, empty room. Starlight shined through the high windows, casting a faint blanket of dusty blue light over the tables.

Aella and Finnlay sat in the center of the room together, speaking in low voices.

Felix silently shut the door behind him and weaved between the tables. He sat beside Finnlay.

"Felix! You made it!" Finnlay said. Felix couldn't see well in the darkness, but he could imagine Finnlay's smile from the tone of his voice.

"I made it," Felix whispered, looking back and forth between the dark shapes of Aella and Finnlay. "Did I miss all the magic?"

"Not at all! Feel free," Finnlay said as he gestured toward the table.

Felix grinned and stood up, keeping his hands on the table in front of him, and shifted into a house cat. He hopped onto the table to sit between Aella and Finnlay. It felt great to transform again. The darkness of the room did not conceal nearly as much with his cat eyes. The view of the room was just as clear as daytime but not quite as colorful.

Finnlay beamed at him. "Wow! That's amazing!"

Felix tried to ask Finnlay to show him more witchcraft, but it came out as a squeaky meow. He forgot how hard it was to form words with an animal's mouth.

"You can't speak?" Finnlay asked.

Felix shook his tiny cat head.

"Interesting."

"Oh my gods, you really are a shapeshifter," Aella remarked. "You're so cute!"

Felix turned to look at her, flicking his tail at her words. He walked across the table and back to his original seat to become human again. "That felt good," he said.

"I bet!" Finnlay said.

"Can you show me some witchcraft?" Felix asked.

Finnlay looked around the hall as if someone might be lurking in the shadows, waiting to catch them. Satisfied they were alone, he faced the table again and whispered, *"Ablight."* A small orange flame blazed above the palm of his hand, bringing the relief of sight with its flickering glow.

"Wow," Felix said, sounding more amazed than he meant to.

"Thanks!" Finnlay said.

"So, what's your plan, Finnlay?" Aella asked.

Felix tried not to let surprise show on his face. Aella had gotten him involved in this plan, but she didn't even know what it was?

"I want to create a cloaking grid," Finnlay said. "Right now, we can't do any magic during the day, because we'll be caught. It's not very practical to sneak out of our beds every night to come here, so I thought it would be a good idea to make an enchantment to disguise us while we figure out an escape plan."

"You don't have an escape plan?" Aella asked.

"Good things take time, Aella," Finnlay said, unbothered by her judgmental tone. "We can't have an escape plan without precautions."

Felix couldn't argue with that. He had been so reckless when he tried to escape that the layout of the camp changed.

Aella sighed. "Fine."

"So, what do you need from us?" Felix asked.

"This enchantment should be fairly simple," Finnlay said. "It doesn't take a wide variety of ingredients to complete, but we will need a great quantity. I need as many flowers as you can find. Can you do that?"

Aella nodded. "Easy."

"Sure," Felix added.

"Good. Please be careful. Attempting magic is obviously not permitted, and if they know anything about witchcraft, they will be wary of anyone harvesting flowers," Finnlay said.

"Is that it?" Felix asked. "Usually there's more to an enchantment than gathering flowers."

Finnlay shot him a sly smile. "Felix, you son of a witch. Yes, there is more to it. I need a secret."

"A secret?" Aella asked. "From one of us? Or from someone else?"

"Preferably from someone else. It's more potent that way, but if we can't manage that, then one of you could share a secret. Only if you're willing, of course," Finnlay said.

Felix and Aella shared an awkward silence.

"Someone else, then," Finnlay said, his smile growing more amused.

"I'll talk to the other people in my hall," Felix said, omitting that they all hated him.

"Me too," Aella said.

"Thank you for your help," Finnlay said. "I don't usually work alone, so I'm grateful to have you both here with me."

"Do you normally work with your sister?" Felix asked.

"Yes," Finnlay said, running his fingers through his hair. "We did everything together until I got captured."

Aella crossed her arms and frowned at Felix, looking him up and down once before returning her gaze to Finnlay. "What happened to your parents? Were they burned at the stake?" Aella asked Finnlay.

Her words were as sharp and painful as if she had struck Felix over the head with them. "Aella . . ." Felix grumbled. Aella ignored him.

Finnlay's eyebrows furrowed as his eyes passed between Felix and Aella. "Uh . . . No. Nothing like that."

"Did they kick you out for having a boyfriend?" Aella asked.

Finnlay's eyes widened and he refused to look at Felix. "N-no."

Felix hadn't known that about Finnlay, but judging by the conversation he'd had with Thomas, it probably wasn't something Finnlay wanted Aella telling people. "Gods, Aella. What's the matter with you?" Felix asked.

Aella shrugged and narrowed her eyes at him. "What? There's nothing wrong with it. And Finnlay doesn't mind. Do you, Finnlay?"

"Actually, Aella," Finnlay said. "That was a secret that I only shared with you because I *thought* you would understand. My own sister doesn't even know that about me." Finnlay pressed his palms together to extinguish the flame in his hands, and the room fell back into darkness. "Felix, perhaps you should be the one to find the secret. If you're still willing, anyway."

Felix understood what he was implying, and it made his heart ache. "Finnlay, I don't care about that. You're not the first guy I've met who's attracted to men. You're not even the second," he said.

"Really?" Finnlay asked. "Who else did you know?"

"Just these two guys I met during my time as a sailor. They

had a romance, but it didn't work out because their families were big competitors in their industry."

"Oh . . . That's sad," Finnlay said.

"Not really. One of them was a huge jerk. The other was better off without him. I hope he, uh . . ." Felix stopped himself, realizing he was about to say he hoped Thomas found someone better, but Thomas never would. He was dead. "Actually, yeah. It is sad," he amended. "Anyway, I'm sorry about Aella. She never learned manners."

"Hey!" Aella said.

Felix laughed. "What? You don't like having your tragic past thrown in your face in front of someone else?"

"Not having manners is not my 'tragic past,'" Aella said.

"It is to me," Felix replied.

The sound of Finnlay's laughter eased the tension.

Aella rolled her eyes and stood up. "Whatever. You're both stupid," she said, and turned to leave. "See you tomorrow." She threw a hand up in the air to wave goodbye.

Felix shrugged at Finnlay. "Sorry," he said again.

"You aren't responsible for her behavior. I am surprised she didn't apologize, though. She should know better," Finnlay said.

"Why?"

Finnlay opened his mouth but didn't say anything, looking like he had been caught in a lie. "Um . . . Oh. This is awkward. I guess I thought you knew, since she told me you were friends. But I now realize that . . . wasn't true."

"She's the same?" Felix asked, looking toward the door where Aella had exited. That didn't make any sense. Aella had always liked to mess with the guys in New Brook. He suspected she gave him as much trouble as she did because he was the only guy who could see the monster behind her beautiful smirk.

"Sort of. She's, um . . . Well, she's got eyes for everyone," Finnlay said with a nervous laugh.

That made more sense. "Ah," Felix said.

"I suppose I'm as bad as her now."

"No. She outed you intentionally."

"Yes . . . That was odd. Can I count on you to get the secret? I'm not sure I trust her as much anymore."

"Absolutely," Felix said.

Finnlay nodded and eyed Felix for a minute before speaking. "I'm afraid of encountering the opposite problem with you, to be honest."

"What do you mean?"

"If someone tells you a secret, are you going to be able to break their trust enough to tell me and Aella?"

Felix hadn't considered that he wouldn't want to break the trust of someone he hadn't met yet. If it were just Finnlay, that would be easy. Finnlay looked like he could keep a secret. He clearly had a few of his own. Aella, on the other hand, could be a problem.

"Hm . . ." Felix rubbed the back of his neck. "If it comes to that, I'll just share one of my secrets."

Finnlay nodded, and in the darkness, Felix could still see his smile. "Okay, good. I'd still prefer a secret from another person if possible."

"Trust me, I'll try. I'd rather not share so much with Aella if I can help it," Felix said.

"Yeah . . ." Finnlay said, and Felix hadn't realized he hoped Finnlay would disagree until that word left his mouth.

Maybe Aella was still a problem.

AT SEA

Thomas focused on the gentle sway of his hammock as he breathed in slowly and let out a measured exhale. It was finally time for his break, but he was afraid that if he let himself sleep, the ship would capsize under his nightmares. Instead, he used his break to work on figuring out his magic.

Rain thundered against the wood panels of the deck overhead. If he had made any progress, it was slow. Every few minutes, a drop of water worked its way between the deck boards and slapped him directly in the center of his forehead, which did nothing to calm his nerves. No matter how he turned, that droplet seemed to find his face.

Footsteps thumping up the hatchway from below interrupted his focus. He opened his eyes to frown at the damp boards above. Trying to relax was useless. He didn't know how he could possibly keep this up for the rest of the journey to Brenton. A solid month of counting breaths would be impossible.

"Hey, Thomas," Charles said, sidling up to Thomas's hammock as he fixed a perfect smile onto his face. Something twisted tight in his stomach at the sight of Charles's smile, and he had to fight his own mouth to not smile back. Why was his body trying so hard to sabotage him?

"Don't talk to me," Thomas said, closing his eyes so he didn't have to look at Charles. "Your life literally depends on it."

"Ooh, is that a threat?" Charles asked.

Thomas opened his eyes to shoot him a dirty look, but the smug look on Charles's face only made him angrier. "Yes," Thomas said. "I am going to strangle you if you don't walk away right now."

Charles pressed his lips between his teeth, fighting back a laugh. "Promise?"

Rain thundered hard overhead.

"Oh my gods!" Thomas yelled, sitting up. "Shouldn't you be working? What do you want?"

"I just talked to your new girlfriend. She told me you need help."

Thomas scoffed, ignoring the accusation that Fiona was his girlfriend. "I need *her* help. Not yours."

Charles frowned. "Wait, is she actually your girlfriend?"

Thomas narrowed his eyes. "Don't be stupid."

"I can't help it," Charles said with a shrug that he probably thought looked casual. "Anyway, Fiona taught me how to control magic. She asked me to walk you through it."

Thomas scowled at Charles but stayed silent for a long time. "I don't think it would be very effective if I learned from you."

A smile tugged at one side of Charles's mouth. "All right. I'll just let you sink this ship and everyone on it, then." He turned to leave.

Thomas grabbed his sleeve to stop him. Charles turned and looked at Thomas with mock surprise.

"You're right. I need help," Thomas admitted.

Charles let his smug smile slide back into place as he faced Thomas again. "From Fiona? Or is there someone else who can help you . . . ?"

"Can you please stop being an asshole for *five* minutes?" Thomas asked through clenched teeth.

"Let's find out," Charles said. He held out his hands as if he wanted Thomas to take them.

"What are you doing?" Thomas asked, eyeing Charles's hands warily.

"Fiona said we have to hold hands," Charles said.

"Bullshit. She did not say that."

Charles only continued holding his hands out and raised his eyebrows.

"Charles, what would that do for me? You're not even a magus," Thomas said.

"It's not about magic."

"What is it about, then?"

"Love."

Thomas folded his own hands under his arms. "This whole ship can fucking sink," Thomas said, lying back in his hammock again. "I don't want to talk to you."

"Oh, come on, Hambleton. You can't even get over our petty rivalry for the sake of your crew?"

"This is *not* a petty rivalry. This is a full-blown enemy . . . ship," Thomas said.

Charles took the edge of Thomas's hammock in his hands. "You may hate me, but I'm not your enemy."

The twist in his stomach tightened. "You are my enemy. Go away."

"What have I done to deserve that title?" Charles asked.

Thomas raised his eyebrows. "Do you really want to get into that?"

Charles paused, seeming to consider it. "No."

"Then I think you already know."

"All right. Fine. I'm your enemy, but you're still just my ex-boyfriend. Let me help you," Charles said.

Thomas glared at Charles for a long time. To his dismay, he found the longer he looked at Charles, the more willing he was to agree. He averted his eyes, but the damage had been done. "Fine. Just know I'm doing this reluctantly."

"Oh, you've made that very clear," Charles said, offering Thomas a hand to help him out of the hammock.

Thomas tried to fling his legs over the side and slip out without Charles's help, but his left foot caught on the edge while the right swung out, tipping him out of the canvas onto the damp floor in a noisy tumble of knees and elbows.

Charles stood in the same spot, his hand still extended. "Dei, Thomas. I wasn't going to hurt you."

Thomas quickly pushed himself up and dusted off his shirt. "You've done it before."

Charles sighed and lifted his other hand. "Fiona really did tell me to hold your hands."

Thomas's eyes roamed his face, searching for a lie. It was probably there, but some twisted part of him refused to call Charles out on it again. He slid his hands into Charles's. They were warm and dry, and Thomas couldn't stop himself from squeezing a little tighter in an attempt to find some of the comfort he had once known in them.

"Do you hear that?" Charles asked, looking up at the dripping boards. The rain had quieted to a patter.

"Please don't," Thomas said, shaking his head. "It's just going to come back."

Charles nodded. "Okay. Close your eyes," he said.

Every instinct in Thomas told him to do the opposite of anything Charles said, but he knew this wasn't really Charles. It was Fiona talking through him.

Thomas closed his eyes.

"Take a deep breath and then exhale slowly," Charles said.

Thomas did as instructed.

"Do you feel the magical energy coming out of you? It starts in your core and flows through you," Charles said.

Thomas tried to focus on his energy. The core must have been his soul. He tried to think about where his soul had been when Mariana fixed it. It was at the center of his chest. When he remembered this, he felt it. A powerful ball of energy waited at his center and flowed through his body, exiting his skin with a mild tingle. "There's so much of it . . ." Thomas said.

"Good. Take a deep breath and try to separate your magical energy from your feelings," Charles said.

Thomas opened his eyes and frowned at Charles. Charles had been watching him curiously, and his expression softened when Thomas looked at him.

Thomas looked away. Rain battered the deck overhead. "I don't know how to do that. What does that even mean?"

"Just try," Charles said.

The ship lurched, and Thomas stumbled into Charles. Charles kept his footing and held Thomas until the ship was stable. His heart ached at the feeling of Charles's arms around him. Despite his sickening desire to stay there, he pushed himself away as soon as he could. "How?!" he demanded.

"Feel your magical energy at your core and separate it from your emotions," Charles said unhelpfully.

Thomas didn't have a choice. Despite Charles's lack of instructions, he had to try until he got it right, or else they could be stuck in this storm all the way back to Brenton.

Charles offered his hand, but Thomas didn't take it.

"Fiona didn't really tell you to hold my hand, did she?" Thomas asked.

Charles lowered his hand. After a long moment filled only by the sounds of the thunderous rain and creaking ship, he asked, "It helped, didn't it?"

Thomas didn't want to admit it, but holding Charles's hands *had* helped somehow. Thomas didn't feel calm around Charles, but maybe he hadn't been lying. Maybe something about their love eased the turmoil, despite the turmoil their love made him feel on its own. He reluctantly nodded and reached for Charles again.

Charles took his hands right away. "Breathe."

Thomas closed his eyes and attempted the breathing exercise again. He took a deep breath in. As he exhaled, he felt the magic pouring out of him, his skin tingling as it left him. His frustration grew at his lack of control, which only made the magical energy move faster. How was he supposed to separate his magic from his anger? They felt the same to him.

Breathing had helped him before he knew anything. There must have been something to it, especially if Fiona said so. Thomas continued breathing deeply and exhaling slowly, focusing on the force of his energy. After the third breath, he managed to get a grip on his anger, and the magic slowed. Keeping his calm seemed to help the forcefulness of it, at least.

"I think I'm doing it," Thomas whispered.

"I knew you could," Charles said.

His concentration wriggled free from his grasp at the sound of Charles's voice. Thomas's eyes snapped open, and he frowned at Charles.

"What?" Charles asked.

"I think I need to do this alone," Thomas said.

"Why? What did I do wrong?"

"Nothing," Thomas said. "I mean—right now, anyway. I just need to . . . not be around you. I think it's messing me up."

"Oh . . ." Charles said. He reluctantly released Thomas's hands, and cold empty air took their place. "Okay. I'll go. Let me know if you need any more help."

Thomas nodded but said nothing. Charles waited a beat longer and then walked away when it was clear Thomas wouldn't give him anything more.

Thomas was surprised to see him go.

Chapter Eight

Tinera

In the morning, Felix had to endure another temple service with Catherine. This time, she let him stay, but he wished she would kick him out again. She preached about how a murderer's soul will never make it to the quiet afterlife, looking at Felix every time she said the word "murderer." Everyone else in the temple picked up on the purpose of the sermon and shot him dirty looks. At one point, he pinched his arm to check he wasn't having a nightmare. This place was awful.

Afterward, Felix hurried to the dining hall. He was one of the first to arrive. After receiving his food and a flagon of water, he sat at the usual table at the center of the room. Aella and Finnlay joined him a few minutes later.

"Whoa, what's the matter with you?" Aella asked. "You look awful."

Felix raked his hands through his hair and sat up straight, trying to appear presentable. He hadn't realized Catherine's sermon had bothered him so much until Aella said something. "I just came from temple. It was—" He stopped. He hadn't told Aella or Finnlay who Catherine was. He glanced around the room once before leaning in close to speak in a lowered voice. "Do you know who the priestess is?"

"Catherine," Aella said with a smile like Catherine was her best friend.

Felix nodded. "Catherine who?"

Aella shrugged. "How should I know? Does it matter?"

"Do you know her, Felix?" Finnlay asked.

Felix hadn't told them that he had lived as Thomas Hambleton before getting thrown in here. It had been a stupid decision, and he knew Aella would tell him so if she found out.

Felix nodded but did not clarify.

Aella and Finnlay exchanged a curious look before fixing their eyes on Felix again. After a moment of silence, Aella asked, "Are you going to tell us?"

Felix pushed the vegetables around in his bowl. "Hambleton," Felix said. "Her name is Catherine Hambleton, and I'm here because I got her son killed."

Finnlay choked on his food and coughed to clear his airway. Aella stared at Felix with wide eyes.

"You did *what?*" Finnlay asked.

"Nice!" Aella said with a grin. She lifted one hand in the air for Felix to high-five.

Felix shook his head. "Aella, he didn't deserve to die."

Aella frowned but didn't lower her hand. "He was a Hambleton," she said. Finnlay shot a look of subtle shock in her direction but sealed it away before she saw.

"The Hambletons aren't killing *us,*" Felix said.

"Aren't they?" Aella asked, giving him a pointed look. She finally dropped her hand.

Felix averted his eyes. "No. That wasn't them."

Finnlay scrutinized Aella and Felix. "How did you get involved with the Hambletons?" he asked.

Felix was grateful for the change in subject. He explained what had happened the night he met Thomas. He told them about their agreement to trade lives, Felix living with Thomas's face and identity and Thomas taking Felix's place on a Southworth crew.

"Wow. How did he get away with that? Do you two look pretty similar or something?" Finnlay asked.

Felix shrugged. "Yeah. He looks like me but more . . . depressed."

"He sounds hot," Aella said.

Finnlay squinted at her. "What is the matter with you?"

Aella shrugged. "What? Come on, Finnlay. You don't think Felix is hot? I know you do."

Finnlay froze, staring at Aella. "N-no. I mean, he's fine. Not like *fine,* but you know. He's handsome. I'm not—" He looked at Felix with desperation. "Felix, I don't look at you like that. Aella's just trying to get under my skin."

"Honestly, it seems like it's working," Felix joked.

Finnlay's face flushed and he stopped stammering.

"So how did you get caught?" Aella asked as she continued eating, completely unfazed by the distress she had caused Finnlay. Finnlay ate his own food in silence too, but he wouldn't look at Aella or Felix.

"I . . . I was trying to get back at Thomas's ex-boyfriend, Charles," Felix explained. Finnlay looked up, fixing his eyes on Felix. "Charles, um . . . well, we don't have to get into that. He sucks. One of the things I did to get back at him was date his sister as Thomas, but I actually fell in love with her. I told her who I really was, and she didn't take it well. Now I'm here." Felix intentionally omitted Rebecca and Charles's last name.

"I'm so sorry that happened to you. That must have been pretty recent," Finnlay said. "Are you all right?"

"I'm getting by," Felix said.

"I thought it was weird that you got caught. You must be the only shapeshifter here," Aella said. "Most shapeshifters are good at slipping away, like you did when your mother was burned."

The shock of that memory hit him as fresh as if it had happened yesterday. He had tried everything in his power to save his mother, but instead he stayed too long for an event he never wanted to attend. "Why do you keep bringing that up, Aella?" he asked quietly.

Aella seemed speechless for a second while Felix and Finnlay watched her. Finnlay looked a bit nauseous, and Felix could tell he knew exactly what had happened. It was probably something he feared as a witch himself.

"Because that was the last time I saw you," she said, and there was something in her voice that Felix had not heard before. Compassion, maybe? Fear? "All this time, I didn't actually know if you made it out alive. I thought you might be dead."

"Why did you care? You've always hated me," Felix said.

"No, I've never hated you . . ." Aella said. Her brow furrowed and her lips parted like she wanted to say more, but she seemed to sober from her moment of kindness quickly. She sat back in her seat and crossed her arms. "So how did you get the Hambleton kid killed?"

That sounded more like Aella. "The Southworth ship I was on got lost at sea after he took my place. They think it was sirens."

Aella scoffed. "Sirens? I doubt it. He probably starved to death."

Felix hadn't considered Thomas might not be affected by the sirens. "Wow. Now I feel *worse*. Thanks."

"Felix," Finnlay said gently, "you don't really believe that was your fault, do you? He chose to take your place. It was a mutual agreement. Besides, if it wasn't him, it would have been you."

"He was a Hambleton," Aella said again. "It just means one less piece of trash in the world we have to worry about. You did us a favor."

Finnlay pursed his lips. "Aella, you don't know anything about this person. What if he was different? Maybe he could have helped us."

Felix stood from his untouched bowl of stew. "I'm not hungry. I'm going to go for a walk." All this talk about death made him feel queasy. He didn't think he could stomach this nasty food anyway.

"Wait, Felix, I'm sorry," Finnlay said. "I didn't mean to say—"

"Don't worry about it," Felix said as he walked away.

At Sea

As the days passed, Thomas tried to focus more on his breathing and less on Charles. Breathing seemed to calm the energy and stop it from leaving his body, but he still couldn't quite separate it from his feelings, whatever that meant. On this ship, it was proving impossible to keep his anger down.

The captain was ruthless, and he rarely let his crew rest. Caldwell did not believe the size of the crew made a difference to their energy level, and he cared little that the amount of work assigned to each sailor was almost triple the normal amount expected of an average merchant crewmember.

Thomas worked most watches, but he didn't mind. If the captain was going to overwork anyone on the crew, Thomas preferred it was him.

One day, Thomas was enjoying a rare moment of rest. Midday began its descent into afternoon, and Thomas watched the dark, blustery sea while he practiced his breathing. Rain continued to fall, but it had slowed from a heavy downpour to a light sprinkle. The change in weather gave him the confidence to believe he could get a handle on his magic.

The captain's bellowing voice cracked the calm he had managed to cultivate. Harsh words rang loudly in the air. It wasn't abnormal to hear him shout commands at the crew, but this was different. He was angry.

Thomas turned away from the sea. He let out a sigh of relief when he found the captain wasn't yelling at Charles, and then he tried to convince himself he hadn't been worried about that to begin with.

His relief didn't last long. A crowd gathered on the middle deck, where the captain stood over a sailor lying on the ground. Thomas flanked the crowd to get a look at the sailor, who was propped on his elbows, squinting up at the captain.

"Get up," the captain demanded.

The sailor tried to push himself up but fell face-first onto the deck. He groaned as he wobbled up onto his hands. He couldn't even keep his eyes open. "I'm trying," he croaked.

"Try harder," the captain said. "Stop being lazy. We can't all be napping on the job, or this ship wouldn't get anywhere."

"I've only had one break since we departed," the sailor said.

"What?" Thomas asked before he could stop himself. Thomas had taken at least three breaks himself, and he didn't even need them.

The captain looked up, a glimmer of amusement hiding in his eyes. "Look who it is. Our model sailor," he said with a sick smile. He turned to the sailor again. "Mr. Hambleton never gets tired. Why should you?"

The sailor stared miserably at Thomas. Thomas didn't know

what to do. It wasn't fair of the captain to expect the same amount of work from the rest of the crew. They were mere mortals.

"I'm sorry, Mr. Hambleton," the sailor said. Despite his exhaustion, a tremble hid in his tone. "I'll do better. I promise." The sailor tried to push himself up but collapsed again.

Thomas became nauseous at the thought that this sailor feared him to the point of working himself to death. Thomas eyed the rest of the crowd, who somehow watched without looking directly at him. They looked away when he tried to make eye contact. All except one sailor.

Charles was with the rest of the crew, watching Thomas with the same sickened frown. Why wasn't Charles doing anything?

What *could* he do? The captain was a tyrant.

Thomas's head spun as he realized that, as a Hambleton, he was the only person who could do anything about this. Without wasting another moment, he hurried toward the exhausted sailor and kneeled beside him. "Don't hurt yourself," Thomas said quietly. "What's your name?"

"Julian," the tired sailor answered promptly.

Thomas put his arm around Julian and lifted him off the ground. "I'm going to take over for you, Julian. You need to rest."

"What are you doing, Hambleton?" the captain asked.

Thomas frowned at the captain, struggling to hold Julian up, who was too tired to hold his own weight. "I'm helping my crewmate. You're going to work him to death."

"We don't have enough people to allow for such frivolous breaks. We need as many hands on deck as possible," the captain argued.

"I'm taking his place," Thomas said.

The captain's dark eyes looked Thomas up and down. "Julian is our strongest sailor. You alone could not take his place."

"I'll help too," Charles said, stepping forward. "Two of us will be enough."

The captain sighed heavily, eyeing Charles like he didn't think Charles added much value. "I suppose . . ." He glared at Thomas and Charles, then his narrowed eyes fell on the other sailors. "Get back to work! This ship won't sail itself!" he barked before disappearing into his cabin.

"I'm—I'm sorry, Mr. Hambleton," Julian stammered. "I've hardly slept since we left Dufonn."

"I know," Thomas said. "It's okay. Let's get you to the living quarters."

"Let me help you," Charles said, rushing to Julian's other side. He threw Julian's other arm around his shoulder, relieving some weight from Thomas's shoulders.

"Thank you," Julian said. "I don't know what I would've done if you hadn't stepped in."

They slowly led Julian down the hatchway and found his sleeping area. He fell into his hammock, pulling himself deep into it.

Thomas rolled his shoulders. Julian was a big guy, and Thomas wasn't used to carrying so much weight. Charles wasn't fazed by the effort. "Julian, can I ask you a question?" Thomas asked.

Julian mumbled in response.

"Is this how it's always been?" Thomas asked. "Has working on a Hambleton ship always been so . . . difficult?"

Julian didn't answer. Thomas began to suspect Julian had fallen asleep, until he said, "No. I love working for the Hambletons."

Thomas sighed and shook his head. "Get some rest. I'll take over for you until you feel better. Don't come back until you feel well enough to work, okay?"

"Yes sir," Julian said.

Thomas frowned at Charles. Charles smiled back.

"What was Julian's role?" Thomas asked. "What are we supposed to be doing?"

"The rigging," Charles said.

"Wow. The captain was right. I couldn't do that alone," Thomas said.

"Good thing we've got each other," Charles said with a wink.

Thomas looked at the hatchway to distract himself from whatever nice feeling was trying to pull itself from the ashes of his anger. "Thank you for volunteering to help."

Charles nodded. "Anytime."

"Are you going to be okay? I could work until we got to Brenton, but I know you're already exhausted."

"I'll be fine. Don't worry about me," Charles said.

Thomas pressed his lips together as he scrutinized Charles. "Let's go," Thomas said quietly, nodding toward the hatchway.

Thomas tried to ignore the other sailors' eyes on him as they returned to the main deck. He wondered for the thousandth time what they truly thought about the Hambletons.

He focused on Charles to keep his mind occupied. "How are my friends doing?" he asked. Charles had been tasked with taking care of the prisoners.

"They're as good as they can be. They ask about you a lot," Charles said as he began to check Julian's work.

"What do you tell them?" Thomas asked, following close behind him.

Charles turned to smirk at Thomas. "You want to know what I say about you when you're not around?"

Thomas took a deep, steady breath. "Yes," he said evenly.

"Hm . . . I tell them you're doing well with controlling your magic, but that you won't talk to me. They think you should spend more time with me."

"Bullshit," Thomas said.

Charles laughed. "You got me. They actually think it's good that you're staying away from me."

"Yeah."

"Anyway, I like your friends," Charles said.

"Me too. I'm glad you get along with them," Thomas said.

"Really? Why?" Charles asked, pausing to hold Thomas's gaze.

"Because they're my friends," he said, too defensively. "And you're . . ." He sighed. "Well, you know . . ."

Charles's smile widened. "How did you meet them?"

Thomas was surprised Charles didn't pull at that loose thread. "I met Faya and Fiona on this ship as prisoners. I met Fyavine and Ametta in Chratan. Fyavine was a siren, and I met Ametta in jail when I was arrested."

"You got arrested? For what?" Charles asked with laughter in his voice.

"For being a magus. I didn't even know I was one."

Charles raised his eyebrows while he continued to inspect the ship. "Hm . . ." His hand ran over the gunwale, and Thomas was surprised that the sight of his elegant fingers over the rough wood of the ship didn't seem out of place. Charles's hands were strong, and the muscles in his forearms were toned like he had actually been working during his time at sea. He wasn't just a spoiled rich boy anymore.

"Thomas," Charles said. Thomas flinched, but he watched Charles attentively. "Do you realize when you're staring at me? Or do you just not care?"

Thomas forced himself to look somewhere else. He decided on the main mast of the ship and kept his eyes there. "Um—" He cleared his throat. "Yeah. I know I'm doing it. I guess I'm just not used to this."

"Not used to what?" Charles asked.

"Being allowed to look at you."

"Oh," Charles said in a lighthearted tone. "Who said you weren't allowed?"

Thomas glared at him but only became more frustrated at the amused smirk on Charles's face. Gods, he was so irritating.

"You're welcome to stare at me," Charles added. "I just want to understand why."

"I don't need to explain myself," Thomas said.

Charles tilted his head. "I didn't mean to pry."

Thomas crossed his arms and turned his glare at the mast again. "No, I mean . . . I think you can figure it out."

"Oh . . ." Charles said. Thomas felt Charles's eyes on him. "So you're just going to leave it at that and let my imagination get away from me?"

Thomas closed his eyes and exhaled through his nose. "Yes." He doubted elaboration would make things any less uncomfortable, and whatever Charles imagined was probably not far from the truth.

Charles shrugged and got back to work. "Okay."

"Hambleton!" the captain shouted.

Thomas and Charles both jumped at the booming voice. Thomas turned to find Captain Caldwell strolling toward him, looking very somber.

"Yes, Captain?" Thomas asked.

"Come with me. Let's talk," the captain said. Something beneath his calm expression seemed to wait for the right moment to emerge, but Thomas couldn't identify it.

Thomas glanced at Charles. Charles raised his eyebrows and shrugged. Thomas turned to follow the captain.

Caldwell stood in the captain's cabin, on the other side of the table, with his hands folded behind his back. He watched steadily as Thomas shut the door behind himself.

"Hambleton," Caldwell said calmly.

"Caldwell," Thomas said.

This only sharpened the hidden look behind Caldwell's stoic frown. "I am your captain. You will address me as such."

Thomas crossed his arms. "Do you need something, *Captain?*"

Caldwell narrowed his eyes. "You're nothing like your father."

Thomas resisted the urge to say *Thank Dei for that.* Instead, he said, "How do you mean?"

"Your father appreciates hard work. He would never allow this kind of insubordination from his sailors. The only reason I allowed it from you is because I think you can learn from this experience."

Thomas didn't know what he could possibly stand to learn from abusing the people who worked on his ship. The only thing he had learned was how *not* to act as a leader. "What should I have learned?" he asked carefully.

"I want you to go out there and tell Lee that he's on the next two watches," Caldwell said.

"Lee?" Thomas asked, looking at the door behind him as if he could see beyond it. "Lee has been working since yesterday morning. He can't work until tomorrow morning too."

"He can and he will. You're going to tell him," Caldwell said.

"No," Thomas said, looking Caldwell in the eyes. "I'm not going to do that."

"Either you tell him he's on the next two watches, or I'll tell him he's working the next three," Caldwell said. "It's your choice."

"You can't be serious. These people need to rest," Thomas argued.

"They knew what they signed up for when they volunteered to work on a skeleton crew."

"Three days without a break is inhumane. I can't let you do that to my crew," Thomas said.

"*Your* crew?" Caldwell stepped around the map table to approach Thomas. "This is my crew, Thomas. I don't care who your father is. Out here in the middle of the ocean, you answer to me."

Goosebumps prickled across Thomas's skin. Caldwell's words felt like a threat. "And what if I don't?"

"I suppose there's nothing I can do about that." Caldwell stepped back and eyed the ceiling. "Maybe you were right about the prisoners. They would make a good replacement if something were to happen to a member of our crew, particularly if that crewmember were responsible for their care. I would hate for it to come to that, of course."

Thomas felt sick. *Charles*.

Something dark settled over Thomas's thoughts. He needed to get Caldwell away from his friends somehow, but they were all stuck out here together in the middle of the ocean.

A thought itched in the back of his mind. There was a way to get the captain off this ship, but he refused to acknowledge it. His brain refused to draw the connection that would save his friends, his crew, and the world.

When Thomas looked at the captain again, his blood went cold. It wasn't just his thoughts that had darkened. The room had darkened as well. Not even the low lantern light could penetrate the shadows taking hold of the small cabin. A dark figure loomed tall behind Caldwell, wearing a power-hungry smirk to match his.

Tetra.

Thomas watched, waiting for her to speak.

"I know what you're thinking, Thomas," Tetra said, her smile growing. "Because I'm thinking it too. I want *him*." Tetra towered over Caldwell as she eyed him hungrily.

Why hadn't Thomas thought of it before? Of course Tetra wanted Caldwell. But did Thomas want to live with *Caldwell* in this world for eternity? Did he want to face Caldwell in a duel?

Thomas slowly shook his head, fighting to find words.

In unison, Tetra and Caldwell tilted their heads. "Are you refusing?" they asked as one. Caldwell narrowed his eyes as he spoke, but Tetra said it like she already knew what Caldwell would say. Tetra let out a low growl of a laugh that slowly grew into a loud, terrible cackle.

"If you don't give me Caldwell, I'm going to take your boyfriend," Tetra said.

"You can't do that," Thomas said.

"I'm in charge, Thomas. This is *my* crew," Caldwell answered.

"I almost had him," Tetra said. "He agreed to be mine, and he would have been if only your stupid god hadn't ruined it."

"What? What are you talking about?" Thomas asked. He didn't remember Charles agreeing to be Tetra's servant. Charles had said no. Twice.

Tetra's sourceless laughter echoed through the room. Thomas winced like the sound was a weapon.

Caldwell furrowed his bushy black brows.

"I told him I was going to make you my servant in death. It was a lie, of course, but he didn't know that. He offered to take your place," Tetra said.

"No way," Thomas said. "Charles didn't do that."

"Have you lost your mind, Hambleton?" Caldwell asked, but Thomas hardly heard him over the sight of Tetra.

Tetra released a growl of a sigh. "In hindsight, his act of selflessness was sickening. If I could feel nausea, I would throw up from the memory of it."

"That didn't happen. You're messing with me," Thomas said.

"Get the hell out of my quarters," Caldwell said, rounding the table to push Thomas toward the door. "If you don't talk to Lee, I will. And don't come back here until you've got your head on straight."

"Maybe," Tetra said. "If you don't believe me, I guess you'll never know. Because you definitely won't believe *him*," Tetra said as Caldwell shoved Thomas into the light rain drizzling over the middle deck, slamming the door behind him.

Tetra's sinister laughter followed Thomas from the cabin and met him on the deck. She now loomed at the center of the deck, tall and dark. Out here, she looked almost human. Her inky black hair fell down to her waist in curling tendrils. Her skin was ghostly white, and her eyes were jet black. She smiled, showing a mouth full of sharp teeth.

It was the middle of the day, but the sky was as dark as night. The other crewmembers didn't seem to notice.

Thomas looked up at Charles working aloft, his strong silhouette suspended from a line while he trimmed the sails. Would Charles really offer his soul for Thomas? It didn't seem like he would, but . . . maybe it was true.

The light drizzle fell a little harder. Thomas turned away from Charles and found himself looking into Tetra's deathlike face. It did not help the weather.

Tetra eyed the cloudy sky then lowered her narrowed gaze onto Thomas again. "You know what it takes to become a servant, don't you? You went through it yourself."

"All I had to do was say yes," Thomas said.

"Yes, and?" Tetra asked, stepping toward him.

Thomas took a step back, looking around to check if other sailors could see this monster. Thunder rumbled in the distance. "What?"

"You died, too."

Thomas was unwilling to understand what she meant. "So?"

"So . . . You would have had to die to become Mariana's servant whether I killed you or not," Tetra said. "You can't become immortal if you don't shed your mortal skin."

Thomas shook his head. "What are you saying?"

"I'm saying . . ." Tetra took another step toward him. "You have to kill your captain."

Thomas clung to the forecastle step railing as a wave smacked the ship's hull and rocked the deck at a steep angle. Tetra's violent smile sharpened.

"No," Thomas said. "I won't."

"You have to," Tetra hissed. "You promised you would."

"I didn't know!" Thomas said.

Tetra shrugged. "That's not my problem. Kill Alastair Caldwell, or I take Charles."

"I . . . I ca—" Thomas had already sacrificed his mortality for Charles. He wouldn't let it be for nothing. He had to figure out how to handle this without giving Tetra an opportunity to go back on her word.

"You can, and you will do it quickly," Tetra said. "I've seen your own blood do much worse than murder. I know you have it in you."

"You just said you don't want Charles anymore. He makes you sick," Thomas argued.

"Yes, it seems we've got a lot in common, then, doesn't it?" Tetra asked.

Thomas tried not to let her words get to him as she laughed. "I *don't* want him," Thomas said.

"Right. Neither do I," Tetra said with a mocking smile in her voice.

"You can't take him unless he agrees, anyway," Thomas argued.

"Maybe. Maybe not. He won't have much choice if he's dead," Tetra said.

"You can't do that," Thomas said, his magic moving through his body. Now that he recognized it, he could feel it inviting water toward him.

"Oh, but I can," Tetra said as rain began to pour again. The water seemed to miss her entirely, falling right through her. "I *love* this weather, by the way. Thank you for bringing a little more darkness into the world."

Thomas didn't know what to say. He didn't want to help her, intentionally or otherwise.

Tetra glided toward him and patted his cheek with a cold, clawed hand. "You're really living up to your name, you know."

Thomas thought he would throw up if he tried to speak.

Whether he had it in him to kill Caldwell or not, this couldn't happen. He couldn't live with Caldwell in the Pantheon forever. If Tetra got what she wanted, she would use Caldwell to make the world a living nightmare, and then she would have him kill Thomas in a duel to the death.

But if Thomas didn't give her what she wanted, she would kill Charles, bring the sirens back, and continue ruining the lives of innocent people all around the world.

Thomas had no choice.

Chapter Nine

Felix tried in vain to find a secret. As a resident of Oleander, it was impossible. His fellow magi wanted nothing to do with him. Not even the only other shapeshifter in the building would speak to him. The only people he spoke to were Finnlay and Aella, who were unwilling to share secrets themselves.

Days passed, then weeks. Aella and Finnlay made good progress with finding flowers, but Felix was stumped. How would he convince *anyone* to confide in him? Why would anyone trust a murderer?

Every couple of days, Aella would say she got a secret from someone, but she never made it the whole day without spilling. She was not good at holding onto other people's information. Finnlay told her he'd rather wait for Felix to find something, and eventually, Aella agreed.

This only complicated the problem. It meant he would have to find a secret that Aella could hear but not tell.

It was impossible.

Felix took a walk by himself during free time on a sunny afternoon. Dry mud caked the sparse grass, but the occasional flower bobbed in the wind. It was a beautiful spring day.

Felix came upon the main entrance building, approaching it from the north. The sparse forest of trees partially concealed him.

An open window on the north side of the building revealed two people having a serious conversation. One of those people was Catherine.

Felix stepped behind a tree before they caught sight of him. This could be a good opportunity to get a secret. Finally.

Their voices carried on the wind, but not loudly enough to hear what they were saying. He would have to get closer.

The sound of dull footsteps behind him sent a spark of fear through his body. He whipped around. Luckily, it was only Aella.

"Hey Felix!" she said. Her steps quickened. "What are you—"

"Shh!" Felix placed a finger to his lips. He beckoned her closer, and she ducked her head with raised eyebrows as if to ask what he was doing. "Catherine is talking to someone, and the *window is open*. I'm going to go listen," he whispered.

Aella's eyes moved to the space beyond him and widened when she spotted the room. "I'll come with you!" she whispered back.

"No! If we both go, we're more likely to get caught. You're terrible at keeping secrets, anyway."

Aella puckered her lips to one side of her face and squinted at him, then released the expression with a sigh. "Gods, fine. Go on your adventure without me."

Felix nodded and rounded the tree, stepping quietly toward the window. Before he could make any progress, Aella yanked him back by the collar of his shirt and pulled him behind the tree again.

"Are you out of your mind?" she asked. "You're just going to walk directly toward the window?"

Felix shrugged.

"No, you definitely need my help. Come on," she said, taking his hand and pulling him to the left, toward the front fence. "You'd think a shapeshifter would know how to be sneaky."

"I can usually hide in plain sight. I've never really had to sneak anywhere," Felix said.

Aella pressed her index finger to her lips, and they continued their walk in silence. They reached the dirt incline at the fence and carefully stepped closer to the main building. Neither Catherine nor her companion were visible from here, which meant Aella and Felix weren't visible to them either.

When they reached the edge of the building, Aella crouched to keep the height of her head below the windowsill. Felix followed her lead until they were safely under the window and out of sight.

Aella sat beneath the window, and Felix sat beside her. They stayed still and quiet as Catherine's voice drifted out. She sounded like she was crying.

"Where did you hear this?" she asked.

"Commissioner York in Dufonn sent notice to your husband today, and he wanted you to know as soon as possible."

"Thank you," she cried.

"You're welcome, my lady. There are a few other details that Commissioner York wanted to make you aware of as well."

"Go on," Catherine said, sniffling.

"He seems to have befriended three magi and a mermaid, and he refused to let them board the ship as prisoners. All have escaped before, so we must be careful. We will not let them get away this time. One of them is a witch, and her brother is already here. We've managed to keep him contained."

"Who is it?" Catherine asked.

"Finnlay Ferguson."

Aella clapped a hand over her mouth and watched Felix with wide eyes. Felix's jaw dropped. Finnlay had been so certain his sister escaped, but she was doomed to the same fate as the rest of them. He would be so disappointed.

"With their knowledge of magic, they could be dangerous together," the man said.

"Their knowledge of magic won't help them here. This place is entirely magic-proof," Catherine said.

"Don't underestimate them. They are identical twins, and they have the same base magic. Their combined power is dangerous."

Felix noted that his suspicion about Finnlay being an identical twin was correct, but again decided it didn't matter. He hadn't known twins shared the same base magic.

"Maybe you're right. It could be difficult getting them here if my son has befriended them. He may try to stop us," Catherine said.

Felix turned fast to face the window, as if looking at the direction of her words would make them make any more sense. Her son? Her son was dead. She chided Felix weekly in front of an entire audience about getting him killed.

But Thomas was *alive?*

"We'll do everything in our power to predict the ship's arrival, but it's hard to say exactly when that will be," the man said.

"Of course," Catherine said. "Thomas's return is confidential information. Do everything you can to keep this from getting to the Southworths. They have grown too comfortable with their position in our industry as the only family with a living heir. They believe we are doomed to fail without Thomas, so they have lost their competitive edge."

"He's alive," Felix whispered before he could stop himself.

Aella slapped a hand over his mouth and watched the windowsill closely.

"What was that?" Catherine asked. Footsteps tapped against the hard floor, approaching the window.

Before Felix could decide what to do, Aella swung her leg over his lap and kissed him, pushing him against the wall beneath the window. It took him a baffling moment to understand why she had done it. When he realized it was for show, he put his hands on her waist to seem more genuine. Aella took it as encouragement.

"Excuse me, what do you think you are doing?" Catherine's voice called loudly overhead.

Aella pushed herself away from Felix but kept him pressed into the wall so Catherine couldn't see who she was straddling. "Oh Dei!" Aella acted like she just noticed they weren't alone. "I didn't realize there was anyone in there. Sorry, Catherine!" she said with a nervous laugh.

Aella kept her fake smile aimed through the window until Catherine's hands reached out and pulled the open panes closed. She locked them with a sharp click of the latch.

Aella hastily pulled Felix up and away from the window, dragging him toward the courtyard as fast as she could without seeming suspicious.

Felix rubbed his face, struggling to process the last sixty seconds. "Thomas is alive," he whispered, running his fingers through his hair. A laugh escaped him. "I'm not a murderer."

"Congratulations, man. That's a secret though, right?" Aella asked.

Felix nodded. "Right. You're right. This is a good secret. You won't tell anyone, will you?"

Aella shrugged. "As long as Finnlay doesn't tell anyone, we're set. Or as long as the person the secret is being kept from doesn't find out about it, which is *just* the Southworth family. Lucky us."

Felix nodded again. "Right. Okay." He couldn't believe it. Thomas was alive, *and* they had found a secret that Aella couldn't give away. "I'm going to go talk to Finnlay. He needs to know about his sister."

"Okay, handsome. Don't blow it," she said with a wink.

Felix turned to leave, but the way she spoke stalled his thoughts. Did Aella think their kiss meant something? "What?"

Aella shrugged. "Don't let the secret slip until it's time."

Felix shook his head. "No, I know ... Did you just call me ... handsome?"

"Yes."

"That kiss wasn't real, Aella. That was just for show. You know that, right?" he asked.

Aella frowned and tucked a strand of pale hair behind her ear. "I know that, but ... Felix, I ..."

Felix let the silence drift wide between them, fighting to find something to say as much as Aella seemed to be. "Um ..." He knew he should say real words, but he was blanking. "Aella ..."

Aella sighed and looked at her feet, then looked up with a smile. "I know I haven't always been a good friend to you, but I have always liked you. Before you left, I was going through something, and I've never been comfortable with—with ... Well, I guess I'm still not comfortable with it. Anyway, it doesn't matter. I just want you to know that I—I'm sorry." The last word came out fast, like it was hard to make herself say it.

"O-okay. Thanks," Felix said.

Aella nodded but wouldn't look him in the eyes. It was strange to see her look insecure.

"Uh ... Do you want to come with me to find Finnlay?" Felix asked.

"No thanks. I think I'm going to go look for flowers," Aella said. "I'll see you later."

"See you." He watched her disappear between the trees, then he headed for Larkspur, the discomfort of their interaction still wriggling under his skin.

The residential hall was alive with murmurs of hushed conversations. Finnlay lay flat on his bed, tossing a ball of thread in the air and catching it.

"Finnlay!" Felix called out.

Finnlay caught the ball and sat up, searching the room until his eyes landed on Felix. "Felix!" A smile blossomed on his face, and he stood up.

"No, sit down," Felix said, sitting on the bed across from Finnlay's and gesturing to the space where Finnlay had just been sitting.

Finnlay's smile slowly disappeared, replaced by confused optimism. "What's the matter?" he asked, taking a seat again.

"I need to tell you something important. Well, two things. Do you want good news or bad news first?"

Finnlay rubbed his chin and inspected the ceiling. "Good news, I suppose."

"I have a secret for you. It's a good one," Felix whispered.

Finnlay's face lit up. "That *is* good news. I imagine that's the extent of the good news since you can't tell me yet?"

Felix laughed. "Yeah, I guess so."

"What's the bad news?" Finnlay asked.

Felix's upbeat attitude rearranged into dread. He scratched his head and looked away. "Aella and I were eavesdropping on Catherine, and I heard something that I thought you should know."

Finnlay's smile fell away. "What is it?"

"They were talking about some new intakes they'd be receiving soon, and they said one of them was . . . well, it's your sister."

Finnlay's eyebrows shot up. "No . . . Are you sure?"

"Yes. They said your name. They think you'll be dangerous together."

A mischievous grin spread across Finnlay's face, and he laughed. "I can't say I blame them. This place will be in trouble if we're both here." His smile withered and his gaze fell to the floor. "I don't want her to go through this, though."

Felix nodded somberly. "At least you won't have to worry about her anymore."

"No . . . I think I'll worry more," Finnlay said with a sigh.

Felix sat in silence and wondered how it felt to be in Finnlay's position. Felix would give anything to see his brother again. "At least you know she's alive," Felix said.

Finnlay looked at Felix again. "I can't say it hasn't crossed my mind that she wasn't. I don't know if I could handle news like that."

Felix didn't know how to respond. Losing his family had left him in a dark place for a long time, and he had yet to hear words that made the pain better.

"Are you all right?" Finnlay asked.

Felix cleared his throat. "Yep," he said. "Even though the circumstances are grim, I'm looking forward to meeting your sister. I bet she's great."

Finnlay laughed. "Yeah, she's all right. You two will get along."

"What makes you say that?" Felix asked.

"Because we get along," Finnlay said. "Don't we?"

"Yeah," Felix said. He considered it and came to a surprising discovery. "Gods, Finnlay . . . Are we *friends?*"

Finnlay laughed. "I hope so."

Felix laughed with him. "Me too."

"So, it seems we have everything we need." Finnlay lowered his voice as his eyes scanned the room. "Aella and I have found plenty of flowers. If you really think this secret will be strong enough to hold a boundary, we can do this tonight. What do you say?"

Felix grinned. "I'll see you tonight."

At Sea

Charles's fingers ached as he gripped a line to keep the storm from washing him away. The ship rocked over the wild black sea while he dangled over the violent void of water, only one slip-up away from losing his life. It was not uncommon for sailors to die at sea, but Charles couldn't let himself join their ranks. That was exactly what his father wanted.

As soon as the captain had requested to speak to Thomas alone, Charles knew the storm would return. He took it upon himself to trim the sails, but in the current storm, everyone struggled to do their jobs.

Finally, Thomas pulled himself onto the forecastle and squinted up at Charles. He jumped onto the bulwark and climbed the ratlines to join Charles aloft.

"Are you insane?" Charles yelled as Thomas perched himself beside him.

"We need to finish trimming the sails or this ship is going down," Thomas yelled.

"Or you could just breathe!" Charles yelled back.

Thomas shook his head and climbed even higher. Charles watched with a slack jaw until a nervous laugh came out of his mouth, then he also got back to work. Charles, Thomas, and two other crewmen finally got the ship upright through the heavy rainfall and crashing waves.

It was a constant battle for the rest of the watch. There was no rest for any sailor while the storm raged on. Julian was the only exception.

The only reprieve from the squall was the call for dinner. Due to the all-hands order, sailors were only permitted to take their meals two at a time. Since Thomas and Charles were covering the work of one person, they were set to go together. When their time came, however, Thomas told Charles to go without him.

"I really think you should eat something," Charles argued.

"I don't need to. It's a waste of food. It's a waste of resources. Other sailors need it more than me. I need to keep this ship afloat," Thomas fired off his arguments like he'd had them at the ready.

"Maybe you don't need food, and maybe you feel the need to personally keep this ship moving, but I *need* to talk to you," Charles said.

"I don't want to talk about this," Thomas said.

"Thomas, please!" Charles begged. "Just give me a few minutes. It won't take long."

Thomas let his head roll back and he sighed. "Fine, but I won't talk about the storm."

"Fine," Charles said.

Thomas eyed him suspiciously but did not argue when Charles grabbed his arm and led him below deck.

The rumble of rain was loud but calm compared to the conditions above. The dry air was warm against his drenched skin and clothes.

Charles pulled Thomas into the galley and shut the door behind them. He led Thomas to the table's bench, where Thomas sat down, looking like an angry wet cat. Charles grabbed two pieces of hardtack and two pieces of dried meat for them, handing one of each to Thomas before sitting beside him at the table.

Thomas took it but did not eat. "What did you need to talk to me about so desperately?"

"What did the captain say to you?" Charles asked.

Thomas's eyes widened. "Oh my gods, *Lee!*" He lurched forward like he was going to run for the door but stopped himself. He turned to look at Charles with a pale, gaunt face and wide eyes.

Charles did not believe Thomas could go without food. He looked unwell.

"Sit down," Charles said.

To his surprise, Thomas sat.

"Eat your food," Charles said.

Thomas brought the hardtack to his mouth but only held it there, lost in his own thoughts. "I can't do this," he said quietly, looking at nothing.

"Do what?"

"Any of it."

"The breathing exercise isn't working for you anymore?" Charles asked.

Thomas shook his head. "That's not what I mean. I—I—" He dropped the food onto the table with a clatter and held his head in his hands. "I'm not strong enough to save anyone. I can't save the magi, and I can't save you."

"I don't need to be saved," Charles said.

Thomas shook his head. "Dei, Charles, you have no idea."

Charles let the silence linger a moment, turning Thomas's words over in his head a few times. "Did the captain threaten to kill me? Because you don't need to worry about me, Thomas. I can take care of myself."

Thomas only let out a long sigh that became a groan, and he laid his head against the rough wood of the table. "No. Well, yes, actually . . . But it's not him I'm concerned about."

"Wow. Someone *else* threatened my life?"

Thomas didn't answer.

"Thomas?" Charles asked.

"It's Tetra. She wants me to . . ." He lifted his head and scanned the empty galley with tired eyes before continuing. "*Kill* Caldwell. She wants him as her servant," he whispered. "If I can't, she's going to take you instead."

Charles scoffed. "She can't take me unless I agree. You know that, don't you? You're a servant yourself."

Thomas fixed his eyes on Charles and didn't say anything for a long time. "Charles, did—" He quickly shook his head and looked away. "Never mind. Yes, I know that, but she's going to kill you anyway. Apparently you *have* to die before you become a servant. That's why I have to kill Caldwell."

"Wow . . ." Charles said.

"Yeah. And I can't control my magic, and I can't save my friends on *my own* ship, and I have no clue what I'm going to say to my parents when I get home. I'm not strong enough to do any of this. I don't know anything. I'm just a dumb rich kid with no skills and no useful knowledge."

"Hey, come on. That's not true. You're very smart. You were always at the top of the class."

Thomas rolled his eyes. "Yeah, sure. Maybe I can discuss the symbolism and themes in *Eternality* and bore Caldwell to death."

Charles laughed. "That's not a bad idea. That lesson almost did me in."

A small smile found its way onto Thomas's mouth, and Charles realized how long it had been since he actually saw Thomas smile. He had been obsessed with drawing smiles from Thomas before everything fell apart. Thomas was adorable when angry, but he was divine when he smiled.

Charles cleared his throat. "Listen, uh . . . I know I made a huge mistake that ruined both of our lives and irreparably damaged our relationship, and I am very sorry for that, but . . ."

He hesitated. "I hope you know that I still love you just as much as I did back then."

"Charles, stop." Thomas's smile disappeared. "Don't talk to me like that."

"Hear me out," Charles said. "I'm only saying this to you because I want you to know I would do anything for you. I would *kill* for you if I had to."

Thomas urgently shook his head. "No. Stop. I don't want to hear any more of this. I would never ask you to do that."

"I know you wouldn't. You don't have to ask."

Thomas continued shaking his head. "Because I *wouldn't*. You're offering, and I'm refusing. Don't ever speak of this again, and don't try to '*help*' me without my consent. This is my problem, not yours."

Charles nodded. "All right. I won't do anything unless you agree to it, but I don't mind being part of your problems."

"Yeah, that's pretty obvious," Thomas said.

"Wait, that's not what I—"

"All I need from you is for you to keep yourself alive. You've done that just fine for the last seventeen years, do you think you can manage?" Thomas asked.

Charles frowned. "Yes."

"Good." Thomas stood to leave.

"Wait," Charles said, standing to join him.

Thomas turned, pinning his flat gaze on Charles. To anyone else, Thomas probably appeared mad, but Charles knew him better. Thomas was tired and stressed, and he probably didn't know how angry he looked.

Charles grabbed the food Thomas had left on the table and held it out. "You need to eat. You look ill."

"No," Thomas said, and then he left the galley.

Charles sighed and stared at the door separating him from Thomas. Thomas had a lot of problems to deal with, but his two biggest problems were being too independent and too kind. He wouldn't let Charles help with his issues, and he would never kill another man. If he didn't let Charles help, Caldwell would never die.

And then Charles would die.

This wasn't just a matter of helping Thomas, it was a matter of life or death for him too.

But it was hard to be upset. Knowing Tetra had used Charles's life as motivation for Thomas was flattering in a twisted way.

Charles took this opportunity to feed the magi in the brig as well, since the all-hands order did not include his duties to them. This would be their only opportunity to receive food. He grabbed four more servings and snuck to the hold, fearing the captain would punish him for doing this job at the wrong time.

The brig was silent when he entered. Each prisoner watched him move through the room and wordlessly accepted their serving of food. Charles had a limited amount of time before the captain noticed he was gone, so he didn't mind the lack of conversation.

Before he departed, Fiona stopped him. "Charles, wait," she said, sitting up and pressing herself against the bars. "Can I ask you something?"

"Sure," Charles said, moving to stand in front of her cell.

"Do you—" She stopped talking and frowned. Her eyes flickered behind him at Faya and then moved to him again, but she didn't speak.

"Do I what?"

Fiona closed her eyes and sighed. "Please don't tell Thomas I said this, but it's been eating at me. Being stuck in here knowing that Thomas is a Hambleton . . . yet we're *still* stuck in here." She shook her head. "He seemed so upset when we saw him down here last, but I don't know."

Charles raised his eyebrows and turned to Faya. Faya was

frowning at him, but she looked away when Charles caught her eye. "You think Thomas did this to you on purpose?" he asked.

"Well . . . No. Not really. I think I'm usually a pretty good judge of character, but . . . Okay, yes. I have been wondering if we made a mistake trusting him. How stupid could we be? Of course we ended up here," Fiona said.

"You're not stupid," Charles said. "There is nobody I would trust more in the world than Thomas."

"How can you be so certain?" Fiona asked.

Charles smiled. "I've known him my entire life. I used to think he was just a stereotypical bigoted anti-magic Hambleton, but he's not like that at all. He went out of his way to talk to me one day, and it was immediately obvious that he was actually . . . a decent person, which was hard to believe at the time."

Fiona shook her head. "I'm finding it hard lately."

Charles nodded. "I would be wary in your position too, but I can honestly tell you that you don't need to be afraid of Thomas. His first reaction when I told him about the Hambleton magus camp was shock, followed immediately by determination to end it. He only wants to help, and that's not even to mention that he is a magus himself."

Fiona considered his words. A hesitant smile flickered over her face, but it was gone as quickly as it appeared. "I can't help but wonder how they found us," she said. "If Thomas didn't tell, then how did they find out about us?"

"Maybe the same way I did," Charles said. "At the docks."

A quiet moment passed. Fiona's face paled. She was obviously remembering her meltdown at the docks where she announced to the entire city that she was a magus. "Oh . . . Right," she said.

"I wouldn't waste another thought worrying about his integrity. To be honest, you are better off down here. It's brutal up there," Charles said.

"It's just that . . ." Fiona said, pulling herself up to stand face-to-face with Charles. "If he's a Hambleton, then why are we still in here?"

"The captain doesn't care that he's a Hambleton. It does nothing to help him out here in the open sea. Trust me, Thomas is worried about you. He asks about you a lot, and if he ever learned that you doubted him, he'd be distraught."

Fiona's eyebrows pulled together. "I know. I feel terrible even thinking it, but I also feel terrible being locked up."

"You would feel worse if you were swinging from the topsails in a hurricane," Charles said.

"A hurricane?" Fiona asked. "Is he still having trouble controlling his magic?"

"Yes. Your advice worked for a while, but he doesn't like to talk to me. I understand his hesitation, but I don't think it's good for him to be so isolated from all of you *and* from me," Charles said.

Fiona bit her thumbnail and eyed the wood paneling of the wall. "Do you think you could distract the captain long enough that he wouldn't notice Thomas paying us a quick visit? I would like to talk to him."

"He threatened to throw you all overboard if he caught Thomas down here," Charles said.

"Yes, I heard," Fiona said.

"And you want to risk that?"

"A little water never hurt anyone!" Fyavine called from behind him. Charles turned to find Fyavine and Faya both watching with interest.

"It has killed quite a few people, actually," Charles said.

Fyavine waved the comment away like it was a transparent lie. "If they throw us overboard, I'll be there to swim everyone to safety."

"We're hundreds of miles from land," Charles reminded her.

"You don't think you could distract the captain?" Fiona asked. "If he doesn't notice, we have nothing to worry about."

Charles turned to Fiona again. He nodded as he thought about it. The captain was shrewd, but so was Charles. "Yeah . . . Maybe."

"Will you at least ask Thomas?" Fiona asked.

Charles nodded again. "Yes."

He would take any excuse to talk to Thomas.

Chapter Ten

Aella and Finnlay were already at the table when Felix arrived at the dining hall at midnight. They sat beside one another, eyeing a wide collection of colorful flowers over the dim light of a small flame hovering above Finnlay's palm. Finnlay picked up an orange flower with his free hand and rotated it by the stem.

Felix sat across from them and admired their flowers. "Wow, nice scavenging."

"It was all Aella," Finnlay said with a wide smile.

Felix thought Finnlay was just being modest, especially when Aella sat up a little straighter and smiled. "I just like pretty flowers. Where are your flowers, Felix?"

Felix's mouth fell open. He had been so focused on the secret, he hadn't even tried to find flowers. He stammered for a minute until Finnlay stopped him.

"Felix has the secret," he said.

Felix nodded, but the secret seemed like nothing compared to Aella's garden of flowers.

"Would one of you mind grabbing a lantern off the wall?" Finnlay asked.

Felix jumped up and did as he said, suddenly feeling useless. Finnlay lit the lantern with the small flame and pressed his hands together to extinguish the fire in his palm.

"Thank you," Finnlay said. He rifled through the toppling garden and plucked out several unique flowers, leaving the wild weeds and daisies in a clump together. "Hold these for me?" He offered Aella the flowers, which she silently took. Finnlay returned his attention to the common flowers. "Felix, can you fetch me some water in a bowl or a pail?"

"Sure," Felix said, eager to help however he could. He fumbled around in the kitchen for a while, making his way to where he thought the pails would be until his eyes adjusted to the darkness again and he was able to identify each blurry shadow.

When he returned to the table, Finnlay said, "You can set that on the floor. Thank you." Orange lamplight illuminated his smile.

Felix set the bucket down with a splash.

Finnlay stood and examined the table full of flowers. After a moment of consideration, he hovered his hands over them. Their stems expanded and twirled around one another, growing and intertwining into one long green rope. Finnlay plopped the stem end of the flower rope into the bucket of water and continued growing its length.

Felix watched in utter amazement. He knew earth elementalists could reach the point of mastery that allowed them to manipulate life itself, but he had never seen it in person.

"Finnlay, that's amazing!" Felix said in a hushed voice. "I've never seen anyone do that before."

Finnlay's smile grew like the flowers beneath his hands. "Thank you! It really isn't that hard."

Felix shook his head. "Are you kidding? It's incredible." The ability to create life out of a flower and a bucket of water was extraordinary. Felix couldn't believe Finnlay brushed it off like it was nothing.

Finnlay shrugged and looked away. "I've already carved the sigil into the stone beneath the table. We just need to wait for this rope to finish growing, and then I'll have you share your secret to complete the obscuring enchantment."

"Sure. Whatever you need," Felix said.

"Great," Finnlay said, gesturing to the table. "Take a seat on the other side."

Felix sat beside Aella while Finnlay draped the growing rope around the perimeter of the table. When he was done, he took the unique flowers from Aella and braided their stems into the rope at even intervals. He sat opposite Felix and rested his hands on the tabletop, palms facing up. "We should hold hands. If you don't mind," Finnlay offered.

Aella rolled her eyes. Felix shot her a confused look that she ignored.

Felix placed his hands in Finnlay's. Finnlay smiled and closed his eyes. He muttered a few inaudible incantations as a pale light glowed from somewhere beneath his shirt. "All right, what's your secret?" Finnlay asked, opening his eyes to look at Felix.

Felix swallowed, suddenly worried his secret was not enough. Finnlay was incredibly powerful to create life from nothing and do magic from a magicless prison. What did he care about Hambleton-Southworth drama?

Finnlay raised his eyebrows. "Felix?"

"I'm worried it's not enough," Felix admitted.

Finnlay frowned. "Tell me anyway."

"Right. Um." Felix looked away. "Thomas Hambleton is alive.

The Hambletons are keeping it a secret from the Southworths because they think it'll give them some sort of advantage."

The bordering rope of flowers glowed from the inside, its crevices lit with white light. After a couple seconds, the light dimmed and left the room aglow in soft starlight once again.

"That's great news!" Finnlay said with a smile. He released Felix's hands.

"Yeah," Felix said with a short laugh. "It is. I hope I see him again someday so that I can apologize."

"Why would you want to apologize to a *Hambleton?*" Aella asked with a crinkled nose.

"Because I almost got him killed," Felix said.

"I guess . . ." She shrugged. "Finnlay, did Felix tell you about your sister?"

"Yes," Finnlay said, all remains of his happiness disintegrating.

"Is she really your identical twin?" Aella asked, twirling a strand of platinum hair around her index finger and eyeing Finnlay with a subtle but severe gaze.

Finnlay's eyes widened. "Where did you hear that?"

"Eavesdropping on Catherine," Aella said.

Finnlay watched her with horror for a moment. He forced a smile. "Yes, she is my twin. But more importantly, look at what we've done!" He spread his hands over the table to gesture to their work.

"She's your *identical* twin?" Aella pried, narrowing her eyes. "Does that mean you—"

"I don't want to talk about that," Finnlay said. His forced smile abandoned his face, and he watched her with a severe gaze that matched hers. Felix had never seen him so serious before.

Aella raised her hands in defense. "Sorry . . ."

Finnlay's stern expression wavered through guilt before he looked at Felix. His eyes and lips were tense as he scanned Felix's expression, and he seemed relieved to find Felix had no idea what was happening.

Finnlay laughed nervously and fixed his eyes on the table. "Um . . . So, have either of you thought about what to do next?"

"You don't have a plan?" Aella asked.

Finnlay shrugged. "Getting this set up was the plan, and now we need a new plan. Having an area where we can do magic every day will be a huge help. We can do almost anything."

Felix thought back to everything his mother had taught him. She had tried to teach him about witchcraft when he was young, but he never cared for it. He wished now more than ever he had listened to her.

"My mother spent a long time working on a potion that could help us, but I don't know if she ever completed it, and I can't remember the recipe," Felix said.

Finnlay looked up. "What kind of potion?"

"The area we lived in was full of bigoted unmagic people," Felix explained, shooting a look at Aella. Aella's eyebrows rose and she nodded. "My mother was always trying to come up with ways to protect us from worst-case scenarios. This was her biggest project. She said it would grant immunity to magic suppressants, but I don't remember much about it."

When Felix finished, he looked up to see Finnlay watching him with wide eyes, gripping the edge of the table. "That's incredible. Do you remember *any* of it? Or anything about it? Was it successful?"

Felix scratched his head and admired the deep blue of the night sky through the high windows. "I don't know if she ever got it to work, but she came close," he said, racking his brain for any piece of information about the potion that cared to flutter through his conscious memory. "I don't remember much else. She was so proud of herself for figuring it out because the solution seemed so obvious. She was amazed nobody else had thought of it."

"Obvious?" Finnlay asked. "Immunity to magic suppressants? There's an *obvious* solution to that?" His gaze wandered away as he became lost in thought.

Felix perked up as he remembered something. "One of the ingredients was blood of a loved one."

Finnlay locked his wide eyes on Felix again. "Why?"

"No, wait . . ." Felix said. "Maybe it was just the blood of someone who loves the brewer. I'm not sure if it had to be mutual. You know more about potions than I do. What would be the purpose of something like that?"

"Permanence," Finnlay said immediately. "Or protection. Was it permanent? Did you drink the potion she made?" he asked, leaning forward.

"I didn't drink it, but I don't think it was permanent. Or maybe it was . . ." Felix groaned and rubbed his eyes. "I'm sorry. I'm useless when it comes to witchcraft or remembering important things."

"Aw it's okay, bud. It's not like our freedom depends on it," Aella said.

Felix frowned at her. She grinned, and for the first time he realized she might actually be a little funny. He let himself smile back. "I'm trying," he said. He folded his arms and stared at the tabletop as he tried to summon his memories, but nothing came. "Do you think you could recreate it with the amount of information I've given you?"

"I'm not sure . . ." Finnlay rubbed his neck and eyed the flower rope around the table. "I only know the purpose of the potion, one ingredient, which I don't have, and a piece of information that does not tell me very much. I don't know how to figure out what is 'obvious' about this recipe."

Felix nodded. "I'll try to remember. In the meantime, maybe

your sister will show up and give you some of her blood," he joked.

Finnlay did not laugh. His gaze fell to the table again.

"Sorry . . ." Felix said.

"It's all right. She'll be here soon enough. Maybe we actually *can* wait," Finnlay said with a pained expression. He clearly didn't like this option.

"No we can't," Aella said. "Catherine said your sister was coming here with that Hambleton guy. Once he's home, the Southworths will know he's alive, and our cloaking grid won't work anymore."

Finnlay's head snapped up. He stared at Aella with wide eyes. "Oh no," he said. He looked at Felix. "How soon did she say they'd be here?"

Felix scratched his head. "She didn't say . . . But they're coming from Dufonn. That journey is about a month, right?"

"Yes." Finnlay slid his hands up over his face and threaded his fingers through his hair. "This complicates things. We'll just have to hurry up and figure it out before then, won't we?" He gave a short laugh, but his pained expression returned as he fixed his gaze on the empty space behind Felix. "They could find out at any moment," he muttered.

"I should've known better than to give you a secret with an expiration date," Felix said.

Finnlay focused on Felix again and sat up. He straightened his shirt and smiled warmly. "Almost every secret has an expiration date. I suppose I should consider us lucky that we know when it is."

"That's a good point," Aella said. "It seems like a well-kept secret. The potion will probably go pretty fast once we know how to do it, and Finnlay's the smartest witch I've ever met. I'm confident he can figure it out."

Finnlay smiled. "Thanks, Aella."

"Yeah, we can do this," Felix said. "We just need a good night's sleep and some space to think. We accomplished something big tonight. We don't have to hurry into this."

Finnlay nodded as if trying to convince himself. "Yeah," he said quietly. "We've got this."

⌐

AT SEA

Charles climbed back onto the main deck, scanning his surroundings for the captain. Caldwell was nowhere to be seen. His cabin was dark. Charles wasn't sure whether Caldwell was asleep or away. It wouldn't surprise Charles if the captain had decided to sleep through this storm while his crew was hard at work getting the ship moving.

Charles hurried to the forecastle, where he and Thomas had been before their meal. The rain had slowed since Charles was last here.

Charles searched the jungle of lines and halyards until he found Thomas's hazy silhouette against the watery backdrop of rain. Despite the bad weather and harsh conditions, Thomas looked more at home out here than he ever looked at Blackwater or in Brenton.

As always, Thomas eventually noticed him. Charles leapt onto the bulwark and climbed the ratlines to get to him, pretending he had just stepped onto the deck so Thomas wouldn't suspect Charles had been watching him.

"What do you want, Charles?" Thomas asked when Charles reached him. He didn't look up, yet somehow he had sensed Charles's approach.

"Well, I—" Charles paused and glanced around to make sure no one was nearby. "When is your next break?" he asked quietly.

Thomas whipped his head around to eye Charles warily. "Why?" he demanded.

Charles bit his lip to fight back a laugh. Thomas was clearly suspicious of his intentions. "As much as I want to ask you on another cute date to the galley, your friends requested to see you," Charles said. "They want me to distract the captain so you can sneak down to the brig. So, when are you free?"

Thomas's eyes widened. "They could get killed if Caldwell catches me."

"I won't let him."

"Don't be ridiculous. There's no way you can keep the captain distracted. He'll notice I'm gone. He always does."

Charles glanced down at the captain's cabin and immediately regretted it. His head spun at the distance to the deck below. He locked his eyes on Thomas. "We'll plan to do it while the captain is asleep and we both have a break. So, when's your break?"

Thomas narrowed his eyes. "Tonight, but I'm not going to risk my friends' lives on the hope that *you* can deal with Caldwell if he wakes up, because frankly, he reminds me of your father."

Charles froze at the mention of Alfred. He hadn't thought about it, but Caldwell *did* look and act like him. He shook his head. "I can do it."

"Are you sure?" Thomas asked with raised eyebrows.

Charles nodded, but drawing that connection had shaken him.

Thomas's eyes wandered below as he considered it. He did not seem perturbed by their elevation, and Charles admired him for it. "It would be nice to see them again . . ." Thomas said.

"I'll come get you at the start of the first watch. How does that sound?" Charles asked.

Thomas sighed heavily. "Fine."

As soon as they were both free from their duties, Charles found Thomas standing near his hammock. "Are you ready?" Charles asked.

A small smile flashed across Thomas's face, but it was gone devastatingly fast. "Is the captain asleep?"

"Yes," Charles said. "I haven't seen any sign of him on deck, and the cabin is dark."

Thomas nodded. "Don't get yourself in trouble, Charles. I don't trust Caldwell."

Charles arched an eyebrow with a smile and raked his fingers through his damp hair. "Aw, you're worried about me?"

"Shut up," Thomas said, rolling his eyes as he walked away.

Charles waited until Thomas had dropped into the cargo hold before returning to the main deck. To his relief, the cabin was still dark. Everything was going as planned.

Charles perched on the middle deck between the two sets of forecastle steps to keep an eye on the captain's cabin. A cool breeze blew across the sea. The ship moved through the light rain, rocking steadily. If Charles wasn't careful, he could fall asleep to the sway.

Only a few minutes passed before orange light flickering to life inside the captain's quarters woke Charles from his sleepy daze.

Charles jumped up and took a step toward the cabin, but he stopped. Caldwell would not react well to a knock at his door, but Charles couldn't let him step outside and find Thomas missing. Thomas was right, Caldwell *did* notice when he was gone.

Charles took decisive action to knock on the door. Caldwell didn't spend much time in there except to sleep, and he would exit soon anyway.

Charles gave three light raps on the door and waited until Caldwell emerged. His long black hair was not tied back as usual. His scowl was as severe as ever, and he was not fully dressed. He wore an undershirt only, which fell open at the collar and revealed a black tattoo of a skull over his heart.

Charles's greeting caught in his throat at the sight of it. He recognized that mark. It was the mark of a pirate.

Charles stared for one second too long and forced himself to look into Caldwell's eyes, which narrowed to dark slits as they met Charles's. "Southworth," Caldwell growled. "What do you want?"

"Um—" Charles's mind went blank. The comparison between Caldwell and his father had already thrown him off, but he fell into debilitating uncertainty knowing Caldwell used to be a pirate.

Or maybe he still was.

Caldwell scanned the dark deck and tightened the drawstring of his shirt to hide the mark. "Since you insist on being nosy, you may as well come in," he said, nodding toward the interior of the cabin.

Charles stayed glued to where he stood until he forced his feet to move forward, following Caldwell—a pirate—into his cabin. Alone.

Caldwell shut the door firmly behind Charles and watched him with lowered brows. "You better not speak a word of what you saw to your crewmates. I've nothing to hide, but I don't need rumors spreading on an already unpleasant voyage."

"I won't tell. The Hambletons pay you well, eh?" Charles tried to joke.

Caldwell did not laugh. "They do. I believe in redemption, which is why I believe in the Hambletons' mission. Who else would spend all their resources on saving a group of people who've no desire to be saved?"

"You, uh . . . You got me there," Charles said, trying not to argue over what was clearly a violation of human rights. A pirate wouldn't know anything about that.

Caldwell did not acknowledge his response, turning to the chest against the wall to continue dressing. "Don't waste my time, Southworth. What is it?"

"I only wondered if you could tell me which route we are on," Charles said.

"Why?" Caldwell demanded without looking up.

"I want to know which route would be experiencing so many storms at this time of year. It's unusual," he said.

"You are the last person on this crew who will know the trade route, Southworth. You're only going to share this information with your rat father for personal gain. I know your type," Caldwell said.

Charles was deeply offended at being compared to his rat father. "Alfred does not deserve the information I bring home as a result of him banishing me from my own fleet."

Caldwell scoffed. "You still think it's your fleet?" He shook his head as he shrugged on his overcoat and turned to fix his dark eyes on Charles. "Do you really believe you can talk your father into letting you back into your family after you show up in Brenton with a resurrected Hambleton? You're out of your mind."

Charles ignored the sting of his words for the sake of the conversation. "So why is it a problem to share the trade route with me, Captain?"

"Because I think your father might be stupid enough to do just that if you come home with a valuable piece of information," Caldwell said.

"But not something as insignificant as one of the many well-known trade routes."

Caldwell stood up straight, looking taller than he ever had before. He glanced at the door, then scrutinized Charles with narrowed eyes. "Seeing as this is a matter of Hambleton business and we have a Hambleton aboard this ship, perhaps we should ask *him* if it's okay to share this information?"

Charles bit back his immediate urge to disagree, but his heart beat hard. He had promised Thomas he wouldn't let Caldwell catch him, but he wasn't performing his best when he felt like he was speaking to a vicious pirate and his own father at the same time. "I'd rather not bother Thomas with something so trivial," Charles said.

"No? But you're so keen to bother him about all other trivial matters," Caldwell said.

It was true. Every excuse Charles found to bother Thomas, he took it. "Yes, and he's asked me to stop."

"What are you up to, Southworth?" Caldwell demanded, strolling toward the cabin door.

Charles let him, hoping his relaxed demeanor would dissuade Caldwell from checking on Thomas, but inside he was spiraling. "Why would you think I'm up to something?" he asked, turning to follow Caldwell to the door.

Caldwell pulled open the door, and a cold wind swept through the room. "If you're so innocent, then perhaps we should ask him together?" He stepped out onto the deck and searched the rigging for Thomas. His head moved from the fore of the ship to the aft, but Thomas was nowhere to be seen. "Is Hambleton taking his break?"

Charles followed him onto the middle deck, ignoring the question. "We don't need to talk to Thomas. I asked *you* about the trade route because you know the ins and outs of the voyage best. You're the captain, after all. You made the call."

Caldwell folded his arms and turned to Charles. The wind whipped his black hair across his face, framing his narrowed eyes in a way that made Charles's skin prickle. No wonder Tetra wanted him. "Your flattery won't work on me," he growled, and he turned to head for the hatchway.

"Captain, wait!" Charles shouted, quickly losing control of the situation. "Listen, you're right. If I can be frank with you, some of the other crew members are trying to mutiny," he said quietly, pushing past Caldwell to drop himself below deck first, but the captain grabbed him by the collar of his shirt before he could reach the steps.

"This crew wouldn't dare," Caldwell said with a sneer. "I've met too many weasels like you. Do you really think I can't recognize a half-baked scheme?"

Charles hadn't thought the captain would be so perceptive, but he hadn't known Caldwell was a pirate. He might have prepared a better lie if he had.

"Okay, there is no mutiny and no scheme," Charles admitted. "I just want to talk to Thomas alone."

Caldwell shoved him away from the hatchway and stomped down the thin wooden steps without saying anything else.

"*Shit,*" Charles hissed. He didn't know how he had let this spiral so far out of his control.

Chapter Eleven

Tinera

Felix arrived at the dining hall the next morning as early as possible, but Finnlay and Aella were already there. Finnlay stood inside the circle, tidying the mess they had left the previous night. When he spotted Felix, he grinned. Aella sat across from him with her head resting in her hand.

Felix grabbed his morning serving of stale bread and sat down beside Finnlay. "Good morning," Felix said. "How'd you sleep?"

"I didn't," Aella grumbled.

"Me neither. I was too excited about this." Finnlay looked over both shoulders, then smiled at Felix and Aella. "Nobody can see us. Not really, anyway," Finnlay explained. "We are still visible, but nothing about the sight of us will be interesting or remarkable. The same is true of our conversations. People can still hear us, but they won't care about what we say. We are effectively invisible."

"Wow, that's amazing," Felix said. He thought for a moment, and then asked, "Why was I able to see you when I walked in?"

"You were in the circle when it was created, so it doesn't affect you," Finnlay explained.

"Wow, I didn't know such a thing was possible. So I could eat my breakfast as someone else?" Felix asked.

Finnlay beamed at him. "You can!"

Felix shifted into Aella and shot her the smug look she always gave him.

Aella sat up to look him up and down with the same look on her face. "You've never been cuter," she said with a wink.

Finnlay watched with amusement and then said, "Anyway, I've been trying to figure out Felix's mother's recipe all night, but it's not as obvious as she thought. Have you remembered anything else?"

Felix shook his head and shifted back into himself. "Sorry."

Aella sighed. "Felix, I don't mean to sound rude, but . . . I know so many magi who would kill for such a potion. Have you considered that your mother was lying to you?"

"She wasn't lying. She considered it her life's work," Felix said.

Aella raised her eyebrows and shrugged. "It was just a thought. Parents aren't perfect."

"I have an idea," Finnlay said. "Felix, why don't you tell me everything you know about making potions. Maybe something you know about potions came from that one in particular, and it will help me understand it."

"Sure, yeah . . ." Felix rubbed his neck as he tried to find a starting point. "I'll start with bases, I suppose." Finnlay nodded and watched him expectantly. Aella looked on with just as much interest. "I know there are five standard bases; experimental, reversal, enhancing, longevity, and mending." Felix paused, haunted by the ghost of a memory. "Hold on, I think there was something strange about the base . . ."

"It wasn't a longevity base?" Finnlay asked.

Felix shook his head. "I don't think so."

"But she used your blood?"

Felix nodded. "What else could it have been?" He rubbed his chin as he went through the list in his mind again. He was impressed Finnlay's suggestion was already working.

"I did find it odd that the second base you listed was reversal. That's usually the one people forget because it can be finnicky, so it isn't used often. Is it possible . . . ?" Finnlay trailed off and looked away, then his eyes widened. "Is that what was obvious about this potion? It used a reversal base with the longevity trait added through a separate ingredient?" He watched Felix as he waited for an answer.

Felix stared right back, his mouth hanging open. "Finnlay, you're amazing. That was exactly it. I can't believe this worked," he said through a laugh.

Finnlay grinned. "That *does* seem obvious, but I never would have thought of it. Your mother was a very smart witch."

"Do you think you could make it now that you have this new information?" Felix asked.

Finnlay rubbed his chin. "I'm not sure. If I do it wrong, I'm afraid I'll take away someone's magic forever."

"You can test it on me," Felix said. "That'll probably happen to me either way."

Finnlay frowned at him. "Don't talk like that."

"Why do you think that?" Aella asked.

"I'm a prisoner here. They won't let me out whether I have my magic or not because of what happened to Thomas," Felix said.

"But he's not even dead anymore," Aella said.

The injustice hit Felix all at once. "Wait a second, why *am* I a prisoner? They have no reason to keep me here now that they know Thomas is alive."

"Well, Felix . . . I don't think you're really here because of Thomas," Finnlay said with a pained smile. "You're here for the same reason as the rest of us."

Felix sighed and rubbed his hands over his face. "You're probably right. Either way, you can test your potion on me. I brought you this idea, and I'm willing to sacrifice my magic for the good of the world."

"Are you sure?" Finnlay asked with a furrowed brow.

Felix nodded. "My mother would have done the same."

Finnlay smiled. "I'll get it right, Felix. Don't worry."

"Does this place have what you need to make a reversal base?" Felix asked.

"Yes, the base is easy. I am a little worried about the other ingredients, though. I can assume based on the residential hall names that they are using hemlock, larkspur, oleander, and belladonna. The only other one we've found so far is wisteria, but if they are using any other magic-suppressing flowers on us that we don't know of, the potion will be useless. It has to block everything."

"So what should we do?" Aella asked.

Finnlay ran his fingers through his hair. "We can't exactly ask. I guess we'll have to search a little harder."

Aella hung her head back and sighed loudly.

Although Felix had volunteered, losing his magic was the last thing he wanted. He had faith in Finnlay's abilities, and he trusted his mother's recipe.

It had to work.

At Sea

Thomas walked away from Charles and dropped himself to the lower decks, heading for the brig as fast as he could. He had limited time to safely speak to his friends before Caldwell caught on.

Thomas shoved the brig door open with his shoulder and stumbled into the room.

"Faya? Fiona? Fyavine?" Thomas asked as he walked through the room.

Faya and Fyavine sat back to back against the slat of wood that separated their cells. Ametta sat at the back of Faya's cell and played with a piece of rope, unraveling it and tying each piece into many smaller knots. It looked tedious, but it was probably entertaining for a six-year-old stuck in a cage.

Fiona stood gripping the bars of her cell, watching Thomas with a grin.

"Hi Felix!" Ametta said, waving wildly. She looked surprisingly lively for a child prisoner. It probably helped that she wasn't separated from her mother this time.

"His name is Thomas, my love," Faya said.

Ametta's mouth fell open as she stared blankly at her mother, and then at Thomas. "Oh."

Thomas smiled at Ametta. "Hi Ametta." He looked at Faya. "Are you all doing okay? I've been so worried about you. Is Charles taking proper care of you?"

"Yes. He's surprisingly nice," Faya said.

Fyavine scoffed. They clearly disagreed on that.

"He is," Fiona agreed. "He had a lot of nice things to say about you."

"Really? What did he say?" Thomas asked before he could stop himself. "Never mind, that's not important. It's so good to see you guys." He tried to fight the burn in his cheeks.

"It's good to see you too," Fiona said. "How is it going with your magic?"

"Not good," Thomas said. "Can't you feel the storm? It's awful."

"Did Charles explain to you how to control it?" Fiona asked.

"Charles is not a magus."

Fiona watched him for a moment with a patient smile. "So he didn't tell you?" she asked.

"No. He said to separate my magic from my emotions, and I have no idea what that means or how to do it," Thomas complained. "The only useful advice he gave me was to breathe."

Fiona pursed her lips. "He didn't tell you about magical activation? I explained it all to him."

"No. This is the first I've ever heard of 'magical activation,'" Thomas said.

"Oh boy," Fiona muttered. "Okay, I have a lot to explain, then."

Thomas nodded. "Great. I'm listening."

"Every magus has a set amount of magical energy to use on top of their normal energy. Using magical energy is a little bit like using normal energy. You use normal energy to move your body, so when you intend to move your arm," she said, lifting her arm in demonstration, "you will. It's the same with magic. You can activate your magical energy with intention. When you intend to use your magic, you will. We call this 'intentional activation.' Are you following so far?"

"I've never intentionally used my magic," Thomas said. He recalled Mariana mentioning something about intention too. "So, I can control water if I just . . . *intend* to? It's that easy?"

"Yes, you can," Fiona continued. "I'm aware that you haven't done that yet, which brings me to my next point. There is another kind of magical activation called 'emotional activation,' which is what you have been experiencing. This happens when we have big feelings that we can't control, which you may have noticed can happen with normal energy too. Have you ever been so upset that you said or did something you didn't mean to do?"

Thomas considered this for a moment. "Yes."

Fiona nodded. "Right. This is basically what emotional activation is with magic. It happens to everyone, particularly younger or more inexperienced magi. It's worse when you have a lot of unused magical energy, which seems to be the source of the problem for you. It's the only way someone could use as much magic without dying."

"I *do* have more energy now . . ." Thomas sighed and shook his head. "What can I do about it?"

"Charles was right when he said you need to separate your emotions from your magic, but I understand your frustration with his lack of explanation. That doesn't entirely address the issue. You're not truly *separating* your emotions from your magic but instead identifying the feeling alongside your magic and letting it pass without letting your magic pass with it. Even the most skilled magi sometimes struggle with this. Sit with your emotions and focus on how magic moves through your body. Practice quiet introspection when you can to identify how your magic feels. It's important to do this when you're not feeling big emotions too."

"So I need to make myself stop feeling emotions to stop my magic?" Thomas asked.

"That's not what I said. Let yourself feel it."

"That doesn't make any sense. Won't that just make it worse?" Thomas asked.

"Maybe very briefly, but sometimes things have to get worse before they get better," Fiona said. "The important thing is that it *will* get better."

"That doesn't make sense!" Thomas was frustrated. He still didn't understand, even with Fiona's explanation.

The sound of footsteps thundering overhead stopped their conversation. It didn't sound like the usual patter of a sailor at work. These footsteps were angry and determined.

Heavy feet thumping against hatchway steps was followed by arguing voices. Thomas recognized Charles's voice, and then Caldwell's. It sounded like they were in the living quarters one deck above. Thomas didn't have much time to get out.

"I have to go. I wasn't here," Thomas said, backing away from Faya's cell, wishing he had more time to say goodbye.

He pushed open the door to the brig as quietly as he could and leapt behind a stack of crates in the dark hold just as Caldwell began to descend the steps.

"Captain, nothing is happening down here. I promise you," Charles said. Thomas recognized the urgency beneath his practiced composure that only seventeen years of knowing him could reveal.

Caldwell wasn't buying it. "We'll see," he growled, stomping through the room.

Thomas shrunk behind the stack of crates hiding him from view. Caldwell's footsteps stopped just behind them. Thomas's heartbeat was so loud, he worried it would give him away. He held his breath and waited for Caldwell to move on.

"Captain—" Charles started.

"*Quiet,*" Caldwell hissed.

Thomas continued holding his breath and squeezed his eyes shut as if it would keep him hidden.

Caldwell waited. And waited. Thomas was grateful he didn't actually need to breathe. That was probably just what Caldwell was waiting for. There was no light in the cargo hold, so it was nearly pitch black. The only way Caldwell could catch him was by listening.

Finally, Caldwell growled a heavy sigh. The creak of the brig door told Thomas he was safe. He released a slow breath before creeping toward the hatchway steps as quickly and quietly as he could.

"I knew I would catch you in here," Caldwell's deep voice growled through the room.

He hadn't actually left.

Thomas froze with fear but made himself scramble up the portal. He ran through the living quarters to get to the hatchway leading to the upper deck.

His crewmates watched him cautiously. Sitting against the railing of the ship was Lee, the sailor Caldwell had commanded Thomas to overwork. His eyes slowly drifted shut as he leaned his head back to rest. Thomas's heart sank. He had avoided giving Lee the order to work the two extra watches because he didn't think Caldwell would really force a sailor to work three extra shifts, but Caldwell hadn't been bluffing.

Thomas had let his crew down.

Caldwell blazed up the hatchway steps. When he spotted Thomas, he strode toward him with fire in his eyes. "Hambleton. I told you what would happen if you visited the brig, didn't I?"

Charles scrambled up the deck after him but stopped when he saw Caldwell and Thomas.

"I wasn't in the brig. I was in the hold," Thomas said.

Caldwell narrowed his eyes. "Don't lie to me, Hambleton. I know Southworth was helping you."

Thomas glanced at Charles, who shook his head.

"Don't be ridiculous," Thomas said.

A muscle in Caldwell's jaw flexed as he fixed his angry eyes on Thomas. After a moment, his gaze flitted behind Thomas to where Lee sat against the railing. "Lee! Stand up!" he shouted.

Lee jerked awake and hurried to push himself upright.

"Leave him alone. He's exhausted," Thomas said.

"Don't tell me how to run my ship, Hambleton," Caldwell said.

"It's *my* ship."

Caldwell looked around at the crew watching the spectacle, then at Charles, his gaze finally settling on Thomas. "You *are* organizing a mutiny. Is that what this is?" Caldwell challenged.

Heavy silence filled the humid air until a crew member at the stern shouted, "Yeah!" He was as overworked as everyone else and clearly ready for the abuse to end.

Other crewmen began to join him in their cheers. Thomas didn't know what to do. He didn't want to mutiny. He didn't know how to be a captain, but he didn't want to work for this horrible man anymore.

"Yes," Charles said. "It's a mutiny."

Thomas gawked at Charles. Charles smiled.

"Very well. If it's a mutiny you want, you'll have to fight me for it," Captain Caldwell said, drawing his sword. "Who will it be?"

Caldwell would obviously fight for his position, but Thomas hadn't expected him to duel so willingly. Would he really kill Thomas over this? He had to know he would lose his position if he murdered his employer's son, but maybe he didn't care. Maybe he was just sadistic.

Of course he was. That's why Tetra wanted him.

Charles was surprisingly calm considering the captain wanted to kill them. He watched Thomas with a somber smile before turning to the captain and opening his mouth to say something.

Thomas pushed Charles out of the way and stepped forward. "Me," Thomas said, glaring at Charles.

Charles stepped toward him. "Thomas—"

"Shut up," Thomas said. "I have to do this."

"I really think you should let me—"

"No, Charles. You could die."

"So could—" Charles stopped, and his face paled as he realized he was wrong. Thomas couldn't die.

The captain looked him over with disgust. "Where's your weapon?"

Thomas took a step away from the captain. He didn't have a weapon, and there was no way Caldwell would *lend* him one for a mutiny. Thomas looked at Charles, who shrugged back at him. Charles's eyes quickly darted back to the captain and widened as he grabbed Thomas's arm and yanked him back. The captain's sword slashed the air where Thomas had just been standing.

Thomas stood frozen, watching the captain as the reality of the situation hit him. Caldwell was trying to kill him, and if he was going to kill Caldwell, it had to be now.

This was it.

CHAPTER TWELVE

Tinera

Felix awoke earlier than usual to the sound of a loud bell ringing through the residential hall. He sat up in bed and rubbed his eyes, squinting at the guard by the door waving the bell around.

"Wake up, residents!" she yelled. "Gather yourselves in the courtyard immediately."

It took Felix a moment to register what was happening. This was new. They had never gathered in the courtyard before. Felix pushed himself out of bed with a yawn, filing out of the room behind his forty-nine roommates.

The sky was a dark shade of periwinkle, brightening near the horizon. Residents from every hall trickled out onto the cold muddy grass. Felix searched the crowd for Finnlay and Aella and found them standing together with the other Larkspur residents on the opposite side of the courtyard.

When every prisoner arrived, a tall, angry woman walked to the center of the square. "It has come to our attention that someone has been attempting magic," she began without introduction. She paused to look at each sleepy magus. Felix didn't dare look at Aella or Finnlay, no matter how much he wanted to. "Wildflowers around camp have suddenly gone missing. Flowers are often used in witchcraft."

The silence in the air was heavy. His fellow prisoners looked at one another, surely wondering who was responsible. It had been a few days since Felix, Finnlay, and Aella had created the cloaking grid, after spending a month gathering flowers. Now that Felix wasn't burdened with finding a secret, he had also been collecting flowers. The flowers around camp were noticeably sparser now that they were searching for the magic-suppressing ones.

"Magic is not possible within bounds of the fence, and all attempts are forbidden. If you are found with any evidence of witchcraft on you, you will be punished. Your belongings are being searched at the moment, and we will begin bodily searches shortly," the angry woman continued.

A groan swept through the crowd but quieted as fast as it began. Felix tried to stay calm, but his heart pounded. He chanced a look at Finnlay, who stared straight ahead, calm as ever.

Felix also looked straight ahead, trying not to look guilty, but he had no reason to worry. He didn't keep his flowers with his personal belongings. They were hidden underneath a large rock near the edge of the grounds.

Finnlay was smart. Surely he found a safe hiding place as well. Felix wasn't sure how Aella was storing her things, but hopefully she was being careful.

The search was agonizingly long. The guards moved slowly through the line of prisoners, feeling them up and down and searching their pockets. They took their time on people with longer hair or tattoos. Despite his shorter hair, the guards were extra careful with Finnlay. It was obvious by his many tattoos he was a witch. Finnlay kept a calm expression as two different guards searched him multiple times.

Finally, it was Felix's turn. He held his breath as the guard approached him. She ran her hands over his clothing and made him turn out his pockets. He had nothing, but he worried his guilt hung on him like a sign.

When she moved on, Felix released his breath.

Aella smiled at the guard when it was her turn. She even threw a wink at the woman as she walked away. Felix didn't understand how she and Finnlay were so calm.

Felix breathed slowly through the remainder of the searches. They hadn't been caught. Not yet.

Finally, a guard emerged from Larkspur with a small bouquet of flowers. Everyone watched the guard walk to the center of the field.

Felix glanced at Finnlay, but Finnlay kept all emotions hidden. Aella did not seem worried. The flowers had to belong to one of them, but which would be so careless?

"Larkspur bed number forty-three!" the guard called out. He passed the line of prisoners and walked toward Aella. To Felix's relief, the guard passed Aella and stopped at a frightened young woman three paces away. "We found these flowers under your mattress."

The woman's mouth opened and closed as she tried to speak, but she was clearly too terrified to respond. Finally, she said, "You must be mistaken."

The guard dropped the flowers and squished them into the mud with his boot. "It's no use lying. You heard our captain. Any evidence of witchcraft will be punished." The guard grabbed the woman by the arm and dragged her away, stopping in the center of the courtyard to present her to the rest of the prisoners. "Let this be a lesson to all of you. Magic is forbidden here. If you try to use it, you will lose it."

Felix gasped in the cold morning air as the line of prisoners around him fought back their muffled expressions of surprise. This was the first time they had ever used magic removal as a punishment. Until now, they had treated it like a reward. Like salvation.

"What?!" The woman struggled to get out of his grip. Two more guards approached to restrain her as she fought harder. "Let me go! I wasn't doing magic! I never agreed to this!" she yelled as they dragged her away to the temple building. "Somebody help me!"

Nobody moved. Nobody wanted to share her fate.

Aella watched the woman get dragged away with disinterest. Finnlay closed his eyes and turned away. The only sound in the entire camp was the woman's pleading and crying.

The camp quieted as she disappeared behind the temple door. Several agonizing seconds passed before the woman started screaming.

Felix squeezed his eyes shut. That could have been him if he had been a little less careful. It could have been any of them.

"Remember this moment!" the guard captain yelled over the woman's screaming. "Magic is pain. It does nothing but hurt us, and if we hold onto it too tightly, it hurts to let go. You can easily be free of this pain and fear if you choose."

Finnlay glowered at her. Aella still looked bored. The screaming stopped.

"You are dismissed." The captain's voice was quiet but audible in the dead silence.

The crowd dispersed immediately. Felix lingered in the courtyard, wondering if he should speak to Finnlay and Aella. Aella meandered away. Finnlay watched her walk away, looked at Felix, then eyed the temple before also turning to leave.

Felix was second to arrive at breakfast. Finnlay was already sitting at the table with his untouched hunk of bread waiting on his plate, staring at nothing. He looked ill. Felix sat across from him, breaking him from his trance.

"Hey, Finn," Felix said. "You all right?"

"That was awful," Finnlay said quietly. "I wish I had done something to help. I feel terrible."

"What could you have done? They just would have done the same to you," Felix said.

Aella bounded into the room and sat beside Finnlay. "Hello, boys," she said. "That was close, wasn't it?"

Finnlay shrugged. "Not really. I don't keep anything in the residential hall. Do you?"

Aella laughed and snatched up Finnlay's chunk of bread. "Are you going to eat this?"

Finnlay shook his head. Aella took a bite and eyed the long line forming around the room. Felix and Finnlay exchanged a wary look.

"I hide everything under a rock. What about you, Aella?" Felix tried.

Aella swallowed the bite of bread and narrowed her eyes at Felix with a twisted smile. "Yeah, I hide my stuff in the residential hall."

"You're joking, right?" Felix asked.

Aella tore off another bite of bread and chewed. "Relax, they won't catch me."

"What makes you so certain?" Finnlay asked.

"They confiscated everything I had this morning. I'm not stupid enough to hide it under my *own* bed."

Finnlay's jaw dropped. "Aella!" he yelled. "Are you serious? That woman had her magic taken away because of *you?*"

"Better her than me," Aella said with a shrug.

Finnlay watched her eat the last of the bread before turning to look at Felix. They seemed to realize at the same time the particular danger they were in.

Aella could not be trusted.

She sighed. "She deserved it. She called me some ugly names just for flirting with her, so good riddance to her and her nasty magic."

"Nobody deserves to go through what she experienced today," Finnlay said.

"Whatever, Finnlay. You wouldn't know what it's like to have your heart broken by a beautiful woman. It hurts, and I would argue that it hurts more than when a man breaks your heart, because men are just dumb. Felix knows what I mean."

Felix did not know if Aella was trying to relate to his experience being heartbroken by women or if she was calling him dumb. He looked at Finnlay.

Finnlay was glaring at her. "Have you ever considered that maybe you don't like men, Aella? If women hurt you so badly?" Finnlay asked.

Aella twirled a lock of hair around her index finger and eyed Felix up and down with a smile. "I've considered it."

Felix averted his eyes. "What are we going to do?" he asked without acknowledging her.

Aella sighed. "They're onto us. They took all of the flowers I collected. You hardly found any last time, so I know we won't have enough to make your mother's miraculous potion. Not to mention *you don't know the recipe.*"

Finnlay frowned at her. "I've mostly figured it out."

"And I found more flowers this time," Felix argued.

Aella shrugged. "It just feels like no matter what we choose to do, we are going to lose. If we play their game, we lose. If we fight back, we lose. It's impossible."

"Maybe we need to take a break," Finnlay said. "It's not as hopeless as it seems, but today was tough."

"That will just give them more time to find us," Aella said.

Finnlay sighed. "All right, why don't you two take a break, and I'll figure it out."

"Okay," Aella said with another lazy shrug.

"Wait, no. I want to help you," Felix said. "I'm not scared."

Aella rolled her eyes. "I'm not scared either."

"It's okay to be scared," Finnlay said. "I am very scared, but that's why I'm doing this."

"What do you need me to do?" Felix asked.

Finnlay took a deep breath and closed his eyes on the exhale. "I don't want you to do anything that makes you uncomfortable, but after this morning, we *do* need more flowers," he said, watching Felix carefully.

"I can do that," Felix said.

Finnlay smiled. "Thank you. We should store them at this table if possible. You can continue hiding them under your rock if it's secure, but be *very careful.* I would hate for anything to happen to you."

Aella sighed heavily. Felix and Finnlay looked at her. "Gods. Fine, I'll keep helping," she groaned.

"You don't have to, Aella," Finnlay said. "I understand your hesitation."

Aella frowned at him. "You and your dog won't get very far without my scavenging skills."

"'Dog?' Are you talking about me?" Felix asked. "Aella, you can't—"

"By the way," Aella interrupted without looking at Felix. "I found peonies. They are using more than just wisteria and the namesakes of our residential halls."

Finnlay's gaze moved rapidly between Aella and Felix, clearly not sure which thing to address. "Thank you, that's good to know," he muttered, "but, you do realize you can't call him a dog because he's a shapeshifter, don't you? That's incredibly rude."

Aella shot a sideways glance at Felix. "It was just a joke," she grumbled.

"I know, but it wasn't nice," Felix said.

Aella opened her mouth to say something but decided against it. She stood up. "I'll keep looking. Talk to you guys later," she said, and then she left.

Felix and Finnlay watched her walk away then shared a grim look.

"I'm a little worried she's going to hide flowers under *my* bed," Felix said when she was out of earshot.

Finnlay glanced in Aella's direction before looking at Felix again. "She won't do that."

"How do you know?"

Finnlay opened his mouth to answer but said nothing. He sighed through his nose.

A sense of dread settled over Felix. He tried to shake it off, but he was too disturbed at the familiarity of the feeling. He had felt the same way after Rebecca promised she wouldn't tell anyone he was a shapeshifter. Right before she told the Hambletons.

AT SEA

Thomas ran from Caldwell to the edge of the ship, clinging to the side as he looked back and forth across the deck for a weapon. Loose rope and empty barrels littered the limited pathway, but he found nothing he could use. He felt himself over in one last attempt to find anything weaponlike and stopped at something rod-shaped in his coat pocket. He gasped.

He *did* have a sword.

The sword Mariana gave him in York had been in his pocket

all along. He pulled it out and turned the sparkling stone over in his hand, trying to remember how to use it. The captain prowled toward him. What had Mariana said?

Use your intention.

Thomas hadn't known any magic when he received the sword, but he knew a little now. He knew enough.

"It's not too late to back out," Caldwell said. "Things can go back to how they were. I won't tell your father about any of this."

Thomas focused his intention on the sword, but nothing happened. He flicked the hilt downward as if he could force the blade out. Still nothing. "What's wrong? Are you scared?" Thomas taunted.

Caldwell smirked. "Scared? Of *you?* You're just a spoiled little boy, and you don't even have a weapon."

"Maybe you're not scared of me," Thomas said, breaking away from the bulwark when the captain prowled too close. Thomas moved along the edge of the ship. Sailors made space for their duel as they approached. "But you are scared of what my father will do to you when he finds out you murdered me after my miraculous survival."

"No," Caldwell said, shaking his head. His smirk remained. "I can't wait to see the look on his face when I deliver the news that Southworth killed you and then threw himself overboard."

Thomas could not believe his ears. Tetra really had chosen the worst person. He stared at Caldwell like a deer about to be eaten by a lion.

Caldwell struck. He lurched forward, bringing the blade down overhead. Thomas lifted the hilt of his own sword in defense, desperately trying to use his intention. He didn't know anything had happened until Caldwell's blade was inches from his face, held back by a glittering crystal cutlass.

Thomas wrenched his blade to the side, swinging Caldwell's

sword away from him. Caldwell did not continue his pursuit. He pinned his deadly glare on Thomas. "Was that magic?"

Thomas took a step back, feeling the full weight of the cutlass in his hand. A smile pulled at his face despite the circumstances. "Yeah. It was," he lied.

Caldwell's glare darkened. "In that case, your father won't want you back anyway." He moved forward again, swinging his sword down hard. Thomas barely managed to block it, retreating backward with each new swing of the sword. Caldwell was too fast. Thomas couldn't hang on much longer.

Just when Thomas thought he would lose, Caldwell stopped, stepping back to scoff and shake his head. "You're weak," he said. "If you want me gone, then do it. Kill me." He spread his arms, leaving his torso wide open for attack.

Thomas couldn't move. He found Charles in the crowd of onlookers, and Charles nodded urgently. Thomas held his sword in both hands, painfully aware that his grip and his stance were both wrong. Caldwell could have dealt a killing blow by now, but he was toying with Thomas.

Thomas shook his head. It wasn't going to happen. He couldn't kill another human, and Tetra knew it. "I—I can't do it."

Caldwell dropped his arms to his sides. "How embarrassing. I'll see you in the afterlife, Hambleton."

At his last word, the captain struck, faster than before. Thomas didn't even have time to react before the sharp blade plunged deep into his chest.

Vicious amusement glimmered in the captain's eyes. Thomas didn't know how bad the injury was until he coughed and blood splattered at his feet. Charles watched the scene, pale and wide-eyed.

Thomas wanted to tell Charles it would be okay, but before he could speak, Caldwell withdrew the sword from his heart. Warm crimson blood spilled from his chest. Charles's hand covered his mouth as his eyes ran down Thomas's blood-soaked body.

Thomas didn't know what immortality meant for him. Would he die and come back? Or would he heal quickly? Thomas's heart stuttered, but before Thomas could learn about his immortality, Caldwell stuck the sharp sword into his heart again.

The blood he'd already lost was too much, and it continued spilling out of him. His limbs grew weaker and he fell to his knees. The world around him went cold.

Thomas didn't have the strength to keep himself up anymore. The wind was much colder than it had been a moment ago. He fell to the deck and lowered his head to the floorboards. He would get up again soon, but he needed to rest. Just for a moment.

Chapter Thirteen

Tinera

For the rest of the day, Felix searched for flowers on his own. He was careful not to draw the attention of the patrolling guards, pretending to be on a casual stroll as he scanned the ground for foliage. He managed to collect a handful of daisies, but he was humbled again at dinner when Aella and Finnlay showed their collection of beautiful unique flowers.

"How are you two doing this?" Felix asked.

Aella shrugged and took a bite of stew. Finnlay smiled. "It takes some practice," he said.

"Are you a witch, Aella? Why are you so good at this?" Felix asked.

"Ew, no," Aella said, squinting at him. Finnlay's eyebrows pulled together as he shot her a look. Her eyes darted to him. "No offense."

Finnlay shook his head and rolled his eyes subtly. Felix was surprised at his reaction. Finnlay was usually optimistic, but he was clearly losing patience with Aella. Felix himself was losing patience with her, and he didn't even have to live in the same hall.

Finnlay reeled in his annoyance to smile at Felix. "Just do your best. We'll talk again tomorrow. Hopefully we can get these flowers together quickly so that we can get out of here."

Felix nodded and smiled back at him. "Thanks."

Breakfast the next day came later than usual. The sun was already out by the time the Oleander hall leader let everyone out into the yard to head to the dining hall. Normally, breakfast was at dawn.

When he got there, it was empty. So far, only the Oleander residents had arrived.

Felix got his food and sat at the center table alone. He watched the door and waited for the other halls to arrive, but they never did. Felix ate his food in lonely silence.

After breakfast, the Oleander hall went to the library. Felix sat in a corner of the room, leafing through a small booklet about the spiritual benefits of Pietanism. He had never had a problem with Pietanism itself, but certain members of the religion seemed to believe using magic was a temptation and that to use the magic you were born with was an immoral choice. They truly believed they were helping magi by telling them to reject a fundamental part of their existence, but these beliefs only ever hurt people, including the people who believed it.

About an hour into recreation time, the door to the library opened and Catherine Hambleton strolled into the room, black cloak billowing behind her. She searched the room for one safe second until her eyes landed on Felix.

Catherine flashed him a sickly-sweet smile before marching deeper into the room to sit beside him. "Hello, darling."

Felix said nothing. Why was she here? Was it to tell Felix that Thomas had survived? Would she offer him that courtesy of knowledge?

"It's impolite not to say hello when someone greets you," Catherine said.

"You're not my mother."

"No, but you once believed yourself good enough to be my son, didn't you?" Catherine asked.

Felix pretended to continue reading the booklet in front of him, but Catherine yanked it out of his hands and slipped it into her cloak pocket.

"Thomas is dead because of you, Felix," Catherine said. "Doesn't that make you feel at least a little bit sorry?"

Felix narrowed his eyes at her. Of course she wasn't here to share the good news about Thomas. She just wanted to hurt him. Felix couldn't bring it up himself, because that would be admitting he had listened in on her conversation. "Of course I am," Felix forced himself to say.

"Then say it."

"Say what?"

"Say you're sorry for killing my son."

"I didn't kill him," Felix said.

"You may as well have."

"He *chose* to leave," Felix said. The injustice of this conversation fueled the sleeping anger in his heart and overpowered the careful control he needed to navigate a conversation with Catherine.

"I don't believe that. I think you tricked him, just like you tricked that Southworth girl," Catherine said.

Felix clenched his jaw as much in anger as to keep himself quiet, but he only managed to hold the words back for a few seconds. "I didn't trick her. I was honest with her, but she didn't like my honesty. None of you do."

Catherine tilted her head and squinted with a tight smile. "You are nothing but a liar. You were born a liar, and only through the beauty of salvation will you ever be anything else."

His anger rushed to his head, and he shut his eyes to let it pass. She was calling him a liar for being a shapeshifter; something he couldn't help. "Why are you so fixated on me?"

"You need more help than anyone else here. You're a murderer," Catherine said.

Felix scoffed. "If Thomas were alive, you'd still be pretending he was the person you wanted him to be instead of the person he was."

Catherine sat up a little straighter and scanned the room hastily to make sure nobody had heard him. When she was satisfied their conversation was private, she turned to him again. "I had no issue with the person he was. I loved him," she said as if Felix hadn't seen her seconds ago looking around the room to make sure no one heard her son was imperfect.

"You only spoke to me twice in the three months I lived with you, and I bet if you never noticed I wasn't Thomas—which you wouldn't have if not for Rebecca—you only would have spoken to me twice more. If ever. And if Thomas's ship is ever found and he somehow miraculously survived, you'll just go right back to pretending he's someone else."

Catherine's fake smile melted away, leaving behind a burning scowl. "Watch yourself, Felix," she said as she stood up. "You forget who's in control." She forced the calm smile back onto her face and turned to leave him in the wake of her words.

His mouth went dry as he absorbed their meaning. In his anger, he hadn't considered Catherine had complete control over every aspect of his life. And he had angered her. Again.

SOMEWHERE UNKNOWN

A cool, gentle breeze brushed over the pale sands of the warm beach. Clouds drifted overhead, casting pleasant shade whenever the sun came too close to unpleasant. Ocean waves gushed over the wet sand and then slowly retreated back into the crystal blue sea. The salty breeze carried the smell of petrichor and fresh flowers.

Thomas had been here before.

Was he dead?

This wasn't right. He couldn't be dead. Mariana had immortalized him. But what if she hadn't? Did she mess up somehow? Was he *actually* dead this time? He searched the horizon, but he was alone.

A heavy gust of wind blew over him, as cold as it was strong. The clouds drifted together, darkening the sky and transforming the serene landscape into a rumbling storm. He backpedaled onto the warm sand as a storm cloud darkened into black shadow and twirled into the shape of a large woman. Two red eyes opened over a sharp smile.

"Tetra," Thomas said. "Am I dead?"

Pitch darkness surrounded him, broken only by Tetra's smile. She approached Thomas, coming close enough to touch him. "What do *you* think?" she asked in a low growl.

Hair rose on his arms and the back of his neck. "I think I'm in the afterlife again, but I thought I couldn't die."

"Of course you can die, you fool. You're still human."

"But I'll come back to life?" Thomas asked.

Tetra leaned back and smirked. "We'll see, won't we?" The darkness eased just enough for the beach to become visible, but it was still as dark as a moonless night. Tetra gestured to a portal hanging in the air where the image of his corpse was displayed. His body lay face up in a pool of blood. The captain kept his foot pinned to Thomas's shoulder. Thomas's crystal sword had been stuck into his chest. The captain held himself up on the sword like a walking stick, keeping it plunged directly into Thomas's heart.

"He's even better than Charles," Tetra said.

"Why am I still dead?" Thomas asked, keeping his eyes on the sword in his heart.

"Are you dead? Or are you just not trying hard enough?" Tetra asked, resting her arm around Thomas's shoulder.

Thomas finally spotted Charles in front of the captain with his hand over his mouth. His face was pale, and his eyes were glued to Thomas's corpse.

"He's going to kill Charles if you don't hurry," Tetra taunted. "I know how much you hate that."

"What do you mean?!" Thomas asked, jumping out of her grip. "What am I supposed to be doing?"

Tetra shrugged. "Go back."

"How?!"

"I don't know. You're the first undead human. Figure it out," she said with a sick smile.

With a cool gust of humid sea wind, the darkness blew away, leaving behind dim twilight. Mariana stood with Thomas and Tetra in the surf. Shadows lined her stormy face. "Tetra," she said. "Get away from him."

Tetra raised both hands in surrender and stepped back with an innocent smile. "I'm allowed to speak to the dead."

"*Leave,*" Mariana said, grabbing Thomas's arm.

The amusement on Tetra's face dimmed to disdain. Without another word, she vanished. The beach brightened to overcast daylight once again. Mariana took Thomas's other hand and looked him in the eyes. "Are you all right?"

"Am I dead? I thought I was immortal."

Mariana looked into the portal that showed Thomas's bloody

corpse. "You are." She watched the image for a moment longer, then squeezed his hands and nodded. "Your body is having trouble regenerating because there is a foreign object stuck in your heart."

"What do I do?!" Thomas asked, watching in horror as the captain left the crystal sword embedded in his chest and approached Charles, carrying his own bloody sword. "He's going to kill Charles! Help me, Mariana!"

Mariana looked back and forth between Thomas and the portal. She nodded and looked Thomas in the eyes again. "The moment I remove that weapon from your heart, step through the portal back into your body. It will hurt, but it's only temporary. Do you understand?"

"I understand." Thomas nodded in agreement.

"Good," Mariana said and vanished into mist.

The edge of the portal shimmered in a wavelength Thomas had never seen before. His eyes could not comprehend the sight of the physical and ethereal realms meeting. Thomas ran to the portal and looked at the scene below. Caldwell approached Charles, backing him against the edge of the ship. Charles shook his head and said something, but Thomas couldn't hear. He lifted his hand to touch the image, but a flat, invisible barrier kept him out. He placed both hands against the barrier and pushed, but nothing happened. He could only watch and wait like he was staring through a window. What was taking Mariana so long?

Caldwell grabbed Charles by the front of his shirt. Charles shook his head, pleading. Thomas pressed his face hard against the invisible barrier.

A tendril of water spiraled into the air from the sea and snaked around the sword in Thomas's chest, wrapping itself around the hilt before freezing to ice. The frozen tendril tugged the bloodied sword upward with a core-wrenching tear.

The barrier disappeared, and the physical world sucked

Thomas back in. He felt nothing until he landed inside his corpse, where his soul spread through his body like a hand into a glove. Instantly, he was in agony.

His chest screamed with pain. His heart beat slowly and erratically, and he couldn't move. Like when he had died in Tetra's temple, his body was still coming back to life. The bloody crystal sword flew over his head across the deck toward Charles and the captain. With a loud thump, it stuck itself into the wood of the gunwale beside Charles.

Charles and Caldwell turned their heads to look at it, then at Thomas. When Thomas finally had enough strength, he could not contain his groan. The pain was intense.

"Thomas!" Charles shouted. He ripped the sword from the wood and turned it on Caldwell while Caldwell watched Thomas's resurrection. Charles raised the sword and swung, but Caldwell was quick.

He easily blocked the attack. Charles ducked around him and backed away, but Caldwell advanced on him, swinging furiously. Charles blocked every blow. How was this so easy for him? Why was Charles good at everything he tried? Even his stance and his grip looked good.

Caldwell did not go easy on Charles. Every time he swung at Charles, Thomas was sure it would be the end, but Charles held his ground. Just as he started to believe Charles had a chance, Caldwell swept his feet from under him.

Charles lay on his back, looking up at the captain in shock. The crystal sword clattered out of his reach. Charles pushed himself up, but the captain kicked him back down, holding him in place with his foot. "I don't know what kind of blood magic you two are up to that could keep you alive after a fatal injury, but it ends *now*," the captain said to Thomas, then turned to Charles with his sword held at his side.

"No!" Thomas coughed. He searched the deck for someone to

help, but the other sailors only watched. Nobody wanted to touch the undead. Nobody wanted to get in the captain's way. Thomas forced himself to roll over, propping himself up on one arm as he gathered the strength to stand.

Get up, he scolded himself. He couldn't let this be how Charles died. Thomas couldn't let *Caldwell* kill the person he loved just before bringing him into the Pantheon.

Caldwell raised his sword in the air, ready to strike. Charles struggled to get away. Thomas pushed himself up to run but fell flat on his face.

He wouldn't make it. What could he do? What did he have left? His sword was too far away, and he had no control of his magic.

"No!" Thomas screamed, throwing his hand forward as the captain swung his sword down.

The sword stopped in the air mid-swing. Charles's frantic eyes skipped between the captain and the sword. Thomas kept his hand outstretched, the pulse of magic running from his core to his fingertips.

His magic *was* helping him. Thomas intended to stop Caldwell from killing Charles, and he had.

Humans were mostly water.

"What is this?" Caldwell asked. Thomas focused his intention on pulling Caldwell's fingers away from the hilt, and his sword clattered to the deck.

"Magic!" Thomas snarled.

Caldwell stepped back, realizing he still had control of the rest of his body, and kicked Charles in the face. Charles groaned and fell to the side with the motion of the kick.

Thomas's blood boiled. He tightened his control, streaming his intention to Caldwell's core. Thomas pulled his arm back, aiming to pull the captain away from Charles.

Caldwell came tumbling backward and fell flat on his back.

He coughed and gasped for air when he hit the ground, but he wasn't getting back up. That was good enough for Thomas.

Thomas collapsed onto the ground again. He took deep, steady breaths and focused on his injuries. His body was weak. The wound in his chest burned and tingled.

"Thomas!" Charles yelled, rushing to Thomas's side and dropping to his knees. He gently rolled Thomas onto his back. Charles held a hand over his left eye, squinting out of his right to look Thomas over. The captain must have kicked him hard.

Thomas rested his hand on Charles's knee. It was all he had the energy to do. "Are you . . . okay?" Thomas asked in a coarse voice.

Charles nodded. "Are you?"

Thomas didn't know how to answer. He doubted any mortal human had ever felt this terrible before. He would be dead right now if he weren't plagued with eternal life. "You should run before Caldwell gets up again." Thomas had to force the first words out, but they came easier as he worked through the sentence.

Charles glanced behind him where Caldwell lay and then shook his head. "I don't think he's getting up . . ."

Charles was right. Caldwell lay on his side, taking sharp, labored breaths. He gave a ragged cough, and blood splattered onto the deck. "What . . . what did you do to me?" the captain asked hoarsely.

What *had* he done? Thomas thought he was only pulling Caldwell away from Charles, but without proper control of his magic, he must have seriously injured Caldwell as well.

Thomas turned to face Charles again. "Go get Fiona."

"What?" Charles asked.

"He's going to die. Fiona can help him," Thomas said.

Charles didn't move. "No, Thomas. This is what you wanted."

"Charles!" Thomas yelled, grabbing the front of Charles's

shirt. Charles fell forward with the force of the pull and watched Thomas from inches away. "I don't want to be a murderer. That's not who I am."

"You had to do it," Charles reminded him. "For Mariana. For the mermaids."

"I can't live forever with *Caldwell*," Thomas said.

Charles squinted at the captain again before nodding. He stood and made his way to Caldwell, searching his body for the keys.

"Get your filthy hands off me, Southworth," Caldwell growled through rattling breaths.

"Don't flatter yourself, Caldwell. I'm not interested in miserable old sea captains," Charles said, unhooking the keyring from Caldwell's belt. "I'll be right back," he said to Thomas. "Will you be okay?"

Thomas's head felt fuzzy. "I think so." He pushed himself up onto his elbow. His strength was slowly coming back.

Charles nodded and ran to the hatchway.

Caldwell rolled onto his stomach and took heavy breaths. Thomas watched to make sure he survived long enough for Fiona to arrive.

Eventually, footsteps thudded up the hatchway. Fiona burst from the horizontal portal. Her eyes widened when they landed on Thomas, and she ran across the deck to be at his side. "Thomas! What happened to you? Are you okay?" She looked around at the immobile crew. "Are you out of your minds? Why aren't you helping?!" she demanded.

The crew looked at each other and then back at Thomas, but they didn't move.

"I'm fine, Fiona. Help Caldwell. He's going to die."

"*Caldwell?*" Fiona asked. She looked at Caldwell's hunched form, hacking his insides out. "I'm worried about *you*."

"Please," Thomas begged. "You don't understand. Tetra wants

to make him her servant. I don't want to live in this world with him for eternity, and I'll have to if he dies."

Fiona's worried expression softened at the reminder of Thomas's immortality.

"What . . . did you say?" Caldwell gurgled. "*Tetra?*"

Thomas ignored Caldwell. "Can you help him?" he asked.

Fiona stood and cautiously approached the dying captain. Thomas forced himself into a sitting position and breathed slowly. He was feeling much less dead now.

Fiona crouched to the captain's level, keeping a safe distance.

"Don't you dare touch me, evil woman," Caldwell rattled.

"You would rather die than be saved by magic?" Fiona asked.

"I'll survive . . . the *right* way," Caldwell said.

Fiona turned to frown at Thomas. "It's too late for him," she declared with a shrug. "I can't perform magic on him if he doesn't consent. It goes against my beliefs."

"Don't be stupid, Caldwell. Magic is normal," Thomas said. "You're going to *die.*"

"*Magic* did this to me," Caldwell growled.

Thomas's chest tightened. He hadn't meant to kill Caldwell. Tetra told him he had to, but he never thought he could actually do it. "Fiona," Thomas pleaded. "Tetra can't have him as her servant. She'll be too strong. You *have* to help him."

Fiona sighed heavily. "Okay. I suppose if it's to save his life . . ." She dropped to Caldwell's side, aiming her palms at his face. "*Staze.*"

Caldwell stopped moving, staring into the air in front of him, unseeing.

"What was that?" Thomas asked.

"I stunned him. It'll be easier this way, trust me." Fiona held her hands over his body and closed her eyes. "*Exectify,*" she whispered. A pale glow came from under her shirt on her upper right arm. She hovered her hands above his still body, slowing at his center and moving up his torso. She held her hands there for a long moment before she curled her fingers and frowned. Her tattoo stopped glowing, and she opened her eyes. "What happened to him?" she asked quietly.

Thomas swallowed hard. He didn't want to admit what he had done. "I was just trying to get him away from Charles." He squeezed his eyes shut and shook his head.

"Did you use magic?" Fiona asked softly.

Thomas nodded.

"You didn't do anything wrong," Fiona said.

Thomas forced his eyes open to look at her. "Can you save him?"

Fiona took a deep breath and held his gaze for a moment before shaking her head. "I understand you were only doing what you could to save the life of someone you love, but the type of magic you attempted requires years of practice if you want to prevent injury. You should not try that again until you have an intimate understanding of human anatomy, unless you find yourself in another deadly situation."

Thomas's heart pounded and his breathing became shallow. "I didn't mean to kill him."

"I know," Fiona said.

Thomas shook his head and searched the deck frantically. "Where's Charles?"

Fiona moved from Caldwell's side to sit beside Thomas. "He's letting everyone else out of the brig. He'll be up here in a minute."

Thomas sensed the daylight dimming even behind his shut eyes, and when he opened them again he found the midday sky was as dark as night.

He grabbed Fiona's arm. "Stay with me, Fiona," he said urgently.

"Why? What's happening?" Fiona asked, placing her free hand over Thomas's where he held onto her.

"Tetra," he said.

"Tetra?!" Fiona asked, standing and breaking free from his grip.

Thomas grabbed her arm again and stood up with her. His strength was coming back fast. "You're safe with me. Just don't break contact," he said.

The dark sky swirled into a pitch-black vortex until it took the shape of a tall woman in the same way Mariana formed herself from water. Tetra stepped onto the deck, looking almost human. She strutted toward Caldwell's unmoving body and smiled at him for a moment before leaning down to pick him up like he weighed nothing. She turned to Thomas. "Thank you, Thomas. He's perfect."

"He hasn't agreed." Thomas forced the words out.

"He said yes immediately," she said with a sickening smile. She looked Thomas over once. "And just after proving he can kill you with a sword. I couldn't ask for better."

Mariana was right. Tetra wanted to kill him.

"Can I admit something to you, Thomas?" Tetra asked with a fake pout and a tilt of her head. Her black hair tumbled over her shoulder while Caldwell's limp head rolled against her arm.

Thomas couldn't answer.

"You don't have to die to become a servant," Tetra said. "I just wanted to see if I could convince you to kill someone. It was surprisingly easy."

Thomas felt sick. He murdered someone, and he didn't even have to.

Why had he blindly believed her?

Behind Tetra, Charles emerged from the hatchway. He stopped halfway up the steps and watched Tetra with wide eyes.

"Oh, look who it is. The one who got away," Tetra said. "This could have been you, Charles." She held Caldwell's corpse up for Charles to see.

Charles looked away. His eyes followed the trail of blood to Thomas and Fiona, and he made fearful eye contact with Thomas.

Tetra followed Charles's gaze and spotted Thomas's death grip on Fiona. She turned to Charles. "Keep pushing the limits of what Thomas will do for you and he'll love you forever, because he'll have no other choice."

Charles opened his mouth but said nothing.

A cold smile broke across Tetra's face. "Do you hear that?" she asked. The sound of waves splashing against the hull barely covered a thin wailing in the distance.

Thomas searched the deck and saw his crewmates' expressions grow distant. His heart stopped.

It couldn't be true. They had made a deal.

"Sirens?!" Thomas demanded. "You said you would fix the sirens if I found you a servant, and you have your servant!"

"No, Thomas. I said I would stop *creating* sirens," Tetra said. "These ones already existed."

"That's not what I meant, and you know it!" Thomas yelled.

Tetra shrugged. "Maybe next time you should say what you mean." She smiled and winked at Thomas. "See you soon," she said, then she disappeared into the shadows with Caldwell.

The world brightened back to daylight. Thomas let go of Fiona and looked around the deck. The singing wasn't loud enough to get the sailors running yet. "We have to do something," Thomas said.

Fiona was as pale as Tetra. Her mouth hung open and her brown eyes were wide. "What *can* we do?"

"Grab the sailors at the bow. I'll get the stern. If they're still lucid, tell them to plug their ears, and we'll lock them all in the brig," Thomas said. He looked at Charles, who was watching Thomas with a horrified expression. "Charles!"

Charles raised his eyebrows.

"Gather the crew from the living quarters and lock them in the brig. Including Faya and Fyavine!" Thomas said.

"What about us?" Charles asked.

"We'll be fine," Thomas said. "I'm immune to sirens. You will be too."

"You are?" Charles asked with a furrowed brow. He leaned back as if shocked by the revelation. "I don't think I am, Thomas."

"Just go!" Thomas yelled, annoyed Charles was wasting time. He obviously didn't understand sirens.

Charles narrowed his eyes and shook his head. He plugged his ears and descended below deck.

Thomas turned to collect the sailors at the stern while Fiona ran to the bow.

The two sailors at the stern were semi-distracted, coming back to reality with each noisy crash of the ship against a wave that briefly covered the singing, which grew louder every second. When the ship crashed back into the sea against an oncoming wave, Thomas put the sailors' hands over their ears.

They blinked rapidly as awareness returned to their eyes. "Sirens! Get to the brig!" Thomas yelled.

The sailors shared a worried look before nodding and running toward the hatchway. On the opposite side of the deck, Fiona dragged Julian, who kicked and fought the entire way. Thomas was impressed at Fiona's ability to hold him. He ran to help but stopped when his sailors dropped their hands and ran for the edge.

Thomas sprinted to catch them. He grabbed one sailor by the back of his shirt, but the other slipped through his fingers, and Thomas could do nothing as he fell into the sea.

The sailor he had caught was struggling to get away. This man was bigger and stronger than Thomas, and Thomas couldn't hold on much longer. What could he do? After the incident with Caldwell, he wouldn't dare use his magic. But Fiona might.

"Fiona!" Thomas shouted. Julian's hand pushed Fiona's head while her arms were wrapped around his body to keep him restrained. Fiona could barely open her eyes to look at Thomas. "Stun him!"

Fiona's eyes widened. She hesitated for a moment, then shouted, *"Staze!"*

Julian stopped moving. Fiona dropped him and ran to Thomas, who was now struggling to keep hold of the surviving sailor. The sirens' singing was deafening.

Fiona only made it a few steps before swearing loudly and running in the other direction. The last two sailors had emerged from the lower deck and were running for the side.

Fiona stunned one of the sailors and tackled the other, pinning him to the ground. She breathed heavily, sitting on him to keep him from running. "I'm running out of energy. I need a second," she said, panting through her words. "I might pass out if I stun him, and everyone else will wake up if I pass out."

"Take your time," Thomas said as his sailor elbowed him in the face.

At that moment, Charles ran up the hatchway. Finally. "Charles, help me!" Thomas yelled.

Charles stopped and blinked hard, shaking his head. He looked at Thomas. "What?" he asked.

"Help me!" Thomas said again. His grip on the sailor was weakening.

"How did I get up here?" Charles asked. He looked away from Thomas, and his expression fell into desperate longing.

Charles wasn't immune?

Why wasn't he immune? What did that mean?

Charles ran for the edge.

"Charles! No!" Thomas yelled.

Charles stumbled over his feet and stopped for a brief moment but quickly continued forward. He had reacted to the sound of Thomas's voice and snapped out of it when he looked at Thomas. Thomas couldn't let go of the sailor, but he had to stop Charles.

"Charles, stop! Stop running! Turn around!" Thomas desperately yelled.

Charles stumbled again but didn't stop at Thomas's demands. It wasn't *just* the sound of Thomas's voice. He only reacted when Thomas said his name. What did that mean? It didn't make sense, and Thomas only had seconds to figure it out.

Charles swung one foot over the side of the ship, and Thomas panicked.

"Charles! I love you!"

Charles stopped and turned his head. His eyes were on Thomas. His mouth fell open, and his eyebrows angled upward.

"Don't look away!" Thomas pleaded. "Get down from there, but don't look away from me!"

"I love you too," Charles said.

Thomas nodded. "Carefully, don't trip. Don't look away or you'll die," he begged.

"Okay . . ." Fear flashed through Charles's eyes as he swung his leg back onto the ship while maintaining eye contact with Thomas.

The ship lurched against a high wave, and the sailor in Thomas's arms kicked him in the stomach as they stumbled apart. Thomas fell onto his side. The sailor scrambled up and climbed onto the edge. Thomas grabbed at the sailor, but the sailor slipped out of his hands by mere inches and threw himself over the side.

Thomas had lost both sailors. They were gone forever.

He pulled himself up and ran to the edge, greeted only by a crowd of claws and snarls. How could he have let this happen?

Again.

Thomas turned to make sure Charles was still looking at him, but the railing where he had been sitting was empty. Thomas frantically searched the deck, but he only saw Fiona and her three sailors.

Charles was gone.

Chapter Fourteen

Tinera

Another mealtime passed with no sign of Finnlay or Aella. Felix's hope that the new dining hall schedule was just for breakfast had died. At least he would get to see them during outside time.

But when the end of lunchtime came, they were not let outside as usual. The residents of Oleander were ushered back into their hall and forced to wait in their beds with nothing to entertain them. Felix hoped it was only to let the other halls eat their meals, but the time dragged.

Finally, Matthew rang the bell and announced that they were free to leave the hall if they wished. Felix was quick to reach the door, hoping outside time hadn't also been separated by hall.

But the courtyard was empty.

Dread sat cold in the pit of his stomach. Catherine knew more than she let on. They had searched everyone in the camp not because it was necessary to find who was doing witchcraft, but because they wanted people scared. And now, isolated.

Catherine probably suspected Felix, and she knew he would be working with someone else. He obviously wasn't receiving help from anyone in his own hall.

Felix meandered to Larkspur, wondering if there was a way he could sneak in and talk to Finnlay and Aella, but as he came closer he noticed security had been tightened. Now, an alert and attentive guard stood by Larkspur's door, scanning the grounds. The guard's eyes locked on Felix as he walked by. Felix continued on as if it were merely a coincidence he had walked past Larkspur.

This wasn't good.

He didn't hold out hope that he would get to see Finnlay and Aella at dinner, and he was disappointed to be correct. All meals were now completely separate from other residential halls. There would be no more interaction between different magical types, and no more opportunities to interact with peers that weren't closely monitored by hall leaders and guards. No chance to scheme.

As Felix lay in bed that night contemplating the new changes, he considered their options. How would they complete the potion now that they couldn't communicate? Was there any way to communicate? The only safe method would be using their hidden table in the dining hall, which had not been found yet.

Maybe Felix could leave a note. But he had just had library time, and even if he had the opportunity to steal a blank page, they were never given writing utensils.

What would Finnlay and Aella do? Together they had probably come up with something. Felix had the disadvantage of being alone.

In the past, they snuck out and met at their table in the middle of the night. Maybe they were planning to do that again. Maybe they were counting on Felix to have the same idea.

He had to try.

Night fell, and Felix waited for the gentle sounds of sleep to fill the room before quietly peeling his covers off and tiptoeing through the room. Matthew was as soundly asleep as the rest of the room, leaving the door unguarded.

Felix took the cold doorknob in his hand and slowly turned it, cringing against the creak of the door as it opened. Maybe this would actually work. Maybe he could—

"Hey! What do you think you're doing, resident?"

The halls weren't just guarded during the day. Felix stared silently at the guard and cast a desperate look at Larkspur across the muddy field.

Leather-clad guards roamed the grounds in search of disobedient residents. In search of *him*.

"Um . . . I just needed some air," Felix said.

"Go back to sleep. You'll get 'air' in the morning," the guard snapped, shoving Felix back into the dark, sleepy room and slamming the door shut behind him.

Felix stared at the shadowy door in disbelief. If he couldn't see Finnlay and Aella at mealtimes, outdoor time, or at night, when would he get another chance?

He might never see them again.

At Sea

"Charles!" Thomas screamed, running to the other side of the ship. He threw himself against the bulwark to look into the water. The sirens clawed at the hull, but Charles was gone. Before Thomas knew what he was doing, he climbed over the edge and positioned himself to jump.

"Thomas, don't! Are you mad?" Fiona yelled as she struggled

to keep her sailor down. She looked up through lowered eyelids. Her wild hair fell over her face, and she breathed heavily.

"I'll be back!" Thomas said.

"Wait—"

Thomas jumped, landing among the sick mermaids, but they did not reach for him. He pushed and kicked the sirens away to get beneath them and found the dark shape of a siren taking off to the depths with a sailor.

It was Charles.

Thomas dove beneath the sirens, swimming as fast as his human legs would let him. The siren was much faster.

"Mariana!" Thomas tried to call, but it only came out as a quiet voice muffled by air bubbles. He hoped she understood. "Help me!"

No response. Thomas's heart dropped as he remembered Mariana couldn't see inside herself. He was alone.

He swiped through the water until his lungs burned, swimming as fast as he could. The darkness closed in until Charles and the siren were a dark blur beneath him. There was no way he would make it in time, but he had to try.

Thomas reached forward, letting his magic flow through his palms. He focused on the water in front of Charles and the siren and tried to pull it back, hoping against all hope it wouldn't injure them. He only wanted to slow them down.

As he pulled, he continued kicking down into the dark depths of the sea. He couldn't tell if it was working. The dark blur was still small, still far away.

But then the blurry shape started to grow, giving Thomas the encouragement he needed to swim faster. Every second was important. Each moment brought Charles closer to death. Slowly, the blur took the shape of Charles and the siren swimming in place. His magic was working.

Thomas grabbed Charles by the collar of his shirt and kicked the siren in the chest. The siren shrieked as Thomas took away her prey. Her sharp claws sliced Thomas's leg in a desperate attempt to keep her hold on Charles. The cold salt water stung the cuts as Thomas wrenched Charles and the siren apart.

The moment Thomas pulled Charles into his arms, it was as if the siren couldn't see them anymore. The shrieking stopped. She floated in place for a few seconds, then she shot up to the surface to rejoin the other sirens. Thomas had been prepared to fight, but it was over.

With the exertion it had taken to swim to Charles, Thomas felt like he would die without the small amount of air in his lungs. He couldn't die, but Charles *would*. Thomas took Charles's face in his hands and pressed their mouths together. He tried not to think about the familiar feeling of his lips. This was not a kiss. It was a breath of air for someone on the verge of death. Thomas exhaled all the air left in his lungs into Charles's body, then forced himself to break away.

Thomas firmly gripped Charles's arm and swam up. He thought they would break through the surface at any moment, but they just kept swimming. How far down had they gone?

Finally, the water gave way to open sky. Thomas inhaled a deep breath of air as he yanked Charles up. The panic in Thomas's body eased as Charles gasped for air beside him. Charles was alive.

"Charles!" Thomas called through his own heavy breaths. "Are you okay?"

Charles could not answer as he coughed and struggled to breathe.

"Keep looking at me and don't let go," Thomas said, looking around. He couldn't hear the sirens anymore, but he wasn't going to risk it. The ship had gotten away from them fast, its silhouette sailing toward the horizon in the distance.

"Thomas," Charles gasped.

"Keep breathing," Thomas said, turning in circles as if help would miraculously appear. He swore loudly and tightened his grip on Charles. He had saved Charles from the quick and painless death of the sirens only to strand him in the ocean.

"Thomas," Charles said again. "What happened? Where are we?"

"Sirens," Thomas said. A tall wave washed over them. Thomas held on tightly as they briefly lost sight of each other. It would only take a moment for them to be separated forever. He pulled Charles to him and indulged in a hug. "I'm so glad you're okay," he murmured against Charles's shoulder.

"Y-you are?" Charles asked.

Thomas only pushed away from the hug but didn't answer the question because he felt it was stupid.

"You're immune to sirens?" Charles asked.

Thomas nodded. "Yeah, I . . . I assumed you would be too. I'm sorry I didn't listen to you."

"Why?" Charles asked.

"Because I thought you were gay," Thomas said. The moment he said it, he realized what it meant. Charles wasn't gay. Maybe he never even liked Thomas.

It didn't matter, anyway. That ship had sailed. Just like the one shrinking on the horizon, *gods damn it.*

"I'm so confused . . ." Charles said.

"What are we going to do?" Thomas asked, watching the speck that was their ship as though it would turn around and come back for them.

"Why don't you ask Mariana for help?" Charles asked.

Thomas shook his head. "She won't help me." Historically, Mariana had been painfully unhelpful when Thomas needed her.

"How do you know that? Have you tried?"

Thomas rolled his eyes. "Mariana?" he called, certain she wouldn't answer.

Mariana twirled out of the water and lay on the surface with her head in her hands. "Hi Thomas! What are you doing out here?" she asked, looking around the empty ocean landscape.

Thomas gawked at her. He didn't want to say anything, reluctant to admit that Charles had been right.

"Do you need something?" Mariana asked.

"Is she here?" Charles asked.

"Yes," Thomas begrudgingly answered both of them.

"What's the matter?" Mariana asked with a tilt of her head.

"We fell overboard. Sort of," Thomas said. "Can you find us a boat? Without killing its crew first, please."

Mariana rubbed her chin in thought. "I'll look." She splashed back into the dark water, leaving Thomas and Charles alone in the vast ocean. The cold waves continued rolling over them. Thomas breathed slowly, struggling to stay calm. If he lost control of his magic now, he could drown Charles. The very thought of it didn't help.

Mariana quickly returned, wearing a big smile. "I found you something!"

"Great," Thomas said. "Where is it?"

"It's underneath you!"

Thomas looked down to see a large, dark shadow widen beneath his feet. His instinctual panic told him to swim away, but he forced himself to stay put, holding onto Charles. Mariana wouldn't intentionally put them in harm's way. Not over this, at least.

The boards of a flimsy boat hit his feet, then his butt, then lifted out of the water until he sat at the bottom of a dinghy, still clinging to Charles, waist deep in water. Water streamed off the sides of the boat as it rose from the ocean. With a flourish of her hand, Mariana pulled the remaining water from the inside of the boat.

"There you go! A new boat!" Mariana said.

Water slowly seeped through the floorboards and pooled around their feet. The boat had a leak. Of course it did.

"You couldn't find a functional boat?" Thomas asked, already ankle-deep in water.

"Do you really think any boat I could find for you without killing its crew is going to be functional?" Mariana asked. "You're welcome, by the way."

Thomas gestured at the rising water. "For what? This boat is not going to last five minutes!"

"Just patch it with ice," Mariana said. "You're a water elementalist."

Panic rose faster than the water beneath him. The salt water he had swallowed conspired with his nausea. He felt like he would vomit. "I-I don't know how to do that."

"What do you mean? I fixed your soul. You should be able to," Mariana said.

Thomas shook his head urgently. He had stopped the siren with his magic, but that was different. Charles's life was on the line. He had no desire to try to learn his magic right now after Caldwell's death, especially when he knew Mariana could do it. She had pulled the sword from his chest by freezing a tendril of water. "Please, Mariana. Can you do it for me? Even if I did know how, I . . ." Thomas stopped talking, still shaking his head and squeezing his eyes shut.

"Okay, Thomas. Sure," Mariana said in a gentle tone he hadn't heard before. Was it sympathy? He opened his eyes to see Mariana and Charles watching him with concern.

Mariana waved her hand over the boat. The boat rose partially out of the ocean, water draining out of its large gaps. It crackled loudly as the remaining water paled and hardened with thick ice, covering the exposed sections of the hull.

The boat wobbled against oncoming waves. Mariana had effectively created an entirely new hull made of ice. "Better?" she asked.

Thomas nodded. "Thank you."

Mariana sat on the edge of the boat and frowned. "What happened?"

Thomas's mouth fell open as he struggled to respond. "Tetra got her servant," he finally said. "He's an evil, terrible man, and she made me kill him because she thought it was funny. She told me servants need to die to become immortal, and I believed her."

Mariana's eyebrows furrowed. "Why didn't you talk to me? I would have told you the truth."

Thomas didn't know what to say. It hadn't even occurred to him to ask Mariana. Why would he believe *anything* Tetra told him? "I don't know."

"Next time another god tells you to do something, come to me first," she said.

Thomas felt like he was suffocating. "I'm sorry," he whispered. A wave rocked the ship, and Thomas held Charles's arm tightly.

"You didn't know," Mariana said.

"I killed him." Thomas covered his face with one hand. "I'm a monster."

Rain began to fall from swirling storm clouds overhead. Thomas knew he should breathe, but he couldn't stop this. It was too much.

Charles put his arm around Thomas's shoulder and pulled him close. "It's okay," he said. Thomas buried his face against Charles and took a deep breath, fighting back the grief.

"Not really," Mariana said. "If anything, you gave him extra life. You knew he wouldn't truly die, anyway. On the bright side, now that Tetra has her servant, she'll get her nasty disease out of my mermaids and the sirens will be gone."

Thomas lifted his head. The last thing he wanted to do at that moment was break the news that he had failed her, but he had no other choice. She had to know. "Mariana . . . I made a mistake. Tetra promised to stop making sirens, not cure them. I wasn't careful with my choice of words."

Mariana's optimism dripped away. "What?"

"The sirens are still around. That's why we fell overboard. Charles almost died," Thomas explained. "I jumped after him, but they didn't chase me."

Mariana's eyes darted to Charles for a moment before landing on Thomas again. "I see. So, we still have a siren problem."

Thomas nodded miserably.

Mariana sighed her bubbly sigh and looked across the turbulent landscape of shifting water. "They didn't attack you?"

"No. Do you have any idea why?" Thomas asked.

Mariana's stormy blue eyes landed on him again. "Probably because of your godservant protections. Because your soul belongs to me, no other god can harm you. That must include the sirens, since they were created by Tetra."

"Tetra couldn't hurt Charles when I held onto him in her temple. Does that mean he's safe if we're making contact?" Thomas asked.

Mariana nodded. "Yes. He is safe with you."

Thomas sighed with relief. He had been on edge this entire time, knowing there was a chance his theory was wrong. "What should we do?"

"First, I need to get you back to a proper ship," Mariana said, looking around again. "Then we can figure out a plan."

"Can you tell our crew where we are?" Thomas asked.

Mariana returned her attention to him. "I'll see what I can do. I'll be back when I know more."

"Thank you," Thomas said gratefully.

"Of course." She splashed back into herself, leaving Thomas and Charles alone on the drifting dinghy.

Thomas sighed heavily. The wood of the boat creaked as large waves rocked the small vessel. Raindrops smacked against the wet ice at the bottom of the boat. "Are you all right?" he asked, keeping his arms around Charles.

"Are *you?*" Charles asked.

A long silence passed between them.

"Thomas . . ." Charles started. When Thomas didn't respond, he said, "Did you kiss me? Underwater?"

Thomas glared at him. "No. I gave you air."

"I know you gave me air . . . but it felt a lot like a kiss."

"Shut up, Charles. Gods . . ." Thomas sat up to get away from him, keeping one hand on Charles's arm. He was mad, but not because Charles was wrong. He was mad that Charles was so relentlessly observant. "I was just trying to keep you alive."

"Right . . ."

"Why would you care if I kissed you, anyway? You're obviously not gay," Thomas said.

"Why would you say that?" Charles asked.

Thomas gestured to the ocean around them. "We would not be out here on this boat if you were. You ran to the sirens."

"I don't see what the sirens have to do with that," Charles said.

"Are you joking?" Thomas asked. "I'm immune to them *because* I like men."

Charles stared at him with furrowed eyebrows. "Are you not attracted to women?" Charles asked.

"Are *you?*" Thomas asked.

Charles's jaw dropped. "Well, yeah. Have you *seen* women?"

"Yes, I've *seen* women," Thomas said. He released a heavy sigh. "I wish I were attracted to women. Then I wouldn't have to put up with you."

"You don't have to be rude," Charles said.

"I don't get it. Why would you bother risking everything to be with me when you could just be with a girl?"

"Because I like you!" Charles said. "I can't stop myself from liking you just because I can also like women. And in case you forgot, I *did* have a girlfriend, but she dumped me when I told her I like men. I've told you that!"

"Is that really why she left you? Or did you actually cheat on her?" Thomas asked.

"Wow, Thomas. I thought you understood, but you're just like her. Instantly suspicious that I'm a cheater the moment you find out I like more than one gender," Charles said, looking straight ahead at the sea. "You know what? We don't have to talk to each other." The boat wobbled as he stood.

The moment Thomas and Charles were no longer touching, the faces of hungry sirens broke the surface of the water. Thomas grabbed Charles's arm and yanked him back down. The sirens disappeared beneath the waves again.

"It's not safe," Thomas said.

Charles glared at him. "So what? Just let me die if I'm such a fucking problem."

"What are you talking about? I am constantly fighting off gods and murderers and monsters to keep you alive!" Thomas said.

Charles threw his free hand up. "Yeah, and I don't understand why, since you obviously hate me."

"I *obviously* don't!" Thomas yelled. "What is wrong with you?"

"I don't know what you want from me!" Charles said. "You're mad that I can't stay away from you on a gods-damn *brigantine* with a skeleton crew, but you just told me that you loved me and then you kissed me. Now you're mad at me for asking about it! Sometimes I think you're the only person who still likes me, but the rest of the time I think you despise me more than anyone. What do you want?!"

Thomas was speechless. He could only stare at Charles as he tried to find an answer, then tried to understand why he didn't have one.

The only conclusion he could come to was that Charles was right. Thomas was mad at him, and he just couldn't get over it no matter what Charles did. Charles could be annoying sometimes, but he hadn't done anything wrong since Blackwater. He had actually done a lot *right*.

"Maybe I'm not being fair to you," Thomas said. "I don't know what I want. I wasn't expecting you to be on my ship, so I don't have the space I need to sort out my feelings. About you, but also about my parents, and my friends being imprisoned because of *my* family, and my new immortality, and my uncontrollable magic, and Tetra's servant . . . Everything is so overwhelming. And with my friends locked up, I've felt . . . so alone."

Charles listened quietly, and then he nodded. "I don't want you to feel alone, but I understand that's probably not something *I* can help you with. What can I do?"

"You *can* help me with that, Charles. I know you can, because you were the first person in my life to ever make me feel like I wasn't alone, but . . ." Thomas shook his head. "I don't trust you anymore."

For a long time, the only sound was the heavy patter of rain. Finally, Charles asked, "What can I do to get you to trust me again?"

"I think that's part of the problem. I don't know if I ever will."

Charles's eyebrows rose as the heavy silence built.

"What if I answered any question with complete honesty? Is there anything you want to know? I will give you a full, direct, honest answer," Charles offered.

"You should be doing that anyway," Thomas said.

"I should, but sometimes I unintentionally skirt the truth."

"That's just as dishonest as lying."

"What do you want to know?" Charles asked.

Thomas sighed and watched the choppy water as he considered what question might restore his trust.

Suddenly, he remembered what Tetra had told him about the night he became immortal. Tetra thought he would never believe Charles if Charles told him the same story. Maybe this was his chance to hear the truth.

Thomas looked at Charles again to find he was watching him with tired eyes. He offered Thomas a weak smile.

"I do have a question for you," Thomas said.

Charles's smile disappeared. "What is it?"

Thomas eyed Charles carefully. Would he really tell the truth? "What happened in Tetra's temple between the moment I died and the moment I came back?"

Charles's eyebrows shot up. His mouth fell open, and his eyes stayed locked on Thomas. "I don't think you'll believe me," he finally said.

"Tell me."

Charles swallowed and nodded, lowering his gaze to his feet. "I . . . I couldn't believe you were dead again. I couldn't believe it was my fault. By some amazing stroke of luck, or by some miracle, you were alive. I got you back, and then I immediately lost you again. And it was my fault. *Again.* I don't remember much after I realized you were dead. I know I was crying. I wouldn't let you go." Charles paused to rub his eyes.

"Are you crying right now?" Thomas asked softly.

Charles's eyebrows pinched together, but he didn't answer. "Do you have any idea how hard it is to hold the corpse of the person you love, knowing it's your fault they died? It's the worst feeling in the world. Gods, it was so hard to let you go when you asked me to leave. It's hard not to be with you now," Charles said, looking Thomas in the eyes.

Thomas admired his bright hazel eyes under the dark sky. "So, what happened?" he asked quietly.

Charles scanned Thomas's face before he looked into the sea, wiping away a tear. "She tried to trick me. I thought she was going to make you her servant, but I didn't think you would want that. I knew how much you hated the idea of living forever." He paused to shoot an apologetic look at Thomas.

Thomas shrugged.

Charles looked away again and opened his mouth, but he did not speak for a long time. Finally, he said, "I offered to take your place. I didn't want to be the reason you died, the reason your life was miserable, *and* the reason you suffered for eternity. I mean, I don't want to be any of those things, but it's a little too late for . . . well, all of them, I guess."

To his own surprise, Thomas laughed. "You offered to serve Tetra?"

"Yeah. I did."

"She told me, but I didn't know if it was true. You're being honest?" Thomas asked.

"I swear on my mother's life."

Thomas watched him closely. As far as he could tell, Charles was being truthful. "Okay," he said quietly. "I believe you."

Charles hesitated. "You do?" he asked with a cautious smile.

"Yes. I suppose I should thank you."

"Don't thank me. I didn't do anything."

"You were willing to sacrifice your eternal soul so that I could rest peacefully. It didn't happen, but the fact that you offered tells me everything I need to know," Thomas said. "If that's not love, I don't know what is."

Charles looked up to meet Thomas's gaze. "I do love you," he said. He lifted his hand and caressed Thomas's face.

Thomas took Charles's hand, ready to pull it away. After a moment of contact, he lowered his hand but let Charles's remain.

Charles's eyebrows twitched. His eyes roamed over Thomas's face, pausing for a moment on his lips before looking in his eyes again. He caressed Thomas's cheek with his thumb. "I'm so grateful you survived. I've missed you so much."

"I've missed you too," Thomas admitted. He reached to brush aside the damp locks of dark hair covering Charles's face. Charles flinched at his touch but didn't pull away. A dark bruise was already forming under Charles's eye where Caldwell had kicked him. For a moment, Thomas didn't regret what he had done. "I'm glad you're here."

A smile slid onto Charles's face. Thomas's heart fluttered at the sight of it. He wanted to kiss it, but he couldn't admit that aloud.

Thomas must have stared too long, because Charles's smile slipped away again as his eyebrows drifted upward.

"Charles, can I confess something to you?" Thomas pulled Charles's hand off his face and folded it between his own.

"Of course," Charles said.

"I did kiss you."

The smile was back, fighting a laugh. "I know. You can't hide anything from me, Hambleton."

"I didn't mean to," Thomas said, looking into the water. His face warmed at the admission. "I think it was just familiarity. I mean, I wasn't trying to take advantage of you. It was an accident."

"Thomas, it's okay. I know you're not like that. You could kiss me anywhere—land, sea, or sky—and I wouldn't mind."

"Really?" Thomas asked, arching one eyebrow as he looked at Charles again. "I haven't been very nice to you."

Charles shrugged. "I was *never* very nice to you."

"Yeah . . ."

A smug smile snuck onto Charles's face. "How can I make it up to you?"

Thomas couldn't help laughing. It was the same question Charles had asked right before they kissed for the first time. "You've used that line on me before."

Charles's smile widened as though he was pleased Thomas remembered. Of course he remembered. "Is it working?" Charles asked, leaning forward until their faces were inches apart.

Before Thomas could answer, Mariana sprung up from the water beside the boat. And thank the gods she did, because it *was* working.

"Thomas!" she yelled.

"Mariana," Thomas said, and then he saw she wasn't alone. Fyavine had emerged from the water several feet from the boat.

Mariana grinned at Fyavine, then turned to Thomas. "I came to tell you that your mermaid friend is on the way to save you, but she swims very fast."

"Fyavine! Are you okay? Is Faya okay?" Thomas asked, leaning against the edge of the boat to get closer to her.

Fyavine threw a salty look at Charles before beaming at Thomas. "We're okay."

"Thanks for coming back for us. How did you and Faya stay safe from the sirens?" Thomas asked.

Fyavine lifted her hand from the water and dangled the dripping shell bracelet from her fingers. "I took it off and Faya put it on."

Thomas nodded. It was a smart solution. Sirens didn't affect merpeople. "Right. Good thinking."

Fyavine smiled at Thomas. "I brought it out here for . . ." She narrowed her eyes at Charles again. "For *him.* Just in case the sirens come back." Fyavine chucked the bracelet at Charles. It slapped him in the face and clacked to the floor of the boat.

Thomas frowned at her as he picked the bracelet up. "That was rude."

Charles sighed and rubbed his face. "It's fine."

"No, it's not fine," Thomas answered. "You may not like him, Fyavine, but I do. Please be nice to him." Thomas could see Charles watching him in his peripheral vision.

Fyavine stared at the sky as she blew bubbles into the water. "Fine," she groaned, bringing her eyes back down to Thomas. "But only because I like you."

"Thank you," Thomas said, turning the shell bracelet inside out. He slipped the loop of shells around Charles's wrist and tightened the rope. Charles watched with interest. "Let me know when you're ready to be a merman."

Charles's mouth fell open, and he looked up at Thomas. "This will turn me into a merman? Is it magic?"

"Yes," Thomas said. "Is that okay?"

Charles grinned. "Yes! I'm ready!"

Thomas couldn't help but smile at Charles's enthusiasm. He began working the bracelet right-side out. As soon as the inside of the last shell lay flat against Charles's wrist, the transformation began. Charles's legs fused together and sprouted fins where his feet had been. The scales of his tail shimmered rich brown speckled with gold under the cloudy daylight. Thomas could not look away.

"Wow," Thomas said. "Your tail is beautiful."

"Thanks," Charles said with a smile that was even more beautiful than his tail.

"Thomas," Mariana cut in, "an emergency Pantheon meeting has been called. I need you right now."

"What does that mean?" Thomas asked.

"Come on," Mariana said, pulling him up by the arm. She yanked him out of the boat.

Thomas expected to feel the sting of icy seawater against his skin as he fell in, but instead he landed on a cold, hard floor.

Thomas stared at the cool marble beneath him, trying to understand. When he looked up, he found he was nowhere near the ocean. He sat on the floor beside a huge marble table. Large people occupied its seats, each composed of something different. Some looked entirely human, but some looked like sculptures made of rock or fire or ice, and they were all moving.

Gods.

Thomas stood. The room was incomprehensibly large, and the oval table was much bigger than he could have seen from his vantage point on the floor. He couldn't count the number of gods that were seated, but most were looking directly at him.

Mariana took a throne-like seat made of sea-green stone lined with shells of all shapes, sizes, and colors. With a wave of her arm, a smaller wooden seat pulled out from the table beside her. She pointed at it and smiled at Thomas.

Thomas took hold of the chair's high back and brought himself around to sit on the blue cushioned seat. He turned to Mariana on his left. "What is this?" he whispered.

"Thomas," Mariana said with a grin, "welcome to the Pantheon."

Chapter Fifteen

Charles could not believe his eyes. Thomas had disappeared right off the edge of the boat. He had been pulled up by an unseen force and then stumbled backward like he was going to fall overboard, but instead of a splash, he was gone.

The rainclouds were finally starting to part, making way for the bright sun. Mariana must have taken Thomas somewhere. He had seemed confused before he vanished.

Charles leaned forward against the side of the boat and looked into the dark blue water. The inability to move his legs independently reminded him he had a fish tail. He fell forward, clinging to the edge of the boat for support. He turned to look at his tail, then down at Fyavine. Her tail shimmered golden under the seawater. Hers was so beautiful, and his was just *brown*.

"What the hell?" Fyavine asked. "What happened to Thomas?"

"I don't know. I think Mariana took him somewhere," Charles said.

"Is he coming back?"

Charles shrugged.

Fyavine sank back into the water and frowned. "Well, do you want to swim back with me, or should I tow you back to the ship?"

Charles looked around at the interior of the boat. There was no rope for Fyavine to tow with. The ice patches on the hull were weakening by the second, and neither Thomas nor Mariana were around to fix them. He didn't know how to swim with a tail, but he could learn. The sirens wouldn't hurt him in this form.

"I'll swim with you," Charles said. "I may be a little slow."

Fyavine gave him a flat frown. "Okay. Let's go, then."

Charles nodded and took one last look around the boat before sliding into the cool water. He writhed, flipping upside down and spinning around in an attempt to gain his bearings. His nose and mouth filled with salty water, but it didn't burn. It felt as normal as air. He could *breathe* down here. Everything came easy, except swimming. Swimming with a fish tail was impossible.

Fyavine took a firm grip on his arm and pulled him upright. Her curly black hair flowed around her head gracefully, and her golden tail shimmered like magic. Dim blue light from the surface danced across her dark brown skin. Charles hadn't seen her outside the brig before, and he was struck by the beauty the water brought out in her.

"What?" she demanded.

Charles shook his head. "I'm really bad at this," he said, knowing Fyavine would not respond well to a compliment from him.

Fyavine looked him over, assessing his flaws. "You're not using the upper half of your body. You can't rely only on your tail to swim around. You have to use your whole body."

It seemed obvious when she said it, but Charles realized he had expected his fish half to do all the fish work. He engaged his arms to regain balance. It was much easier.

Fyavine nodded in reluctant approval. "The ship is that way," she said, pointing behind herself. "Let's go." Without waiting, she took off.

Charles followed, keeping balance with his arms stretched out in front of him as Fyavine did. She swam very fast, but occasionally she glanced back and slowed her pace to allow him a chance to catch up.

"You're a fast learner," Fyavine said.

"Thanks."

They swam in silence for a few awkward minutes before Fyavine stopped abruptly and stared into the darkness below.

Charles searched the darkness, looking to see what she was seeing. A few yellow points of light spotted the dark abyss, but not much else was clear. As he looked longer, blurry lines of large structures appeared. It was a city. The city was tall, and the structures ended in spires about a hundred feet below them. The dark, lurching silhouettes of sirens haunted the tops of the buildings.

Fyavine hadn't moved since she stopped. Her expression hadn't changed.

"Fyavine?" Charles asked. "Are you all right?"

Fyavine tore her gaze away from the city to frown at Charles. She grabbed his arm and swam, not bothering to let him swim for himself. After dragging him for a few minutes, she stopped again and stared back in the direction from which they came.

"Charles . . ." Fyavine said. "Do you know where we are? In relation to land?"

"Uh . . ." Charles glanced around the wide blue sea, as if that would help him find the answer. "I couldn't tell you right now, but

I can pinpoint our location once we get back to the ship. The captain should have been charting the course."

Fyavine nodded and turned to face him again but kept her eyes locked on something distant and imaginary.

"Do you recognize that place?" Charles asked.

Fyavine didn't answer for a long time. Finally, she looked into his eyes. "Can I ask you something?"

"Sure," Charles said.

"If you fell in love with a merperson, would you ever be willing to live underwater with them?" she asked. "Would you give up the world you know to be with them?"

Charles considered her question for a moment. He tried to imagine Thomas as a merperson, and how he would feel about living underwater with him. If Thomas wanted him to, he would. Their last interaction left him confused about where they stood, but either way, Charles would do pretty much anything to be with Thomas. "Yes. In a heartbeat," he said. "Why?"

Fyavine glanced back one more time. After a short pause, she said, "Let's keep going." She grabbed his wrist and pulled him through the water again.

"Fyavine, what was that?" Charles asked.

Fyavine didn't answer as they came up under a large oval shadow. It took a moment for Charles to recognize it as the hull of the ship. He had never seen a ship from this perspective.

"Where are the sirens?" Charles asked.

Fyavine frowned at him and tugged at a strand of her curly hair. "They took all the men. Fiona almost had a hold on three of them, but she didn't have enough energy to keep them all down. We found her passed out and alone on the deck when we finally felt safe enough to come up. She's inconsolable."

"Dei, that's horrible," Charles said. He crossed his arms over his chest and peered at the darkness around them as guilt hung heavily on him. He would have died if it weren't for Thomas. He was lucky Thomas cared about him enough to jump into a horde of sirens. "How do we get back up?"

"Faya is waiting for us to return. She'll help us up," Fyavine said.

"Oh, great. Let's go," Charles said as he began swimming toward the surface.

Fyavine grabbed his arm before he could get far. "Charles, wait. Please don't say anything about what we saw."

Charles stared at her. "The city?"

Fyavine nodded.

"O-okay . . . Why not?" Charles asked.

"Just please don't say anything," she said.

"Your secret's safe with me."

Fyavine smiled at him. "Thank you," she said, then dragged him to the surface.

The humid air warmed his face as he came up. Breathing air was just as easy as breathing water had been. This body was amazing.

"Faya!" Fyavine shouted.

Faya leaned over the edge and grinned at Fyavine. "You're back!" she yelled.

Fyavine beamed at her. "Can you help us up?"

Faya looked left and right, then back at Fyavine. "Where's Thomas?"

Fyavine and Charles exchanged an uncertain look. Neither knew how to explain what had happened to Thomas. "He's helping Mariana with something," Charles finally said. "He'll be back."

Faya seemed to accept this answer. She disappeared for a moment and returned with a net, which she threw over the edge. "Hang on. I'll pull you up."

Fyavine gestured toward the net. "Gentlemen first."

Charles frowned. "That's not how the saying goes."

"Neither of us are very ladylike, are we?" she asked.

Charles huffed a reluctant laugh and swam to the net, holding on tight. Faya pulled him up and helped him onto the deck, then lowered the net for Fyavine. Charles collapsed onto the floorboards and stared into the sky, hoping Thomas would come back soon.

Faya pulled Fyavine onto the deck and caught her in her arms. Fyavine giggled. "Wow, you're so strong."

Faya grinned. "Thanks."

Fyavine's question was starting to make a little more sense.

TINERA

At breakfast, Felix didn't sit at the magical table. He headed to a table with only one other occupant.

His hall leader, Matthew, sat across from him. Matthew looked up with surprise before glancing around the room as if someone had put Felix up to this. "Hello, Felix. Can I do something for you?"

"I want to know why the halls have been separated," Felix said. It was a risk to ask, but Matthew's job was to help residents.

"Oh!" Matthew said with a smile that almost convinced Felix he was safe. "We didn't want to alarm anyone, but the witch hasn't been caught yet. Flowers are still going missing. But don't worry, we're keeping a careful watch on everyone to make sure we catch the people involved."

Felix nodded, hiding his disgust. The woman was innocent, but they didn't care they had taken her magic away. Of course they didn't. It was a reward in their eyes.

At least he knew Finnlay and Aella were safe. "So it'll go back to normal when the witch is caught?" Felix asked.

"That's what I've been told," Matthew said with a good-natured shrug. Was he really this brainwashed, or was he a good liar? It was more likely that he was simply brainwashed, but Felix did not want to believe any magus hated themselves enough to give in to this place. It was too sad.

"Thank you, Matthew," Felix said. He picked up his plate and moved to an empty table, not wanting to spend the next thirty minutes in the hall leader's company.

Throughout his hall's dedicated crafting time, Felix pondered their conversation. Would they really let the halls speak to each other again after the witch was caught?

What would happen next? Would the witch lose their magic? Judging by what they did to the woman from Larkspur, it seemed likely. In that case, it meant Felix wouldn't see Finnlay and Aella until one of them got caught and lost their magic, which could not happen. But if it didn't, he would never see them again.

They were screwed.

As the long hours passed, Felix convinced himself that this was the end of their plans. Catherine had thwarted them. She had much more power than any of them, even with their magic. It was no wonder he had never heard of an escapee before. When they began to suspect a developing escape plan, life at the camp became a nightmare. They separated friends and tightened security. How many times had this happened before? Was Matthew being honest when he said it was temporary?

The situation commanded his thoughts. Finnlay and Aella were his only friends here. Catherine had turned his entire residential hall against him and then reorganized the camp so they were the only people he saw. Felix was stuck, targeted by a mad woman who claimed he had murdered her son.

What could he do?

He felt no enthusiasm to get through recreation time like he usually did. Normally, he would get to see Finnlay and Aella afterward. But it was all the same now. No matter what time of day it was, he was alone.

When Matthew stood up to announce it was time for lunch, Felix dragged his feet. He ambled to the back of the line and stared at the ceiling as he waited to receive his daily serving of dirt water.

Would he continue sitting at the magic table? There was no reason to sit there any longer, but there was also no reason not to. His eyes worked their way around the room, eventually landing on the magic table.

Finnlay was there.

Finnlay had been watching Felix, and when Felix made eye contact, Finnlay gave a small wave.

Felix tried not to react. He forced his smile down and stepped out of the lunch line as calmly as he could, heading for the table.

"Finnlay! What are you doing here?" Felix said as soon as he was safely across the line. He let his smile unfurl.

"I waited for you," Finnlay said, returning the grin. "I figured out your meal comes after ours. I sat through the Belladonna lunch too, but it wasn't bad. It gives me a chance to do magic again."

Felix sat down across from Finnlay. "It's so good to see you. I was starting to lose hope."

"Yeah, it's rough. Aella didn't want to come with me. She's convinced I'll get caught and thrown in the cave," Finnlay said.

Felix scratched the side of his face and eyed the guards at the door. "I kind of agree with her. I know she's annoying but . . . she's right. How do you plan on getting back to your hall without getting caught?"

Finnlay scoffed. "Easy. I'll just slip out with the crowd when lunch is over and then sneak back to my hall. These guards are not as observant as they seem."

"But there are more of them than ever."

"I'll be all right," Finnlay said with a shrug.

"Finnlay, we are in danger," Felix said, leaning forward. "My hall leader told me that the restrictions won't ease until they find the witch. And then they'll take the witch's magic. That's us!"

Finnlay nodded as if Felix had merely shared a fun fact. "Don't let them scare you. We can still do this. Aella and I think we can finish the potion tomorrow evening. We'll meet you here at dinner, and then we'll all stay here for the rest of the night until it's done. How does that sound?"

Felix leaned back. "Seriously?"

"Yes! There's still hope for us."

"How are you and Aella still collecting flowers without getting caught? They're *always* watching me," Felix said.

Finnlay scratched his face. "Perhaps Catherine has the guards keeping a closer watch on you."

Felix sighed. "Yeah. You're probably right."

"You don't have to keep looking, Felix. I don't want you to get in trouble. Aella has stopped searching too, but that's okay. I think I can make it work."

"Really? You think we can do this?" Felix asked. He was hesitant to let himself feel hopeful.

"I really do."

Matthew stood from his table and informed the hall lunchtime was over.

Felix swallowed and looked at Finnlay. "I don't want you to get caught. Maybe you should just wait here until dinnertime," Felix said.

"That's four hours from now!" Finnlay said, standing. "I'll be fine. Don't worry."

Felix nodded and stood up with him. "Are you going to exit through the kitchen?"

"Nope." Finnlay crossed the boundary of the cloaking grid and headed for the main door.

Felix stood frozen in shock at Finnlay's confidence that the guards wouldn't catch him but quickly followed after him.

Finnlay turned to Felix. "Just talk to me and act normal. How have you been?"

Finnlay was right. If Felix acted weird about him being here, the guards would notice something was up. He relaxed and let himself get into the conversation. It was a hard question to answer without sounding suspicious, because everyone around them had been stuck with each other for the last two days. "It was weird that Catherine stopped by the library, wasn't it?" Felix asked, realizing he hadn't told Finnlay about that.

Finnlay eyed him. "Very. She didn't talk to me. Did she talk to you?"

Felix and Finnlay walked past the door guards. The guards scanned the crowd, but as Finnlay predicted, they didn't notice anything out of place. Felix tried not to look surprised.

"Yeah. She told me to apologize," Felix said.

Finnlay's eyebrows shot up. *"Really?"*

Felix nodded.

"But—" Finnlay started.

"Yep," Felix said. "I know."

"Did you say something to her?"

Felix cringed. "I didn't correct her if that's what you mean. But I certainly said some things that probably didn't help my situation."

Finnlay snickered. "I wish I had overheard *that* conversation."

Felix couldn't help laughing with him. "Yeah. She was angry."

"Excuse me," a voice cut in. It was Matthew, waiting at the

edge of the crowd as the residents of Oleander walked through the field. "Who are you?"

"Finnlay. Why do you ask?" he said with all the innocence of someone who belonged in Oleander.

"What are you doing here, Finnlay?" Matthew asked. His usual friendly demeanor was tinged with irritation.

Felix tried not to panic as he watched their exchange, but Finnlay stayed calm. "Heading back to my hall, same as everyone else?" Finnlay said.

"You're not a resident of Oleander," Matthew said.

Finnlay shrugged. "Since when is that against the rules?"

Matthew waved a nearby guard over.

"Oh, there's no need for that," Finnlay said with a short laugh. Felix could hear his nerves slip through. "I can find my own way back."

Matthew shook his head. "You realize our halls have been divided for a reason, don't you? It goes without saying that you are breaking the rules by being here outside of your hall's designated time."

"Matthew, come on. He's harmless," Felix said. Matthew narrowed his eyes at Felix.

The guard approached, a tall man with black hair and broad shoulders. "Yes sir?"

"Finnlay is with the wrong hall. Take him to the appropriate lodgings, please," Matthew said.

"Wait—" Felix started, but Matthew shushed him and pushed him back in line with the other residents.

The tall guard grabbed Finnlay's upper arm and began dragging him across the courtyard. Finnlay watched Felix with panicked eyes as he stumbled backward, then he turned around to follow the guard. Instead of heading for Larkspur, they walked toward the corner of the camp, where they had taken Felix after his escape attempt.

At dinner the next day, Felix was alone.

Chapter Sixteen

Thomas had never been more uncomfortable. Hundreds, possibly *thousands* of eyes were on him. The room was filled with walking personifications of anything and everything. A god made of fire sat in a dark stone chair, scorching black marks into it. Farther down the table, a god made of ice crackled and glowed with an aura of pale sublimation.

At one shadowy edge of the table, a black throne lurked in the darkness. A smaller seat sat beside it. Tetra was here, and she had brought Caldwell with her. Any attention that was not on Thomas was on Caldwell.

A bright column of silver light flashed at the center of the table. It extended down from above, shining even beyond the impossible distance of the ceiling that seemed to end where the sky did.

The column of light molded itself into a humanoid figure, much like sea water took the shape of Mariana. The figure did not seem to be man or woman. The light that composed their figure was too bright to make out any facial features.

The figure placed their hands on their hips and looked around the room. "Wow, you all got here fast!"

Thomas glanced around, gauging the reaction of the gods. They all maintained their bored and mildly irritated frowns. Thomas looked up at Mariana. "Who is that?" he whispered.

"Shh . . ." Mariana responded without looking at him.

"It's been a while, hasn't it?" the silvery god said. "Normally I would just make you all wait until the decennial Pantheon to meet the first human servant, but mere *days* after the first, we have a second! How fun!"

Thomas blinked, fixing his eyes on this strange entity. This god was as silly and carefree as Mariana. He suddenly realized their featureless face was pointed at him. Was he supposed to say something?

"Um . . . Hi," Thomas said.

The god threw their head back and laughed. "Humans!" they said. "Amazing." Quiet snickers echoed through the large room. Thomas didn't understand why that was funny. "I don't think these two will last long considering who they belong to, so . . ." The god clapped their hands together, spraying white sparks into the air around them. "Let's get started!"

Thomas felt sick. This must not have been the first time Mariana and Tetra had caused problems, and now he was part of their eternal feud.

"Thomas Hambleton and Alastair Caldwell, please come here," they said.

Thomas glanced at Mariana, who nodded toward the table. Thomas climbed onto it and approached the center, which was surprisingly far from where he had been sitting. Caldwell approached from the other end of the table, staring him down the whole way.

As they met at the middle, Thomas got a better look at the mysterious shining god. This person was larger than either Mariana or Tetra and made completely of silver light. Thomas still could not determine their gender or what they were the god of.

The god glanced back and forth between them quickly. "Wow, it's cute to see the two of you up close," they said. "My name is Dei. I am the god of gods."

Thomas clapped a hand over his mouth to contain his gasp. Caldwell's eyes were wide, and he abandoned his intimidating sneer for the moment.

"You two have been chosen by your gods to serve them for eternity," Dei said. "Before you can begin your eternity, I have two rules to explain to you."

Thomas resisted the urge to look at Caldwell, knowing he wouldn't know anything more than Thomas. Mariana had never told him about any servant rules, and he couldn't imagine Tetra had said anything to Caldwell either.

"First rule," Dei said. "You *must* do everything your god tells you to do. If you don't, your god may force you to do it through whatever means necessary."

Thomas gawked at Dei. "Wait, wh—"

"Second rule. You cannot have children with another human, or your child will be destroyed. You are now members of the Pantheon, which means you are above human, and you have a responsibility to your species not to disrupt the natural order of things. Do you understand?"

Thomas finally looked at Caldwell to see what he thought of the second rule. "Fine," Caldwell said with a bored shrug. "It wouldn't be my problem anyway."

"Ugh, gross," Thomas said. "What is wrong with you?"

Caldwell ignored him. Tetra had definitely chosen the right man.

"Thomas?" Dei asked.

"I don't understand why that would disrupt the natural order of things," Thomas said.

"Because you're immortal. Your offspring would be immortal too. That trait can't spread."

"Okay," Thomas said. It was unlikely he would ever have to worry about that.

"Good. You may have noticed," Dei said, gesturing to Thomas, "that you can't die. Not completely, anyway. You'll die for good only if your god dies or if another servant kills you with their sword. Also, you won't age past the last stage of development for a human, which is around twenty-seven years. Thomas, you'll continue aging until you reach this age. Alastair, you can return to this age if you'd like."

"I want people to fear me, not fear that I'll wet the bed," Caldwell said.

Thomas rolled his eyes. He was relieved he wouldn't be eighteen forever. He'd had enough of it already.

"One last little thing," Dei said, turning to Thomas. "Thomas, since you were the first human to enter the Pantheon, you will be the leader of all humans of the Pantheon going forward, as well as all godservants, human or otherwise."

Thomas did not know what to say. What did it mean to be the leader? Did he have to keep everyone in line? Did they have to listen to him?

"I don't want to be the leader," Thomas said.

"You can pass it onto Alastair if you'd like. What do you say?" Dei asked.

Thomas could think of nothing worse than letting Caldwell have control over him in any way. "No," he said. Caldwell scowled at him.

"That's probably wise," Dei said. "I don't have time to talk to humans, so I need you to find each new godservant as they come and explain the rules."

"Find them?" Thomas asked. "How?"

"When the time comes, you'll know where to go," Dei said with a wink. "Also, you'll have to report any immortal children to me, Thomas. We can't let that go unchecked. Imagine a world of immortal humans." They pretended to shudder. "Gross."

Thomas frowned. He didn't think he would be able to sentence a baby to death merely for being born. "Okay," he said anyway. Pantheon be damned, he had a responsibility to his species not to be a monster.

"That's all. Any questions?" Dei asked. Thomas opened his mouth to speak, but Dei said, "No? Good." At Dei's words, a whirlwind of silver light descended. When it vanished, Thomas and Caldwell were alone on the platform.

Thomas stared at the spot where Dei had been. They were nothing like Thomas would have expected. Humans around the world prayed to Dei, but They thought humans were *gross*. He was starting to suspect none of the gods had the ethereal grace people believed they did.

Thomas turned to face Caldwell. "I hate that I have to spend eternity with you."

"Likewise," Caldwell said with a sneer.

They walked away from their places on the platform, both subject to the curious stares of the many gods lining the edge of the table. Thomas took his place beside Mariana, while Caldwell sat beside Tetra.

"While we are here, are there any urgent disputes that need settling?" the voice of Dei asked from all around.

Mariana stood up. "Tetra is messing with my ecosystem!" she shouted. "She's possessing mermaids and drowning innocent human men."

A silence filled the empty air while all the gods watched Mariana. Just as Thomas was beginning to believe Dei wouldn't answer, They said, "You have a servant for a reason, Mariana."

Thomas held his breath. Dei meant Godservant duels. He had no sword skills whatsoever, and he was not prepared to engage in another battle with Caldwell.

"I don't want to settle it that way. This shouldn't have happened to begin with. It isn't fair," Mariana said.

"What *is* fair, Mariana?" Dei asked.

"She was breaking the rules before I met Thomas. I'm not going to risk losing my servant over this," Mariana said.

"We created this system for a reason. You and Tetra are always fighting. I can't mediate your squabbles every day. Use the system, or I will destroy both of your humans and revoke servant privileges for all gods," Dei said.

Mariana fell back into her seat and crossed her arms. Thomas had never seen her upset like this before.

Across the table, Caldwell grinned at Thomas while Tetra spoke to him, likely explaining godservant duels. Thomas had already lost to Caldwell in a duel once. He wouldn't stand a chance.

"Is this happening right now?" Thomas asked.

"No," Mariana said. "It happens when I choose, as the prosecutor."

"So you *can* choose not to have me fight that sadistic monster again?" Thomas asked.

Mariana frowned at Thomas. "Yes, but I'm starting to think it's the only way to solve this problem."

"There has to be another way," Thomas said.

"Do you have any suggestions?" she asked.

Thomas racked his brain but found nothing. "No, but if I fight him, he's going to kill me. He's already killed me once. It's the solution for Tetra, not for you."

Mariana sighed again. "Fine, we'll put this idea on hold for a while. You can practice your sword work in the meantime."

"Great," Thomas said. His stomach turned at the idea of dueling Caldwell again. He would kill Thomas slowly and make sure it hurt.

"What'll it be?" Dei asked.

"Later," Mariana replied.

Thomas looked across the table to see Tetra's knifelike smile. She gave him a taunting wave.

"Welcome to the Pantheon. You are dismissed," Dei said.

Gods all along the table vanished. Mariana turned to Thomas with a frown. "Thomas," she said, "I don't want to lose you. This is incredibly important. I need you to find someone to teach you how to use a sword, and you need to do it fast."

"How fast?" Thomas asked.

"As soon as you can. Sailors will just keep dying and mermaids will stay sick the longer we put off this duel."

Thomas nodded. "I'll see what I can do. I learn quickly."

Mariana looked sideways at Tetra briefly before returning her gaze to Thomas. "Thank you. I'm sorry I didn't prepare you for this. I had some hope that this wouldn't happen so soon."

"Why?" Thomas asked. "What is it about Tetra that made you think there was an ounce of mercy in her cold, dark heart?"

Mariana sighed and looked at Tetra again, and her expression could almost be mistaken for longing. She didn't respond.

Tetra interpreted the look as an invitation and slid through the darkness of the room with Caldwell in tow. She leaned against the marble table beside Mariana. Her sharp smile curled up. "So, you want to duel me?" Tetra asked.

"I won't have to if you let the mermaids free," Mariana said.

Tetra cackled loudly, showing every single violently sharp tooth. "Mariana, you're no good at threats." Tetra eyed Thomas up and down. "And you chose the flimsiest little man I've ever seen."

"Hey!" Thomas said as Caldwell laughed. "I'm not flimsy."

"Uh huh," Tetra said, keeping her eyes on Mariana. "Don't worry, Mariana. This will all be over soon. You don't want to fight me now, but you will *very* soon," she said with a wink. "You'll have no other choice." She squeezed Mariana's shoulder with a clawed hand. Mariana winced and pushed her hand away.

"Leave me alone, Tetra," Mariana said.

Tetra shrugged. "Okay. Let's go, Alastair." She yanked her new human servant into the shadow realm by the arm. Thomas almost felt bad for Caldwell.

Almost.

"Are you okay?" Thomas asked.

Mariana glared at the tabletop and shook her head. "I'm fine. Let's go."

"Okay. Can you please take me back to wherever Charles is?" Thomas asked.

Mariana nodded once and placed her hand on his shoulder. Just as suddenly as Thomas had appeared in the Pantheon, he was gone. He fell a short distance through the air and landed on the wooden deck of his ship with a painful thud. He leaned back and groaned, rubbing his knee. "Did you have to drop me?" he asked, but she was gone.

"Thomas!" Charles yelled. Thomas looked up to find Charles lying shirtless on the deck. He was propped up on his elbows with his beautiful brown-gold tail laid out behind him. He smiled at Thomas, and Thomas forgot all about the pain in his knee. "Where were you?"

"You're back!" Faya shouted. She sat with Fyavine near the edge of the ship but stood when he appeared. "Where did you come from?"

"Are you okay?" Fyavine asked from the floor, unable to stand as a mermaid.

"I'm fine," Thomas said. "Mariana brought me to the Pantheon to meet the other gods."

"The Pantheon?" Charles asked. "Did you meet Dei?"

Faya rolled her eyes. "I hate to break it to you, Charles, but Dei is not real. The Pantheon only has *real* gods."

Thomas did not know how to break to either of them that Dei was real and did not care about them. "Uh, yeah. I did, actually. They're really . . . odd."

Faya's eyes widened. Charles furrowed his brow. "Odd? *They?*" he asked.

"I don't think Dei has a gender. I don't know," Thomas said.

"You couldn't tell?" Charles asked.

Thomas shrugged. "Does it matter? I didn't think you cared about gender."

Charles scoffed but didn't argue. After a pause, he said, "No, I guess it doesn't."

"Are you all okay?" Thomas asked. "Where is everyone? Where's Fiona?"

His questions were met with a long silence.

"Fiona is below deck with Fiametta," Fyavine finally said.

"What about the other sailors?" Thomas asked.

Faya and Fyavine exchanged a grim look while Charles inspected his hands. "They didn't make it," Faya said quietly. "Fiona did not have enough energy to hold a stun on two people while physically restraining a third. She passed out and, um . . ."

Thomas ran his fingers through his damp hair to distract himself from the dread squeezing his heart. He nodded. "Is she okay?"

"She's pretty down on herself about it," Fyavine said.

"It's not her fault," Thomas said.

Fyavine nodded. "We know that . . ."

Thomas rubbed his face and sighed. He knew those sailors' deaths were on his hands. He had let two of them go and did not stay behind to help Fiona. Instead, he went after Charles. But Charles would have died if Thomas hadn't jumped in the water.

"Let's go see her," Thomas said.

"I don't know if she wants that," Faya said. "She really wanted us to leave her alone."

"Are you joking?" Thomas asked. "She feels responsible for the death of three people. The last thing she needs is to be alone with that guilt."

Faya nodded slowly. "Yes . . . you're right. I don't know what I was thinking."

Thomas sighed. "It's okay. This was all very unexpected, and we're probably still in shock," he said. "We'll have to carry them below deck," he added, pointing to Charles and Fyavine.

Faya and Fyavine smiled at each other. Faya picked her up with ease and marched to the hatchway. It was hard to believe Faya had despised Fyavine not that long ago.

When Faya and Fyavine were out of sight, Thomas was alone with Charles. Charles watched him with something like love in his eyes. "Are Faya and Fyavine gay?" Charles asked.

"Y—well . . . Fyavine is. Faya is like you."

"So yes."

Thomas shrugged. "I guess so."

Charles frowned at him. "Why did you act surprised when I told you I liked women if you already knew someone like me?"

"I don't know," Thomas said, approaching Charles. "I guess it defied who you were in my mind."

"I'm still the same person."

"I know that. It's just new to me. I'm sorry," Thomas said. "Fyavine told me what 'gay' means. Maybe she can answer your questions about yourself too."

Charles rested his head in one hand and raised his eyebrows.

"I don't have questions about myself. I want to know about *them.* Are they together? You didn't tell me you knew another gay couple."

Thomas looked toward the hatchway where Faya and Fyavine had disappeared, fixating on the phrase *another gay couple.* He didn't know if *any* of the four of them belonged to a couple. "I . . . I guess I don't know," Thomas said.

"Fyavine said something strange to me earlier," Charles said. "She asked me if I would be willing to leave land and live underwater if I fell in love with a merperson."

"What did you say?" Thomas asked.

Charles shot him a sly smile. "I had to imagine it was you, but I said yes."

Thomas turned his face away while the butterflies in his stomach tried to convince him to smile. "Do you think she was talking about Faya?" he asked when he could safely look at Charles again.

Charles shrugged, eyes closed. "I'm not making any assumptions, but it seems awfully strange she would ask me that question when there is another beautiful gay woman waiting for her on this ship."

"Yeah. Maybe you're onto something," Thomas said, crouching down beside him. "Can I pick you up?"

"I don't know, can you?" Charles asked. "I'm bigger than you."

Thomas scoffed. "Barely."

Charles eyed him hungrily. "You *have* gotten stronger during your time at sea. Sure, you can pick me up with your big strong sailor arms."

Thomas laughed and slid his arms around Charles's back and under his tail. He lifted Charles from the deck while Charles held onto him.

"You're so strong . . . and handsome and smart and funny," Charles said, watching him adoringly.

Thomas began walking to the hatchway. "I don't know what those last three things have to do with this."

"Nothing. I just like you a lot," Charles said.

Thomas couldn't fight back his smile this time but tried to turn away before Charles saw. He still hadn't sorted out his feelings, and this wasn't helping.

"I can see you smiling. Let me see it," Charles said.

Thomas tried to reshape it into a grimace as he turned. "Does this look like a smile to you?"

Charles laughed his genuine laugh as Thomas carried him to the lower deck. "Yes, and it's adorable."

Thomas couldn't keep it back anymore, freeing a giddy laugh from that sickening twist in his stomach. Charles was his weakness.

Below deck, Faya and Fyavine sat on either side of Fiona, and Ametta sat off to the side. Fiona's face was buried in her palms. Faya patted her on the back and muttered something Thomas couldn't hear.

Thomas set Charles down near Fiona and sat next to him. "Hey, Fiona," Thomas said. "How are you doing?"

Fiona dropped her hands, revealing her tear-streaked face. It quickly brightened with a relieved smile. "Thomas! You're okay!" She moved toward him but stopped herself. "I was so scared you were gone for good. When the storm stopped, I thought . . ."

Thomas extended his arms for a hug, and Fiona sprang forward to tackle him with a tight embrace. "I'm okay," he said.

Fiona leaned back and smiled briefly as her eyes landed on Charles. "You saved him," she said.

Thomas nodded. "Yeah . . . I wish I could have done more."

"You did more than me," Fiona said quietly.

"You did everything you could," Thomas said. "I wouldn't have asked you to stun them if I knew it would drain you so fast."

"It's not your fault. I should have known better, but I wanted to save them all," Fiona said. She sighed and looked away. "I couldn't save anyone."

"It would have been a miracle to save any of them," Thomas said. "The only reason I got Charles back was because I have the power of a god on my side. If I had done that as a mortal, we both would have died. It was stupid of me to jump in. We're lucky there are any survivors at all. Well . . . *you* would have survived, Fiona, but the rest of us are lucky to still be here."

"No thanks to me," Fiona said.

"Fiona," Faya said from beside her, "We were all only capable of saving ourselves. Thomas only saved Charles because he cannot die. You tried, and that's what matters."

Fiona shook her head. "No, that's not what matters. Their lives mattered, and now they're gone."

Thomas did not know what to say. Nobody seemed to. How could they argue against that?

"At least they aren't suffering anymore," Faya said.

Thomas hid his face behind his hands and sighed. The members of this crew had been former magi. Their souls had been broken. Mariana had told him the afterlife alone couldn't fix their broken souls. It would take several lifetimes to heal.

"I suppose . . ." Fiona said.

Thomas lifted his head. "Are you feeling all right physically? Passing out from magic overuse can't be good for you . . ."

"I'm exhausted, but it's hard to rest," she said. "And now that you're back, I need to make another self-sailing enchantment, but I don't know if I have it in me. I can barely keep my head up."

"We're not in any hurry," Thomas said.

"We can't just drift along with the current," Charles said. "We'll lose the course, and we could collide with another vessel."

Thomas frowned at him. He knew that, but he didn't want Fiona to stress about it.

"Do you want me to show you how to make it so that you can learn a little bit of magic?" Fiona asked Thomas.

Thomas froze. His heart beat hard, and his throat felt tight. Nausea twisted his insides. "No."

Fiona raised her eyebrows. "Really?"

Thomas shook his head. "I don't want to do magic," he said. "Ever."

"Why not?" Fiona asked.

Caldwell was alive again, but the horrible feeling of taking another person's life was still fresh. His magic had killed someone. "It's dangerous. I don't want to hurt anyone. Maybe it was a mistake for me to get it back. Maybe they took it from me for a reason."

Fiona exchanged a worried look with Faya. "Thomas . . . It was a mistake for them to take it from you."

"I killed someone, Fiona . . ." Thomas said quietly.

"Only because you're a grown man who was never taught how to use your magic. That's not your fault. Besides, that was self-defense. You won't hurt anyone if you learn proper magic, and I can show you," Fiona said.

Thomas shook his head and tucked his hands under his arms. "No, I can't do it. Magic is too dangerous. I never should have gotten it back."

Fiona and Faya's faces pinched with unease. Charles watched them with the same look.

"What?" Thomas demanded. "Why are you all looking at each other like that?"

Charles turned his attention to Thomas and smiled carefully, resting one hand on his arm. "It's just a little frightening to hear . . . *you* talk about magic like this."

Thomas's heart dropped. He couldn't believe he had let himself express his distrust of magic in front of magi. "I didn't mean it like that. I'm sorry," he said, shaking his head urgently.

"I'm not . . . I'm not like them. I didn't mean . . . It's not magic. It's *me*."

"It's okay," Charles said softly. He squeezed Thomas's arm. "We know you're not like that."

Fiona smiled uncertainly. "You know, it might be good for you to practice so this fear doesn't get out of hand. One bad moment doesn't define you."

"I don't know . . . I don't feel comfortable trying witchcraft when I can't even control my water magic," Thomas said.

Fiona nodded somberly. "All right. Are you willing to try, Faya?"

Faya scratched her head. "Yes, I can try. I've never done witchcraft before."

"I can walk you through it," Fiona said.

Faya nodded once. "What do we need?"

"Tobacco, a sailor's belonging, and a jar," Fiona said as she struggled to push herself up but fell back down immediately. She breathed heavily, leaning against the wall to rest. "I thought I could at least help gather ingredients, but I can't even stand up."

"Don't exert yourself," Faya said, pushing up from the floor. "I'll gather everything for you."

"Do you need help?" Thomas asked.

Before Faya could answer, Fiona cut in. "No, Thomas. Stay here. I need to talk to you." Faya shrugged at Thomas and walked away to rifle through the sailors' belongings.

"Oh—Okay," Thomas said.

"Should we go?" Charles asked, gesturing to himself and Fyavine.

"No. It's nothing serious," Fiona said.

"What is it?" Thomas asked.

"I would like you to reconsider learning magic. Now that I'm not stuck in that cage, I can show you how to safely manipulate water. It feels bad right now, but take some time to rest and recover, and talk to me again tomorrow. I won't have enough magic to show you anything for a while, anyway."

Thomas wanted to argue. He wanted to say no and avoid her for the rest of the trip. "Can I ask you something, Fiona?"

"Of course," Fiona said.

"I don't know anything about magic. I'm a magus, obviously . . . but is there some way to know where my magic came from? Ametta clearly got her magic from Faya, so I know it's genetic somehow. I just can't figure out which of my parents is magical. It doesn't seem likely that either of them are."

"Oh . . . I could tell you, but typically that's information we keep within the community." Fiona pushed herself up to sit a little straighter and eyed Charles and Fyavine. "Um . . . no offense, you guys, but I should have this conversation with Thomas alone."

"Faya already told me," Fyavine said. She fixed her golden eyes on Charles as if daring him to speak.

"Wow, really?" Fiona asked. "That's . . . um . . . surprising. Typically, magi only share secrets with unmagic if they expect to spend their lives together."

Fyavine smiled wide and covered her mouth with her hand, tapping her fingertips along her lips.

Charles and Thomas exchanged a knowing look. Maybe Charles was right about Faya and Fyavine.

"Or maybe she thought it was okay because you're a mermaid," Fiona said with a shrug. After a pause, she nodded. "Actually, yeah that makes sense. Mermaids are basically honorary magi. I forget you're a mermaid sometimes." She laughed sheepishly.

Fyavine's bright smile dimmed a little, but it didn't leave her face. "Oh."

"Fiona . . ." Charles said, slipping on a charming smile. "What if I promised to marry a magus. Would you let me in on the secret?"

Fiona's eyebrows rose. "No."

Thomas snickered as Charles's smile fell away.

"What if I got engaged to a magus right now? Would you tell me?" Charles pried.

"Ugh. Shut up," Thomas said, rolling his eyes.

"I'm flattered, Charles, but I'm not going to marry you," Fiona joked.

"Are you sure? I'd take good care of you. You'd be incredibly wealthy. I know my father would let me back into the family if I brought a woman home," Charles said.

Thomas snapped his head to the side to glare at Charles, failing to pretend Charles flirting with Fiona right in front of him did not fill him with hot jealousy.

Charles moved his gaze from Fiona to Thomas. His casual smile was back. "What's wrong? Are you jealous?" Charles asked with a wink.

"Obviously."

Charles's eyebrows shot up. He clearly wasn't expecting that answer.

"Money isn't everything, you know," Fiona said, interrupting their quarrel. "Anyway, no. I wouldn't tell you, but if Thomas is just going to tell you anyway, there is no point in me keeping it from you now. Thomas?"

Thomas turned his attention to Fiona but could only stare at her stupidly. Was she implying Thomas was going to spend his life with Charles? It wasn't the direction he expected his life to go, but it was starting to seem more likely with every conversation that passed between them. They still loved each other. That much was obvious. And watching Charles flirt with Fiona was torturous. How could he ever accept Charles being with someone else?

Still, he couldn't imagine letting Charles back in, even after his admission on the dinghy.

Whether Thomas ended up with Charles again or not, he probably *would* tell Charles. He had trouble keeping things from him.

"You won't tell anyone?" Thomas asked.

Charles's taunting smile took on something a little more honest. "You're willing to tell me?"

"Don't get any ideas. Fiona's right. I probably would have told you anyway," Thomas said.

Charles's amusement fell away. "I promise I won't tell."

Fiona's eyes danced between Thomas and Charles. "Okay . . ." she said uneasily. "Basically, a mother's firstborn child gets her magic, and a father's second born child gets his magic. That is always how it happens, which means that any combination of that birth order can result in inheritance of multiple magical abilities or none at all. For example, if you were your mother's first child but your father's second, you could have gotten your magic from either of them."

"Wow . . . So your brother has different magic from you?" Thomas asked.

Fiona rubbed her neck and gave a nervous laugh. "No. That's different. I should have said the children from a mother's first pregnancy gets her magic. Finnlay is my twin, so we inherited the same magic because we were in the womb together."

"Finnlay is your twin? You've never mentioned that," Thomas said. "Are you identical?"

Fiona pursed her lips and furrowed her brow. "Um . . ." Her lips parted as she prepared to answer, but he realized it was a stupid question before she could.

Thomas slapped his palm against his forehead. "Obviously not. He's a man," he said.

Fiona smiled and swept a spiral of ginger hair away from her face. "I was trying to keep the magi birth order simple for you. I didn't think you would ask about my brother."

"Oh. I'm sorry," Thomas said.

"No, no! I'm flattered you want to know," Fiona said with a smile. "Anyway, considering your family history, you probably got your magic from your mother. Unless you think your father could have had a child before you and never mention it."

Thomas took a long moment to consider it. That didn't seem like something his father would do, but he had learned a lot about his parents recently. Thomas couldn't imagine either of his parents as magi, but it only seemed more likely he had a secret half-sibling as he continued to speculate. "I just can't imagine my mother as a magus," he said. "She's too . . ."

Fiona watched him warily, and he realized he had to choose his next word carefully.

"Conservative," he finally said.

Fiona seemed to approve of his word choice. She nodded. "Your father isn't?"

Thomas sighed. "Yeah, he is."

"Hmm . . ." Fiona said, rubbing her chin. "So as far as we know, you inherited your magic from your mother."

"That's the only reasonable answer," Thomas said.

"Oh, I know!" Fiona suddenly said. "Many magi have recognizable names within the magic community, because the magus child takes the last name of the parent from whom they received their magic. Do you know your mother's maiden name? Maybe I will recognize it."

"Really? So if it's my mother, I wouldn't be a Hambleton?" Thomas asked.

Fiona grinned. "No, I guess you wouldn't be."

"Her maiden name is Fontaine," Thomas said. "Does that mean my name should be Fontaine?"

Fiona's jaw dropped. "You're a *Fontaine?*"

Thomas shrugged and looked at Charles. Charles shrugged too. "Is that more surprising than Hambleton?" Thomas asked.

Fiona laughed. "No, but you definitely got your magic from your mother. The Fontaine line is one of the oldest known lines of water elementalists. I can't believe she took an unmagic name. I can't believe a Fontaine became a Hambleton, and then turned her firstborn child into a Hambleton too. Why is she trying to end that name?"

Thomas scratched his head. "Well . . . It's going to end with me, anyway."

Charles laughed. "No, it won't."

"Charles, I'm *not* interested in women," Thomas said.

"That's not what I meant," Charles said. "I only meant that your name will never die because you will never die."

"Oh . . . Right." Thomas was not excited to live forever and tried to avoid thinking about his eternal future. Or maybe not so eternal if he couldn't find someone to teach him how to use a sword. "What else do you know about the Fontaine family?" he asked.

"Well, they have generational wealth from—"

"Wait, stop," Thomas said. "Please don't tell me that the other side of my family is evil too."

Fiona laughed. "They're not evil. They develop communities around lakes and rivers and then use their money to take care of the people in cities they have created. They put a lot of effort into providing clean water to those cities. That effort extends to nearby towns as well. The Fontaines are good people with a genuine interest in caring for their own."

"With one exception," Thomas said.

Fiona's smile crumbled. "Right. Your mother."

"Why do you think she would want to abandon that?" Thomas asked. "Why would she marry someone who is actively trying to destroy magic?"

"I can't imagine why any magus would put themself in that situation," Fiona said.

"Are you sure your father is the one trying to destroy magic? What if it's your mother?" Charles asked.

"Why would she do that?" Thomas asked.

"I don't know, but your father doesn't seem . . . um . . ." Charles looked away.

"What?" Thomas demanded.

"He's just not very bright. I wouldn't expect him to be able to organize something on this scale and successfully keep it hidden from you."

"Just because he doesn't talk much doesn't mean he's stupid," Thomas argued.

Charles raised his eyebrows and looked away with his shoulders up. "Honestly, I would think he was smarter if he spoke *less.*"

"What makes you think my father is stupid, aside from the things your father says about him?" Thomas asked.

"Yeah . . . Alfred does badmouth him a lot," Charles admitted. "Maybe you're right. I used to think you were stupid too, but you're the smartest person I know."

Thomas scoffed and crossed his arms. "Bullshit."

Charles smiled. "You are."

"No, I meant there is no way you thought I was stupid. I outranked you every year. Not to mention you were always on my ass about something because you wanted me so bad," Thomas said.

Charles laughed. "Okay, you're right. I just didn't think it was fair that you were smart *and* hot, so I tried to convince myself your parents were paying the school."

"Nope. All me," Thomas said.

"I'm just saying you didn't get it from your father," Charles said, raising his hands in the air in a gesture of surrender.

"Fine. Maybe he is stupid, but I wouldn't know. He doesn't talk to me," Thomas said.

"Your father doesn't talk to you?" Fyavine asked. "Ever?"

Thomas shook his head. "No. In fact, I think he avoids me."

Fiona, Fyavine, and Charles watched him silently.

"What?" Thomas asked with a shrug.

"Nothing, that's just . . . sad," Fiona said.

The casual conversation Thomas thought he had been having was suddenly an embarrassing detail of his life he wished he hadn't shared. "It's fine," he said.

"Does your mother talk to you?" Fiona asked.

"Yeah, I guess so."

"What does that mean?" Fiona asked.

"It means she talks to me. I don't know," Thomas said. He stood, ready to leave this conversation.

"Wait, Thomas, don't go," Charles called after him.

"I'll be back," Thomas said, ascending the hatchway.

The quiet evening wind blew across the empty deck as the sun sank behind the horizon. Dried blood staining the wood planks to his right gave the drifting ship an eerie aura.

Thomas approached the edge of the ship and peered into the dark water. "Mariana," he said to the swirling sea. The sun was still hidden behind a thick layer of dark gray clouds, which only seemed to thicken in the aftermath of the conversation about his parents.

As the ship crashed into the waves, water moved up the hull of the ship and perched itself on the edge, smiling at Thomas with Mariana's face. "Hello, Thomas," she said, but her tone was off, and her smile was more twisted than usual.

"Hi, Mariana."

"Do you need something?"

Thomas wrung his hands. "Is there any way . . . I mean, is it possible . . ."

Mariana crossed her arms. "Spit it out."

Thomas hesitated. "The sailors we lost. Can you get them back?" he asked.

Mariana laughed. "No."

Her reaction was jarring. She had never been particularly sympathetic, but earlier she had been much more compassionate and understanding. She seemed to have lost that soft edge. "I know you can't see inside yourself, but I thought maybe you could help. You pulled that boat out of the sea . . ."

"I had help finding that. Your crew is gone," Mariana said. "Don't be sad. Death is natural."

"Their death was untimely," Thomas said.

"Everyone dies, Thomas. Get over it." Mariana watched him with a bored frown.

"Why are you acting like this?" Thomas asked. "I just want people to stop dying."

"You want it to stop?" Mariana asked. She slid herself off the bulwark and walked toward him. She leaned down to his height. "Then learn to fight. Save them yourself."

Thomas took a step back, feeling on edge at her approach. Mariana was not usually so brusque.

"I'm trying," Thomas said.

She narrowed her eyes. "Are you?"

"I—Yeah!" he said.

"Try harder."

"Mariana, I am doing everything I can. I have no idea who to ask for help."

"You haven't asked *anyone* for help."

The only people left on this ship were Faya, Ametta, Fyavine, Fiona, and Charles. He didn't think any of them knew how to use a sword. "Okay. I'll ask."

"Good. Now, while you're working on that, I need something else from you," Mariana said, stepping closer. "I need your help."

Thomas took another step back. "With what?" He knew he couldn't refuse.

"I want to know what it feels like to be human."

"I don't know how to help you with that," Thomas said.

Mariana grinned. There was something terribly familiar but distinctly off about her smile. "Don't worry about that," she said. In a moment, she disappeared into the air as dark mist. The cool mist wrapped around Thomas, settling on his skin and dampening his clothes. Thomas backed away in an attempt to get away from it, but his skin absorbed the mist like a sponge.

"Mariana?" Thomas asked, looking over himself and searching the deck.

I'm inside you, her voice said in his head.

"What?!"

You don't have to speak. I can hear all your thoughts. I know everything about you.

"Get out!" Thomas yelled. "I don't like this!"

Shh, she said. Suddenly, Thomas could not move. His body was moving, but he was no longer in control. Mariana had possessed him. Her presence inside his body felt magnitudes larger than his own, because she *was* magnitudes larger than him. It was as if he were trapped at the bottom of the ocean, trying to move all the water in the sea at once.

Get out of my body, Thomas screamed inside his head, but Mariana didn't answer.

He was trapped.

Tinera

Day after day, Felix hoped to see Finnlay at their table again. Day after day, he was disappointed. His concern for Finnlay was mounting. Matthew wouldn't tell him anything. Felix could only guess at how long Finnlay would be locked up.

Felix didn't even want to entertain the thought that they might have taken his magic away. Of everyone in the camp to lose their magic, it couldn't be Finnlay.

No amount of staring at Larkspur could tell Felix what happened. The worrying was driving him mad, so he decided to do something about it.

It had been easier for Finnlay to wait for Felix at the table because Larkspur's mealtime came before Oleander's. In order for Felix to wait for Finnlay and Aella, he would have to wait until the next meal.

Four days after Finnlay was dragged to the main building, Felix waited at the table as his fellow residents filed out of the room after lunch. When the room emptied, he stayed behind at the concealed table.

The sounds within the kitchen stopped, and Felix ventured inside. The large fireplace with the giant empty kettle loomed unlit to the left. On the right was a stone tabletop used as a preparation area with piles of raw carrots, celery, and turnips next to a neat lineup of knives. He felt sick at the sight of the vegetables. That vegetable stew got old fast.

On the other side of the countertop was a stack of long loaves of bread and wheels of cheese, destined to be cut up into small hunks and handed out for breakfast or dinner. That day's preparation group had already cut up enough for dinner, but Felix was focused on the untouched loaves.

He grabbed three loaves of bread and an entire wheel of cheese to bring to the magic table. On his way out, he snagged a knife from the counter and rearranged the lineup so nothing looked amiss. After dropping the food and knife off at the table, Felix returned to the kitchen to fill a pail with fresh water, just in case Finnlay had recently been released. He decided to snatch a few fresh vegetables too. Maybe they tasted better raw.

Felix returned to the hidden table and waited.

The hours passed slowly, but it was nice to have the large space to himself. It was better than walking around the muggy courtyard or lying in his bed and listening to the censored conversations of his neighbors.

Felix waited through Hemlock's dinnertime until eventually, the residents of Larkspur began to trickle in. The line extended to the door before Felix caught sight of anyone he knew. Then Aella walked in alone.

Moments later, Finnlay trailed behind her. He shuffled his feet and rubbed a hand over his face, fixing his eyes on the serving table at the end of the long line. Aella watched him with a pinch of concern between her eyebrows. She said something, and he only nodded in response. Gods, had they taken his magic? Why did he look so broken?

Aella sighed and let her eyes wander to their table. Her eyebrows shot up when she spotted Felix, but she did not acknowledge him. She elbowed Finnlay and whispered something.

Finnlay lifted his head to look. When he made eye contact with Felix, he stood up a little straighter and smiled. His eyes immediately fell to the food Felix had stolen. He said something to Aella. Aella nodded and began walking toward the table. Finnlay followed her.

"That looks delicious," Finnlay said, sliding into the seat beside Felix.

"I snagged it for you. I thought they might have thrown you in that cave," Felix said.

Finnlay nodded and snatched a loaf of bread, reaching over Felix. "Thank you," he said as he took a hungry bite. "They did."

"Are you okay?" Felix asked.

Finnlay continued eating. "I'm fine."

"We were actually going to wait for *you* today. Have you been here since lunch?" Aella asked, picking at her own loaf. It was the first time Felix had seen her since the camp tightened restrictions, but she acted like they'd just spoken yesterday.

"Yes," Felix said. "How are you doing, Aella? It's been a while."

Aella shrugged. "I've missed you, but you don't want to hear that."

"I've missed you too," Felix said, and he was surprised it was true. It was awful being apart from his only two friends in the camp.

Aella's bitter expression softened. She smiled. "We're going to get out of here tonight. Are you in?"

"Yes," Felix answered too fast, leaning forward. "I'm ready. Whose blood are you going to use?"

Finnlay stopped chewing and remained silent for a beat. He swallowed and said, "We can make do without it. It doesn't have to be permanent. It just needs to work long enough for us to escape."

"Why don't you use Felix's blood?" Aella asked. She raised her fork and smiled wolfishly at Felix. "It wouldn't be too hard to draw."

Felix did not take his eyes off the utensil. Was she threatening him? He couldn't tell if Aella loved him or hated him. Or both. Whatever it was, she was passionate.

Finnlay glared at her. "Put that down."

Aella frowned at Finnlay and set the fork down. "I'm just saying, Finnlay. I don't think it's smart to stray from the recipe just because you *think* you don't have all the ingredients."

"It's more dangerous to use a wrong ingredient than to forget an ingredient," Finnlay said.

"You can use my blood, Finnlay. Just don't let Aella draw it," he said, glancing at the fork. Aella winked.

Finnlay met Felix's gaze. "Don't be silly. You don't love me."

Felix scratched his head, not sure what to say. They hadn't known each other long, but they had already been through a lot together. Felix didn't know how he would have survived this without Finnlay. He cared about Finnlay and hoped they would still be in each other's lives when this was all over. There was more than one way to love someone.

Maybe Finnlay didn't feel the same way. Maybe that's why he refused to let Felix use his blood for the potion, but their love didn't need to be mutual.

"Yeah I do," Felix said. "You're like a brother to me."

Aella sucked air through her teeth as though Felix had said something rude. Finnlay scowled at her. Instead of responding, he reached for the raw vegetables and tossed them out of the bowl Felix had placed them in. "We can use this for the base. It won't take much to make, and I can do it right now." He paused. "Like I said before, a missing ingredient is better than a wrong ingredient."

Felix crossed his arms and frowned. It was mildly insulting that Finnlay thought he was lying. "But a right ingredient is better than a missing one."

"I'm not willing to take any risks," Finnlay said. "We only have one chance to do this right, and it doesn't have to be permanent. Besides, any 'love' you have for me at this point is not permanent."

"My mother taught me that all love is permanent. No matter how much you hate someone you once loved, your love for them lives on in your heart like a stain," Felix argued.

"Like a *stain?* Yikes," Aella said.

Felix ignored her. "Come on, Finnlay. It's not a risk."

"It's fine," Finnlay said. He dug a bundle of daisies out of his pocket and set them next to the bowl. Aella followed his lead and slapped a small pile of colorful flowers onto the tabletop. Finnlay plucked petals from a daisy, dropping them into the bowl.

Felix sighed and gave up trying to convince Finnlay. Maybe he was right. Finnlay knew more about witchcraft than Felix did. If he thought there was no point in adding blood, then Felix believed him.

Felix and Aella watched Finnlay work in silence. Once his collection of daisy petals was in the bowl, he carefully poured in water from the pail. Then, he stirred the water with a spoon. After a minute, he switched the spoon to his left hand and stirred counterclockwise with the handle submerged. The liquid shimmered as he muttered an incantation over it. When he finished, the shimmering dimmed. A twinkling bowl of orange liquid was left in its place.

"That's all it takes?" Aella asked.

"For the base, yes," Finnlay said. "It's the next part that will take me a while. Aella, can you start grinding up the wisteria? I'll do the hemlock. Felix, you can take the oleander."

Finnlay and Aella began pulling flowers from the pile and placing them on their plates.

"Um . . . Which one is oleander?" Felix asked.

Finnlay wasted no time flinging a few white flowers in his direction until Felix could identify them himself.

The trio ground up flowers into a paste with stones Finnlay had brought from outside and shaped with his magic into three small pestles. Felix fidgeted through his own hall's dinnertime. As soon as his hall left, he was in it for good. The building was finally empty, leaving the three alone in the dimming afternoon light.

"How much longer is this going to take?" Aella asked a while later from two tables down. She had finished grinding the wisteria and peonies and had been pacing the rows of tables. Now she stood with her arms crossed, watching from a distance. Felix had finished as well, but he moved on to help with the larkspur while Finnlay worked on the belladonna.

"I'm almost done," Finnlay said, keeping his eyes on the paste on his plate. He had made it through most of the stack of flowers, leaving only a small mound of bright yellow flowers.

Aella sighed and resumed pacing. Felix finished his stack of flowers and then watched Finnlay carefully work through his. Finnlay's flowers were the most toxic and needed to be handled with care. When he finally finished, he sat back.

The sun had set a while ago, and the high windows were the deep navy of the night sky. A chill settled in the room as night took its hold. "Are we done?" Felix asked, rubbing his eyes and yawning.

"Almost." Finnlay picked up the spoon from his table setting and scooped the paste from his plate. He dipped it into the base mixture, gently stirring without touching the edges of the bowl. He proceeded to do the same with the other pastes. The orange base shifted into a sunny yellow, then eased into a leafy green. Finnlay withdrew the spoon, letting the last of the droplets fall back into the bowl before setting it on the table.

"Now it's done," Finnlay said.

Aella perked up and turned to face them, looking more like a dog than Felix ever had. She hurried back to the table and sat beside Finnlay, staring into the bowl with wide eyes. "What do we do now?" she asked.

"We shouldn't all drink it at once. Just in case it doesn't work," Finnlay said.

"What do you mean?" Aella asked. "I thought you were confident in your work."

"I am. It's basic safe practice," Finnlay said, frowning at her.

"I'll drink it first," Felix said. "I already volunteered to let you test it on me. I don't mind."

"I bet you don't. You're so *generous*, offering to be the first to drink it," Aella said.

"Aella, we're all going to drink it if it works," Finnlay said, irritation in his voice. He looked at Felix and his expression softened. "Are you sure you want to do this? I understand if you'd rather not."

Felix nodded. "I'm sure," he said, but he wasn't. Not really. Finnlay had skipped an ingredient, and this was not a well-known recipe. None of them understood it. It was all guesswork.

But Felix had brought him the recipe, so it was his responsibility to test it.

"Okay. Are you ready?" Finnlay asked.

Aella sighed and crossed her arms.

"Yes, I'm ready," Felix said.

Finnlay pushed the potion toward Felix. Felix lifted the bowl to his mouth and drank the sparkling green liquid. It tasted like sweet apples and honey. Felix had never tasted anything so beautiful in his life. Finnlay had clearly done something right.

"This is delicious," Felix said, placing the bowl back on the table. "I had no idea potions could taste like this."

Finnlay smiled. "How do you feel?"

"I feel . . ." Felix trailed off as something tingled at the center of his chest and expanded, reaching through his body and extending down his limbs. Then, his skin prickled like it did before a transformation. He stood and stepped away from the table.

"Are you all right?" Finnlay asked, standing up with him.

Felix felt his body change, but he wasn't sure what he had changed into. Finnlay and Aella were both staring at him with wide eyes.

"What is this?" Aella asked, crinkling her nose. "Are you obsessed with me or something?"

"What are you—" Felix was surprised to hear Aella's voice leave his mouth. "Am I *you?*"

"Well, yeah," Aella said like it was obvious. Maybe it should have been, but Felix didn't mean to shift into her.

It didn't make sense. Felix only stared back at her until he fell to the ground and landed on four little paws. He opened his mouth to speak but meowed instead.

"It's working," Finnlay said.

Felix tried to disagree but could only meow. He tried to shift back into a human to tell them something was wrong, but nothing happened.

This was not good.

Felix was not in control of his magic.

Chapter Seventeen

Charles sat with Fiona, Fyavine, and Ametta as Faya searched for ingredients for the enchantment. He couldn't keep his thoughts off Thomas. Thomas had never talked much about his home life, and Charles had never asked. He assumed it was as bad as his own.

Footsteps thumped down the hatchway from the upper deck and Thomas strode into the room, smiling at Charles. He was relieved Thomas was feeling better, but the sudden change in mood was unexpected.

Thomas sat himself on Charles's other side. "Hey!"

"Hi," Charles said. "Are you feeling all right?"

Thomas smiled and leaned his head against Charles's shoulder, wrapping both hands around his arm. "I'm good," he said, closing his eyes.

Charles's heart beat faster. He was afraid to move for fear of scaring Thomas off. What did this mean? He took the opportunity to stare at the pretty boy on his arm. If Thomas couldn't see him, it was okay to look.

Faya emerged from the cargo hold with a bottle filled with tobacco, a bundle of twine, and a slip of paper with scratchy handwriting on it. "I found everything you asked for, Fiona," Faya said. Her face fell when she looked up and noticed Fiona was asleep. "Oh great," she muttered as she approached the group. She sat close beside Fyavine.

"Hi Faya," Fyavine said with a big grin.

Faya tore her gaze away from Fiona to look at Fyavine, an adoring smile replacing her frustration.

"Should we wake her up?" Charles asked.

Faya jolted and looked at him like she just remembered he was there. "Who?"

If he had any doubts about their relationship before, they were gone now. "Fiona," Charles said.

"Oh!" Faya said with a nervous laugh. "I'd hate to wake her up, but our ship is just drifting. We could get pulled into a bad storm or run aground somewhere."

"I wouldn't worry about that," Thomas said.

"Oh, do you have a new sense for that sort of thing?" Charles asked.

Thomas looked him in the eyes and smiled. "Yes."

Charles watched Thomas carefully. Something was off. He got the same feeling as he did when Felix wore Thomas's face, but there couldn't possibly be a shapeshifter aboard this ship.

No, Charles was just paranoid. Maybe he wasn't used to Thomas being nice to him again yet. He smiled back at Thomas, then focused on Faya. "It's up to you, Faya. You're the witch now."

Faya laughed. "I'm no witch. I can't do any of this without Fiona."

"I think we should wake her . . ." Fyavine said. She threw a nervous glance at Charles. "We're in a school of sirens. Charles and I have to stay like this until we're safely away from them." She gestured to her beautiful golden tail and Charles's dull brown one.

Faya watched Fiona, who was sleeping peacefully with Ametta. "The poor girl is exhausted," she said.

"Fiona!" Thomas yelled.

Fiona jumped awake and looked around at the group watching her. She rubbed her eyes and blinked hard. "So sorry," she said. "I fell asleep. Is everything okay?"

Charles frowned at Thomas, who smiled in return. It was very unlike Thomas to be so insensitive. "Why did you do that?" Charles whispered.

"We need her help," Thomas said.

Faya sighed. "I'm sorry, Fiona. We're ready to make the enchantment now, but you're the only one who knows how to do it."

"Oh, that's okay. Don't worry about me," Fiona said, yawning and stretching her arms over her head. Ametta continued snoozing. "I can show you what to do, but I don't think I'll be able to do it myself. Is that all right?"

"Yes, of course," Faya said.

Fiona eyed the gathered ingredients. "All right. Put the tobacco inside the—oh, it already is. Good. Roll up the note and stick it in the bottle—yes, just like that. You're a natural," she talked as Faya did as she said.

Thomas's eyes were on Charles while Fiona and Faya worked to save the half of the remaining crew who were attracted to women. Charles forced himself to smile at Thomas. Thomas smiled back, sneaking one hand from Charles's arm and around the other side of his fish tail. The action was innocent enough, but something about it was so unlike Thomas. It made Charles uneasy.

Charles tried to clear his mind and enjoy the moment. It had been a long time since they could be together. He was probably responding to the familiar way Thomas acted toward him in this unfamiliar environment of kind and accepting people. He held Thomas around the waist and pulled him closer, appreciating their nearness.

Charles kept his eyes on Fiona and Faya. Faya unsteadily followed Fiona's directions while Fiona forced herself to stay awake to explain. Fiona drew a sloppy sigil on Faya's arm and said a string of unfamiliar words while Faya squinted at her. Faya tried to repeat them, but Fiona shook her head and stopped her. She walked Faya through the words one at a time. As they finished the spell together, the enchantment glowed white.

Charles had not seen much magic in his life, so he was disappointed when Faya stood and ascended the hatchway to hang the enchantment on the mast. It had all ended so quickly. Fiona laid her head against the wall and drifted back to sleep. Thomas fiddled with the collar of Charles's shirt, brushing his fingers against Charles's chest. Fyavine sat nearby, pretending not to see it. Several minutes passed before the ship creaked and groaned as it came to life, as if a ghost crew had suddenly pulled its rigging back into place.

"It sounds like it worked," Fyavine said, looking around the dim room. "Do you think Faya is okay? That mast is tall."

"She's fine," Charles reassured her while Thomas slid his entire hand underneath Charles's shirt. Charles gently pulled his hand out again and held it in his own to stop Thomas from feeling him up in front of Fyavine.

Fyavine scratched her head and frowned at Thomas. "Do you want me to give you two some privacy?"

"No," Charles quickly said. "You should not become human until we're certain the sirens are out of range."

"You'll be safe if you're with me," Thomas said, much closer than before. "I won't break contact."

Charles's heart rate increased, but he didn't know if it was a positive reaction. He simply stared at Thomas. Words would not find him, and neither would an explanation for the feeling that he did not want to be left alone with Thomas. The number of times Charles had fantasized about being alone with him just in the last week was not something he would admit aloud to anyone, not even Thomas himself, yet he didn't want it now. Why?

Charles watched silently as Thomas pulled the bracelet from Charles's wrist and handed it to Fyavine. His brown fish tail disappeared, transforming into his usual legs. Fyavine slipped the bracelet on her wrist, grew her own pair of legs, and ascended the steps to join Faya on the top deck.

Thomas snuck his hand under Charles's shirt again, watching him hungrily.

"Thomas," Charles whispered. "We're still not alone."

Thomas frowned at Fiona and Ametta, then he aimed the frown at Charles. "It's fine. They're asleep."

Charles shook his head. "Even so, I don't understand . . . *this*." He gestured between himself and Thomas.

Thomas shrugged. "What is there to understand?"

"Are we . . . ?"

Thomas watched him impatiently, pretending he didn't know what Charles was trying to ask. "What?" he demanded.

"Are we together again? What are you doing?" Charles asked.

Thomas leaned back and sighed, rolling his eyes. "Who cares? Why can't we just enjoy each other's company?"

"I care," Charles said. "I realize I've been unkind to you in the past, but I really do love you. I'm not interested in doing this if you're just messing with me. What is this?"

"*Messing* with you?" Thomas asked, eyes narrowed. "Why would I be messing with you?"

Thomas would've answered the question if this was serious.

"You *are* messing with me, and I'm honestly a little surprised you're so eager after everything we just went through," Charles said.

Thomas was angry. He glared at Charles for a long time before speaking. "You're right; today was hard. I learned something new about you, and I'm starting to doubt you ever liked me at all."

Charles scoffed. "That's stupid."

"Oh, it's stupid? You sound just like you did at Blackwater. It's always *me* being stupid and never you taking accountability for your actions," Thomas said.

"I haven't *done* anything," Charles said.

"Not yet."

"What is that supposed to mean?"

"You know what I mean."

Charles rolled his eyes. "Oh, fuck off. You're being mean."

"So what? I thought you were into that, but clearly you've never been into me at all."

Charles couldn't believe what he was hearing. Would it always be this way now that Thomas knew he liked women too? "Why are you being like this?"

"Why are *you* being like this? Why won't you just prove to me how much you like me?" Thomas asked.

"I shouldn't have to! Why don't you trust me? Still?!" Charles asked.

"Maybe it's because you accused me of assaulting you when *you* were the one who pulled me into bed with you, even though *I* asked *you* to stop!"

Charles didn't know what to say. He hadn't realized he had come closer to being the assaulter in that scenario than Thomas ever had. "I'm—I'm so sorry."

"It's fine," Thomas answered. He pushed himself up against

Charles and looked into his eyes. "You can make it up to me now."

"I don't—I'm uncomfortable," Charles admitted.

Thomas frowned at him. "What? Why?"

"You're not acting like yourself."

"What do you mean?"

"You're being pushy and rude. I don't like you like this," Charles said.

"Well, I don't like you like this either," Thomas argued.

"Like what?"

"Like—someone who likes girls."

Charles narrowed his eyes. It wasn't fair for Thomas to be upset that he liked women. He couldn't help it any more than Thomas could help his attraction to men. "We've already talked about this. I can't change that."

"Maybe you should find yourself a girlfriend, then."

Charles arched an eyebrow. "Yeah, maybe I should." He didn't mean it, but Thomas was making him angry.

Thomas scowled at Charles. Then he stood, breaking all physical contact. "Fine," he said, and then he walked away.

"Wait—Thomas, don't leave! What about the sirens?!" Charles called after him. Thomas ignored him, climbing onto the upper deck.

Charles panicked. The only reason he felt safe taking off the enchanted bracelet was because Thomas was with him. Now that he was alone and human, the sirens would come back. He only had moments to figure out how to save himself. He frantically glanced around the room, but he was out of time.

The sirens were already singing.

Faya's worried face against a backdrop of stars filled his sight a moment later. One arm was around his body and the other had a firm grip on his wrist, where the shell bracelet was pulled tight against his skin. He was sitting on the bulwark, his brown tail draped over the side of the ship. Inky seawater waited for him below.

Charles let out a startled gasp and clung to Faya.

"It's okay," Faya said in a shaky voice. "You're okay." She carefully pulled him back onto the deck and set him on the damp floorboards beside Fyavine, who was rubbing her head and looking as confused and disoriented as Charles felt.

It seemed only moments had passed between Thomas leaving him below deck and now, but that was clearly not the case. Charles did not remember running up here at all, but he felt the exertion in his body from dashing up the steps and across the deck.

Charles let himself fall onto his back and sighed, watching Faya's upside-down figure storm away.

"What the *fuck* were you thinking?" Faya shouted.

Charles exchanged a surprised look with Fyavine and rolled onto his stomach to get a better look at the unfolding drama.

"We all could have died! Are you out of your gods-damned mind?!" Faya yelled at Thomas.

Goosebumps prickled Charles's skin as he met Thomas's eyes. Thomas wasn't listening to Faya at all. He was staring at Charles, unsmiling. Something about the look in his eyes made Charles feel sick. He almost seemed . . . amused?

Something wasn't right. Charles averted his eyes and listened to Faya berate Thomas about how irresponsible he had been with their lives, but there was no point.

A stranger had worn Thomas's face once before, and Charles had noticed immediately. There couldn't be a shapeshifter aboard this ship, but Thomas never would have let this happen.

"What happened, Charles?" Fyavine asked quietly. "Why did Thomas let you go?"

Charles shook his head. "I don't know what's going on," he replied, "but that is *not* Thomas."

Chapter Eighteen

"What are you doing? Stop messing around," Aella said.

Felix grew from his small feline body back into a human and sighed with relief. He stood and brushed himself off, but Finnlay and Aella stared at him like he was still a cat. "Something is wrong. I—" Felix stopped when he realized, again, he wasn't using his own voice. It was Thomas's. His hands flew to his face to feel the differences in facial structure, confirming his suspicion.

Finnlay narrowed his eyes and looked Felix up and down. "Who—"

"There's no time!" Felix said as soon as he realized he would not stay in this form much longer. "I can't—"

Felix turned into a crow and fluttered to the floor. He flapped his wings and cawed loudly.

"You can't control this?" Finnlay asked.

Felix cawed again.

"Oh no, I'm sorry Felix," Finnlay said, slapping his forehead with the palm of his hand. "The reverse base with suppressants must be forcing you to use your magic instead of stopping the effects of them." He paused as his eyes widened. "Oh no . . . The blood *was* for protection from the effects of the suppressants. It wasn't for longevity."

Felix looked up at Finnlay with one bird eye.

Aella groaned. "Great job, Finnlay. The potion is ruined because you couldn't get over your crush on Felix long enough to accept his brotherly love."

Finnlay glared at Aella. "I do *not*—" He shook his head. "It doesn't matter. You should get out while you're still a bird."

"Wait," Aella said. "If this potion is forcing Felix to shapeshift, it could kill him. We have no idea how long it will last."

Finnlay ran his fingers through his hair as his eyes scanned the dark ceiling. "You're right. I thought it would stop as soon as he got away from the camp and the suppressants, but I don't want to risk his life on a guess."

"It's a little too late for that, *Finnlay*," Aella snapped.

Before Finnlay could respond, Felix shifted back into a human. He rubbed his head and frowned at his companions. "This sucks," he said with Thomas's voice. "Ugh! I'm Thomas again!"

"Thomas?" Finnlay asked, looking him over again. "Thomas Hambleton?"

Felix looked down at his temporary body. "Yes," he said.

"Why do you keep turning into him?" Aella asked.

Felix thought about the pattern and realized he was shapeshifting in backwards order of his shifting history. He had turned into Aella briefly after they created the cloaking grid, and before that he shifted into a cat to show Finnlay his magic. He had lived as Thomas for a while, and he turned into a crow every time he wanted to see Rebecca so he could climb through her window. If his theory was correct, he would shift back and forth between Thomas and a crow for a while.

Felix quickly explained this to them.

Finnlay grabbed his hair by the roots and grimaced. "I'm so sorry, Felix."

"It's not your fault. I gave you half of a recipe that I didn't even understand," Felix said.

"We have to do something before he gets seriously hurt," Aella said.

"Uh . . ." Finnlay looked around, his eyes landing on the potion. "I can probably make an antidote, but it'll take a few minutes."

"Are you joking? We don't have time for you to mess up another potion!" Aella said.

Finnlay winced.

Felix watched her with a frown, knowing it would look more like a scowl with Thomas's unfriendly face. "I am willing to risk my life for freedom," Felix said. "I don't want to be here anymore. Maybe we can all drink the potion and make the antidote together on the other side. We can each escape with our own form of magic, can't we?"

Finnlay nodded slowly at first, and then more assuredly. "Yes, that's a good plan. Let's do it."

Aella's jaw dropped. "Are you joking? You two are going to get yourselves killed!"

"We can fix it outside of the camp," Finnlay said.

Aella arched an eyebrow and scanned Finnlay from head to toe. "No offense, but I wouldn't trust you with an antidote."

Finnlay sighed and rubbed his face.

"Aella, it was half of an unknown recipe with ingredients we found inside a barren field. Give him a break," Felix said, then he turned into a crow again. He let out an angry squawk.

"Oh my gods. Stay here. I'll be back," Aella said. Felix and

Finnlay watched her leave the dining hall but did not try to stop her.

"Where is she going?" Finnlay asked.

Felix flapped his wings.

"Right, stupid question."

Felix fluttered up onto the table and pecked at the bowl of potion, trying to tell Finnlay to drink it so they could escape.

Finnlay wrung his hands. "You want to leave without Aella?"

Felix nodded.

"That's not fair to her. She helped us," Finnlay said.

Felix wanted to remind Finnlay about all the horrible things Aella had said to him just in the last five minutes. That wasn't even including everything she had said over the last several months. She was not nice, and whatever she was doing at that moment would probably screw them over anyway.

"She said she would be back . . ." Finnlay said.

Felix turned into Thomas again, sitting on the tabletop.

"Oh, thank the gods," Felix said through heavy breaths. The shifting was wearing him out. "Finnlay, listen. We made this potion so that we could escape. We did not leave Aella out of this plan. *She* chose to leave for whatever reason, and to be completely honest I think she might be turning us in. If we don't leave *right now*, we'll never get out."

"Come on, Felix. She isn't turning us in. Why would she do that?" Finnlay asked.

"Why would she relentlessly insult the only person in this camp willing to help her? She's an awful person."

Finnlay pursed his lips.

"She had her chance to come with us, but she didn't take it because she didn't believe in us. It's now or never," Felix said.

Finnlay considered this for a moment, then he nodded. "Okay. You're right." He lifted the bowl of potion from the table. "I shouldn't drink it yet. I don't want to cause an earthquake, and I should save my energy for the antidote."

Felix clapped his hands triumphantly. "Yes! Let's go!" he hopped off the table and ran for the door.

Finnlay followed him into the dark night. They snuck around the edge of the building, keeping watch for the dark silhouettes of guards lurking among the tall trees. There was no easy way to stay hidden while running from the dining hall at the center of the camp, so they moved as quickly and quietly as they could through the squishy earth and toward the back fence.

"Hey! What are you two doing?"

It was a guard.

"Run!" Finnlay hissed, pushing Felix forward as he increased his pace.

The footsteps followed them until they reached the sparse forest, but they could not create distance between themselves and the guard. He was too fast.

Felix fell into a puddle when he unexpectedly turned back into a crow. "CAW!" he shrieked as he writhed in the thick mud.

Finnlay reached down to fish Felix out of the mud, holding the bowl carefully in his other hand.

"What is that?" the guard demanded as he ran closer.

Finnlay ignored the question. The moment he had Felix in his hand, he ran for the fence. Finnlay was much faster when he didn't have to wait for Felix.

Felix flapped his wings, trying to clean them quickly so he could fly, but the mud was heavy on his feathers.

"Get back here!" the guard shouted from behind them.

"Can I throw you over the fence?" Finnlay asked. "You may not be able to fly like this, but you can still flutter safely to the ground, can't you?"

Felix cawed.

"I don't know what that means!" Finnlay said.

Felix cawed louder.

"No, I shouldn't. What if I can't follow you?" Finnlay asked.

Before Finnlay could make up his mind, Felix transformed back into Thomas and brought them both toppling into a cold puddle. The potion spilled onto the grass while the bowl rolled toward the guard. It would be impossible to recover any of it.

Finnlay gasped, pausing a moment as their hard work soaked into the soil. He shook his head and pushed himself up, glancing behind him before he grabbed Felix's hand to continue running. "I'm sorry, Felix. I really messed this up."

"It's okay, Finnlay," Felix said. "You did your best. We both did."

Finnlay smiled but quickly looked away. "Do you think you'll be turning into a bird again?"

"I think so. Throw me next time. I don't care if I don't have an antidote."

Finnlay took a moment to reply. "We lost the potion, Felix. I can't come with you to create the antidote, and I don't want to do anything that will put you in critical danger. It goes against my beliefs to do anything that might cause harm."

"Please, Finnlay! I'm begging you. If you throw me, I'll get help. I'll get us both out of here," Felix said.

"I'm sorry, Felix. I can't put your life at risk."

"Then what are we doing?!" Felix asked.

Before Finnlay could answer, Felix transformed into a crow again. He squawked, but Finnlay just picked him up and kept running without answering. When they reached the fence, he didn't throw Felix.

The guard was on them instantly, but he seemed uncertain about what to do with a witch and a shapeshifting bird. Finnlay walked backward until his back was pressed against the tall wooden slats of the fence, keeping his eyes on the guard. There was nowhere to run. If Finnlay wouldn't throw him, they would be stuck inside the fence forever. They were as good as caught.

Felix felt the prickle in his skin that meant he would transform again. He braced himself for the energy loss his body couldn't afford, but at least he would be able to speak.

Unfortunately, it wasn't just birds and Thomas Hambleton all the way back.

Felix's body pulled from his energy reserve to grow his bones and skin past the size of a human until he was much larger, on all fours, his claws digging into the cold dirt and mud. Fur covered his body. He gave in to the instinctual urge to rear his head back and let out a long howl.

Felix bared sharp teeth at the guard, knowing he wouldn't dare approach a werewolf, even if it wasn't real. Finnlay stepped behind Felix, looking at the half-moon dangling between the stars.

Felix gave a low growl, but the guard stood his ground.

"Um . . . Felix," Finnlay said from behind him.

Felix turned and found they were surrounded. Two guards flanked them, and another snuck toward them from the forest.

"That's him!" Aella's voice came from behind the guards. "The werewolf!"

"Aella?!" Finnlay said. "What are you doing?"

Felix had tried to warn him. He was not surprised, but he was disappointed.

"I saw my fellow resident in trouble and went for help," Aella said.

"Why would you do that?" Finnlay asked shrilly.

"Felix needs help," Aella said. "He's not in control."

Another guard approached, raising the pewter bowl Finnlay had used as a cauldron. "They dropped this while running," he said, tentatively sniffing the inside. "I think it's a potion."

"I don't know what that is," Finnlay said. "It's probably just old soup."

Felix shrank into a crow and fluttered to the ground with muddy wings. Finnlay lurched for him, grabbing his little bird body, but he still didn't throw Felix over the fence. It felt like Finnlay was trying to *prevent* him from flying away. Finnlay held Felix close while he cawed and struggled to get out of his hands.

"I'm sorry, Felix," Finnlay said quietly. "I don't want you to die."

Felix continued shrieking with the volume of an angry crow. Finnlay couldn't do this to him. Of all people. *Finnlay* was keeping him trapped here. He expected it from Aella, but never from Finnlay.

The guards were on them instantly, ripping Felix from Finnlay's hands and holding him so tight he couldn't breathe. The guard clamped his beak shut. "They know it's a potion. This one obviously drank it," she said.

"He didn't do anything wrong. It was all me," Finnlay said, a pair of guards holding him back.

Felix thrashed in the guard's hands, but her grip was tight.

"You," the guard with the bowl said, pointing at Aella. "What do you know? Which of these two men are responsible for this potion?"

Aella eyed the potion again, then looked steadily from Finnlay to Felix. Finnlay scowled at her with clenched teeth. Felix could not move.

She pointed at Felix. "The bird. He did everything." Her eyes hovered over Finnlay. "Finnlay doesn't know anything about witchcraft. He's innocent."

"Liar!" Finnlay yelled. "I am a witch! You helped me make that potion!"

Aella shook her head. "You can't be a witch. You're not a woman," she said with a shrug.

"You know that's not true!" Finnlay yelled.

"Oh, you *are* a woman?" Aella asked.

"That's *obviously* not what I meant!" Finnlay snarled. Felix had never seen him so worked up. He didn't know Finnlay *could* get so worked up.

The guard lost her grip on Felix as he changed back into Thomas and fell onto his hands and knees before collapsing into the remarkably comfortable mud. He breathed heavily from the prolonged effort of frequent shifting. He couldn't keep himself up. If this potion didn't wear off soon, he might actually die from exhaustion.

The guard beside Aella crouched in front of Felix, pushing his shoulder to roll him face-up. "Open your mouth," the guard demanded.

"*Why?*" Felix spat back. He just wanted to sleep forever on the cold ground.

"I'm going to help you," the guard said.

Felix needed help, but he knew what it meant when these people said it. "How?"

The guard fished something out of his pocket and presented it to Felix. It was a small vial of milky white liquid. "This is an antidote. It will stop the effects of your potion."

Aella *had* done him a favor by telling the guards. Felix opened his mouth without hesitation.

The guard yanked the cork from the bottle and dumped the contents into Felix's mouth carelessly, spilling some on his face. Felix swallowed what he could and immediately felt himself shift back into the comfort of his own body. He sighed and closed his eyes.

The guard that had given him the potion started shouting again, but it wasn't directed at Felix.

Felix lifted his head with great effort. Aella had taken the potion bowl from the unsuspecting guard. She was smiling.

"She licked the bowl!" the guard yelled, looking at the other guards as if they could do anything about it.

"So what? It was empty," another guard said.

Aella threw her head back and laughed. The wind picked up, blowing cold gusts of air over them. The guard who had been holding Felix tried to stop Aella, but she raised her hand and knocked the guard back with a wall of wind.

Aella ran to Felix and grabbed him by the arm to yank him up, creating a tunnel of air around them that kept them a safe distance from everyone else. The tunnel produced a noisy tornado of mud and grass that occasionally escaped its boundaries to whip Felix in the face with debris.

"Come with me," Aella said, taking both of his hands and looking him in the eyes. "I can get you over the fence."

Felix looked back at Finnlay through the chaotic mess of air that separated them. Finnlay watched helplessly from the captive arms of a guard. "What about Finnlay?" Felix asked, expending great effort just to form the words.

"He'll be fine," Aella said, shaking her head. "They think it was all your idea."

"We wouldn't have made it this far without him, Aella. We can't just leave him behind," Felix said.

Aella's hopeful expression settled into her usual judgmental frown. "He's smart. He can make another one."

"I'm not leaving him," Felix said.

"Are you stupid?" Aella demanded. "This is your only chance to get out of here, and they think it was you! If you stay, you're going to lose your magic!"

Felix pulled his hands out of hers and shook his head. "You're selfish, Aella. I would rather be stuck here with Finnlay than go anywhere with you."

"Felix, please." Aella took his hands again. "I—I've always—" Whatever she wanted to say beat against the boundaries of her expression, pleading to be free, but she couldn't do it. Sincerity did not come easy to her.

Felix pulled his hands away again and took a step back. He didn't want her to say it. "No."

The wind whipped Aella's pale hair around her face and splattered mud across her legs as the pleas in her expression shriveled back into disdain. "Fine," she said, stepping closer to Felix. "Then I'll take this for the road." She placed one hand around Felix's neck and the other against the back of his head, and then she licked his jaw.

Felix stumbled back, alarmed at the sudden warmth on his face. Before he could react, Aella forced the tornado away from her, pushing Felix and everyone else back as she ran to the fence and jumped over, aided by a powerful gust of wind. After a few moments, the strong gales shaking the trees beyond stopped.

She had licked his face for the antidote. It was probably the only reason she wanted him to come with her.

A female guard who Felix recognized as the angry woman from the body search wiped her face, the cleared mud leaving behind a scowl. "Go after her. Do *not* let her get away. We haven't had an escapee yet, and I'll be damned if the first one happens under my watch."

Two men nodded and ran off. She aimed her scowl at Felix. "I'm taking Mr. Warren to meet his savior." She smiled, but it wasn't friendly. Felix's stomach turned. Before he could move, two large men grabbed his arms and dragged him to the back of the camp.

"No!" Finnlay screamed. He lunged forward as they dragged Felix away, and the guards struggled to keep him back. The angry woman joined forces with Finnlay's guard to restrain him. He writhed against their grip, but the guards were stronger.

The excessive shifting had taken so much out of Felix. He

knew what came next, but he did not have the energy to fear or fight it.

He was going to lose his magic.

♪

AT SEA

Thomas stood paralyzed under the stars as sick mermaids wailed around him. Mariana would not let him move. Not even when Faya shouted at him to help as she chased Fyavine across the deck. Not even when Charles emerged from the hatchway, pushing past Thomas to get to the water Thomas had *just* rescued him from.

Mariana made him stand still and watch the chaos unfold. He had been certain he was about to watch Charles's life end as he climbed over the side of the ship, but luckily, Faya had kept her eyes on Fyavine. She remained lucid as the sirens began singing, just as Charles had been when Thomas called his name.

Faya grabbed Fyavine before she could throw herself overboard, pulling the bracelet from her wrist as she wrenched Charles back by the collar of his shirt, not looking away from Fyavine the entire time. She blindly wrestled him to get the enchantment around his hand. As soon as she tightened the string of shells, the singing stopped, and it was safe for her to look away from Fyavine.

Faya wasted no time confronting Thomas about the situation, using colorful language. Mariana kept Thomas's eyes fixed on Charles, who watched from the floorboards of the deck with confused, fearful eyes. If Thomas could have felt sick, he would have. He did not like being feared, especially not by Charles.

Beneath Faya's yelling, Thomas swore he heard Charles say, "That is *not* Thomas."

How does he know? Mariana's voice hissed inside his head as she forced his feet to move them below deck.

Thomas didn't bother answering. Mariana had access to all of his thoughts and memories, so it wasn't a secret that Charles knew Thomas better than anyone else. Thomas had been relieved and surprised Charles didn't succumb to Mariana's charmless attempt at seduction. When he realized what Mariana was trying to do, he felt so disgusted that he didn't want to be in his own body. He was so sure that Charles would jump at the chance to be with him, but Charles knew something was wrong.

Mariana marched Thomas through the living quarters and down to the brig, where she kept him awake all night.

It was torture. She wouldn't let him sleep, sit, or move. Worst of all, she would not let him go back to apologize. She forced him to stand in the darkness between the cells and dug around in his memory, bringing to the forefront every bad thing Charles had done to him.

Every time Charles had laughed at a wrong answer in class. Every time Charles rolled his eyes passing by in the hall when Thomas was only trying to be cordial.

He repeatedly asked why she was doing it but was only met with a worse memory than the previous one.

The morning Charles tripped him in the courtyard after it rained and his uniform was muddy for the entire day. The day everyone in school pretended he didn't exist and ran into him without acknowledging him or simply refused to speak to him, and later finding out that Charles had set it up. The time Charles stole his homework and threw it in the lake.

Thomas began to wonder why he even liked Charles at all.

Eventually, the sun came up, and the thoughts quieted. His autonomy returned to his body as slowly as ice melting beneath his skin. A cloud of mist twirled out of Thomas's chest, taking the shape of a tall woman at the center of the room. The relief of control returned completely. He crossed his arms over his chest as though the action could keep her out.

Mariana observed him solemnly. "Good morning."

Thomas took a step back but did not take his eyes off her.

"Are you all right?" Mariana asked.

"Am I *all right?*" Thomas demanded. "You've been torturing me all night! You almost killed Charles!"

The ship lurched, and Thomas's shoulder violently met the hard metal of the cell bars. He clenched his teeth and squeezed his eyes shut, giving into his anger. He couldn't keep it apart from his magic.

Cold water splashed against his shoulders, and he forced his eyes open. Mariana held him in place, watching him with a furrowed brow. "Thomas, I know you're mad, but you have to calm down."

"Don't touch me!" Thomas yelled, stepping aside to get away from her.

Mariana lifted her hands in the air in compliance, removing them from Thomas's shoulders. "Listen carefully," she said. "I don't have long before it gets bad again. The storm cleared up while you were possessed because I was in control. It was the only thing I could do to get us back to each other."

Thomas took another step back as she spoke. "What are you talking about?"

"I can only speak to you because the sun is out right now. If you pull another storm over us, it will be too dark," Mariana said.

"Why does that matter?" Thomas demanded.

"Do you remember why Tetra calls herself Tetra?" Mariana asked, glancing at the ceiling as though she could see the sky through it.

"Yeah, so what?" Thomas snapped. "You can't just spend the

night making me miserable and then expect me to want to help you with your stupid feud with Tetra. Why did you—"

"Just listen to me, Thomas!" Mariana cut him off. "I am trying to explain it to you. I'm sorry about last night, but it wasn't *me*."

Thomas's anger drained away to make room for the void of dread as he began to piece the situation together. "What—what are you saying?"

"Tell me how she got her name," Mariana said.

Thomas swallowed his fear so he could speak. "She's called Tetra because she's the god of four domains. She killed three other gods and stole their power."

Mariana nodded and fixed her eyes on him. "Do you think she would stop at four?"

"Are you saying . . . ?" He stopped. Something was moving beneath the surface of her translucent skin. A dark shadow darted along her edges as though searching for a way out. "Mariana, what is that?" he asked, watching the shadow roll around the boundaries of her body.

Mariana's eyes widened when she spotted it. Thomas had never seen her scared before. He didn't know she *could* be scared. "It's Tetra."

"How? Why?" he asked, frozen in place.

"Look at me," Mariana said. "It's important you do whatever you can to keep the storms away. She can't influence me where it's daytime, but she can where it rains. The darkness created by the rainclouds gives her a natural hold on me, and if she has that part of me for an entire day and an entire night, I'm gone. You're my last line of defense. If you can keep the rain away wherever you are, I will stay alive. Normally, she shouldn't be able to control you because of my protection, but when it's dark she can. We're only safe when the sun's out."

It was a lot to process. Thomas would have to keep the clouds away to keep Mariana alive? It was impossible. "Are you going to be okay?" he asked.

"I'll be all right," Mariana said solemnly. " I've got some things I need to get sorted, but I'll talk to you before the sun goes down again. Try to keep the clouds away."

"Okay. I'll do my best."

Mariana gave one last smile before dripping between the dark floorboards without another word. Thomas stared at the damp planks as he processed their conversation. If he didn't get a grip on his feelings quickly, he would lose Mariana. How could he do that?

Now that Fiona was free, she could help with his magic. But Charles was a big source of turmoil for him. With Charles around, the storms would never go away. Could he fix that? Would he have to completely mend his relationship with Charles?

Mariana was going to die.

He took a deep breath and forced his feet to move through the doorway and across the hold. The living quarters were dark. Fiona was still asleep, curled around a spare sail and clinging to it like it would keep her safe. Thomas needed her help more than ever, but he remembered how Mariana—or *Tetra*—had rudely awoken her, so he let her sleep. Fyavine and Ametta slept close beside each other on the opposite side of the deck. Charles and Faya were missing.

Hushed voices cut through the dark room from the direction of the galley. Thomas tiptoed toward the sound, careful not to awaken his friends.

He pushed the solid door inward. It creaked, high and shrill, and the voices stopped. Thomas slipped through the narrow opening to avoid waking the others.

Faya turned to watch him enter from her seat at the galley

table. Charles sat across from her with his head down. Faya did not smile at Thomas. "Thomas," she said.

Thomas nodded once. "Hello."

Faya narrowed her eyes. "Thank all of the gods Fyavine and I were together. I wouldn't have caught Charles otherwise."

"Thank you for saving him. I'm glad you're all okay," Thomas said.

Charles lifted his head. He looked like he hadn't slept. Dark skin ringed his left eye where Caldwell had kicked him, but the skin around his other eye was also dark with exhaustion. His hair stuck out around his head, messier than Thomas had ever seen it. He was not well.

"You should be ashamed of yourself," Faya said.

"It's all right, Faya," Charles muttered. "Can I talk to Thomas alone?"

Faya sighed, then shot a glare at Thomas again. "Fine, but I'm not done with you," she said as she stood from the table.

Thomas watched her leave the galley until he was alone with Charles. Charles fixed his eyes on the table below.

The wooden bench creaked as Thomas took Faya's seat opposite Charles and watched him for a moment, wishing he had thought of something to say. He hadn't expected Charles to be sad. He expected anger or resentment, but not this. "Charles, I—"

Charles's brown eyes darted up to meet Thomas's. "Don't apologize."

This was not what Thomas expected. "W-Why not?"

Charles's eyebrows knitted together as he looked away. "I know you, Thomas. You wouldn't pick a fight with me just to be mean. I don't know what happened, but that wasn't you, was it?"

"I'm impressed you could tell," Thomas said.

"What happened?"

"It was Mariana. Well, actually it was Tetra. Um . . ." Thomas rubbed his neck. "It's . . . complicated, but Tetra possessed Mariana, sort of, and then Mariana possessed me."

"How is that possible?" Charles asked.

"Tetra is trying to kill Mariana. The storms are making it easier for Tetra to get in, and I need to somehow get my emotions in control. The only way I could think to do that is by sorting things out with you." Thomas scrubbed his hands over his face.

When Thomas dropped his hands, Charles was smiling. "You want to sort things out?"

Thomas forced himself to breathe deeply, fighting away the memories Tetra had forced him to relive all night. "I am not saying I want to get back together. I just want peace."

Charles rubbed his chin and eyed Thomas. Thomas had to look away. "Sure. I'd like that too," Charles said.

"Okay, good." Thomas cleared his throat. "So . . . I guess the most immediate concern is, uh . . . are you okay? I know last night was weird and . . . gross. You seem unwell."

Charles focused on the table again. "It did get a little weird, but I think what really got to me was what you said. I know it wasn't you, but Mariana had to get those thoughts from somewhere, right?"

Thomas crossed his arms and shrugged. "I don't agree with anything she said."

Charles shook his head. "How can you *not?* Before you were possessed, you asked me why I bothered pursuing you if women were an option. Like you were just the hard choice of many easy choices."

Thomas didn't know what to say. He was scared to admit that he still didn't quite understand why Charles would choose Thomas when he could have a normal life.

"You don't see what I'm saying, do you?" Charles asked.

Thomas hesitated a moment, then shook his head.

Charles sighed and rubbed his face. When he dropped his hand, he left behind a frown. "I know we're not together, but you've said you love me. I don't think you would love me if you had a choice."

Thomas's eyebrows rose. "What? No, that's—that's not true," Thomas stammered, but he hadn't thought about it.

"Then why would you ask me that?" Charles demanded, his tone growing frustrated.

"Because—I mean—look at you!" Thomas said, gesturing toward Charles. "You're the ideal man. You're smart and charming and . . . *so* attractive. Everyone adores you, and I don't understand how someone like you could love . . ." Thomas stopped to return the gesture to himself. "*Me.*"

Charles's anger melted away, and his eyebrows pulled together. "Dei, Thomas . . . I wish you could see yourself how I see you."

Thomas shrugged. "What do you see?"

"When I look at you, I see . . . comfort." He paused, tilting his head as he admired Thomas with a smile. "You are everything I didn't know I needed. I feel safe with you in a way I didn't think another person could make me feel."

Thomas didn't know what to say. He opened his mouth to reply, but nothing came out. The familiar pleasant twist in his stomach made itself known. "I had no idea I meant that much to you," he finally said.

Charles's smile fell away. "I suppose that's my fault. I should have told you sooner."

"I wouldn't have allowed it," Thomas said.

Charles smiled sadly. "I've told you I love you, and you've said you believe me. How can you say you didn't know?"

"It's easy to say I love you. It's hard to explain why."

"For you, maybe," Charles said.

"That's not what I meant," Thomas said.

Charles locked his hazel-brown eyes on Thomas. "Why do you love me, then?"

Thomas pursed his lips and maintained eye contact with Charles as he searched for the answer. The question wasn't hard. It shouldn't have been, anyway. There were many reasons, but he couldn't put them into words.

Charles sighed and shook his head. "It's okay. You don't have to answer the question. It *is* hard."

"It's not hard," Thomas said decisively. Taking away the option to answer reminded him of every reason. "You understand me in a way no one else does. I am impressed that you can tell me apart from strangers wearing my face. I've gone my entire life without a single person trying to understand me, or downright *refusing* to. Nobody ever bothered to try, until you. You make me feel like I belong, and that's new to me."

A smile grew on Charles's face. "What else?"

Thomas squinted at him. "That wasn't enough?"

Charles laughed. "No, I mean what else do we need to settle to create peace?"

"Oh . . . Wow, that's a tough question." The answer was obvious, but Thomas struggled to say it out loud. The memories Tetra had resurfaced all night itched at the front of his mind, and he couldn't let them go. "Let's talk about the years of torment you put me through. I was so infatuated with you last year that I looked past all of it, but it's crazy that I just let it slide, isn't it? Do you remember how mean you were?"

"I just wanted your attention," Charles said.

Thomas crossed his arms. "Maybe you did, but that's not an excuse. You've never even apologized to me. Do you remember the incident in year ten when you paid Vanessa Florence to ask me out because you thought it would be funny? Do you have any idea how uncomfortable that was? What about when you stole the custodian's keys and locked me in the bathroom overnight?"

Charles's expression stiffened into horror. "Please don't remind me—"

"Why not?" Thomas interrupted him. His anger was getting to him, and he couldn't reel it back in. It wasn't fair that Charles had spent so many years making Thomas miserable, and all he got in return was a loving relationship. "You don't want to confront the fact that the person who makes you feel safe, comfortable, and loved lived in discomfort for so many years as a direct result of your actions? Do you want to just pretend it never happened?"

"Of course not, Thomas, but I *did* apologize to you. The first time we spoke. I apologized for the way I treated you," Charles said.

"That wasn't a real apology."

"Okay, so should I apologize again? What do you want me to say? I'm sorry about Vanessa, and I'm sorry about the bathroom thing," Charles said.

Thomas could not believe this. "Are you joking? That apology was even worse."

"Does it matter? You won't remember anyway."

Thomas's jaw dropped. "What is wrong with you?" He stood. This conversation was not going as he expected, and if he didn't leave the room immediately, he would pull another storm in.

Charles sighed. "Wait, I'm sorry. I—Come back, please."

"Shut up, Southworth." Thomas walked toward the door. "Does that sound familiar? Because that's how you used to talk to me."

"Please don't go," Charles said as he rose from the table.

Thomas stormed out of the galley, firmly shutting the door behind him. He had arrived thinking he could make amends, but that wasn't possible with Charles on the other end of the conversation.

"Thomas," Faya said from his right. She waited for him in the darkness near the galley door. Her arms were crossed, and she frowned at him. "Come here."

"No," Thomas said in a harsh whisper, glancing at the sleeping people around them. "I'm sorry you're offended by whatever Charles told you I said, but I'm not talking to you about it right now."

Faya raised her eyebrows. "Are you all right?"

Thomas shrugged. "Does it matter?"

"Of course it does."

"It doesn't."

"Come here," she said, more gently this time.

"No, Faya. Leave me alone."

"Thomas—"

Thomas walked away before she could scold him more. Every terrible feeling he had experienced in the last week churned in his gut, creating a disgusting emotional soup he wished he could purge.

He returned to the top deck, hoping no one would follow. For the first time in many days, the yellow morning sun struck the deck, illuminating the surface of the ocean and warming his skin. The mast waved through the sky as the cold sea batted the vessel around. Dark gray clouds lurked on the horizon.

"Thomas!" Mariana called.

Thomas turned to face her. "What."

Mariana stood on the empty deck with a bemused look on her face. "I have something for you."

Thomas pursed his lips and nodded.

She smiled and lifted a silver chain dangling from her clenched fist. It swayed in her grip as the ship moved. A small stone hung from its end. "I made this for you," Mariana said.

Thomas stepped toward her and placed his hand behind the cool chain to admire it. The polished stone was translucent, warping the image of his hand behind it. An elegant silver thread coiled around the stone to keep it attached to the chain. "Uh . . . thanks? It's very, um, pretty . . ."

Mariana laughed. "It's a piece of me." She plucked the gem from the palm of his hand and held it up for him to see. "This is a diamond. My good friend Terra helped me create it. Inside the diamond is a small amount of pure seawater from the sunniest place in the world. If you wear this, I'll be able to join you everywhere you go."

Thomas took the necklace and watched the diamond swing back and forth. "Why would I need this right now? I can't get away from you even if I try."

Mariana nodded. "Yes, well, I was going to give this to you when you reached land so that I could continue to help you, but I think it can help us out here too. The diamond protecting that seawater is unbreakable, so I am completely protected in there. I think you should start wearing it now. It may keep you safe from any tainted version of me."

Thomas draped the chain around his neck. "Thank you. I won't take it off."

Mariana smiled sadly. She opened her mouth, hesitating before she spoke. "If I'm going to survive this, you're going to have to learn to use a sword much sooner than I thought."

Her words felt like his soul had been ripped out of his chest again. Knowing there was a possibility Mariana could die terrified him. What did that mean for the world? Would the ocean become a dark, deadly place? Would he die too, or would he become Tetra's servant?

"How soon?"

Mariana's smile fell. "The best time would have been five years ago, but we'll have to settle for now. Right now."

Thomas swallowed the lump in his throat. "I don't know if anyone on this ship has experience with a sword."

"If you don't know, then ask," Mariana said. "It's a question that could save the world."

Thomas nodded. "Right. Okay."

Mariana kneeled to his level and took his hands in her cold, watery ones, looking into his eyes. "I understand you have a history of wishing for death, but I really need you right now. Please don't look at this as an easy way out. I need you alive and fighting. I need you to win."

Mariana's candor left Thomas speechless. Finally, he nodded. "I will fight for you, Mariana. I don't want to die," he said. "Not anymore."

Mariana smiled. "Good."

"It's because of you. I owe you a lot."

"Frankly, I'm happy to hear that too. Now is a good time for you to owe me," Mariana said with a laugh.

The idea of being indebted to a god would have scared him not long ago, but Mariana did not scare him. He would do a lot for her.

"I will save you, Mariana. I promise."

Chapter Nineteen

Charles watched the rough wood of the galley door for a long time after Thomas left. He couldn't believe he had become so defensive when Thomas brought up the way Charles used to treat him. He should have just apologized, but it was clearly still a sore topic for them both.

Why in the world had he felt he had any right to be upset? It was beyond reasonable that Thomas would want the person who made his life a living hell for seventeen years to apologize more than once.

Charles felt like an ass. He held his head in his hands and rested his elbows against the splintery wood of the table, refusing to move so he didn't subject anyone else to his selfishness.

After a few minutes of listening to the ship creak against the waves, the galley door squeaked open, and the table bench groaned in complaint as someone sat beside him.

Charles let out a sigh and lowered his hands, expecting to see Faya sitting with him, but it wasn't Faya.

"Fyavine!" Charles coughed her name out in surprise. "Um—I don't know where Faya went."

Fyavine shook her head, long dark curls swaying around her shoulders with the movement. "I'm not looking for Faya. I wanted to talk to you."

It was one of those rare moments when Charles didn't know what to say. Fyavine had only ever been begrudgingly tolerant of his presence, and he couldn't blame her. "Why?" he finally asked.

A reluctant smile settled onto her face, and she moved her gaze away from Charles to a barrel in the corner of the room. "You said the captain was charting the course?" Fyavine asked, tucking a strand of hair behind her ear.

"Oh . . ." Charles said, fixing his eyes on her and remembering her request. Earlier, Fyavine had asked Charles to find out where they were in relation to land. "Yes, I can do that. Let's go to the captain's cabin."

They walked in awkward silence through the dark living quarters and up the hatchway onto the main deck. Charles stopped briefly when he caught sight of Thomas near the edge of the deck fiddling with a stone hanging from his neck. Thomas stared out at the sparkling sea, seemingly so absorbed in his thoughts that he didn't notice Charles and Fyavine.

"Hi Thomas!" Fyavine called.

Thomas turned to look, smiling for Fyavine, but the grin was gone as soon as he spotted Charles. He fixed his sullen gaze on him until Charles gave a brief wave and a smile of his own. Thomas's eyes flickered over to Fyavine. "Hi Fyavine." He turned to make his way onto the quarterdeck.

Charles sighed and shoved the look of Thomas's disappointed frown to the back of his mind as he continued toward the captain's cabin. He wrenched open the door and gestured inside. Fyavine stepped through uncertainly, and Charles followed.

The captain's belongings were organized in the same tight

severity with which he conducted the crew. The small bed was neatly made, the thin sheets tucked beneath the slender mattress. An unlit lantern rocked against the panels of the wall with the movement of the ship. On the center table, four pins stuck a wrinkled world map in place. There wasn't much else to the room.

Charles approached the map table and peered down at the thin black lines illustrating the irregular edges of the continents' borders. The captain had stuck a small silver pin into one of many red trade routes traced across the sea. This particular line fell south from Dufonn to the middle of the Panthea Sea, then back up north to the eastern coast of Tinera. Caldwell could have chosen a short and dangerous route or a long and safe one, but he had chosen a long and dangerous route for no apparent reason. The season didn't call for it, and neither did the weather. On top of that, it ran through a known school of sirens.

When they had stopped on their way back to the ship, they appeared to be several miles off the coast of the island Miceani. "This is where we were when we found the underwater city," Charles said, pointing to the map. "So if you ever want to return home, find passage back to Miceani island."

Fyavine's head snapped up to look at him. "I never said that was my home."

Charles silently held her gaze.

Fyavine looked away but said nothing for a long time. "Charles, can I admit something to you?" she finally asked.

Charles was shocked Fyavine, of all people, would want to confide in him. "That city was your home?" he guessed.

A smile pulled one side of Fyavine's mouth up, but it soon fell back into a nervous line. "I'm not . . ." She glanced at the door, then looked at Charles again. "I'm not sure I want to go home, even if the other mermaids are cured."

Charles did not know what to say. "Oh. Really?"

Fyavine nodded. "I'm in love with Faya, but I don't know if she feels the same way about me."

"Well, are you two, um . . . ?" Charles scratched his head and looked away, trying to find the right words. "I mean, does she at least know that you have feelings for her?"

"Yes. We've been spending a lot of time together and we talk about our future a lot, but I'm afraid to tell her that I love her. I don't know if it's as serious for her, especially since she just lost her husband and she has a child. There are more important things in her life than a lost mermaid."

Thomas had spoken about Fyavine like she was the authority on gay relationships, but here she was, asking *Charles* for help. He was out of his depth. His only gay relationship was a tragedy. "I'm not sure about that, Fyavine. You talk about your future? That sounds pretty serious."

Fyavine smiled sadly. "Yes, but I don't think she means it."

Charles did not understand. "Why would she talk like that if she didn't mean it?"

"It's fun to fantasize."

Charles shook his head. "No, Fyavine. She's not fantasizing. I mean, she *is*, but I'm sure she means it. Do you think Faya is cruel?"

Fyavine's eyes widened. She shook her head, her long curls bouncing around her with the movement. "No! She's wonderful."

"Then why do you think she would lead you on?" Charles asked.

Fyavine pulled at a long coil of hair and bit her lip. "I don't, but she just seems . . . too good to be true."

"You should tell her," Charles said. "Be honest about what you saw and tell her that you want to be wherever she is. I don't think you have anything to worry about. It sounds like she feels the same way about you."

"But what if she doesn't, and then I'm far away from home again? How will I get back?"

"She does," Charles said. "And if she doesn't and you decide you want to come home after everything is settled, I will personally bring you back."

Fyavine smiled, but it drifted away. "How do you know?"

"The way Faya's face lit up when she saw you in the water told me everything I need to know."

"Really?" Fyavine asked.

"Yes," Charles said. "I remember being scared to tell Thomas that I loved him for the first time. To think that he might not feel the same way was terrifying. But the moment when he said it back . . ." Charles shook his head with a smile. "Dei, Fyavine. There is no better feeling in the world." Of course, they had broken up mere minutes later, but he wouldn't mention that.

"Thanks, Charles," Fyavine said with a warm smile. "Maybe I was wrong about you. You're all right."

Charles scratched his head. "No . . . You were right. I'm an asshole."

Fyavine laughed like he was joking, but he was not. She playfully pushed his shoulder. "Nah, an asshole wouldn't waste time helping a sad lesbian with her relationship problems." She hesitated, then she added, "I think Thomas will come around."

Her words instantly broke a dam of thoughts he had desperately been holding back. Being with Thomas again was always on his mind, but to hear someone other than himself or Thomas talk about it in a positive way ignited an obsession that he would not be able to keep away.

Maybe it *was* possible.

AT SEA

Thomas was determined. He had a goal, and he knew what he had to do.

But who could help him?

Faya and Charles were probably not eager to talk to him after the way he had left things. Faya probably didn't know how to use a sword, anyway. Charles didn't know anything. Fyavine might not even know what a sword is. Ametta, obviously, would be no help.

But Fiona knew everything. Aside from Mariana, Fiona had helped him more than anyone. He would ask her first.

After passing the early morning hours alone on the quarterdeck, Thomas finally made his way to the hatchway and descended the steps to the living quarters.

To Thomas's dismay, Fiona had company. She sat on a tall pile of rope with Charles beside her, engrossed in conversation. Ametta sat at their feet, setting fire to small pieces of twine and watching the flame eat the material until it reached her fingertips, then she laughed and dropped the charred remains to the ground.

It seemed dangerous, but Fiona wasn't concerned. Or maybe she wasn't paying attention. Judging by the way Fiona and Charles were looking at each other, their conversation must have been very interesting. An unpleasant feeling lurked in the pit of Thomas's stomach. He ignored it.

Thomas shuffled through the room and placed himself in front of them. Charles looked up at Thomas while Fiona talked about haircare oils, but Thomas kept his eyes on Fiona.

"Hi Thomas!" Ametta shouted from below him.

Thomas smiled at her, relieved she finally knew his name. "Hi Ametta. How are you?"

"Good!" She jumped up and lifted the most recent spindly victim of her arson. Gray smoke spiraled from her fingertips. "I'm burning rope."

"That looks, um . . . fun," Thomas said.

Ametta giggled. "It is!"

Fiona finally noticed him. Her eyebrows shot up and she smiled. "Hey!"

Thomas nodded in greeting. "Are you feeling okay?" Everyone on the crew had been through a nightmare the day before, but Fiona carried the heavy guilt of loss more than anyone.

Fiona sighed. "Yeah, I'm okay. Thanks." She smiled with pinched eyebrows. "Did you need something?" She shot an uncertain glance at Charles, who was staring at his hands in his lap. "How is Mariana?" she added in a whisper.

Thomas rubbed his neck. Charles had clearly told her about the situation. "I'm not sure. Without getting into detail, I need to find someone to teach me to use a sword. Fast. Do you happen to have experience with a sword?"

Charles's head snapped up, but Thomas ignored him. Fiona twisted her mouth into a half-smile. "Sorry, love. I wish I could help you, but sadly, I know nothing about swords."

Thomas crossed his arms and frowned at the floor. "All right. Thanks anyway," he said. "I guess I'll see if Faya knows anything."

"Thomas, you're not going to ask *me*?" Charles asked.

Thomas glared at him. Charles's eyebrows drifted halfway up, waiting in an antagonistic liminal state. A smile hid behind his inquisitive frown. "No, I'm not going to ask you. You don't know anything useful that I don't already know," Thomas said.

Charles let his eyebrows rise higher. "Really? Because I actually *do* have experience with a sword." He released his hidden smile with a wink.

Thomas gritted his teeth. "Is that a joke? Don't be gross."

Charles's jaw dropped. He covered his mouth with his hand to hide a laugh. "Thomas Hambleton-Fontaine, you naughty boy! I was not making a joke," Charles said through his laughter.

Thomas's glare remained as he glanced back and forth between Charles and Fiona, who were both laughing at him, and then down at Ametta, who thankfully didn't seem to know why they were laughing.

Thomas didn't like Charles and Fiona laughing together. At him. And Charles had let her hear his real laugh, which, until now, he had only ever let Thomas hear. "You do not know how to handle a sword," Thomas said.

Charles grinned. "Well, you would know. Now I *am* making a joke."

Thomas's face burned. "You're an idiot."

"Yes. But I will teach you how to use a sword," he said.

"I didn't ask *you*."

Charles frowned. "It sounds pretty urgent."

Thomas recalled Mariana's words. *It's a question that could save the world.* Thomas was extremely lucky to have someone on board this ship who knew anything about sword fighting. He just had to swallow his pride and ask for help. Thomas clenched his fists and exhaled through his nose. "How do you know anything about swords?" he begrudgingly asked.

"My parents wanted me to stay safe from threats at sea, so they hired a swordsman to teach me the basics," Charles explained. "Your parents didn't do that for you?"

"My parents haven't done anything for me," Thomas said.

"Except let you live in their giant house and give you money and buy you whatever you like," Fiona chimed in.

Thomas looked up at the ceiling and shook his head. "Yes, thank you, Fiona." When he looked down again, Fiona and

Charles were exchanging an amused look. "She told me to start today if possible."

"Oh, did you want my help? That's funny, I didn't hear you ask. Did you hear him?" Charles asked Fiona. She shook her head. Charles locked his golden-brown eyes on Thomas again with a dreamy smile.

"I don't want your help, but I do *need* it," Thomas said.

Charles raised his eyebrows, his stupid beautiful smile still pasted to his horrible perfect face.

"Will you help me?" Thomas grumbled.

"Of course I will, Thomas. Anything for you. Shall we get started?" Charles stood and pointed toward the hatchway. "This is an upstairs activity, I think," he added, and then he made his way to the main deck.

Thomas frowned miserably after him, watching him climb the steps. Fiona seemed to think the situation was funny. Ametta was very invested in a blazing piece of rope.

"Ametta, does your mother know anything about swords?" Thomas asked.

Ametta looked up with her big golden eyes and shook her head emphatically. "Nope."

"Damn it," Thomas muttered, turning to join Charles on the top deck.

Charles was watching the glimmering afternoon sea as Thomas crawled through the hatchway, but he quickly turned his attention to Thomas.

Thomas dragged his feet until he met Charles at the center of the deck.

"Do you have a sword?" he asked, looking Thomas up and down once in search of a weapon, and then one more time without purpose.

"Yes," Thomas said, pulling the aquamarine sword from his

pocket. The sparkling blade quickly extended from the hilt. It was easy now that he knew how to do it.

Charles stepped forward and eyed the sword from pommel to point several times. He lifted his hands. "May I?" he asked.

Thomas held the sword out. Charles gingerly took it, brushing his fingers against Thomas's hand more than necessary in the exchange. He held the weapon as though it would break if he looked at it wrong. After eyeing it for what felt like hours, Charles looked at Thomas again. "Is this the sword we used against Caldwell? It doesn't look very strong."

"Yes. Mariana gave it to me. It's unbreakable," Thomas explained as his fingers grazed the diamond necklace.

"This sword was made by a god?" Charles asked.

Thomas shrugged and nodded. "Yeah, I guess so."

Charles laughed. "Thomas, you are the only son of a bitch who would handle a god-made sword and not care about its origin."

Thomas smirked. "It's just a sword."

"No, this is not just a sword." Charles took a step back before swinging the blade a few times. Thomas admitted to himself that Charles *did* look like he knew what he was doing. "This is amazing," he said, grinning at Thomas.

Thomas didn't feel very amazed by the sword. Looking at it made him sick. Its presence in his life meant that he must kill or be killed.

Charles noticed his lack of response and frowned. "Why do you need to learn to use a sword?"

"To keep me safe from pirates," Thomas grumbled.

"Like Caldwell?" Charles asked.

"What?" Thomas asked, his mouth going dry. How did Charles know?

"I didn't tell you?" Charles asked, leaning forward. "Caldwell had the mark. He was a pirate before he worked for your family."

Thomas didn't know he could feel relieved and sick at the same time. Charles *didn't* know why Thomas needed to learn to use a sword, but Thomas also hadn't known Caldwell was a pirate. "Oh . . . That explains a lot."

Charles scoffed. "Yeah. He was awful."

Thomas nodded. "Are you going to show me how to use that thing, or are you going to swing it around all day?" he asked, desperate to move on.

"Both," Charles said with a smile. He came around to Thomas's right side and placed the sword back in Thomas's hand, keeping his own hand around Thomas's. Thomas glared at him, and he raised his hands in surrender. "I'm just showing you the proper grip. Is that all right?"

Thomas sighed. "Fine."

Charles adjusted Thomas's hand on the hilt, wrapping his hand securely around it and forcing it into a tight grip. "It's interesting that Mariana gave you a cutlass," Charles said. "Cutlasses are good for close combat, such as combat that happens on a ship at sea, so this grip is best."

Thomas looked at the sword in his hand, noting his firm hold on the sword. "Okay. I probably could have figured this out on my own."

"As for your stance," Charles continued, ignoring his comment, "keep your feet shoulder width apart."

Thomas widened his stance. Charles scrutinized it, then nodded. "Good. Now, angle your right foot a little. Perfect, you're a natural."

"I'm just standing."

"Yes, and you're very good at it," Charles said.

Thomas pursed his lips before asking, "What's next?"

Charles hesitated. "Before I teach you anything substantial, you have to tell me why you need to learn how to use a sword."

"Mariana told me to learn," Thomas said.

"There's more to it than that."

Thomas took a deep breath and shook his head. "You don't want to know."

"I wouldn't have asked if I didn't want to know."

"You don't have to pretend to care about me anymore. We broke up," Thomas said.

Charles frowned. "I've never had to pretend to care about you, because I *do* care about you. And I would like to un-break up with you, but you're being stubborn."

Thomas accidentally laughed, which made Charles smile. Thomas forced himself to stop. Charles had not actually admitted he wanted to get back together prior to now, but it wasn't exactly a surprise. "Fine. I'll tell you, but you have to promise not to get upset," Thomas said.

Charles's smile fell away. "No."

Thomas groaned. "All right, then at least promise you won't back out of this arrangement if you don't like it. Mariana's existence depends on it."

Charles let out a slow sigh. "Fine. I'll continue teaching you, even if I disagree with the reason."

Thomas nodded, trying to find the words. Charles patiently listened while Thomas explained the Pantheon's godservant rules. His neutral expression soured as Thomas detailed the situation with Mariana, Tetra, and Caldwell.

"You have to fight Caldwell *again*? With a sword?" Charles asked.

Thomas nodded.

"Why did you think I wouldn't want to continue training you? I want you to eat, sleep, and breathe sword training until the day you face Caldwell. Are you kidding? In fact, why didn't you tell me this sooner?"

"I didn't know you were a master swordsman."

"Oh, you didn't?" Charles asked with a sly smile.

"Shut up," Thomas said, fighting back a laugh.

Charles continued teaching Thomas how to handle the sword, starting with a lesson on defensive tactics. Thomas realized his assumption during the duel that Charles was just good at everything he tried was wrong. Charles held his ground against Caldwell because he knew what he was doing.

The sun had started to set, and Thomas hardly noticed he had spent the entire day with Charles. When it became too dark, Charles stopped the lesson.

"I think that's enough for today. You're doing very well," Charles said.

"I've hardly done anything but blocking," Thomas said.

"Blocking is important, and you've picked up the form very fast."

Thomas retracted the blade and dropped the hilt in his pocket again. "Thank you," he muttered. "So . . . how long have you been doing this?"

Charles shrugged and looked at the sky. "I started learning when I was eight."

"Gods, Charles. You have *nine* years of experience?"

Charles brought his gaze back down to Thomas and squinted. "Well . . . I couldn't really keep up with it while I was at Blackwater, so . . . more like five years. Although I did practice during summer breaks."

"That counts!" Thomas said.

Charles smiled, and Thomas suspected he was flattered. "We'll pick up again tomorrow for a full day of practice. You should get some rest before then."

"Okay," Thomas said.

They stood quietly for an awkward moment.

"Um," Charles started, rubbing his neck as he looked away. "You probably don't want to hear this, but I'm . . . I'm sorry. I'm sorry for everything I did to you growing up, and I'm sorry I wasn't nicer to you. I got defensive because I hate who I used to be. I know it's not an excuse, but my father used to tell me to never go easy on you because you're the same as your father in his eyes. I think that's why it took so long for me to realize that the strong feelings I had for you were not hatred, but . . . something else." He shook his head and sighed. "I am disgusted, and I regret it more than I can express. I should have said it sooner, but I'm very sorry, Thomas."

"Oh . . ." Thomas lacked a response as he processed the apology. Charles's words twisted something inside his chest that felt a lot like a thorn being pulled from his heart. "Thank you. That's exactly what I needed to hear."

Charles finally met Thomas's eyes, and he smiled. "Oh. Good."

The sun dipped below the horizon, leaving periwinkle reflections over the twilit sea. Dark clouds in the distance threatened their peace. The soft light of post sunset was much more beautiful gracing the lines of Charles's face.

Thomas couldn't take his eyes off Charles, but not because he was beautiful. Something strange was happening. The world was darkening fast. Charles did not seem to notice.

A clawed black hand slid onto Charles's shoulder from behind. Thomas's nerves fired all at once. He quickly grabbed Charles's hand and pulled him away.

The space Charles had been standing was now occupied by Mariana, wearing a deranged, sharp-toothed smile. Her dark waves blew away from her in fast, jerking movements, claws dripping black water that seemed to stain the wood below. Charles gave no indication he could see her, only watching Thomas with concern.

"*Thomas*," Mariana-Tetra growled as her smile widened. It was Mariana's voice with the cold undercurrent of Tetra's harsh whisper. Goosebumps ran along his arms.

Thomas squeezed Charles's hand, keeping his eyes fixed on the tainted version of Mariana watching him like a lion about to attack its prey.

"Thomas, what's wrong?" Charles asked.

"It's Tetra. Don't let go."

Mariana threw her head back and cackled, sounding like both Tetra and Mariana. When she lowered her head to face him again, Tetra's presence was far more apparent. "You can't protect him from me, because you can't protect yourself from *your own god.*"

"You're not my god," Thomas said.

She pouted. "What do you mean? Of course I am. It's me. *Mariana.*" She cackled again.

Thomas felt sick. Tetra was wearing Mariana's skin like a puppet. It was grotesque. "Leave me alone, Tetra," Thomas said.

She stepped toward him with purpose, her sick smile washing away. She reached for Thomas, and Thomas pushed Charles away when he realized Tetra *could* touch him. Before Tetra got to him, a pale blue mist swirled from beneath his shirt and spilled onto the floor in the familiar, healthy shape of Mariana.

"Go away, Tetra," Mariana said.

Tetra could no longer pretend. Her frown became an angry grimace. "Get out of my way. That's *my* servant."

"No, he isn't," Mariana said. "And this isn't your domain. I noticed that you're only able to occupy the water. Are you having trouble controlling it?"

Thomas realized for the first time the ocean was calm. If Tetra had control of the ocean, surely she would try to sink the ship. And Mariana had kept the storms away when she and Tetra had possessed him together. Beneath Tetra's threatening smile, Mariana still had some control.

Tetra slashed at Mariana's misty surface with watery black claws. "I *am* the water!"

Mariana folded her arms. "Quit harassing my servant. We won't let you get away with this."

Tetra turned her attention to Thomas. After a moment of contemplation, she smiled with narrowed eyes. "You're scared, aren't you? I can feel it."

"I'm not scared," Thomas said.

"You are." Tetra nodded. "You're trying so hard to find any reason to find comfort in the arms of the person who hurt you the most. The person who will hurt you again if you let him back in. Give it up, Thomas. You're never going to control your magic. You never knew how, and you're too stupid to learn now. You're not strong enough to learn sword fighting in time to save Mariana. You're too socially inept to save your friends from your parents. And Charles will *never* love you the way you want him to."

Thomas didn't know what to say.

"Don't listen to her, Thomas," Mariana said. "She's just using your fears against you."

"You know I'm right," Tetra said. "Do you really think he's sorry for all he did to you, or do you think he would simply say anything to convince you to trust him?"

Thomas turned to look at Charles. Charles met his gaze with fearful eyes and raised eyebrows.

Thomas looked away. Tetra was right. Charles was great at doing bad things and apologizing for them, but he never seemed to do the right thing from the start.

"Thomas, don't listen to her. That's an order," Mariana said with more firmness in her tone. "Look at the sky."

The dark clouds that had been lingering on the horizon were now much larger, looming overhead. Cold wind blew over the deck, carrying the smell of impending rain.

"She's doing this so that darkness will follow you. None of that is true," Mariana said.

"It is true," Thomas said quietly. "It's all true."

"Thomas, *no*," Mariana said as Tetra laughed in the background. "How do you not see what she's doing? Your fears are not real!"

"My fears *are* real, Mariana! Why else would I be scared of them?"

"I thought you said you weren't scared," Tetra taunted.

"Be quiet!" Mariana shouted.

Tetra snickered. "Don't get mad at me because you chose a kid to serve you. That's on you."

Thomas cringed at himself for being so emotional. He wished he could go back to the days where he felt nothing if only so he could save Mariana. He had no idea what to do about the powerful, confusing emotions tormenting him.

"I'll leave you alone for now," Tetra said with a dripping smile. "But I will see you very soon, Thomas Hambleton." She melted away in a splash of dark water that evaporated into a wisp of shadow tendrils.

Thomas swallowed hard, feeling the heavy weight of her words. Mariana turned to face him with a frown. "I chose you for a reason, Thomas. I have complete faith in you."

"You only have faith in me because you have no other choice," Thomas said. "Tetra's right. I'm just a dumb kid. I don't know how to use my magic or a sword or my social status or—*anything*. I'm useless."

Mariana watched him with a tight-lipped frown. "She's the god of fear, and she's using her power to weaken you. Get a grip!"

"I'm trying!" Thomas yelled. Thunder rumbled in the distance.

Mariana raised her eyebrows. "I don't think you are."

"Thomas," Charles said, resting a hand on his shoulder. "I—"

"Don't touch me, Charles." Thomas shoved Charles's hand away. Whatever peace they had found was gone. He didn't know how he had accepted Charles's apology so easily. He had apologized for the years of bullying, but he hadn't even mentioned the event that broke their relationship.

Charles took a step back. "Whoa. What did Tetra say?"

"Nothing. It's not your problem," Thomas said, walking away from Charles to return to the living quarters.

"Thomas, wait—" Charles said, but Thomas dropped himself below deck before Charles could try to apologize again.

CHAPTER TWENTY

The half-moon cast pale blue light across the swaying blades of grass and shivering tree branches as the guard dragged Felix across camp. A cool breeze chilled the air and carried the sweet fragrance of mountain flowers.

Felix was so tired. He couldn't fight back. Finnlay's shouting in the distance barely registered.

The guard dragged him through the forest toward a small building with a heavy wooden door. The temple. The guard pulled the heavy door open and yanked Felix through the entryway.

The musty smell of old wood and dust hit him first. The dismal little room was somehow colder than the chilled wind outside. Long pews sat in rows on either side of the room, where he and his fellow residents gathered during the day to listen to Catherine preach about how their existence was a mistake.

The guard dropped Felix just inside the doorway and closed

the door. The clang of a metal lock echoed through the dusty room. There was no escaping this.

Felix's limbs felt heavy. He lay there a moment longer, waiting for something to happen.

"Felix."

Felix lifted his head. Catherine stood in her usual position at the front of the room. She offered a sweet smile that would have been comforting on any other face.

A large throne-like chair with leather straps built into the arms towered behind Catherine where the lectern once was. That hadn't been there before. "What is that?" Felix asked, pushing himself up a little to get a better view.

"Have a seat, darling," Catherine said, gesturing to the chair.

Felix shook his head. "I am not sitting in that thing."

Catherine stepped down from the stage and kneeled beside him, placing a gentle hand on his shoulder. "There's no reason to worry, my dear. I'm here to help. You are going to feel much better when we're done. Please sit," she repeated with a flourish of her hand. Her black robes flowed around her arms with the movement.

"No."

Her pleasant smile dissolved as she yanked him upright.

Felix shuffled toward the seat and reluctantly lowered himself into it, unable to stop himself. His hands trembled as he rested his wrists into the arm straps. He was not moving of his own will.

It hit him all at once. The black robes. The obsession with magic. His sudden loss of autonomy.

He didn't know how he hadn't seen it before.

"You're a witch," Felix said.

But how was she using magic? This whole camp was magic-proofed. Was the temple an exception? Surely, someone would have noticed by now. *Finnlay* would have noticed.

"No, I'm a priestess," Catherine said.

"You're using magic."

"Not magic, Felix. Divine power."

Felix didn't argue. She clearly wouldn't tell the truth.

Catherine wrapped her hands around the high back of the chair and leaned down. "I normally wouldn't share this with someone I'm about to save, but this is a special case. There's a small town on the west coast that you might know. New Brook?"

Felix froze. Why would she bring up his hometown? "What about it?"

"A great tragedy happened there a few years back. As much as I would like to rid the world of evil, violence is never the answer. As soon as I heard about it, I sent my people down there to rescue any lingering magi. We must have missed you."

Felix swallowed. "How did you know I lived there?"

"Oh, Felix . . ." Catherine said, patting him on the shoulder with her cold hands. A witch would never touch him without asking. A witch would never perform magic on him without his consent. Catherine was something far more sinister. "Because we found something very interesting. Do you know what it was?"

Felix said nothing.

"The abandoned home of the witch they burned. Her children were gone. Husband dead. Nothing was left of her but spell books and potion recipes. I found one particularly interesting. It needed a little work, but I got it there in the end."

Felix refused to believe it. It was simply too terrible. "That wasn't yours to take," he said through clenched teeth.

"Whose was it, then? Her only living son didn't care enough to take it."

Tears stung his eyes. "*No!* It should have been *you!*" Felix yelled as he strained against the straps, but they only tightened over his wrists as he thrashed. Catherine had stolen his mother's potion recipe. His mother would be rolling in her grave knowing that her life's work had been stolen to hurt magi.

"Yes, well . . . Now you know how *I* feel." The sensation of ice-cold fingers against his temples made the situation horribly real. She was going to take his magic away. "This will only take a second."

"No! Let me go!" Felix yelled, but it was far too late. This was happening.

Catherine didn't answer. The cold at Felix's temples became a flurry of intense, freezing pain. It started with a headache like cold fire and burned its way into his heart. The pain cut into his core and extracted something warm and comfortable from deep within him, something he hadn't known was there, and he hadn't known he had been protecting with his entire being. He wanted to fight back, but he couldn't move. "Please stop," he sobbed. "Please!"

"It's almost over."

Felix's body fought against the thieving forces as hard as a body could fight an invisible battle, but soon the warmth was gone and only a frigid void remained. Catherine said something, but he didn't hear it.

Felix felt naked. His body could no longer fight off the cold. The restraints had been undone, and he hadn't even noticed.

"You should be thanking me," Catherine said. "I've saved you from the magic that tainted your soul. You are finally free from evil."

Felix knew he was here to lose his magic, but hearing her speak the words made it real. The news should have shocked him, but he felt nothing. He thought about Rebecca turning him in. Nothing. His mother's potion recipe. Nothing.

"You took my magic away?" he asked feebly.

"Yes. Congratulations."

"I . . ." Felix muttered, but he had nothing to say. What could he say? Would it make a difference?

"Move along now, darling. Go enjoy your new life."

Felix didn't move for a long time. What was he supposed to do now? What was the point of living without magic?

Two strong hands lifted Felix from his seat and dragged him down the aisle. His feet scraped against the wooden floorboards. The hands dragged him outside and dropped him carelessly onto the scratchy grass. Felix instinctively lifted a hand to rub his eyes and found his face was wet with tears. He sat up and looked around. Dying grass blanketed the camp, each blade cowering away from the cold dark sky.

Felix stood. A deep fatigue settled into his limbs, but he had to get as far away from Catherine as possible.

You should be thanking me. Her voice repeated in his head. She was delusional. This was a waking nightmare. His entire essence had been stolen.

He didn't even feel like a person anymore.

AT SEA

The ship slammed against a large wave as Thomas landed in the living quarters. He stumbled forward, nearly running into Fiona but catching himself on a beam. Fiona fell on her butt.

"Oh, hello," Fiona said, looking up at him with mild surprise. "Are you struggling with your magic again?"

Thomas only frowned.

"I'm not trying to antagonize you. Do you need help?" she asked.

Thomas sighed and slumped against the beam. He had refused her help after the siren attack, but that was before he knew Mariana would die if he didn't learn to control his magic.

As much as he didn't want to, he needed her help. "Yes," he grumbled.

"Don't fret. You'll get the hang of magic in no time now that I'm not stuck in a magic-proofed cell and you're not under the command of a tyrant," Fiona said with a smile.

Thomas smiled back and pushed himself off the beam to offer his hand.

She let him pull her up, and her eyebrows rose as she stood. "Wow. You really *do* have a lot of magic coming out of you."

"You can feel it?" Thomas asked.

Fiona nodded. "That must be difficult."

"What can I do?"

Fiona rubbed her chin and eyed the boards overhead. "You could channel some of that energy into a storage vessel. Or maybe I could create an enchantment that redirects the flow of your magic, but that could be dangerous. I might be able to cast a spell to help, but those are only temporary. A curse would only cause problems. You could *try* to use it up, but I don't know if your magic *can* be used up, considering your immortality and the storms you've been causing. No, that wouldn't work. You could also—" She stopped talking when her eyes landed on Thomas again. "Oh. You look confused."

Thomas hadn't realized he was making a face. He unfurrowed his brow and closed his mouth. "I, uh . . . don't know what any of that is or how to do it."

Fiona nodded with a careful smile. "Let's just start with the basics then."

An idea suddenly struck Thomas. "Could you make me something to suppress my magic?"

Fiona frowned. "I'm not sure that's a good idea. It's better to learn to use your magic than force it down. It could be catastrophic when you finally take it off."

Thomas sighed and slid his hands over his face. "Of course it can't be easy," he muttered beneath his palms.

Fiona gave a lighthearted laugh. "Yeah, sorry. Guess you'll just have to let me teach you magic."

"Yeah, okay."

Fiona led him back up to the top deck so they had access to water. Charles stood alone by the captain's cabin, staring at the sky. When he heard them approach, he side-eyed Thomas like a scared dog, then he smiled at Fiona.

Fiona smiled back. "Hi Charles," she said. When she turned to Thomas again, her smile fell away. "Is something wrong?"

Thomas decided he needed to pay more attention to his expression, especially around Fiona. "No. I'm fine."

Fiona smiled like she didn't believe him. "All right. Let's do some magic!"

"Okay."

"Aren't you excited? You get to do *magic*. For the first time ever!" Fiona said.

Thomas scratched his head. "Not for the first time."

"Right . . ." Fiona said with a grimace, but she smoothed the discomfort out of her expression quickly. "Shall we get started?"

Thomas tried to smile. His face didn't listen and instead twisted into a pained grimace. "Yes," he said unenthusiastically, letting his face return to its usual stoic frown.

"Great. Lift your hand," Fiona said, politely ignoring his failure to mask his emotions.

Thomas did as she said. She whispered something under her breath and raised her own hand, propelling a column of water up from the sea and over the palm of his hand. A white light glowed from beneath the collar of her shirt and quickly dimmed. Thomas examined her arms, noticing that if he paid attention, he could see her tattoos. Otherwise, her skin was bare.

"Why do I keep forgetting you have tattoos? You have so many," Thomas said.

Fiona grinned. "One of my tattoos is a sigil that keeps them hidden, unless I intentionally point them out or someone is looking for them. They're pretty apparent when I'm doing magic, but if someone is watching me do magic, I'm probably not trying to hide them."

"Wow, that's amazing. They glow when you do magic?" Thomas asked.

"Usually," Fiona said.

"Why?"

"Casting spells requires the use of sigils. The most important sigils are tattooed on my skin, so I don't have to draw them every time." Fiona unbuttoned the top half of her shirt, pointing directly at a tattoo on her chest. "This is the sigil for water." The water sigil was a set of two wavy lines that fit together, twirling into themselves. She pulled her collar aside to reveal two more sigils inked into her skin beside the water sigil. "This one is fire, and this one is wind." The fire sigil was composed of three thick lines curling into the shape of a flame. The wind sigil was a series of four three-quarter circles set within each other, each facing a different direction.

"What about earth?" Thomas asked.

Fiona's smile grew wider. "I don't need that one. That's my base magic."

"Base magic? What is that?"

"Base magic is the ability you were born with. So, for you it's water. Mine is earth," Fiona explained.

"You're an elementalist too?" Thomas asked with a smile.

"Yes I am," Fiona said proudly.

"Are elementalists very common?" Thomas asked.

"Yes. It's one of the most common types of magic," Fiona said.

"Wow... so we're not that special," Thomas joked.

"Not really," Fiona said with a short shrug and a wry smile.

Thomas laughed. Somehow, Fiona had already cheered him up.

Fiona rebuttoned her shirt. "Okay, I want you to hold this water on your skin," she said. "Just intend to hold it close to you, and it will not fall. You don't have to keep it floating, but you can try if you'd like. Are you ready?"

Thomas suddenly felt nauseous, but he nodded anyway.

With a twitch of her fingers, the cold water poured over his hand, and then it stopped.

Thomas kept his palm face-up as he focused on the dripping water. He directed his intention to keeping it attached to himself. It took so long for anything to happen that the water started to dry from his fingertips. Just before he gave up, the droplets clinging to his knuckles started to tremble. Was he doing this? What was happening?

The water began to burn before he could ask. He sucked air through his teeth and shook out his hand. Steam rose from his reddened knuckles to the dark sky above in a few short puffs before disappearing.

"What was that?" Thomas asked.

Fiona watched his hand with raised eyebrows. "You created steam. You're putting too much energy into it. Let's try again," she said, lifting another bubble of water from the sea.

"Can't you just teach me how to control my magic?" Thomas asked, rubbing his hand as the sting rapidly eased. "I am not interested in learning to manipulate water."

"It's easier to learn to control your magic if you know how to use your base magic. Trust me, you'll understand it better this way," Fiona said.

Thomas felt his frustration rise, but he tried to hide his irritation for Fiona's sake. His aversion to magic was not her fault.

"I don't really care about mastering my base magic. I just need to know how to stop making it rain."

"Yes, and you'll know how to stop doing that as soon as you know how to control water. Rain is made of water," Fiona said in a joking tone, but he wasn't in the mood to joke anymore.

"I know that," Thomas said.

Fiona raised her eyebrows and watched him steadily.

Thomas closed his eyes and sighed. "I'm sorry, Fiona. I'm really struggling with this. It's not you."

She nodded slowly. "I'm sure this is difficult for you. If you really don't want to learn about water, I can teach you about magical energy." She lowered her hand, letting the ball of water fall back into the sea.

"Thank you."

"Like I explained before, if you use too much of your energy, intention doesn't matter anymore. You put too much energy into controlling the water and it got too hot."

"Okay . . . so what do I do?"

"The same as you do with any other part of your body. You have unlimited energy, but you still aren't overexerting your physical self. How are you doing that?"

Thomas took a deep breath before answering her, but steam still rose from the damp boards around them. The loss of control snowballed as his lack of understanding only made him angrier at himself. "I don't know."

Fiona frowned at the rising steam. "I know it's hard, but if you let me teach you how to manipulate water, you will understand what I'm saying. You will have something to apply the theory to. Can we at least try?"

Thomas stepped back. "I don't want to hurt you."

"You won't hurt me," Fiona said gently. "It's just water."

Thomas said nothing, feeling like he would be sick.

Fiona muttered, "*Watrol,*" and waved her hand in a circular motion to lift the steaming water from the deck. The orb of water hung in the air beside her, swirling around itself. "Look at this ball of water. I am in control of its movements, but it still moves on its own. Water prefers you suggest movement rather than completely control it. Would you like to try?"

"Please no," Thomas said.

Fiona frowned at him. "Come on, it won't bite."

"Maybe not, but it might boil."

"That's okay," Fiona said with a smile. The water moved through the air, closer to Thomas. "It won't hurt you if it's not touching your skin. Try it."

Thomas's hands shook as he raised them in preparation to take the water from Fiona. He tried to focus on his intention, but he had no idea how to intend a suggestion.

He felt Fiona relinquish her control of the water as his own shaky control took its place. The smooth motion of the water immediately collapsed into a splashy mess. "Am I doing it?" he asked, holding his arms as far away from his body as possible.

"You are! Isn't it great?" Fiona asked. "Don't forget to breathe."

Thomas took a breath, and then another. The wobbly orb began to bubble. "Oh no. Oh gods, what do I do?" Thomas asked, taking a step back.

"Let go."

"How?!"

The orb exploded. Boiling water seared his skin where it hit him, but the pain only lasted seconds. Fiona held her arms over her face, keeping herself covered.

Thomas dropped his hands. "Oh Dei. Fiona, are you okay?" he asked.

Fiona lowered her arms and smiled. "I'm fine. Are you okay?"

"Are you sure?" He stepped toward her but stopped, afraid he might accidentally boil her blood if he got too close. He folded his hands under his arms and took several steps back. "I'm so sorry."

Fiona stepped closer. "It's okay! I know how to protect myself. I told you, you don't need to be afraid of hurting me."

Thomas shook his head, still stepping backward. "I can't—I can't do this. I'm sorry Fiona. I can't—" His words would not come anymore.

"Thomas—"

Thomas turned around and walked away before he did something she couldn't fix.

CHAPTER TWENTY-ONE

TINERA

Days passed in a blur. Felix could hardly tell day from night anymore, but it didn't matter. He couldn't sleep anyway.

The restrictions hadn't been lifted, even though the "witch" had been caught. Felix had already been alone because of the restrictions, but now he felt lonelier than ever. Aella was completely gone, which was fine. He never wanted to see her again. But Finnlay was gone in his own way. Felix had put his trust in both of them and came out the other side of their escape attempt without magic, and he was the only one to do so.

Finnlay had refused to throw Felix over the fence. Felix could have gotten away and returned with help if Finnlay had listened to him, but now they were both stuck. And Aella wouldn't be coming back for them.

Felix made no attempt to communicate with Finnlay. Their chance at escaping died the night Felix lost his magic. The potion was gone, and they were out of ingredients. There was no reason to talk to Finnlay anymore, and trying would only get them both in trouble.

One afternoon, Felix arrived for lunch and found a folded piece of paper left at the table. He sat down with his bowl of stew and eyed the paper for a long time, until he decided to ignore it. If he didn't know what it said, it couldn't bother him.

He shoveled the lukewarm vegetable water into his mouth, trying not to think about the paper. Halfway through the meal, his curiosity got the best of him. He reached for the paper and unfolded it to reveal a handwritten note in a lovely script, seemingly written in charcoal.

> Hello Felix,
>
> First of all, I am so terribly sorry about your magic. I never meant for that to happen. I wish it had been me.
>
> It's impossible to get my hall leader to give me any information about you, and I'm worried sick. I struggle to get through my meals, but if I wait here for you I'll get thrown in the hole and possibly lose my own magic now that they know I am associated with the escapee.

Felix put the letter down, feeling the pinch of irritation. Finnlay and Aella were only ever worried about their own magic. Never the good of the group. They clearly felt the same about escaping. Finnlay hadn't let him escape because he couldn't come too, and Aella only offered to bring him because she wanted the antidote. The longer he thought about it, the angrier he became. He tried to resist reading the rest of the letter, but he couldn't. As mad as he was, Finnlay was his only companion in the entire world, and this letter was the only valuable human contact he had.

If you see this letter, will you please let me know you're okay? I've left a piece of charcoal at this table that I created by burning a fallen branch, and I stole this page from the back of a library book. You can write your response to me on the back, which I've left blank. You don't have to write much. I just want to know that you're okay.

I hope to hear from you soon,
Finnlay

Felix tossed the letter aside. If a response meant he was okay, he would not respond.

Another day passed. And then another. And another. And then a second letter appeared.

Again, Felix tried to resist the temptation to read it, but again he failed.

Felix,

I know you read my last letter because it was not in the same place I had left it. I can only assume this means you are not okay.

I want you to know that I have not given up. I have been trying to nurture the wildflowers around camp so that we can try again. If you're willing to help, I think I can do it this time. I promise I won't let you drink the potion until I'm certain it works. I feel horrible that I let you try the last one untested.

Please let me know if you are still willing to let me use your blood.

Please answer me, even if you're not okay.

Finnlay

Felix threw this letter aside too. Finnlay only wanted Felix for his blood, just like Aella only wanted him for the antidote. Neither cared about him. They both wanted to use him and get out.

Felix grabbed the letter and flipped it over, clutching the piece of charcoal in his hand so tightly that it snapped in half. He held the charcoal stub over the paper to write "No," but then he thought of something more definitive. Something that would keep Finnlay from writing any more letters. He scrawled four large words on the back of the paper and got up without finishing his food.

At dinner that same day, the pieces of charcoal were gone, but the letter with his response was still there. The words he wrote were smudged but still legible.

Felix's anger began to cool when he received no response.

His answer to Finnlay had been coldhearted. He had acted out of anger and a desire to be left alone, instead of his true feelings. Finnlay was probably just as lonely as Felix. Nobody wanted to be associated with them. They were trouble, and trouble brought "salvation." Finnlay probably didn't have any other friends in his hall either, even though he was the nicest person Felix had ever met.

Deep down, Felix knew he would have died if Finnlay had let him go. He didn't have an antidote, and he didn't know how to make one. Finnlay wanted to come with him so he could make the antidote. Felix was kidding himself to think he could have found help before the potion killed him. Finnlay hadn't even wanted to attempt to escape without Aella, despite all the horrible things she had said. Finnlay wasn't selfish. Of course he didn't hold Felix back for selfish reasons.

Felix could trust Finnlay. Clearly, he could trust Finnlay more than he could even trust himself. Finnlay watched out for Felix when the situation was desperate, urgent, and life-threatening, which showed impressive judgment in the face of dire circumstances.

Finnlay was his best friend, and he did not deserve this treatment.

Felix took the note and used his fist to rub away the words:

MY BLOOD WON'T WORK

The page was a dark gray blur of charcoal, but the ghost of his vitriol remained in faint, shameful lines. Finnlay had taken the charcoal, leaving nothing to write with. Felix couldn't apologize, and he couldn't take it back. Even if he could, he feared he had broken something that couldn't be fixed.

Felix flipped the page over, where Finnlay had written his second letter to Felix. Felix's only chance at communication was using this letter. He examined it until he found his own message within Finnlay's words, and then he smudged the letters until it read:

my last letter   was

not okay.

I want   to

try again.   you can do it this time.

I'm certain

I feel horrible

Please

use   blood.

Please

Finnlay

His appropriation of Finnlay's letter started stronger than its desperate ending, but he hoped Finnlay got the gist of it.

Felix spent that night regretting his four-word message to Finnlay. He wanted nothing more than to go back in time and write something nicer. He wanted to reassure Finnlay that he was fine and Finnlay didn't do anything wrong, that Felix had let his distrust of Aella get in the way. Finnlay was the only person who had proven to be trustworthy. He hated thinking about how Finnlay might be feeling at that very moment, unable to read the amended note until the morning.

At breakfast, the note was gone. At lunch, nothing.

Felix began to feel the way Finnlay had described in his first note; so sick with worry that he could not eat. It was his own fault for pushing away his only friend in the entire world. His only *family*, even.

Finnlay deserved a real apology.

Felix decided to wait through lunch and sat at the table until dinnertime. He waited through Hemlock's dinner until Larkspur arrived.

Finnlay was one of the last to enter, shuffling into line behind his peers with his head down. He didn't look up, keeping his arms folded around himself until he reached the food table, where he received his dinner and headed for the center table.

He only looked up when he was a few feet away from the table. He had dark circles beneath his eyes. His hair was a mess. His eyelids drooped with exhaustion, but they snapped open when he spotted Felix.

They stared at each other for an awkward moment. Finnlay's eyebrows pinched together, and he opened his mouth to speak.

Instead, he turned around and walked to a different table.

AT SEA

Charles emerged from the lower deck with two broomsticks in hand. The early morning sun bathed the deck in a warm glow.

"What are those for?" Thomas asked. Despite his anger, Thomas had no choice but to spend time with Charles for sword lessons. Thomas had to learn.

"We're going to spar," Charles said.

Thomas glanced up at the mast.

"Not that kind of spar," Charles said with a smile. "We're going to duel without landing real blows."

"Me and you?" Thomas asked.

"Yep. Me and you." Charles winked.

Thomas felt frustration building in his chest. "Why?" He didn't acknowledge the flirting.

"Because you need to practice." Charles tossed a broomstick to Thomas, which he clumsily caught.

Thomas stared at the wooden pole in his hands. "This is not a sword."

"Oh my gods, you're right. Silly me," Charles said, slapping his palm against his forehead.

Thomas glared at him.

Charles dropped his hand, still smiling. "It's the best substitute we have that won't seriously injure us if one of us messes up."

"Do you mean me?" Thomas asked.

Charles closed his eyes and shrugged. "One of us."

When Charles opened his eyes again, he pretended not to notice the angry look on Thomas's face.

"So, how do we, um . . . *Spar?*" Thomas asked.

"Get into a proper stance, for one thing," Charles said, nodding at Thomas's feet. Thomas suddenly noticed Charles was in a perfect swordsman's stance, his broomstick-sword held at his side.

Thomas adjusted his feet and moved the pole in his hand to a firmer grip.

"Now try to block my blows," Charles said, preparing to strike.

Thomas lifted his fake sword defensively, but Charles kept his own at his side. Charles relaxed and raised his free hand. "Whoa, calm down. I barely moved and you're already taking a defensive position. What if I didn't choose to strike overhead? You've left the rest of yourself completely open."

Thomas exhaled forcefully. "Why don't you just hit me, then?"

"Because I'm not doing this as an excuse to hurt you. I'm trying to help you," Charles said.

"That's a surprise."

Charles sighed and dropped his stance. "Thomas, if we're going to practice, you are going to have to temporarily set aside whatever's pissing you off about me today."

"Don't be a dick," Thomas said.

"I'm not. You're mad, and I have no idea why."

"Don't you?" Thomas asked.

"No! I don't!" Charles shrugged. "I thought we were in a good place after I apologized to you, but Tetra somehow made you hate me again."

"You should already know why I'm mad. I think it's pretty obvious."

"Are you joking? I can't read your mind," Charles said.

Thomas shook his head. "Forget it. We don't have to talk. Just fight me," he said, raising his sword again defensively.

"I *want* you to talk to me, though."

"I don't want to talk to you," Thomas said.

"Then stop acting like a baby." Charles lifted his sword. "Are you ready?"

Thomas gritted his teeth, fighting back another rude comment. "Yes."

Charles raised his sword as if going in for an overhead attack. Thomas took the same defensive stance as before, but Charles reoriented his fake weapon and swiftly jabbed Thomas in the side.

Thomas dropped his broomstick. "Damnit! Why did you do that?"

"You left yourself open," Charles said with a casual shrug, as if they hadn't just engaged in combat.

"You did that on purpose!"

"Yeah," Charles said. "We're sparring."

"Can't you go easy on me? I've never done this."

"Why should I? You're not making anything easy for me," Charles said.

"I think I've made it *very* easy for you. I shouldn't even be talking to you, but *somehow* we ended up on the same ship back to Brenton."

"Is that why you're mad?" Charles asked. "If I didn't get on this ship, I never would have gotten home. No other ships at the dock would let me on."

"So what? Why do you want to go home anyway?! You hate it there, and your father doesn't want you back either," Thomas snapped without thinking.

The anger on Charles's face receded into a hurt frown. Thomas's heart lurched.

"I-I'm sorry, Charles. I didn't mean that," Thomas said.

Charles fixed his expression back into the forced calm of a teacher with his most obnoxious student. "Get back in position. We'll go again."

"Charles—"

Charles impatiently tapped the ground near Thomas's feet with his broomstick. "We need to stop wasting time if you want to win."

Thomas raised his sword, hiding the discomfort of his blunder behind his defensive stance.

Charles went for the overhead strike again. Thomas blocked but made sure to watch for a change in direction. Sure enough, Charles went for the same maneuver. Thomas blocked that move as well, then blocked a third strike to his middle.

Charles stepped back and nodded. "Good. See? You learned."

"Yeah . . ."

"Let's go again until one of us successfully strikes the other," Charles said.

Thomas nodded, and Charles attacked again. It was only a few seconds before Charles jabbed the broom handle against Thomas's ribs, much harder than the first time.

Thomas let out a string of swears as he stupidly realized Charles had not yet taught him offense. "You *are* doing this on purpose!"

"Don't be ridiculous." Charles lazily leaned against the broomstick.

"I'm not! You haven't taught me any attacks, but you just told me to fight until one of us got a hit in. You did that just to hurt me," Thomas said.

Charles narrowed his eyes. "I suppose we're even, then."

Thomas threw his broomstick down with a loud clatter. "You're an asshole!"

"You're no better than I am, Thomas. You're always complaining about how mean I am, but you're mean too."

"Why shouldn't I be?" Thomas yelled. "I have no reason to be nice. All you do is hurt me. *Intentionally.*"

Charles rolled his eyes. "I did not hurt you intentionally."

"Yes you did!" Thomas said. He was vaguely aware of the clouds rolling in from the horizon. "Maybe not today, but you did, and we still haven't talked about it. Why, Charles? Why did you do it?"

Charles's angry eyebrows eased back into a guilty pinch at the center of his brow.

Thomas was surprised the question finally found its way out. "You were everything to me," he continued quietly, his eyes and throat burning. "I never knew I could love anyone as much as I loved you. I wanted to spend the rest of my life with you. And I trusted you, even though you *told* me not to. I was so stupid to think it would ever work."

"No, Thomas . . . You weren't stupid," Charles said, taking a step closer.

"I was! I don't understand why I'm still here with you after everything, and we're just acting like it never happened. *Why?*"

Charles sighed and pinched the bridge of his nose. He had never looked more like Alfred than he did at that moment. He dropped his hand and frowned at Thomas. "Let's talk about it, then."

Thomas nodded, fighting back the hurricane of magic and emotions brewing within him.

Charles took a deep breath and exhaled slowly. "You deserve an explanation, but please be patient. This is not easy for me to talk about."

"Do you think it's easy for *me*?" Thomas asked.

Charles shook his head. "Obviously neither of us wants to talk about it, which is why we've waited so long. But I'm talking about something else. The reason behind it all."

Thomas waited for the explanation, but it didn't come. "Well?"

Charles wouldn't look at Thomas as he began. "I thought maybe you would understand at first, but then I got to know you better, and . . ." He shook his head and sighed. "The things you told me about your father made me realize we didn't have the same upbringing. We are simply from the same social class, and our money is from the same industry. I don't know how to talk about this, and I don't want you to think I'm just making excuses."

Thomas watched him carefully, trying to piece everything together. Nothing Charles said made any sense. "I don't understand . . ."

"I lost my mind when I learned you were dead. It put everything into perspective, and I realized way too late that what really mattered all along was you and only you. My father, of all people, broke the news to me. I didn't take it well. I was sobbing and telling him that it was all his fault for putting the ship on a dangerous route, and I finally admitted to him what nobody would acknowledge. I told him that you weren't my friend, but that I loved you." Charles finally looked at him again, a smile haunting his features.

"You said that to your father?" Thomas asked.

Charles nodded, the ghost of his smile disappearing. "Do you know what he did?"

"What did he do?" Thomas asked.

"He hit me. Hard enough that I fell to the floor. Thank Dei my mother was there, otherwise . . . I don't know. I don't like to think my father hates me enough to end my life, but . . ." Charles pursed his lips and shook his head. "If he didn't, I'd be on a different ship right now."

Thomas didn't know what to say. Charles's explanation made him sick to his stomach. He knew Alfred was a bad person, but he had no idea it was this bad. How could he hurt his own child for being sad?

"He has always been that way. If I was ever anything less than perfect, he got violent. I'm terrified of him, and seeing him walk through your door when we were together was the scariest moment of my life. I was afraid he would hurt us, yes, but I also knew I would not be brave enough around him to keep holding onto you. And I wasn't. I'm so sorry."

Light rain began to fall, speckling Thomas's skin and clothes with cold droplets of water. "Charles . . ." Thomas said, shaking his head. "I had no idea."

"I didn't want to tell you. I've never really talked about it, and I didn't know how to bring it up . . . I'm not trying to excuse my behavior. I just want to explain it."

Thomas stepped forward, and Charles let him approach until they were close enough to touch. "I'm so sorry." His words came out on a whisper. "Can I . . . hug you?" he awkwardly asked.

Charles's eyebrows furrowed. He nodded.

Thomas slid his arms around Charles and pulled him close. Charles wrapped his arms around him in return and squeezed tight. The warm space between them was enough to keep away the discomfort of the rain falling over them.

"You didn't deserve that," Thomas said.

Charles squeezed him tighter. "Thank you," he said softly.

They held each other for a long time. "Charles," Thomas finally said softly. "I forgive you."

"What?!" Charles pushed Thomas away to look him in the

eyes. "Thomas, no. I ruined your life. I got you killed. *Several times.*"

Thomas pulled him into the hug again. "I know, but I'd rather be angry at you than grieving you."

"I-I—" Charles stammered. He rested his head against the crook of Thomas's neck and exhaled, his hot breath warming Thomas's skin. "I don't deserve your forgiveness," he finished in a weak voice.

"You don't deserve to be hurt for being in love."

Charles let out a gasp, and Thomas realized he was crying. He ran his hand up Charles's back to hold his head.

"I miss you, Thomas," Charles cried. "You're right here, but I miss you like crazy."

"I miss you too." Thomas wasn't reluctant to admit it. The anger in his heart he had directed at Charles was gone, replaced with an even stronger anger at Alfred.

"You do?" Charles asked, leaning back to look at Thomas. Charles's eyes were red and watery, and he pulled one hand away from Thomas to wipe his tears away. Thomas was surprised by how much he immediately missed their closeness.

"Of course I do," Thomas said. He took a moment to admire Charles up close, and then he closed his eyes and rested his forehead against Charles's.

Only the wind and rain dared to speak in the passing moments. Charles's hands rested firmly around Thomas's waist. "Thomas," he whispered after a long period of silence.

"Charles."

Another long pause. "I . . . I want to be with you," he said decisively. "You probably don't feel the same, but I need you to know. That's what I want. I have the perspective now to see what's important, and it's you. If you give me another chance, I'll never let you go. I'll fight to the death for you."

His words were powerful, and they left Thomas speechless.

His chest filled with something warm and pleasant. It took him only a moment to recognize the feeling as love.

"Yes," Thomas said.

"Yes?"

Thomas pressed his face into the warm skin of Charles's neck. "Yes," he said again. Charles's heartbeat was so loud Thomas could hear it over the wind and waves. Or maybe it was his own heart. "I want to be with you too."

Charles exhaled shakily and pulled Thomas in tighter. "I love you."

"I love you too, Charles."

Charles kissed Thomas's cheek. "I would marry you if I could."

Thomas peeled himself off Charles to look at him. Charles smiled. "Would you really?" Thomas asked.

"Absolutely. I think about it all the time. Can you imagine what you and I could do together? We would be the most powerful couple in the world."

Thomas raised his eyebrows.

"And also I love you very much," Charles added.

Thomas hid his face against Charles's shoulder again to muffle a laugh. "That would be lovely."

Charles was quiet for a moment. "If I were to propose to you, hypothetically, what would you say?"

Thomas lifted his head again to look Charles in the eyes. He slid one hand up Charles's chest to smooth the fabric of his shirt and adjust his collar. "Let's try to make it through one day first."

A smile cracked across Charles's face before he leaned down and kissed Thomas.

It was a different kind of kiss than they had shared in the past. Charles was much gentler. He used to kiss urgently, like they were out of time, but he gave his time to this one. He didn't taste like cigarettes anymore. The absence of cigarette smoke gave Thomas the sense that Charles was safe now. He wasn't toxic.

It wasn't until they parted that Thomas noticed the rain had stopped. The occasional raindrop fell, sparkling through the sunlight, but the clouds had receded, and the light had returned.

"It's not raining." Thomas looked around to make sure he wasn't missing a bigger storm. When he was satisfied, he met Charles's eyes, and Charles smiled at him.

"Are you happy?" Charles asked.

Thomas smiled and turned away, embarrassed at his lack of control over his face. "I guess I am."

Charles placed his hand against Thomas's cheek to turn his face toward him and kissed him again. "Good."

Chapter Twenty-Two

Tinera

Finnlay sat a couple tables down, facing away from Felix at a table with no other occupants.

Felix stood and rounded the table to get closer to Finnlay, careful not to step outside of the cloaking grid. Finnlay would be able to hear him, but nobody else could.

"I didn't mean it, Finnlay. I'm so sorry. I was mad that you didn't throw me over the fence when I asked you to, but I understand now that you did that to protect me."

Finnlay continued eating.

"I shouldn't have been angry at you," Felix went on. "I'm angry at the situation, and I'm *furious* at Aella, but my anger was misdirected at you. You don't deserve it. I should be thanking you for saving my life."

Finnlay stopped eating. After a beat, he stood and joined Felix at the hidden table. When he sat down, Felix saw that his eyes were watery and his nose was pink.

"Are you crying?" Felix asked gently.

Finnlay turned his face away to wipe his eyes with the heel of his hand. "Felix . . . I care about you. I want to get you out of here as badly as I want to get out myself. You probably don't believe me, but it's true."

"I believe you," Felix said.

Finnlay sniffled. "Your note hurt me."

"I know it did. I'm sorry."

Finnlay shook his head. "I don't think you understand how much it hurt. I know I can't control the way you feel about me, but whether you love me or not, *I* love *you*. Not—not like Aella thinks. More like a brother. My history with familial love is complicated and painful, so for you to tell me once that you love me and then to later take it back . . ." Finnlay sighed and turned his head away again. "Maybe I'm stupid to be so hurt over it. I haven't known you very long, but I think we . . . *had* a strong connection."

The last comment made Felix's heart ache. "It's not stupid. I hurt myself with that dumb note too. I do love you, Finnlay. We both have siblings we're missing, and I think we've filled that role for each other in their absence, at least a little bit. I miss my brother like crazy, and I would do anything to get him back. I'm so mad at myself for giving up the brother I *do* have here in this awful place."

Finnlay looked up, finally making eye contact. "I didn't know you had a brother."

Felix nodded. "I did, but he's gone now."

Finnlay watched with horror. "I'm so sorry . . . I can't imagine the pain of losing a sibling. I don't know what I would do without Fiona."

Felix's throat was thick with grief at the memory of his brother. "Yeah. It was awful."

"What happened?" Finnlay asked.

Felix hesitated, trying to find the words to explain. "Did Aella ever tell you about my mother?"

"Not directly, but I gathered from your conversations that she . . . well, I know she was a witch. Was she . . . *burned at the stake?*" Finnlay asked the last part quietly.

Felix ran a hand over his face and sighed heavily. "New Brook is a small town that doesn't get many visitors. The people there aren't very open-minded, so when they found out about my mother, there was no stopping them. I tried to save her, but I almost got killed too. In all the chaos, I don't know what happened to my brother. I searched for him for days and I asked everyone I met if they had seen him, but nobody had. Eventually I made my way to the city of Occimaro on the west coast and found a news printing about the situation in New Brook. It said my mother and my brother were both dead, but that I was missing." Felix stopped talking as the memory hit him hard. He squeezed his eyes shut and sighed. "I left and didn't look back. There was nothing for me in New Brook, so I became a sailor. I miss them every single day."

"I'm so sorry . . ." Finnlay covered his mouth, leaving only his wide eyes showing.

Felix nodded. "I don't know what I was thinking, pushing you away. You're the closest I've had to a brother since I lost mine. I hope you can forgive me, but I understand if you can't."

"I forgive you," Finnlay said.

Felix swallowed the lump in his throat, fighting to stay composed. "Why?"

"You were betrayed by someone you loved, and then again by someone who claimed to care about you. It must be hard to trust anyone after all you've been through."

Felix shut his eyes and rubbed his face. He hadn't even considered his mistreatment of Finnlay was the result of

Rebecca's and Aella's behavior. "But I hurt you the way they hurt me. That's not okay."

"I've been hurt by people who claimed to love me before. The difference now is that you apologized, and they didn't. And do you want to know what makes it worse?" Finnlay asked.

"What?"

"They were my parents."

Felix dropped his hands and frowned. What could Finnlay's own parents possibly hold against him? "Why?" he asked without thinking.

Finnlay forced a smile and rubbed his thumbs together, but his smile quickly fell away and his eyes wandered elsewhere. "I don't normally share this with people, because I don't want *anyone* to know, but you've trusted me with your pain, so I think you deserve the same." He swallowed before continuing. Felix could tell this was hard for him to talk about. "Do you know very much about curses?"

"About as much as I know about potions," Felix said.

Finnlay nodded thoughtfully. "Curses are a very powerful and permanent type of magic. They are almost like spells, but the effects never wear off unless very specific and challenging circumstances are met. It takes a lot of magic to curse someone, and almost nothing but meeting the conditions can undo it once it's been done. Not even magic suppressants will stop the effects."

"Okay . . ." Felix said, unsure where this was going. Maybe Finnlay had simply changed the subject and wanted to talk about magic instead of his childhood trauma.

"I cursed myself when I was fourteen," Finnlay said. "Intentionally."

"What? Why?" Felix asked, sitting up a little straighter. "What kind of curse?"

"Curses aren't inherently bad. They can often be good, in fact," Finnlay said with a trace of defensiveness. "They are seen as bad because they are permanent and can be cast without consent, which causes problems. My curse cured me of an affliction I've suffered with my entire life, but my parents didn't agree. They demanded I undo the curse, but I made the circumstances to undo it nearly impossible. I never want it to break."

"What is it?" Felix asked.

Finnlay took a deep breath. "What you heard from Catherine is true. Fiona is my identical twin. I don't usually introduce her as such, because, um . . . to put it simply, we used to look the same in every single way. My curse fixed that."

Felix scratched his head, trying to unravel Finnlay's words. A perpetual hazy fog stalled the thoughts in his tired, unmagic brain. He didn't feel Finnlay had put it simply at all.

Finnlay didn't want to look like Fiona? Was she too pretty?

No, they were different genders.

Finally, it clicked.

"Your parents didn't like that you didn't want to be a girl?" Felix asked.

Finnlay grimaced and looked away. "I'm not a girl. I never was, and I never will be. Not even if my curse is somehow undone. *This*"—he stopped to gesture at himself—"is who I am."

Felix nodded and looked Finnlay over for a moment. He was an extremely impressive witch to be able to change his entire body permanently at fourteen, especially without his parents' help.

"Wow. Good for you," Felix said.

Finnlay raised his eyebrows. "What?"

"That's amazing. How did you pull that off at such a young age?" Felix asked. "I can't even imagine the power it would take to change your anatomy."

Finnlay let out a shaky laugh. "You do it all the time."

Felix waved away the comment. "That's different."

Finnlay grinned. "Fiona helped me. She didn't understand at first, but after explaining how miserable I was, she just wanted me to be happy. We completed it when our parents were away, combining our magic so that there was enough for the curse. She even cut my hair for me and promised I could use her hair for magic anytime I needed."

"Wow. Your sister sounds great," Felix said.

"She is." Finnlay smiled wistfully for a moment before continuing. "My parents kicked me out of the house when they discovered what I had done was permanent, and Fiona came with me. They told her to stay, but she was just as angry at them as I was. Angrier, even. It's just been Fiona and me ever since."

"That's incredible," Felix said.

Finnlay raked his messy hair away from his face and offered a small smile. "Not many people have been so quick to accept me. Thank you."

"I've been in the wrong body many, many times. I know how unpleasant it can be," Felix said.

Finnlay's smile grew. "Yeah, I suppose you would understand better than most."

Felix offered a weak smile in return. He wished he could give more, but even smiling took a lot out of him.

"That's why I found it hard to believe you when you said you loved me like a brother," Finnlay said. "I couldn't bring myself to use your blood because you didn't know who I really was."

"Yes I did. You've always been honest about that. I just didn't know who the world tried to force you to be once upon a time," Felix said.

The anxiety lingering at the edges of Finnlay's expression departed. "Thank you," he said softly. "So, what are we going to do now?"

Felix took a deep breath and exhaled slowly. "I don't know. I can't help you with magic. I'm not a magus anymore."

"You'll always be a magus, Felix. They can't take that from you."

"They can. They did," Felix said. The memory of Catherine using magic to steal his own crashed over him once again, and he realized he hadn't had the chance to tell Finnlay about it yet. "It was Catherine who did it. She used magic." He let his words hang heavy in the air. "She's a *witch*."

Finnlay shook his head slowly. "How is that possible? This whole camp is magic-proofed."

Felix rapped his fingers along the tabletop. "Catherine knew about my mother. The Hambletons raided New Brook after I left to 'save' any remaining magi, which is how they found Aella . . . but Catherine found my mother's recipe in our empty home. She tweaked it until it worked. She's using *my mother's* life work to hurt people, Finnlay. I can't—" Felix squeezed his eyes shut and clenched his jaw.

Finnlay brought a hand to his mouth. "No . . ."

"I feel so gods-damn helpless. I feel like I've failed my mother. She would be sick knowing her potion is hurting fellow magi. I don't know what to do."

Finnlay hesitated before speaking. "We have to stop her."

"Whatever she did to me goes deeper than magic. She broke something inside me that I don't think I can ever get back. I'm so tired, Finnlay."

Finnlay watched him with a pained expression. "I don't believe it's gone forever. What's lost can be found again, no matter how dire it feels."

"How can you possibly know that?"

"I've been there before. I haven't lost my magic, but . . . there is a familiar dimness in your eyes now that I once saw in myself. I didn't think I would ever get that light back, but I did. I'll do whatever I can to get it back for you too."

Felix sighed and lowered his head to the table. "I don't deserve your help."

"Of course you do. Everyone needs help sometimes."

Felix didn't respond.

"We'll figure it out. Please don't give up," Finnlay said.

Felix didn't want to hurt his friend, but his entire existence hurt. Some days were better than others, and at the moment he felt like it might be okay. Other days, the pain and emptiness controlled him more than he could manage. "I promise," Felix said, but even as he spoke the words, he didn't know if they were true.

"Felix . . ." Finnlay said, lowering his head conspiratorially. "You don't think Catherine *makes* that potion every time she takes someone's magic away, do you?"

Felix scratched his head. "That's not possible. She was ready to take my magic as soon as I arrived."

"That means she has the potion premade and she's keeping it somewhere in this camp. If we can find it, we won't have to bother trying to make it again."

Felix's eyes widened. "Oh my gods, you're right."

Finnlay chewed his lip. "Do you think she keeps it in the temple?"

"It would be stupid of her to keep it within reach of the prisoners," Felix said.

"We aren't prisoners. We're *residents*," Finnlay said sarcastically.

"Right. My mistake."

Finnlay snickered. "It's a good starting point, anyway. Do you know when you have temple service next?"

"Mine was today."

"Hmm . . ." Finnlay rubbed his chin. "Mine is either tomorrow or the day after. I'll look around, and I'll leave a note if I find anything. Meanwhile, if you happen to go to the library, can you please try to sneak in some blank sheets of paper for notes? I can't tear out more than a page or two per library session without being too noisy or suspicious."

"I'll see what I can do," Felix said with a nod.

"Thank you. This feels promising. Do you feel it?" Finnlay asked.

Felix didn't. "Kinda," he lied.

"I really think we're onto something."

"I hope you're right. If that recipe belongs to anyone, it belongs to *me*," Felix said.

"Agreed."

The injustice hit him harder. Catherine Hambleton was using his *mother's* work to hurt other magi. His mother never would have stood for this. He *had* to find those potions. If not to save his fellow magi, then for her. Surely she was not at rest with the world as it was.

Felix shook his head. "You're right. We cannot let this continue."

"Yes!"

"We're going to find her potions. *And* the recipe."

AT SEA

Thomas and Charles made it through a whole day together. They didn't fight at all, aside from sparring. And then another day passed. And another, until an entire week had gone by.

Time flew by. Charles continued training Thomas, and they were both so absorbed by the lessons (and each other) that they hardly noticed the rise and fall of the sun. Thomas's skills were quickly improving. As they began sparring with real weapons, he became more confident in his ability. Charles was an excellent teacher.

For the rest of the journey back to Brenton, every conversation Thomas had with Fiona ended with her asking about his magic, because Thomas would politely excuse himself when the subject came up. He enjoyed her company, but her persistence about teaching him magic made him anxious. She insisted his fear would diminish if he practiced, but he didn't believe her. He didn't need to practice anyway. He hadn't pulled in a single storm since making up with Charles.

Another week passed without issue, until finally, Brenton stretched across the horizon ahead. Thomas stood at the bow with Charles, watching their hometown slowly approach as they silently realized they hadn't discussed anything important in the last two weeks.

Charles looked like he would throw up if the city dared come any closer.

"Are you all right?" Thomas asked.

Charles tore his gaze away from Brenton to frown at Thomas. He opened his mouth to speak, seemed to think better of it, and looked away.

"Charles, talk to me," Thomas said, leaning against the bulwark to face him.

Charles looked at him again, but something new haunted his expression that Thomas could only identify as fear. "Where will we go?" he asked quietly.

Thomas had wondered the same thing himself, but the question was too difficult to answer. Every time he had thought of it, he decided to figure it out later. *Later* had finally come.

"Neither of us can go home," Charles added. "My father doesn't want me back, and your parents would *only* take you. We shouldn't even let the others near them."

Thomas nodded as he considered it. "I can't go home. If they find out I'm a magus, they'll throw me in that camp."

"I doubt that. Your parents care about you."

Thomas scoffed. "No, they don't. They hardly talk to me."

Charles shook his head. "They care. Rebecca was there when your father found out you were lost at sea, and she told me what happened."

This was new information. Thomas had assumed his father was apathetic about everything. "How did he react?"

"It was bad. My father's presence probably made it worse, but apparently he cried."

"Shut up. He did not cry. Your sister is a liar," Thomas said, rolling his eyes.

"Why would she lie about that?" Charles asked.

Thomas shrugged. "Why do any of you lie?"

"We lie because we're scared, but Rebecca is not scared of me," Charles said.

"You lie because you're scared?"

Charles nodded. "You don't understand, because your father actually loves you."

"What do you know about my father? He doesn't love me. He was probably crying over the lost ship."

Charles squinted at Thomas. "You were on a Southworth ship . . ."

Thomas's blood was too hot under his skin. He wanted out of this conversation. He wanted out of Brenton, and he wasn't even *in* it yet. "Then he was crying over *this* ship. There's no way he cried over me."

Charles was quiet for a moment. "I didn't mean to upset you," he finally said. "I'm just telling you what I know."

Thomas took a deep breath and slowly exhaled. "I'm sorry. I just don't understand how he could ignore me for seventeen years, refuse to talk to me when I actually need him, and then act like he cares about me when I die. Why would he be crying over someone he doesn't even want to speak to?"

Charles frowned, then slid his hand around Thomas's back, pulling him into a hug. The sudden display of affection snapped something tense inside Thomas, and his eyes warmed with tears. He buried his face against Charles's shirt, hoping he wouldn't notice.

"Thomas!" Fiona called from the stairway leading to the bow. "Oh—Sorry. Am I interrupting?"

Thomas pushed away from Charles. "No," he said, rubbing his eyes. "Is everything all right?"

"Yes. Well, not entirely. I don't know," Fiona stammered. "It's just that, um . . . is Brenton friendly toward magi?"

Charles laughed, then quickly stopped himself. "Sorry," he muttered.

Fiona forced a smile and scratched her head. "Right . . . Is there anywhere safe we can go?"

"We were just discussing that," Thomas said. He patted his pockets before remembering he had spent all his money on supplies. His eyes fell on the approaching city. "I don't know what to do without money. Gods, I'm the definition of a useless rich boy."

Fiona laughed and came closer. "That's just how it is. I can't do much without money either."

"I can't go home for obvious reasons, otherwise I'd share my wealth with you," Thomas said. "*He* can't go home because his father basically kicked him out, otherwise I'd beg him for money."

Charles rubbed his chin and examined Brenton for a ponderous moment. "You know, my mother *loves* magi." He looked at Fiona. "If I found her before my father and *you* came with me, I'm sure I could convince her to let us *all* stay at the Southworth Mansion."

"Charles . . ." Thomas said.

"What? I'm not saying that I'll pretend she's my girlfriend. The assumption wouldn't hurt, though."

Thomas exhaled through his nose and frowned at his feet. "No, it's not that," he said, although the comment had been a hot spark on the flammable kindling of his jealousy. "I'm worried about you going back home to . . ." He glanced at Fiona, knowing Charles wouldn't want to discuss it in front of others. "Someone who went out of his way to prevent you from coming back."

Charles waved a dismissive hand through the air. "He'll behave in front of a guest."

"But what about when your guest isn't around?" Thomas asked.

"I don't think either of us wants to be alone with the other. It'll be fine," Charles said.

Thomas rubbed his neck. The sick feeling he got when he thought about Alfred was back, but Charles seemed certain. "All right . . . Are you comfortable with that, Fiona?" Thomas asked.

"With standing near Charles while he talks to his mother? Yes," Fiona said.

"Okay, good . . ." Thomas said. The thought of Charles conveniently forgetting to mention Fiona wasn't his girlfriend *did* make Thomas jealous, but he knew mentioning it would only upset Charles. Charles and Fiona got along well, which Thomas would have thought was a good thing if they weren't both so beautiful. "Where will I go?"

"You're really not going home?" Charles asked.

"I can't go home. I don't know what to say to my parents about —about . . ." He trailed off and gestured at Fiona.

Fiona placed a hand against her chest. "About me?" she joked.

"About magi," Thomas said. "So, yes."

"Tell them to quit it," Fiona said. Charles laughed at her answer, which only worsened Thomas's jealousy.

"You know it's not that simple," he said.

"Have you tried?" Charles asked.

Thomas rolled his eyes. "You know what, have a nice life with Fiona."

Fiona cackled. "He wishes!"

Thomas frowned at Charles, but Charles only smiled back. "No. I'm already having a nice life with you."

"Ugh," Thomas said, rolling his eyes. "You're so sweet, it's disgusting."

Charles pulled him close and kissed his face. "You love me."

Thomas couldn't keep his smile back any longer. "Yeah, I do," he said with a laugh.

"You can stay with me," Charles said, planting another kiss on his face. "I'll sneak you in, and I won't even accuse you of anything if my parents see you."

"You're stupid." Thomas laughed again. "How are you going to sneak me in?"

"I have my ways," Charles said. "I used to sneak Penelope in all the time."

"Ugh," Thomas said. He knew Penelope from Blackwater, and she was vapid and cruel. He couldn't wrap his head around Charles dating her. "Fine. As long as you never mention Penelope again."

Charles snickered. "Deal."

"Thomas," Fiona said. "I know you don't like to talk about magic, but I have to say I am impressed you've managed to keep the clouds away all this time. Have you finally gotten a handle on it?"

"Oh, um . . . Yes," Thomas lied. Truthfully, the magic problem seemed to fix itself after he forgave Charles. Every time Charles kissed him, the sun shone a little brighter.

"Hmm . . ." she said, scrutinizing him. "All right. Good job. I'm proud of you."

"Thanks."

"You're a terrible liar," Charles said.

"I knew it!" Fiona said. "You haven't been practicing at all!"

"Charles! What the hell!" Thomas said.

"As your boyfriend, I feel it's my responsibility to protect you from yourself, and I do not think you should be avoiding magic."

Fiona nodded and pointed at Charles. "He's right. How have you been keeping control?"

Thomas sighed and sank into Charles. "I don't know. Being with Charles seems to fix it."

"Aww . . ." Charles said, drawing the syllable out far too long.

Thomas glared at him but couldn't pretend to be angry for very long.

"Your relationship is still fairly new," Fiona said. "What are you going to do when the novelty wears off? Or when you inevitably see your parents again? You need to practice."

"Maybe it's not Charles. Maybe I'm just better at keeping my feelings at bay," Thomas said.

"No, your phrasing gives you away. You shouldn't be keeping them 'at bay,' you should be letting them in and processing them," Fiona said. "Charles is just distracting you. Your feelings are going to come back eventually, and they'll be even stronger than before since you insist on suppressing them."

"You don't know that," Thomas said.

Fiona pursed her lips and squinted. "I'm trying to help you."

"I appreciate that you want to help me, but please stop bringing it up. I'm okay," Thomas said.

Fiona opened her mouth to argue but closed it again. She sighed and turned to walk away.

The ship was docked and ready for the crew to disembark within the hour. Despite the bad memories and people this city held, Thomas felt at ease in the comfort of Brenton's familiarity. The weather was as he expected it to be for this time of year; warm and sunny but eased by the cool wind. The quirks of the uneven dock did not surprise him like they had in Chratan and Dufonn.

A short older man in a military uniform was positioned at the end of the dock, stopping anyone who tried to pass. He held something in his hands, pointing it at people. Once the light flashed a vivid green, they were free to go.

Thomas's heart beat fast. "They're scanning for magic," he said to his friends. "What do we do?"

Faya shook her head somberly and pulled Ametta and Fyavine close. "We shouldn't run. They will definitely catch us."

"We can't just let them scan us!" Fiona hissed.

"Maybe we could try to sneak past?" Thomas suggested.

"How?" Charles asked. "Faya's right. We'll look suspicious if we do anything other than walk calmly into Brenton."

Thomas scratched his face, sweat beading on his forehead as he searched for a solution. This was bad. "Can you go first?" he asked Charles.

Charles rubbed his chin and considered it. "Yes. Good idea. Fyavine, stand behind me."

"What? Why?" Fyavine asked, taking a step closer to Faya.

"Because you're also not a magus. If he decides to keep scanning, I'd rather it be you. Wouldn't you?"

Fyavine grimaced as she locked eyes with Faya. Faya returned the look and turned to Thomas. "But they were going to throw Fyavine in the camp too. Will the scanner detect that she's not human?"

Thomas shrugged, feeling completely useless as a Hambleton. "I'll stand behind Charles. If they try to scan me, I'll . . . I don't know. I'll do something."

Fyavine nodded, seeming relieved.

"Let's go," Thomas said, pushing Charles forward.

Charles led the group, staying near the edge of the dock as

they approached its end. Thomas maintained hope the military man wouldn't see them slip by, but his hope was dashed by a too-cheery greeting from across the wide dock.

"Good afternoon, welcome to Brenton." The man approached, fiddling with the dials on his device as he came closer. He looked up, his eyes widening when he saw Charles. His face went pale when he saw Thomas. "Oh. Mr. Southworth. Mr. Hambleton. Welcome home," he said with a small bow of his head. "Forgive me, I can't let anyone into the city without scanning for magic first. You understand." He looked at Thomas as he said the last part.

"Actually, no," Charles said. "You already know who we are. This is unnecessary." Charles tried to push past, but the man stopped him.

"Apologies, sir," he said with a firmer tone. "You could be a shapeshifter." Before Charles could argue, he pointed the device directly at Charles and held down a button with his thumb. The light flashed bright green.

Charles quickly set aside his shock and fixed a handsome smile onto his face. "Wow, what a lovely color," he remarked. "I've never actually seen one of these before. May I take a look?" He gently snatched the magic meter from the man without waiting for an answer.

"Sir, you can't—" the old man started but stopped again when Charles tossed the magic meter into the sea without a second look. The wooden box sank beneath the churning waves, the green light fading into the darkness faster than anyone could process what he had done.

Charles crossed his arms and shrugged at the old man. "Whoops. I dropped it."

The old man stammered angrily for a few seconds, trying to find some way to tell Charles he was not allowed to throw expensive equipment into the ocean, but Charles clearly knew that. The magic meter was gone, and nothing could be done.

"Sorry," Charles said in a tone that counteracted the apology, then took Thomas by the hand and led him off the dock as their friends trailed after them.

The old man muttered to himself about *no-good Southworth magi sympathizers* and huffed off. Thomas watched him go, amazed Charles got them past the man simply by acting entitled.

"This way," Charles said, nodding in the direction of the shorefront street, away from the man. "I don't want him to send others after us."

"What about the ship?" Thomas asked.

"I'm sure someone will come after your father for the unpaid dock fee," Charles said as he pulled Thomas behind him.

The familiar lineup of taverns faced the sea, waiting right where they had always been. The residents of Brenton milled along the cobblestone road in the morning sun, enjoying the spring day.

Thomas was hit with a strange sense of nostalgia for the place despite being there. It was as if he was walking through a town he had known his whole life, but it was no longer the same place. Or maybe *he* was no longer the same.

People stared at them throughout the city, and it took Thomas until they reached the edge of town to understand it was because Charles was holding his hand. Thomas's heart swelled when he realized Charles hadn't let go. Surely he had noticed the looks too, but he continued to hold on.

"I'm sorry, can we stop?" Faya asked from the back of the group.

Charles stopped walking. "Yes. Is everything all right?"

"Where are we going?" Faya asked.

Thomas, Charles, and Fiona all exchanged the same stupid look. They had forgotten to tell Faya and Fyavine the plan.

"We're going to stay with Charles. His mother loves magi," Thomas said.

"What about his father?" Faya asked.

Thomas rubbed his neck and looked at Charles, hoping Charles could explain. "My father is fine with magi," Charles said.

"Will we be safe there?" Faya asked.

"Yes," Charles said.

Thomas continued watching Charles, hoping he would be honest, but Charles held his blank expression firm. Thomas sighed and looked back at Faya and Ametta. Ametta had been through so much. Even if Charles was certain he could keep them all safe at his home, it wasn't fair to lie. Alfred Southworth was unpredictable and abusive, and Thomas couldn't let Faya bring her six-year-old daughter into the Southworth home in good conscience.

"Not entirely," Thomas said. "His father is not very kind."

"I won't let him hurt any of you. You'll be safe with me," Charles said.

Faya's eyebrows shot up. "*Hurt* us?"

Charles sighed and exchanged a tired look with Thomas. "Why did you have to say that?" he muttered.

"Because I want her to be able to make an informed decision about where she brings her daughter. They've been through a lot," Thomas said. He turned to Faya. "But I'm confident Charles would not put us in a dangerous situation, Faya."

Faya chewed her lip and looked at Fyavine. Fyavine shrugged.

"I'm sorry, Thomas. I want to help you however I can, but I cannot put my daughter in danger," Faya said.

"I understand," Thomas said with a nod. "Where will you go?"

Faya sighed and looked down at Ametta. "We'll find

something safe. And permanent." She looked up again. "And when we do, we'll share it with you. You're family too."

Thomas smiled, but the expression couldn't possibly relay the warmth he felt in his heart from her words. "Stay safe. We'll meet again soon," he said.

Faya squeezed his shoulder and smiled back. "I'm proud of you, Thomas. Don't be scared of your magic. It's part of you."

Thomas averted his eyes as he nodded. Faya waited a moment before passing him to hug Fiona.

Fyavine stepped forward. "It's okay to be scared of your magic," she added, "but if you keep ignoring it, you *will* have a reason to fear it." Without letting him answer, she threw herself on him and squeezed tight. "I'll miss you. Thank you for everything."

Thomas hugged her back. "I'll miss you too, Fyavine. Take care of Faya and Ametta."

"Oh, I will," she said, stepping back to smile adoringly at Ametta. She ruffled the child's hair. "They are my world." Ametta beamed at her, and Thomas felt his heart warm once again. The family they had found together was beautiful.

"And you keep practicing your fire, Ametta. I want to see more tricks the next time I see you," Thomas said.

Ametta laughed. "I can show you tricks right now!" she said as fire sparked from her palms.

Fyavine grabbed Ametta's little fists to stop her. "Not here, baby. People will see you."

"Oh," Ametta said with a pout. Her disappointment was enough to motivate Thomas to fight for them.

"Are you coming with us, Fiona?" Fyavine asked.

"No, I've got to stick with the boys. They won't last a day without me," she said, winking at Thomas.

Thomas laughed, but she was probably right.

Fyavine blew them all a kiss and took Faya's hand. Then, they disappeared into the busy street together toward the outskirts of town.

"I hope they find something safe," Thomas said.

"Honestly, I'd take my chances on the streets before the Hambletons' neighborhood too," Fiona said.

"You can go with them, Fiona," Thomas said. "We'll be okay."

Fiona arched an eyebrow. "I'll be okay too. I've been running from you for years."

"*Me?*" Thomas asked, affronted.

"Yes, Thomas *Hambleton*," Fiona said.

"I'm not a Hambleton. I'm a Fontaine," Thomas argued.

Fiona's arched eyebrow became a skeptical furrow of her brows. "Last I heard, the Fontaines actually used their magic and the Hambletons actively feared it, so ..."

Thomas's jaw dropped. Charles covered his mouth, hiding a laugh. "That's not funny!" Thomas said, mostly to Charles, who he felt should always be on his side.

"It's a little funny," Charles said, lowering his hand to reveal his amusement. "Let's keep moving. I took us the long way around the city to avoid anyone with a scanner." He took Thomas's hand again, and all of his frustration vanished. It was nice to know Charles was no longer afraid of their relationship.

"What's the plan when we arrive?" Fiona asked, walking on Charles's other side.

Charles was quiet as he considered. "I should go in alone first, just to make sure my father won't be hostile. Hopefully I see my mother. I think she actually likes me."

Thomas squeezed his hand. "Where should we wait?"

Charles's hazel eyes examined Thomas for a long moment. "You should hang back more than Fiona, but I'm afraid if you stay in the city someone will recognize you, especially considering the man with the scanner already did. I'm sure news will quickly travel to your family that you're home." Charles turned to Fiona, who raised her eyebrows in response. "You can stand outside the front gate." Fiona nodded. "But Thomas . . . I think you should wait in the back garden. I'll come get you when it's safe."

"Won't your gardeners see me?" Thomas asked.

"Yeah, maybe, but I don't think they'll care. Alfred is so rude to our workers that sometimes I think they try to sabotage us. If they see some dirty run-down sailor wandering the backyard, they'll probably just think it's funny."

"Wow. Thanks."

"We're all dirty and run-down right now," Charles said, lifting Thomas's hand to kiss it.

"Why would you kiss a dirty run-down sailor?" Thomas asked, pulling his hand away.

"Because I love him," Charles said, draping an arm around his shoulder. Thomas smiled and leaned into him.

"You have gardeners?" Fiona asked.

"Yes," Charles said plainly.

"Why? Gardening is one of the greatest joys in life, and you *hire* someone else to do it for you? Why bother with a garden at all?" Fiona asked.

Charles laughed. "Because it doesn't mean as much to us as it does to you."

Fiona walked in silence for a beat. "Can I hide in your garden too?"

Charles paused while he thought. "All right. You can hang back in the front garden."

Fiona's face lit up, and Thomas couldn't help smiling at her reaction.

They made the journey to Charles's home in relative silence. Charles cut through the middle of the city to avoid passing directly in front of Hambleton Manor. Its dark shingles rose above all other rooftops, as if the house itself could see Thomas inside Brenton. Thomas eyed it warily until it was out of sight.

Finally, they reached the Southworth Mansion. Thomas had walked by it in the past, but he was never as determined to put this building in his route home as Charles had been with Hambleton Manor. As a result, Thomas had never gotten a close look before.

It was simple and classic. The pale façade presented its dark, curtained windows and a tall arched doorway that opened to a vast garden. The path to the doorway was paved with smooth gray stones that led to a circular fountain spewing crystal clear water from its top. Hedges lined the garden, creating a buffer between the garden and the dark exterior iron gate that crawled with vines, which obscured the view of the house.

Charles fixed his eyes on the house for a long time, then he sighed and turned to Fiona and Thomas. "Once we're inside the garden, stay out of sight. Thomas, you can head to the back if you stay behind the hedges. Fiona, stay close to me, but don't let anyone see you."

Thomas squeezed his hand. "Will you be okay?" he asked quietly.

Charles raised his eyebrows and eyed the house again. "Let's find out."

Chapter Twenty-Three

Brenton

Cool wind rustled the leaves of the quiet green garden in front of the Southworth's house. Standing between a blue-flowered hedge and a bed of pink flowers, Charles stared up at the tall building he once knew as home. The dark windows hid a sad life that he did not want to return to. Everything in him told him to turn and run. He took a step back, bumping into the garden's central fountain that gushed crystal water over intricate stone carvings.

He took a seat on the lip of the fountain, unable to look away from the house as he worked up the nerve to go inside. Alfred never wanted him back. What if he saw Alfred before he saw his mother? What would he say?

Charles rubbed his eyes and sighed. He should have let Fiona come with him, but Thomas's honesty with Faya made him realize it was selfish to put Fiona in danger for his benefit, even if the danger seemed unlikely. He needed to make sure it was safe before introducing her.

"Charles?!" a familiar voice shouted.

Charles looked up with a start to see Rebecca staring out from her bedroom window. Charles gave a small wave, not sure how she would respond to his return. She probably hated him as much as everyone else in the house. In the city. In the world.

Rebecca audibly gasped. "Charles!" she said again, then disappeared from her window.

Charles waited uncomfortably by the fountain until his sister burst from the front door and ran to him, her long dark hair bouncing behind her. She was smiling.

Rebecca threw herself on him. "Dei, Charles. I'm so happy to see you," she said, squeezing all the air out of his lungs. "I was so worried."

"You were?" Charles asked, cautiously hugging her back.

Rebecca released him. "Of course. Your boyfriend died, and our father's response to your grief was to send you away." She pursed her lips and shook her head. "I didn't know if you'd make it back," she added quietly.

Charles smiled. He couldn't believe Rebecca would speak about Thomas so openly. "I didn't think any of you wanted me back."

Rebecca continued shaking her head as her smile fell away. "I'm sorry I wasn't here when you needed me." She took a step back and folded her arms together, averting her eyes. "I didn't understand, and I think that scared me. But I get it." She looked at him again. "Who am I to judge you for wanting the same thing I want?"

Charles laughed. Rebecca raised her eyebrows, then a smile found her face too. "You can't find someone else to want?" he asked.

Rebecca laughed with him. "I wouldn't have pursued him if I had known. I thought you were just being a jerk to him for no reason. I'm sorry."

"I forgive you."

"It wasn't really him, anyway," Rebecca added.

"I said I forgive you."

Rebecca sighed. "I'm not sure I forgive myself." She rubbed her arms and looked toward the garden entrance. "Do you think Felix is . . . ?" She looked at Charles again. "Is he okay?"

Why was she asking about Felix? He thought she hated Felix for lying to her. "I think he's fine," Charles said.

Rebecca squinted up at him for a moment, then shook her head. "Anyway, you should come inside. You look awful," she said, turning toward the house again.

Charles froze. He couldn't follow her. Even if he wanted to, he couldn't make himself move his feet. Rebecca stopped when she realized he wasn't following. She raised her eyebrows. "Are you coming?"

Charles opened his mouth, but no words came out. He shook his head. Finally, he forced out the words, "I can't."

Rebecca approached him again, hesitating before she spoke. "We want you here. Mom and I do, at least. She hasn't spoken to our father since he sent you away. She was livid."

"Really?" Charles asked.

Rebecca nodded. "Come on," she said with a nod toward the house. "She'll be so happy to see you."

Charles took a step but immediately stopped. "Is-is Alfred home?"

"*Alfred?*" Rebecca asked with a furrowed brow. Her expression loosened and she smirked. "Huh. No, Alfred isn't here right now."

Charles nearly broke his neck looking toward the garden gate, fearing Alfred would arrive at any moment.

"He won't be back for a few hours," Rebecca reassured him.

A tremble had settled into Charles's limbs. He hated what the mere thought of Alfred's presence did to him. "Okay. Um . . . I brought a friend with me. Do you think it would be all right if she stayed here for a while? She's a witch."

"Come on, Charles," Rebecca said, rolling her eyes, "you don't even have to ask. You know Mom would die to meet a witch."

Charles laughed. "Yeah, I know. Let me go grab her."

"Can I come?" Rebecca asked. "I'd like to meet her too before Mom smothers her."

"Um . . ." Charles rubbed his neck. He didn't want Rebecca to spot Thomas, but Thomas should have been waiting in the back garden. He couldn't think of any other reason to say no. "Sure."

Charles led Rebecca to where he had left Fiona behind the hedge. He stopped at the break in the hedge wall near the center of the garden and stuck his head through to make sure she was there.

Fiona was there, but so was Thomas.

They were engaged in a hushed conversation that seemed very serious, but they stopped when Fiona spotted Charles. She pointed at Charles, and Thomas turned with a grim expression. His face lit up when he saw Charles.

"What are you still doing here?" Charles hissed desperately.

"I wanted to make sure Fiona made it inside safely," Thomas whispered.

As annoyed as he was, Charles couldn't be angry at him for taking care of his friends. Thomas had always seemed to have a better sense of morality than him. It hadn't even occurred to Charles that leaving Fiona alone in the garden of a strange home could be dangerous.

Before he could warn Thomas, Rebecca stepped around the hedge. "What's—" She stopped. "Oh my gods. Felix?"

Thomas stared at her with wide eyes and an open mouth. "Um—hi, Rebecca."

Charles closed his eyes and exhaled. "Calm down, Rebecca. That's not Felix."

Thomas laughed nervously, apparently remembering Rebecca had dated "him" while he was gone.

"Who else could it be? Thomas is dead," Rebecca reminded Charles carelessly.

"Wow. Thanks for easing the blow. But no, Thomas is alive," he said.

"Heh . . . Sorry to disappoint," Thomas said with an awkward shrug. Gods, he was cute.

Rebecca crossed her arms and frowned at her brother. "This isn't funny, Charles."

"It's not a joke. Thomas survived," Charles said.

Rebecca raised her eyebrows and looked Thomas over a few times. Her dark eyebrows lowered, and she looked away. Her face flushed. "I'm glad you're okay," she said, refusing to look at Thomas.

"Thanks . . ." Thomas said, scratching his head. "Sorry about, uh . . . Felix . . ."

Rebecca refused to look his way. "We don't have to talk about that," she grumbled.

Thomas shared a look with Charles, pleading with his eyes for Charles to make this less awkward. Charles didn't know if he could, but he would at least change the subject. "Rebecca, this is Fiona. She's the witch I told you about."

Rebecca finally turned to look at Fiona. She forced herself to smile and reached her hand out. Fiona took it and shook.

"Hello," Fiona said with a smile. "Lovely to meet you."

"Likewise," Rebecca said, looking her up and down in that catty way she always did to other women. Charles didn't say anything, because she hadn't actually done anything to Fiona, but the discomfort on Fiona's face was apparent.

"Come on, let's go find Mom. I think she's in the back garden," Rebecca said to Charles, turning to lead them back to the house.

Charles shared a look of horror with Thomas as they realized

Thomas had accidentally avoided getting caught by Charles's mother, of all people. "Rebecca, wait," Charles said, grabbing her arm before she could walk off.

Rebecca shrugged out of his grip and glared at him. "What?" She dusted off her arm where Charles had grabbed her like he was filthy enough to warrant it.

"Please don't tell Mom you saw Thomas here. I was trying to sneak him in, and I didn't expect you to see him," Charles said.

Rebecca's eyes wandered shamelessly down Thomas's figure. She let out a sigh. "All right. But only because you didn't rat me out when he was my boyfriend, even though you were jealous."

Fiona's hand flew up to her mouth. Apparently Thomas hadn't explained the situation with Felix. She leaned in and whispered something to Thomas. Thomas stifled a laugh and shook his head.

Rebecca's eyes rapidly flitted back and forth between them. *She* was clearly the jealous one now.

"Let's go," Charles said, pushing her toward the house. He took Thomas's hand and pulled him along.

The familiarity of the home's interior comforted Charles as much as the memories repelled him. The dark wooden floors shined freshly polished under the murky daylight. Charles's dirty boots clomped against the delicate wood, a noisy reminder that he no longer belonged here.

Charles turned to Thomas. "Wait for me in my bedroom. It's on the second floor. Go up the stairs and turn left. My door is the third one on the right." He took Thomas's face in his hands and kissed him. "Use whatever you need to get comfortable. I'll join you soon."

Thomas smiled dreamily up at him. "Okay. Good luck." Charles watched him head up the stairs until he was sure Thomas found it.

"Your house is beautiful," Fiona said.

"Thank you," Rebecca said cordially, her tone stiff.

"Neither of us are responsible for that," Charles added. "But thank you."

Fiona laughed, and Charles smiled in response.

"The garden is this way. You'll love it," Charles said, gesturing down a hallway behind the staircase. A windowed door lit the hall and revealed the bright green foliage of the vibrant garden beyond.

Fiona grinned as she followed Charles down the hall. Rebecca stayed behind.

Sure enough, the sight of his mother tending to a bed of flowers greeted him the moment they stepped into the back garden. Fiona froze, looking around the garden open-mouthed. His mother looked up from her work with a smile, obviously knowing it wouldn't be her husband. Her smile fell when she spotted Charles. She dropped the spade in her hand and pushed herself up, holding her skirt off the ground as she hurried toward him.

"Charles!" she said when she reached him, pulling him into a hug.

He hugged her back. "Hi, Mom."

She squeezed and didn't let go for a long time. When Charles tried to break free, she held him a moment longer before reluctantly letting go. Finally, she said, "You have no idea how happy I am to see you." She held him by the shoulders as she looked him in the eyes with a teary smile.

Charles didn't know what to say. His mouth fell open, and he shook his head.

"I shouldn't have let him send you away," his mother said.

"I would have hated for you to try to stop him."

His mother's eyes landed on Fiona. "Oh, hello! Who is this?"

Charles stepped aside and gestured at Fiona, making

introductions. "This is my friend Fiona. She's a witch. Fiona, this is my mother, Lucille."

Fiona nodded once. "Lovely to meet you, Mrs. Southworth. I am so honored to be here and to meet the family who is fighting to save magi. Your garden is absolutely gorgeous."

His mother brought her hand to her mouth and gasped. "You're a witch!" She lowered her hand to reveal a smile. "How wonderful. We're happy to have you here, my dear. How did the two of you meet?"

"My ship left me in Dufonn, and Fiona helped me find passage home. She traveled here because her brother was caught by the Hambletons and she is trying to find him," Charles said. He didn't want to lie, but he couldn't mention he had met Fiona through Thomas.

"Oh . . ." His mother placed a hand over her heart. "Bless you, Fiona. Thank you for bringing him home. May I?" she asked, holding her arms out.

"Oh, um . . . Sure," Fiona said with a nervous laugh, leaning in to hug Charles's mother.

"Is it all right if Fiona stays here? She has nowhere else to go," Charles said.

His mother beamed at Fiona. "We would love to have you as our guest. I'll have the housekeepers set up a room for you. She can stay in your hall, across the way," she said to Charles. "Will you please show her there? I'll have some fresh clothes sent up for her, and I'll send someone up to help you with your hair, Charles. I've never seen it so overgrown." She tugged at a lock of hair hanging in his face with an amused smile.

Charles thoughtlessly ran his fingers through his hair and gave a short laugh. He did need a haircut, but he couldn't let his mother send the housemaid up while Thomas was there. "That's all right. I'd like to just relax for tonight if that's okay."

His mother furrowed her brow. "Oh, you didn't come back for the party?"

Charles forced himself to keep smiling and resisted the urge to groan. Of all days to come back, it was a party day. "What party? I just got back to Brenton today."

His mother's eyebrows shot up. "Did you really?"

"Yes, why?"

She watched him carefully for a moment. "Do you know what day it is, Charles?"

He shook his head.

"It's May tenth," she said.

Charles's eyebrows slowly rose. "Oh."

His mother looked away. "The party isn't what you probably think."

"What is it, then?" Charles asked.

She patted his shoulder. "You should go get cleaned up."

"No, please. Do I have to attend?" Charles asked.

"You should," she said, and her smile became sad.

Charles twisted the cuff of his sleeve around his wrist as he tried to figure out what was going on, but he didn't respond.

"Um, Mrs. Southworth . . ." Fiona said, leaning in to insert herself into the conversation.

"Call me Lucille," she said warmly.

Fiona smiled. "Lucille. You don't have to bother your people with this. I imagine your staff is busy preparing for the party. If you send up the scissors with the change of clothes, I can trim Charles's hair for him. My own hair needs some work anyway, and I'd rather do it myself."

Gods bless Fiona.

"How kind of you," his mother said. "A hair trim from a real witch. It's your lucky day, Charles."

"Thank you, Fiona," Charles said. Fiona grinned in response.

"Be back downstairs by seven o'clock for the party," his

mother said, then she hugged him again. "It's so good to have you home."

"It's good to be home," he said. It was almost true.

TINERA

As the day went on, Felix couldn't stop thinking about his mother. Her death infuriated him for a lot of reasons, but the greatest injustice was that, as the town apothecary, she had personally given aid to the very hands that killed her.

Felix had never met anyone as passionate about magic as his mother. The increasing hatred toward magi around the world drove her to work long hours on the potion that could have saved them. Felix should have memorized it, or at least gone back for the recipe. He had been in a state of panic at the time of her death, and he hadn't even considered going back.

He never could have predicted it would fall into the hands of a monster.

Catherine had taken everything from him. She had taken his freedom, his magic, his happiness, and now she had taken what was left of his mother and twisted it into a weapon against magic.

No matter what the cost, he had to stop it.

Finnlay and Felix had agreed to search the temple as well as they could during their halls' services, but Felix couldn't wait that long.

As darkness crept across the sky, Felix sat alone in his bed. Still, nobody in Oleander would talk to him. He was trouble. A bad omen.

He was entirely alone, except for Finnlay.

The chattering quieted as night fell across the camp, but Felix stayed wide awake. He stared at the dark ceiling above, listening for snoring to overtake the final pair of whispering voices. Finally, soft sounds of sleep filled the room.

He peeled the thin blanket from his body and stepped gently through the dark room, careful to avoid squeaking floorboards. He eyed Matthew's bed by the door. Matthew was asleep, as unaware of Felix's whereabouts as ever.

Felix turned the handle, opening the door quickly before the door guard could yell at him and awaken his hallmates. Felix had concluded that the Hambletons probably hired former magi to work inside the camp. If the Hambletons used their prisoners as labor on their ships, why wouldn't they do the same with their guards?

He stepped into the cool night air. "Hey," he said softly. The woman was already looking at him, her mouth parted to expel some stern commands, but she stopped to listen. "I lost my magic recently and I've been having trouble sleeping. I know it's against the rules, but I could really go for a nighttime walk to clear my head. I just . . . can't be in there anymore."

Her stern expression softened, and it was enough evidence to prove his theory correct. She knew how it felt. "Oh . . ." she said in a normal voice. Of course she was just a normal person. He didn't know why he hadn't considered *talking* to the guards all along. "I'm sorry, but I can't let you leave. I could get in trouble."

Felix nodded and looked at the dark courtyard. The other guards' silhouettes marched through the grounds. Even if he could convince this guard to let him go, he probably wouldn't make it far.

"Maybe you can escort me. I don't want to take you away from your post, but everyone in there is fast asleep," Felix said, pointing behind him with a thumb over his shoulder.

The guard pursed her lips and eyed the door. After a moment of consideration, she turned the knob and cracked the door to peer inside. She shut it quietly and stepped back, nodding. "Okay. I don't think that would be a problem."

Felix sighed with relief. "Oh, thank you. You have no idea how much I need this."

The guard nodded and gestured for him to follow as she stepped away from the building. "Just stay close. If anyone asks, I'm relocating you."

"What's your name?" Felix asked as they strolled between tree trunks and sad stumps lit by dim starlight.

"My name is Rose. You're Felix?"

"What a lovely name. Rose. Yes, I am Felix. I didn't realize my reputation among the guards was so big."

"Yes, well. You've caused a lot of trouble. We've been told to watch out for you," Rose said.

"I won't be causing much trouble now that I have no magic. Can't do much without it."

"You couldn't do much *with* it. It's impossible to use magic here," Rose said, eyeing him carefully.

Felix internally scolded himself for saying too much. "Yeah, but what's the point in trying to escape now? I still won't have my magic. I might as well stay here where I get free food and a place to sleep, right?" As he said the words aloud, he wondered how much he meant them. Maybe it was true. There was nothing for him outside the camp.

Still, he had to get that recipe.

"Right . . ." Rose said.

"Were you a magus, Rose?" Felix asked.

Rose paused. "Um . . . At one point, I was. But I've been saved from that evil."

Felix did not know how to respond for a few long seconds. "Do you really believe that? I mean . . . You know how this feels. You must have realized it was a mistake after accepting . . . *salvation*."

Rose took a deep breath and sighed. "I think everyone carries a bit of discontent in their heart, magus or not. All I can say now is that it hasn't gone away. Yet," she said. "Much like you, I have nowhere else to go. Better to lean into it, yeah?"

"No," Felix said. "I may have lost a piece of myself, but I won't accept that it was good for me. I don't think you should either."

"But what if it was? I lived on the streets before this. I didn't even *know* I was a magus until they scanned me. Both of my parents died when I was young. I had no family, no money, no food, no job. This place took care of me when no one else would. All it cost me was something I never knew I had."

"You did though," Felix said. "Don't you feel like deep inside of you something is missing?"

"I won't talk about this with you anymore, resident," Rose said, suddenly taking a formal tone with him.

"Sorry," Felix said. "I'm happy it worked for you."

Rose shot him a nervous look. "Let's just get this over with."

"I'm enjoying your company, Rose. I don't want to 'get it over with,'" Felix said.

Rose fiddled with her leather chest piece while she looked up at him. "You don't seem as bad as they say."

Felix smiled. "Who in this world can decide whether any of us are bad? Only Dei has that power."

Rose nodded, but she did not seem relieved. "Do you think Dei would think you're bad?"

"It would be blasphemous to answer that question," Felix said. "Is that enough of an answer?"

Rose let out a short laugh. "I guess so."

Felix and Rose passed the Oleander resident hall and meandered near the library centered between Oleander and Belladonna. An approaching guard eyed them and stopped when they came close enough to speak. His eyes flickered back and forth between Rose and Felix before he continued walking.

"Wow. The guards really don't care much, do they?" Felix asked. Now that he knew they were all former magi, he could see that look in their eyes. He understood their irritation when they snapped at a resident. They didn't really care about keeping magi locked up. They were just trying to get through the day too.

"We care enough," Rose said.

They rounded the corner of Belladonna. The temple loomed in the forest, dark beneath the cover of the remaining trees. If Felix wanted to get in there and look around, he needed to ditch Rose.

Or maybe not.

He followed her as she walked on. "Thank you for accompanying me," Felix said. "I've enjoyed talking to you. The other residents in my hall want nothing to do with me because of my reputation, so it's nice to have a friend."

"You're welcome. I wasn't sure about you at first, but I know how it is. I couldn't let you stew in your thoughts in good conscience. I hope this helped," she said.

"It did."

She brought him back to his hall. He thanked her, went inside, and fell asleep.

The next night, he did it again. As soon as the rest of the residents were asleep, Felix crept through the room and asked Rose to take a walk with him. It was easier to get a yes from her this time.

They wandered through the shadowy night and talked about their lives before the camp. Felix told her he was from New Brook, and in exchange she explained she was from Pleurane, a river town in midland Tinera. When she came of age, she was kicked out of her orphanage and found by the Hambletons in a nearby village. On their walk, they stopped and chatted with another guard, who did not seem to mind that Felix was out because he was accompanied by Rose. This guard's name was

Newton, and he was also a former sailor. He had requested to not be put on another ship when he was "saved" by the Hambletons, so they let him work as a guard instead. Felix couldn't blame him.

Felix and Rose chatted with a few more guards; a man named Daniel and a woman named Beatrice. They were happy to talk to Felix simply because Rose allowed it.

Felix let Rose walk him back to the residential hall, and again, he went inside and fell asleep.

At lunch the next day, Finnlay had left a note at their table.

Hello friend,

I realized it was stupid of us to be writing each other's names on these notes, just in case (gods forbid) our cloaking grid stops working.

Anyway, I had temple service this morning. Catherine went outside during our short break, and I took the opportunity to look around. My hall leader went with her, and I don't think the other residents of Larkspur noticed or cared that I was wandering.

I wasn't able to do a very thorough search, but I noticed that the lectern has some strange paneling along the side facing Catherine that is not visible to us during the service. I would have investigated more, but Catherine entered the room again shortly after.

I also couldn't help noticing that she leaves through the back door every day. The temple building looks much bigger from the outside, doesn't it? Do

you think she has a back room to work in?
Just something to consider.
Talk to you soon.

Finnlay had left a piece of charcoal. Felix flipped the page over and scribbled a reply.

I've been befriending the guards. We take nighttime walks together. They are former magi, and they are nicer than you'd expect. I'll try to see what I can find, but they have a close eye on me.
Take care.

He wedged the note beneath one of the bowls they had stolen from the kitchen and continued eating his lunch, letting himself feel a glimmer of hope for the first time since losing his magic.

Chapter Twenty-Four

As Thomas walked up the stairs and away from Charles, he could not take his eyes off his surroundings. He had spent so much time wondering what the inside of Charles's house looked like, and now he was actually inside.

The house's interior was brighter and more welcoming than Hambleton Manor. Golden sunset light fell through open windows onto dark polished wood floors. The air smelled like citrus and vanilla. The house was like Charles; classy and beautiful. It made Hambleton Manor look garish.

Thomas headed up the left side of the imperial staircase and continued down a hallway until he stopped at the third door on the right, as Charles had instructed.

Charles's bedroom was as beautiful as the rest of the house. Four tall posts framed his wide bed, which sat directly across from the room's entrance. To its right, a set of windowed double doors concealed a balcony overlooking the back garden. To the left of the bed was another wide window behind a blue sofa. A royal blue rug covered the polished wooden panels of the floor. An arched full-length mirror hung against the wall to his right. Thomas imagined Charles perfecting his stupid flawless hair there.

Thomas approached the bed and ran his hands over the soft bedding. How many times had he tried to imagine it? The image he had created wasn't too far off. The only thing missing was Charles.

He peered through the wide window behind the sofa and spotted Charles and Fiona speaking to Lucille in the garden. Fiona's head moved back and forth as she admired the trees and flowers, and Thomas felt a sudden fondness for his earth elementalist friend who adored flourishing life as much as he loved the sea.

He decided he should probably not stand so close to the window, just in case Lucille happened to look up and spot his bedraggled, ghostly figure in the window.

Thomas shed his salty overcoat and let it fall stiffly to the floor. He reached beneath the collar of his drawstring shirt and withdrew the diamond. Thomas didn't want to imagine what Tetra would have done to him if he hadn't had Mariana's protection around his neck.

Mariana's essence dripped from the bottom of the diamond until she stood before him as her entire bubbly self. "Hello, Thomas," she said.

Thomas forced a smile, startled at her sudden appearance. He was aware she was inside the diamond, but he hadn't expected her to speak to him. She tended to avoid interacting whenever possible. "Hi Mariana. Is everything all right?"

Mariana folded her arms together and frowned. "No. I'm dying. Tetra's grip on me gets stronger with every day that passes. How has your sword training been going?"

Thomas rubbed the back of his neck and looked away. "I've

learned a lot, but I don't know if I can defeat Caldwell yet. I'm still a novice."

Mariana watched him silently. Her gaze was intense, and Thomas was sweating beneath it. "You have to face him soon. Her darkness has almost entirely spread through me, so I'm only safe with you. She could challenge me to a duel and have you killed, but I think she's just waiting for you to cause another storm, because that will be the end. If it storms here, I'm going to die."

"I've gotten that under control," Thomas said, fighting back the panic rising deep within him. He knew what would happen if he panicked.

"Have you really?" Mariana challenged. "Because I overheard an interesting conversation with Fiona earlier."

Thomas sighed and crossed his arms. "She's wrong."

"She knows more about magic than you do."

"I won't let you die."

"You *are* letting me die. You can't just ignore this problem until it goes away, Thomas. I need you," Mariana said, lowering her head to make direct eye contact with him.

Thomas turned his face away. "I'm not ignoring it."

"You are! When are you going to confront Tetra?" Mariana asked.

"Soon! I'm not ready. I need to practice more," Thomas argued.

"You better mean that, because if you're not ready by the next time it rains here, we're both dead. Do you understand?"

Thomas was stunned into silence. All he could do was nod.

"If it rains again, I'm taking over. I know you don't like being possessed, but I can't take that chance. I'm sorry," Mariana said.

Thomas nodded again, but he felt he would be sick if she continued saying such terrible things.

"I hope you understand how serious this is," Mariana said.

Then she disappeared, leaving a cloud of fine mist where she stood.

Thomas took a deep breath, trying to stay calm. The way Mariana had spoken was frightening, but he could keep the clouds away. He just had to keep it up until he was confident with his sword skills. He was improving rapidly. It wouldn't take long.

It was easier to keep the clouds away when Charles was around and Mariana wasn't scolding him, of course.

He continued to breathe slowly and tried to think of anything that would help him relax. He eyed the simple wooden door to his right. That must be Charles's private bathroom. He would feel better if he were clean. And smelled like Charles. And wore his clothes.

Thomas took his time in the bathroom. He admired the marble basin and tub, and the high window against the far wall with a view of the clear blue sky. The bathroom had been unused for the last couple of months while Charles was away, but the faint smell of his rosy soap lingered. It immediately calmed Thomas.

A silver tap stuck from the wall over the tub. At home, Thomas had to request boiled water from the kitchen to have a warm bath. It likely wouldn't be any different here, but he couldn't just wander into the kitchen and ask for hot water.

Of course, he could do it himself. Heating water was just about the only thing Thomas could do with his magic, even if it was by accident.

But Thomas didn't want to take that risk. He would probably end up breaking the tub or ruining their pipes. He turned the tap to let cold water dump into the basin and briefly considered asking Mariana for help, but he suspected he knew what she would say.

Despite the cold water, it felt amazing to scrub the salt and dirt from his skin after months at sea. Fresh water and soap were a luxury he had always taken for granted.

When he was done, he dug through Charles's closet (probably more than necessary) to find something to wear. Halfway through getting dressed, Charles's door opening and closing startled him, and he whirled around to look.

Charles shut the door behind him and kept his eyes on Thomas, who was not yet wearing a shirt. "Well, hello," he purred.

"Hey," Thomas said with a smile.

"Did you have a nice bath? I'm sorry I missed it."

Thomas laughed but struggled to maintain eye contact for a moment. "Sort of. It was very cold."

Charles frowned. "Why didn't you heat it?"

"I'm not going to get caught by kitchen staff just because I wanted to take a hot bath."

"Why didn't you use magic?" Charles stepped toward Thomas.

Thomas crossed his arms and sighed. "I don't think I need to answer that."

Charles came closer and placed his hand on Thomas's waist. "Well, I'm not going to risk getting you caught by asking the kitchen for hot water either, and I am not going to take a cold bath."

"Ask your fake girlfriend for help, then," Thomas said.

"She's busy warming her own bath," Charles said, missing Thomas's salty tone. A mischievous smile curled around his lips. "She asked for her own room."

"Oh . . ." Thomas said, glancing at the door. Then it hit him. "*Oh*."

"Yeah. You'll have to share a bed with me. I hope that's okay," Charles said with a wink.

"Not if you refuse to take a cold bath," Thomas joked.

"I might need a cold bath anyway," Charles said, letting his eyes wander.

Thomas's face warmed, but he laughed and unfolded his arms to embrace Charles.

Charles pulled Thomas against him, squeezing tight. "Do you know what today is?"

"Um . . ." Thomas hadn't kept track of time since he left Brenton. "I couldn't even tell you what month it is."

"It's May tenth," Charles said.

Thomas knew what that date meant, even though Charles had never told him. It struck him just how long he had actually liked Charles. There was no reason for him to know Charles's birthday, but he did.

"Happy birthday," Thomas said, pushing away from the hug to look him in the eyes.

Charles grinned. "Thank you, and happy very belated birthday to you." He kissed Thomas's forehead.

Thomas giggled, feeling very silly. Charles had no reason to know Thomas's birthday either. The quiet obsession was mutual.

"They're throwing a party tonight, so I might have to leave you alone for an hour or two," Charles said.

"A birthday party?" he asked incredulously. Why would Charles's parents throw him a birthday party when they didn't even know he was coming back?

"No, it's just a party on my birthday. I don't know what it's really about," he said, the smile abandoning his eyes. "Anyway, I thought I should warn you."

"I don't know if I can handle being alone that long," Thomas said. Charles rolled his eyes, but Thomas wasn't joking. "Can I come to the party?"

"Yeah, if you want us both to get kicked to the streets. And then what? We go to *your* house? What about Fiona?"

Thomas sighed and looked away. "Damn it. I don't know. I

need to go home at some point, but I'm not ready. I don't know what I'm going to say to them, and I want to make sure you and Fiona are safe before I leave you. Also, Mariana just—Never mind. I just can't go home yet."

"I'll keep Fiona safe if you decide to go home," Charles said. "What did Mariana say?"

Thomas's eyebrows lowered for a moment, but he played it off as he looked at Charles again. "Nothing. Thank you, but I'm still not ready." After a moment of hesitation, he continued. "Will you help me figure out what to say to my parents? You're better at this type of thing."

Charles lifted his hand to caress Thomas's face. "Of course, Thomas. I'll do anything I can to help you."

The tension in Thomas's heart eased. He closed his eyes and leaned into Charles's hand. "Thank you. I'm so overwhelmed."

"I know," Charles said gently. "I'm here for you."

Thomas smiled, and everything briefly seemed right with the world.

TINERA

Nighttime fell over the camp, and Felix once again ventured outside to speak to his new friend, Rose.

Rose was leaning against the wall with her head tilted back and her arms crossed, gazing up at the stars. When Felix stepped outside, she frowned at him.

"Hey, Rose," he said, quietly shutting the door behind him.

"Felix, I'm sorry, but I can't walk with you tonight. It's been taking a toll on me. I always get really tired on my third night, and

I still have to work tomorrow night. I—" She yawned. "I don't have the energy. You have to go back to bed."

"Oh, Dei. I didn't mean to wear you out, Rose. I'm sorry."

Rose shook her head. Felix could see the exhaustion in her eyes. "It's okay. Maybe tomorrow night?"

Felix nodded, trying to keep his calm. He had an opportunity here, but he had to be careful with his words. "I'm pretty restless tonight . . . I don't want to drag you along, but I think I'll just lie awake all night if I can't get it out of my system."

"Hmm . . ." Rose looked out at the courtyard. "I don't know. I could lose my position if something goes wrong."

"Yeah. I would hate for that to happen because of me," Felix said.

Rose eyed him for a long moment. "Maybe it would be okay if you went alone, just for tonight. It's just a walk. Can you promise to be back here in thirty minutes?"

The offer triggered a rush of adrenaline. She was going to let Felix go out on his own. If he timed his approach to the temple, he could get in without suspicion. He just needed to move fast. "Absolutely. Thank you so much, Rose. I won't let you down," Felix said, clasping his hands together.

Rose nodded, but she still seemed uncertain. "Thirty minutes, Felix. If it takes any longer, I *will* come looking for you."

Felix nodded. "Of course. I'll see you in thirty minutes," he said, trying not to look too excited.

Rose watched him all the way past Oleander and then returned to her post. There were no guards as he passed the library, but that meant he would probably stumble across someone just as he reached the temple, so he slowed his pace.

Sure enough, Daniel came into view as Felix rounded Belladonna. Felix continued his casual pace, even going as far as waving at Daniel.

Daniel's pace quickened as he neared Felix.

Uh oh.

"Felix? What are you doing out here alone?" Daniel asked, searching the grounds as he spoke. "Where's Rose?"

"She was too tired to tag along tonight, but I promised her I'd be back in thirty minutes," Felix said.

Daniel turned to eye Oleander, a dark block of shadow in the distance. "All right. But if I catch you on my next loop, I'm taking you back. Don't do anything weird."

Felix wasn't planning on doing anything weird. All he wanted to do was take back what had always belonged to him. "I won't," he promised.

Daniel stood in place, watching Felix until he rounded Hemlock. Daniel's reluctance to move was going to mess up his plans. Felix walked forward a few paces and waited, eyeing the end of this stretch toward Larkspur at the other end of the grounds. Beatrice, the other guard, would surely come around the corner any second.

He snuck away from the residential hall into the sparse forest, making sure to stay out of Daniel's sight as he slipped from one dark tree trunk to the next.

Felix quickly made his way to the back of the camp, where the temple hid between Belladonna and Hemlock. He approached the front door, confident he wouldn't be seen in the dark behind the forest of trees, even if half of them were gone.

He slowly turned the simple brass knob and pushed open the door, wincing against a quiet but shrill creak of the hinges. Each noise was amplified by his nerves.

He slipped into the small opening and pulled the door shut behind him, letting out a breath now that he was safely inside the temple and out of sight.

The darkness was much heavier and more sinister inside the temple than it had been outside beneath the stars, but it didn't surprise him. Whatever witchcraft methods Catherine had developed were based in evil. Any magic that involved taking without consent was not something he wanted to touch.

Felix hurried through the aisle and dropped behind the lectern where Catherine usually stood. He felt the smooth dark wood as his fingers ran over the slit that Finnlay had seen. He felt all around its boundaries looking for a handle or some other way to open the secret door but found nothing. He dug his fingertips into the edges, but he could not get enough of a grip to pull it out.

He rested his forehead against the panel, feeling frustrated at wasting time trying to pry open a secret door. When he rested his weight against the wood, it sank deeper into the lectern.

Felix leaned back to investigate, and the door popped open. He marveled at it for a moment, but quickly moved on. There was not enough time to consider the technology.

Behind the door were two short shelves, both lined with small glass vials. The vials were four different shapes and colors. The vials of the same shape held liquid of the same color, but any of these could be the potion. One set of vials shone crisp green flaked with gold. It was the same color as the potion Finnlay had made, but Finnlay's potion was not made correctly. That might not be it. Another set of potions was milky white, which Felix recognized as an antidote. There was also a set of shimmering violet potions and another set of sparkling orange.

It was impossible to know which was his mother's, and he couldn't simply take them all. He only had two pockets. If he put two vials in one pocket, they would make enough noise to get him caught.

He might be able to figure out the final color of the potion with access to the completed recipe, but he didn't have that.

He bolted up and turned to the back of the temple, eyeing the back door. Finnlay seemed to think there was more to this temple than the service room, and maybe he was right. It *was* bigger on the outside.

He ran for the back door. It had probably already taken him ten minutes to get here because of his encounter with Daniel, and it would probably take him ten more to get back to Oleander on the exact opposite corner of the grounds.

Felix pushed the door open slowly, half-expecting it to open into the night forest beyond the walls of the temple, but he stepped into a dark room lit only by the same small windows that lined the rest of the temple.

Dim blue starlight was the only source of light, revealing a small space piled high with books and papers. There was a desk to his left and short table to his right stacked with more books than even the library had. He headed for the table, thinking a recipe was likely to be kept within a book rather than left out on a desk.

It was almost too dark to read. No matter how much he squinted or widened his eyes, the contents of the room refused to be seen. In situations like this, he would usually just partially shift into an animal that could see better in the dark, but that simply wasn't possible anymore. Not even if he drank the right potion.

If he took his time, he could make out the letters on the cover of each book, but he did not have time to take. He sifted through the books until he found one with a potion-shaped blur on the cover, and he cracked it open. He flipped frantically through the pages, aware he was losing time with each turn of the page. He had to leave within minutes if he wanted to make it back without suspicion, but before he left he needed to find his mother's potion, read it, understand it, and determine which vial was made using her recipe.

His eyes slowly adjusted to the dark and reading became easier. His hope grew as he flipped through the book, but it fell just as fast when he neared the end of the book with no luck. His odds of success were quickly diminishing.

Finally, he reached the last page. A recipe for a potion that eased a sunburn.

He took a step back and rubbed his eyes with a heavy sigh. This was not going well. He should have bargained with Rose for more time.

He dropped his hands and eyed the stack of books again. Maybe there was another potion recipe book among the piles. All he could do was continue searching.

He set the recipe book aside and eyed the title of the next one. It was a list of resident records between a certain number of years. This particular book recorded residents from one year ago in the Larkspur hall.

He set the book aside and saw another Larkspur record from two years ago. The one below that was from three years back.

The potion book he had already found was the only recipe book. The rest of these were just residential records. He picked up the potion book again and frantically flipped through it, desperate to catch something he had missed. Still nothing.

As he moved to set it down again, something stopped him. This *had* to be the answer. It was the only potion book in the room, as far as he could tell. If the recipe was in here, it was in that book.

He inspected the front and then turned it around to examine the back. He flipped the back cover open, and as he did, something slid inside the cover beneath the binding. He closed the cover again and heard it slide the other way. There was a secret compartment in the binding.

Felix set the book down on the tabletop and held the back cover between his fingers, sliding his other hand along its edge in search of an opening. Along the top, he felt a divide. He tilted the book upright and pried it open. The leather binding curved away from the firm board, revealing a hidden space between.

Keeping the hidden pocket open, Felix turned the book upside down and shook it over the table. A piece of paper folded into a square fell out and landed among the haphazardly stacked records. He tossed the recipe book aside and lifted the paper, unfolding it carefully. The paper was not the same quality as the pages of the book. It was pulpy and rough and as familiar in his hands as the sight of the writing. A loopy, elegant script detailed the purpose of the potion at the top of the page before spelling out the recipe below.

It was his mother's handwriting.

Felix let out an involuntary gasp. It had been so long since he had seen her writing. It was as familiar as if he had just seen it yesterday, but it had been two years since he had even heard her voice.

In the margins, someone else had written their notes in a dangerously neat script. It had to be Catherine's handwriting.

He tucked the recipe into his pocket and tried to stack the books how they had been when he walked in.

When he was done, he ran back into the service area, closing the back door behind him. He crouched behind the lectern again as he scanned the recipe.

He had been right about the reverse base. And the blood *was* a vital ingredient. *The blood of a loved one.* The wording implied mutual affection. His mother had very kindly requested his blood or his brother's whenever she dared to attempt the recipe, and Felix had always been happy to help. She promised it would change the world of magic if she could get it right, and he believed her.

Now he was disgusted that it had.

He wondered whose blood Catherine used for the potion. Her husband? Thomas?

Thomas. Felix hadn't considered it until now, but if Catherine was a witch, Thomas probably had magic too. Did he know?

Probably not, considering the weird way he had acted when he learned Felix was a shapeshifter.

A cold silence gripped him as he realized what that *actually* meant. Catherine had probably taken Thomas's magic away.

She was truly a monster.

He shook his head and eyed the recipe again, struggling to keep his focus. Finnlay had gotten a lot right. He had missed a few minor steps, but the only important ingredient he left out was the blood.

Felix sat in stunned silence as he realized Finnlay had not only deciphered Felix's limited explanation of the potion recipe his mother *did* have, but he also figured out a lot that wasn't there. Finnlay, stuck in this prison with no resources and almost no magic, had almost finished his mother's life work.

Finnlay was amazing.

Felix now understood the green potions were either unfinished and needed blood or they were something else entirely. Adding blood to a green potion would probably not turn it orange. If done correctly, the blood of a loved one would give a violet tint to a potion.

It had to be the purple one.

Felix snatched a purple vial from the shelf, moving one of the many purple vials from the back to the front so Catherine wouldn't suspect any had been taken, and then he shut the hidden door.

He did one last scan of the room to make sure he hadn't left behind any evidence before folding the recipe and tucking it securely in his pocket with the vial of potion that would earn their freedom.

He ran as quietly as he could through the cover of the forest to regain lost time, slowing only when he came near a guard.

When he got back to his residential hall, Rose didn't suspect a thing.

Chapter Twenty-Five

By the time Charles and Thomas had cleaned up and taken some time to relax, the party was only a few hours away. Charles and Thomas had spent the last hour napping together. Charles was exhausted, and although Thomas always claimed he didn't need to sleep, he was clearly exhausted too.

The sound of a sharp knock woke them from a calm slumber.

Charles bolted upright. Thomas scrambled out of Charles's bed with the urgency and reflexes of a startled cat, and he noisily fell to the wooden floor.

Charles leaned over the bed to make sure Thomas was okay. Thomas lay on his back with his hand over his mouth, fighting back a laugh. He smiled apologetically before crawling under the bed to hide.

Charles bit his lip, fighting his own laughter before getting up to answer the door. He turned the knob and carefully pulled it open.

Fiona waited on the other side. She had cleaned up as well. Her hair was glossy and vivid, tamed into beautiful ginger waves that fell to her waist. She wore a long-sleeved black dress that hugged her form. He had never seen that dress before, and he wondered where it came from. Wherever it was from, it was stunning on her.

"Wow," Charles said. "You look amazing."

Fiona smiled and tucked a strand of hair behind her ear. "Thanks. Is Thomas all right? That sounded like it hurt."

Charles let his laughter out. "It did, didn't it? Come in," he said, holding the door open.

Thomas stuck his head out from beneath the bed with a big smile, his expression switching to awe when he saw Fiona. "Whoa, Fiona. Look at you! If I were straight . . ."

Fiona giggled at Thomas's compliment while Charles burned with jealousy. "You're silly," Fiona said, reaching a hand toward him. "Are you all right?"

Thomas crawled out from beneath the bed and took her hand. She pulled him upright. "Yes, thank you. I thought you were Alfred. Or Lucille."

"Lucille seemed quite nice. You don't think she'd be okay with you being here?" Fiona asked, turning to Charles.

"No," Charles said.

"Well, you should practice falling out of bed a little more quietly. They will definitely hear whatever that was," Fiona said with a laugh.

Thomas laughed with her. "Noted."

"You two look very dashing in civil society, even in your underclothes," Fiona said, looking from Thomas to Charles. "I can tell you were born into this life."

"Thank you," Charles said. "Are you enjoying your room?"

"Yes, very much. I've never experienced such luxury. How do

you get water running through your house without magic?" Fiona asked.

Charles hadn't thought about it. He knew less fortunate people didn't have pipes in their homes, but he hadn't stopped to consider how it worked. "Um . . . technology, I suppose."

"Hmm. Maybe it *is* magic. Your mother seems to be a fan," Fiona said.

"Could be," Charles said.

Fiona shrugged. "As handsome as you both look, I think your mother was right. You could use a haircut. You too, Thomas. Unless you want to grow your hair out and let me teach you witchcraft," she said.

"No thank you," Thomas said.

Fiona examined him a moment longer and then stepped toward him. "May I?" she asked, lifting her hands to hover around his head.

"Uh . . . sure."

Fiona scooped his blond hair up with her hands and squeezed it into a bundle at the back of his head. She eyed him again and nodded before turning to Charles. "What do you think, Charles? He looks good with his hair tied up like a witch, doesn't he?"

He did look good. His entire pretty face was visible now, not hidden beneath his messy fringe. "Adorable," Charles said.

Thomas lowered his eyebrows and waved Fiona's hand away. "Just cut it. I don't like dealing with my hair."

Fiona frowned at Thomas and then shot the disappointed look at Charles. Charles got the feeling he said something wrong. "I liked it," Charles said. "You didn't even see it, Thomas."

Thomas rolled his eyes. He must have thought Charles was making fun of him.

Fiona walked to Charles. "Can I touch your hair?"

"Yes," Charles said.

She did the same to his hair. "This is what you looked like. Kinda. But nicer and cuter," Fiona said.

"Hey . . ." Charles argued weakly, but he couldn't disagree.

Thomas's eyebrows slowly rose. "Oh, wow. That actually looks good."

Charles gently removed Fiona's hands. "I can't do witchcraft anyway, so there's no point leaving it like this."

"Oh yeah . . ." Thomas said. He sounded disappointed.

Fiona brought them to her room, where she had gotten *very* comfortable. Her discarded clothing was abandoned across the floor. The bath was lined with long strands of orange hair, and the floor was still wet. How could Fiona make herself so lovely while absolutely destroying the room around her in the process?

Fiona pulled a stool up to the mirror and gestured for Charles to sit.

Charles had been afraid to look in the mirror, worried he might see someone different. He did.

He had changed since the last time he saw his reflection. His face was thinner and more somber. A specter of Alfred haunted the downturned corners of his mouth and the disdain in his eyes. Charles forced himself to smile, knowing he could never look like Alfred that way. He kept his eyes down as Fiona cut off long chunks of hair.

"There you go, Charles," Fiona said when she finished. "What do you think?"

Charles looked up to a more familiar sight. He almost looked like himself again. Fiona had somehow managed to get his hair back to how it used to look without him telling her his preferences.

"How did you know to cut my hair like that?" Charles asked.

"I saw a painting of you in the main hall," Fiona said with a slight smile. "Did I get it right?"

"You got it perfect," Thomas said before Charles could answer. "He's never going to look away from the mirror now. He might leave me for himself. Thanks a lot, Fiona."

Fiona laughed. "You're next. Come have a seat. Charles, go away."

"And step out of sight of the mirror? No thank you," Charles joked as he let Thomas take his place.

Fiona smirked at Charles and shook her head. She turned her attention back to Thomas and ran her fingers through his hair. "I haven't seen any paintings of you yet. Would you like the same?"

"Gods, no. Please, give me something practical," Thomas said, flashing a taunting smile at Charles. Charles leaned against the bathroom wall and winked in return.

Fiona laughed. "All right. Maybe I'll just cut your hair the same way I cut my brother's. You remind me of him a little bit anyway. I think it'll be fitting."

"I do? Why?"

Fiona smiled as she combed his hair. "Now that you're happier, I see it. He was depressed when he was younger too. When he fixed what was hurting him, his smile returned and his attitude changed. I see a lot of the same in you now that you have your magic again. I think you would get along if you ever met him. There is a kindness and humility that seems to come with being on the other side of suffering that you both have."

Charles listened to Fiona talk about her brother while guilt crept into his heart. He knew Thomas had been depressed, but he only recently realized how bad it was. Thomas was noticeably happier these days.

"What was causing his depression? I didn't realize there was a fix for that," Thomas said.

Fiona raised her eyebrows and looked at him through the mirror. "You fixed your issue, didn't you?"

"Yes, but my situation was unique."

"So was his," Fiona said, and she got back to work.

"You don't want to tell me," Thomas said.

Fiona shook her head. "I promised I wouldn't tell. Sorry."

"You cut your brother's hair short? Isn't he a witch too?" Charles asked. His mother had always had a fascination with magic, so he knew a lot about witches from her.

Fiona flashed a smile at Charles. "Yes, but he doesn't like having long hair. We did almost everything together before we were caught, so I always told him he could use mine if he needed it. I wonder if he has changed his mind now that we're apart."

"What does long hair do in witchcraft?" Thomas asked.

"It's used whenever an enchantment or a spell deals with time." Fiona grabbed a long chunk of Thomas's hair and held it up. "This piece of hair has been with you for a while." She pointed to the end of his hair. "This part has been with you the longest. Maybe it was with you when you first fell in love with Charles. That's pretty valuable."

Thomas turned his head to steal a look at Charles, and the lock of hair fell from Fiona's fingers. When Charles blew him a kiss, his smile widened and he faced forward again.

"It was with you when you met me," Fiona continued, smiling through the mirror. "And Faya, Ametta, and Fyavine. And Mariana. It was with you when you got your magic back and became immortal. That's *huge*." She paused. "Actually, now that I think about it, you've been through a lot. Are you *sure* you want me to cut off all this history?" She fluffed what was left of his hair.

"It's a little late now," Thomas said, running his fingers through the choppy hair Fiona had already cut. "I don't see myself getting into witchcraft anyway."

Fiona smiled, but there was pain in her eyes. "All right," she said, positioning the scissors over his head again, but it obviously hurt her to continue trimming.

"I had no idea that's why witches had long hair," Charles commented. "I thought it was more mystical than that."

"That's not mystical enough?" Fiona asked, turning her smile in his direction.

"I guess magic just isn't as serious as I thought," Charles said.

"The gods aren't very serious either. You should have seen Dei," Thomas said, shaking his head.

"Hold still," Fiona said, turning his head to face forward again. "You really are like Finnlay. He can't hold still either."

Thomas laughed. "Sorry."

"You actually met Dei?" Charles asked, leaning forward. He couldn't fathom meeting someone as important as the god of their world.

"Yes. They were silly, and They didn't seem to care much about humans at all. It was like They had never met one before."

Fiona nodded like she already knew that. "They probably hadn't," she said. She stopped cutting his hair again and dropped her hands to her side. "You're really going to make me cut off pieces of your hair from when you met *Dei?*"

"That happened like two weeks ago," Thomas said. "Just don't cut it very short."

Fiona pursed her lips, but she must have been satisfied with his answer because she continued chopping.

"I can't believe how casual you are about being a human among gods," Charles said.

Thomas shrugged, and Charles laughed. "I don't really want to be. They don't care about me, so why should I care about them? The only god I really care about is . . . Mariana." Thomas's expression soured, and Charles could practically see his concentration turn inward. Something had happened with Mariana, but Thomas wouldn't talk about it.

"Are you all right, Thomas?" Fiona asked, moving to work on the other side of his head.

Thomas gave a forced smile. "Yes. Just thinking."

Fiona exchanged a worried look with Charles. After a moment, Fiona said, "Charles, you don't have to wait for us if you don't want to. You're probably expected downstairs by now, aren't you?"

"Yes, probably," Charles said, pushing away from the wall. As much as he wanted to stay, Fiona was right. If Charles wanted to maintain his place in this family, he had to act accordingly. "I should get dressed. I'll see you down there?"

"Yes, see you down there," Fiona said.

"Not me," Thomas remarked.

Right. Thomas couldn't come to the party. Charles stepped forward and placed a hand on his shoulder. Fiona stopped trimming his hair and stepped back, letting Charles wrap his arms around Thomas. Thomas hugged him back, squeezing tight around his hips with his head resting against Charles's stomach. "I'll see you later tonight. I doubt anyone will bother you while I'm gone, but I'll check on you in a few hours, okay?"

"Okay," Thomas said, muffled against Charles's shirt. "I love you."

"I love you too." Charles leaned down to kiss Thomas once. He lingered for a moment to savor the kiss, hoping its memory would give him the strength to get through the evening.

After putting on his nicest party attire, Charles returned to the main hall, where his mother and sister waited. They had also put some time into their appearances. Rebecca wore a long navy dress with sparkling diamonds stitched up the bodice and black lace draped around the skirt. It was the most appallingly decadent piece of clothing Charles had ever seen.

His mother carried herself with more humility. Her dress was similar, but it had far fewer diamonds and less lace.

"Look at you. You look much better," Rebecca said as he

joined them in the main hall. "I almost didn't recognize you when I saw you in the garden."

"Thanks," Charles said, scratching his head. Rebecca and his mother watched him, hiding looks of discomfort behind their stoic frowns. He straightened his posture and cleared his throat, folding his arms behind his back. "I mean, thank you."

"Our guests are waiting in the front garden," his mother said. "Rebecca, why don't you go join them? I want to have a word with Charles."

Rebecca nodded and strutted through the front door. Charles was relieved for the extra moments of peace. The last thing he wanted to do after his long journey was attend a party, but he didn't seem to have any other choice.

"Charles, I would like to show you something," his mother said. She slid her right hand into her left sleeve and retrieved a small silver band. She lifted it, and it sparkled in the afternoon light from the tall windows. A small diamond rested at its center, similar to the many diamonds on Rebecca's bodice.

"A ring?" Charles asked.

She nodded. "I should have shown you this a long time ago, but I . . . I don't know. I suppose I was scared." She shook her head. "That's no excuse. We're all scared."

"We shouldn't be," Charles said.

His mother averted her gaze as she nodded, but quickly rested her eyes on him again. "I gave this ring to someone I loved before I met your father. I've kept it with me all this time because . . ." She hesitated. "I suppose my feelings never went away."

Charles didn't know what to say. He watched her struggle to wrangle the next sentence.

"She was the love of my life," she finally said.

Charles gasped. "*She?*"

His mother nodded and held the ring out. "Take it. I want you to have it."

Charles tried to calm the shaking in his hand as he took it. "You don't want to keep it?"

His mother shook her head. "No. She's forgotten me by now, but I want you to know there's still hope for you. Someday, when you've sat with your grief enough to love again, you will find the right man."

Charles's mouth fell open as he stared at the ring in his hand. He never would have guessed his mother was like him. "Thank you," he said. When he finally looked up from the ring, he pulled her into a hug.

She squeezed him tight. "I love you, Charles."

"I love you too," he said. "Mom, I have to tell you something."

"What is it?" She broke away from the hug to look him in the eyes. "Is everything all right?"

"Yeah . . . Yes," he said, glancing at the door. "Better than all right, actually." He laughed and looked at the ring again.

"What is it?"

Charles smiled. "Thomas is alive. And he's here in Brenton."

She gasped and covered her mouth with her hands. "He's alive?" she whispered.

"Yes," Charles said. "Somehow, he survived. And somehow, he forgave me . . ."

His mother lowered her hands to reveal a smile. "Well then, maybe you'll have a use for that ring after all."

Charles laughed. The thought of proposing to Thomas filled him with a whole garden's worth of fluttering, scattering butterflies.

Thomas could be his husband. They could spend the rest of their—well, Charles's life together. And now Charles had a ring to propose with.

"You should invite him to the party," his mother said.

Charles's eyes widened. The thought of running into Alfred with Thomas at his side filled him with dark dread. He gave a small shake of his head. "I don't—but what if...?"

"I won't let your father hurt you. I will die before I let him take my baby away from me again," she said, placing a hand on one side of his face. "All I want in the world is for my children to be happy. Do what makes you happy." She stood on her tiptoes and kissed his cheek.

Charles nodded and smiled. "Thank you." He tucked the ring into the pocket of his coat.

"If you do decide to invite him, I want to talk to him."

"Why?" Charles asked.

"Because I want to get to know the person whose love drove you to reject a life of luxury."

Charles frowned at her. "I didn't reject that life. It rejected me."

Before she could answer, the front door creaked open, startling Charles and his mother. The dark silhouette of Alfred stepped through.

Charles's heart raced and he struggled to breathe. He fixed his eyes on Alfred, waiting for him to say something.

Alfred looked first at Charles's mother. His eyes lingered on Charles for a moment before returning to his wife. "Lucille," Alfred said, "my meeting with the Wembleys went longer than I anticipated. Can you please see that our guests are entertained while I prepare?"

Charles's mother gave a curt nod. Alfred did not even hazard a second look at Charles before shutting the door and disappearing up the stairway. Charles watched him all the way up the steps, but he never bothered to acknowledge Charles's return. He wasn't angry, disappointed, or disgusted that Charles was back in Brenton. He didn't care at all, and that was almost worse.

Charles's mother placed a gentle hand on his shoulder and offered a sympathetic smile. "I would invite Thomas as soon as you can. You will need all the support you can find tonight."

"What does that mean?" Charles asked.

His mother gave his shoulder a squeeze and walked away, disappearing through the front door before he could ask any more questions.

Dull fear ached deep in Charles's heart, and he contemplated whether he should listen to his mother or keep Thomas at a safe distance.

He decided the answer didn't really matter. He would take any excuse to be with Thomas.

TINERA

Felix had temple service the next morning. It was tense.

At breakfast, he had left the potion and the recipe at their table with a note to Finnlay explaining what had happened the previous night. Felix was eager for Finnlay's response, but he had to make it through the morning first. He considered waiting at the table through lunch, but Matthew was keeping an eye on Felix. If Felix ditched a recreation, especially temple, their whole operation could be discovered.

It seemed Catherine was watching Felix the entire session in the temple. He forced a calm demeanor. Slipping up now could cost everything. He didn't let himself look at the lectern or the back door. Catherine watched him with the intensity of a mother bear watching a man approach her cubs, and Felix refused to falter.

When her sermon was finished, Catherine sat beside him in the pews. "Felix, darling. How are you feeling?"

"Terrible, Catherine. I feel like I've died but my body continues walking, so thank you for that."

"It'll wear off in time. One day you'll thank me," she said with a smile so sweet he wanted to run the other way. How was this woman somebody's mother?

"I don't think so," he said.

"I'm sorry about your mother," Catherine said. "I lost myself in the passion of salvation when we last spoke, but truly. I am sorry. It's awful what your town did to her."

"I don't think you mean that," Felix said. "You got something out of it, so nothing else matters."

"Felix, don't talk like that, my love," Catherine said.

"Don't call me that. You don't love me."

"Maybe not, but my son is dead, and your mother is dead. Perhaps we can set aside our differences and try to find that missing connection in each other?" Catherine asked.

Felix could not believe her. He turned his head to face her. "I tried to be your son, and you kicked me out. You are nothing like my mother."

"You don't think so?" Catherine asked, ignoring his scathing tone. "But our life's work is so similar."

Felix clenched his jaw and his fists, squeezing his eyes shut in an attempt to dispel his anger. "Please leave me alone," he said with forced calm.

"But I—"

"Catherine," Matthew said gently from the end of the pew. Catherine looked up, and Matthew beckoned her over.

"We'll finish this conversation in a moment. Please excuse me, darling," Catherine said, patting him on the shoulder as she stood to walk toward Matthew.

Felix kept his eyes on Catherine. It was strange for Matthew to interrupt a private conversation between Catherine and a resident, so it must have been serious. His heart beat hard. They had probably discovered that the back room had been tampered with last night. They noticed a missing potion. They knew it was him. Of course they would know it was him; the guards had seen him out wandering last night.

Matthew whispered in Catherine's ear. Her eyes widened and locked on Felix. Felix's heart beat even harder.

Catherine covered her mouth and stepped away from Matthew, her eyes wildly scanning the room. "I—I—" She shook her head. "Excuse me, everyone!" she announced. "I have to leave for the day, but I will be back tomorrow. If you need anything in the meantime, please direct all questions to Matthew." She headed for the door. The *front* door.

The entire room silently watched her hurry out of the building.

Felix exchanged a quiet look with Matthew, but Matthew averted his gaze almost as soon as their eyes met.

After the adrenaline from thinking he had been caught wore off, Felix spent the rest of recreation racking his brain for what would be important enough to get Catherine to leave during the middle of a service, and he could only think of one thing.

He hoped he was wrong, because it meant their time was almost up.

SOUTHWORTH MANSION

Thomas watched Fiona work through the mirror. Her brow was furrowed with concentration, but she glanced at him every now and then to flash an unconvincing smile. After the third forced smile, she finally paused to watch him. "Thomas . . . Is everything all right with Mariana? You seem a bit stressed."

"Yes, everything is all right," he lied.

"Are you sure?"

Thomas said nothing.

"It's not all right, is it?" she asked.

Thomas sighed and shook his head. "I'm scared, Fiona. I've done absolutely everything wrong, and now the world is on the brink of falling into Tetra's claws and it all depends on whether I can control my magic, but I *can't.* You were right, I've been lying to myself. Charles is the only reason I've been able to control it, and I can't be apart from him. I might lose control while he's at the party, and if I lose control again, Mariana will die."

Fiona considered this for a quiet moment. "Will you let me help you now? You can't stay by his side forever."

Thomas took a deep breath. "I think . . . whether I want to or not, I have to learn."

Fiona nodded with a gentle smile. "I think you're right."

"Thank you for being patient. I know it hasn't been easy for you."

Fiona patted him on the shoulder. "It hasn't been easy for you either."

That was an understatement.

She ruffled his hair. "There you go. How do you like it?" she asked.

Thomas examined himself in the mirror for the first time. He was unfamiliar with the face looking back at him. Even though he had grown, and his eyes were more serious now, there was a light in them he had never seen before. People used to tell him he looked like his father, but he hadn't seen it until now. Fiona had trimmed his hair short on the sides and left longer on top to fall over his forehead, but it was short enough to stay out of his eyes. As it began to dry, it took on the natural wave of his hair. Fiona had made him look far nicer than he ever had before.

"Whoa . . ." he whispered. "Are those scissors enchanted or is it all you?"

Fiona covered her mouth and laughed. "Oh, stop it. I barely did anything. It's your natural beauty."

"No, you're very talented, Fiona. Thank you."

"Of course." Fiona set her scissors on the edge of the sink and began cleaning the space around them using magic. Thomas watched in awe at all she could do. He admired her and worried once again that someday they would be separated forever.

"Fiona, I—" Thomas stopped himself before he could say something embarrassingly emotional.

Fiona stopped and looked up with a smile. "Yes? Is everything all right?"

Thomas nodded. If Fiona was right, and Mariana seemed to think she was, he needed to learn to be okay with being emotional instead of keeping it all down. He forced himself to say, "I think you're my best friend."

Fiona's eyebrows angled upward, and she smiled at him. "Oh, Thomas . . . That's so sweet. It's not Charles?"

Thomas looked away, but his eyes landed on the mirror, so he fixed his eyes on the tub. "Charles is my boyfriend. That's a different kind of friendship."

Fiona nodded with a calm smile. "You're my best friend too, Thomas. Like I said, you remind me of Finnlay, so it's been nice to have your company. I hope we stay friends when this whole mess is over."

"Me too." Thomas sighed, relieved Fiona hadn't laughed at him, and then he wondered why he thought she would. "We'll find your brother. Don't worry."

"Thank you," Fiona said. She clapped her hands together

suddenly and glanced at the sink. "So, are you ready to practice some magic? It's a lot easier than it seems, trust me."

Thomas couldn't help laughing. "Okay, let's try it."

"All right, stand up with me." Fiona offered him her hand. He took it, and she pulled him up. She didn't let go. "Focus on your magic. You can close your eyes if you need to. I find that it helps sometimes."

Thomas closed his eyes and focused on the feeling at his center. A bright pulse of energy moved through him faster than he could stop it. "Okay. Now what?"

"Your magic is very powerful, but you can control it. Being with Charles has helped you because he makes you happy. Your negative feelings are still there, but they are not in control. This is good."

"Oh. Good ..." Thomas said. "So, what do I do?"

"Do you feel the difference between your magic now and back when you had no control?"

Thomas took another moment to feel the magic flowing out of him, but his skin didn't prickle where it left his body. It flowed through him slowly, taking nothing with it. "Yes. It feels . . . calmer."

"That's right! Because *you're* calmer. When you couldn't control it before, it felt too fast, right?"

Thomas nodded. "How did you know that?"

"It's what I do."

Right. Fiona was a witch. She knew everything about magic. "So what do I do when I can't control it?"

"When you can't control it, it's because you aren't letting your strong feelings pass without differentiating the emotion from the feeling of magic. If you hold your emotions back, you won't learn to identify it apart from your magic, and when you feel again, you'll just be in the same situation. This is why breathing helps.

Deep, steady breaths reset our mind and help process our emotions," Fiona explained.

"So when I'm feeling angry or upset, I just breathe until I don't feel it?" Thomas asked.

Fiona squinted and tilted her head in response. "Um . . . No. You should let yourself feel it."

"But isn't that how I lose control?" Thomas asked.

"No. You lose control by *not* letting yourself feel it. Suppressing that feeling is what causes it to react with your magic. Breathing through the feeling helps you let it pass through your mind and body without causing chaos."

Thomas shook his head. "I don't get it. If the emotions are causing me problems, I should try not to have emotions, right?"

"No!" Fiona said urgently. "That way of thinking is probably *why* you're struggling with control. Let yourself feel, Thomas. It's okay."

A sudden, sharp knock came from the bedroom door. Fiona jumped and looked at the doorway behind her. "Stay here," she said, shutting him inside her bathroom.

The muffled sound of the door opening preceded it closing. The bathroom door opened again, and Charles stepped into view.

He looked stunning.

Thomas rarely got to see him anywhere but Blackwater Academy or, more recently, at sea, and he had never seen Charles look like this before. He wore a deep cerulean embroidered waistcoat and an overcoat to match, both tailored to his perfect body. If Charles were a siren, Thomas would have drowned a long time ago.

Charles eyed Thomas, then his familiar sly smile spread across his lips. "Look at you," he said, stepping closer. He ran his fingers through Thomas's hair. "I can see your face again." He kissed Thomas once and leaned back to look at him. "You look good."

Thomas didn't realize he was smiling until a laugh escaped him. "You do too."

"Thanks," Charles said with a wink.

Thomas giggled and took Charles's hand. "Is everything okay? Why are you here? I thought you were heading down to the party. Did you see Alfred?"

Pain flashed through Charles's eyes, but he smoothed his expression back into a smile. Thomas's heart sank, but when Charles placed his hand on Thomas's waist, it fluttered right back up where it belonged. "I spoke to my mother. She told me to invite you."

Thomas's eyes widened. "She knows I'm here?"

"No. I only told her you're still alive and that you're in Brenton. She wants to meet you . . . officially, I suppose."

Thomas was skeptical. "Why?"

"To get to know you better."

"Why?" Thomas asked again.

"She knows we're together," Charles said. "She told me that she, uh . . ." Charles furrowed his brow, almost as if in disbelief. "She almost married a woman." He paused to give the information the space it needed. "She wants me to have what she couldn't."

Thomas reeled back. "What? Why—Did she—Is—" he stammered. Eventually, he just stared at Charles slack-jawed.

Charles shrugged. "No, this is news to me. She said she didn't tell me before because she was scared, and I don't blame her."

Thomas wondered at Charles's ability to understand his stammering. "Wow," Thomas breathed.

Charles lifted Thomas's hand to kiss his knuckles. "Would you like to be my date to the party?" he asked.

"Yes!" Thomas responded before he could consider whether it was a good idea. He would be safe from his magic if he stayed with Charles, and his lesson with Fiona wasn't really sticking. "Can I wear more of your clothes?" he asked, eyeing Charles's fine clothing again.

Charles grinned. "Yes." He took Thomas's hand and leaned in close. "Let's go get you undressed," he whispered.

Thomas hid his burning face behind one hand as he laughed. Charles kissed his cheek before leading him out of Fiona's bathroom. Fiona was standing by the bed, pretending she hadn't heard them.

"Thomas is coming to the party," Charles announced. "We'll be down in a few minutes. You can head down there now if you'd like."

"Without you?" Fiona asked. "I can wait."

"We might be more than a few minutes," Charles said.

Fiona's eyebrows rose. "Oh," she said, looking away. "All right. Um. See you down there, then."

"Is she going to be safe at the party alone?" Thomas asked, trying to ignore the burn in his cheeks.

"Yes. My mother adores her. She'll be fine," Charles said.

"Are you okay with that, Fiona?" Thomas asked.

"Will there be wine at this party?" Fiona asked Charles.

"Yes," Charles said.

"Then I'll be fine. But you and I are not done with this lesson, sir. We will continue later," she said to Thomas.

"Right," Thomas said.

Charles held Thomas's hand as they crossed the hall and slipped into his bedroom. Charles shut the door behind them and eyed Thomas hungrily. "I don't think we've been making proper use of this time," he said, tracing his finger along the edges of Thomas's face.

Thomas leaned into his touch. "No, I don't think so," he said softly. He slid his hand around Charles's neck and pulled him into a kiss. Charles kissed him back, pushing him toward the bed. His hand snuck up Thomas's torso, feeling his body beneath his shirt. Thomas felt dizzy from his touch, and the kissing made him stupid, but he pushed Charles away and said, "Wait, stop."

Charles watched him attentively. "Why? What's wrong? Are you okay?" His eyes ran the length of Thomas's body searchingly before meeting his eyes again.

Thomas was charmed by how much Charles cared. He bit his lip and smiled. "Yeah, I'm fine. I'm good."

"Why did you stop?" Charles asked.

"Because we're going to lock the door this time."

CHAPTER TWENTY-SIX

The sky was dark by the time Charles finally joined the party with Thomas at his side. Thomas stayed glued to Charles, holding him around the waist like the world would fall from his feet if he let go.

It felt good to be honest about Thomas. Thomas was the best thing that had ever happened to him. Charles wanted to show him off to the world, even if the world didn't want to see it.

The world *didn't* want to see it, but they certainly stared like they did. Every guest at the party watched with their ugly faces contorted in disgust. Thomas didn't seem to notice. His eyes wandered around the party with whimsical happiness.

Fiona appeared from behind a mingling crowd. She hurried over to them with a glass of wine in her hand. Her face was flushed, and she was smiling. "Hey guys! You're finally here. These people are delightful!" she said, taking a sip of the dark red wine.

"Delightful is not the word I would have used," Charles muttered.

"Oh, stop being so negative. You should be happy!" Fiona said. "You're at a party with your boyfriend, and your mother wants to meet him. Did you ever think life would be like this?"

Charles hadn't thought about it like that. He *was* grateful to be here with Thomas. He was grateful that Thomas was alive, and that Thomas still loved him, and that he hadn't been kicked out yet. It probably wouldn't get much better than this. Charles had to enjoy it while it lasted. "No, I guess not."

"Cheers! Happy birthday!" Fiona said, raising her glass in the air as if to toast, but she was the only one with a drink.

"This is not a birthday party," Charles reminded her. Nausea crept up as he glanced around. He had a sick feeling about the purpose of this party.

His eyes landed on his mother and Rebecca chatting near the fountain. This was a perfect opportunity to introduce Thomas without Alfred around to ruin it. "Thomas, I know this is uncomfortable for you, but . . . are you willing to say hello to my mother now?" Charles asked.

"Yes, of course. Whatever you want," Thomas said.

"You should come too, Fiona. She will be happy to see you again," Charles said.

"Okay!" Fiona said a little too loudly.

They walked to the fountain together, sidling quietly into the conversation. "Hello, mother. Rebecca," Charles said cordially.

His mother's face lit up when she saw him, brightening more when she saw Thomas. "Oh, Thomas! It's so good to see you. I'm so happy you're here. And Fiona. Hello, dear."

Fiona raised her glass in greeting.

Thomas wore a forced smile. "Hello, Lucille," he said. Charles squeezed his hand.

Rebecca refused to look at Thomas, keeping her eyes fixed on the grass with the same sick look Charles had felt on his own face all evening.

"I'm so happy you found your way back to each other. I am very sorry I didn't help you when you needed it."

Thomas's uncomfortable smile remained. He shrugged.

"How is—" Charles's mother paused, glancing at Fiona briefly before continuing. "How is your mother?" she asked Thomas.

Thomas rubbed his neck and threw her a sideways look. "Do you know my mother?"

"Oh." Charles's mother laughed. "Hardly. We were acquaintances years ago. I doubt she remembers me."

Thomas's eyebrows rose. "You were?"

Charles's mother tucked a loose strand of hair behind her ear and smiled. "Yes. Do tell her I say hello if you get the chance."

"Sure," Thomas said. He exchanged a wary look with Charles. Charles shrugged. He also had no idea their mothers were ever friends.

"Lucille, I believe we should—" Alfred strolled up to the group but stopped when he spotted Thomas. His grim expression held firm. Charles let go of Thomas's hand and stepped away. Thomas whipped his head around to stare open-mouthed at him, and he immediately felt the familiar flood of guilt that his reaction at seeing his father was to distance himself from Thomas.

"Thomas Hambleton," Alfred said. "Aren't you supposed to be dead?"

Thomas forced his gaze away from Charles to frown at Alfred. "Yes, I guess I am."

Alfred narrowed his eyes. "You're not another shapeshifter trying to ruin my daughter's life, are you?"

"Not your daughter. Just your son," Thomas said.

Fiona gasped and covered her mouth.

Alfred clenched his fists and released them, stretching his

fingers out. The anger in his eyes calmed, and he looked away. "I don't have a son."

Charles looked at his feet. The warmth in his heart from just minutes ago had gone dead cold. He forced the storm in his mind to calm, clenching his jaw to fight the feeling.

"Alfred . . ." Charles's mother said softly, but Alfred shut her down with a burning scowl.

"As I was saying," Alfred continued, "it's time for the announcement. If you two would please join me," he said to Rebecca and his wife. His bored eyes fell on Charles. "I suppose you can come too if you want." He turned to walk away without waiting for a response.

Charles's mother placed a gentle hand on his shoulder and squeezed. "You're still part of this family, my love. Of course you should join us."

Charles nodded.

"And Thomas, you are welcome to join us too," his mother said.

Thomas had been scowling at something in the distance but brought his angry frown back to the conversation to address Charles's mother. "No thank you."

"I rather think you should, darling," Charles's mother said, throwing an uneasy look at Charles. "If Charles does."

Thomas crossed his arms and exhaled through his nose as he glared at a nearby hedge.

"Thomas, I'm sorry," Charles said quietly. "I—He caught me by surprise."

Thomas shrugged. "Go on. Go be a Southworth," he said, nodding toward the center platform Alfred had taken.

"Will you still be here when it's over?" Charles asked.

Thomas sighed and looked at him. "Yes, Charles. I'll still be here."

"Okay, good . . ." Charles took Thomas's hand, but Thomas

pulled away. "I'm sorry."

"Come on, Charles," his mother said softly, pulling him away from Thomas.

Thomas watched him leave with a flat stare. Fiona looked around at anything and everything else.

Charles hated himself. How did he fall so easily back into the behavior of a scared little boy the second his father saw him and Thomas together? Thomas had every right to be angry.

Charles followed his mother and Rebecca to the clearing at the front of the party where the guests had gathered for Alfred's announcement. Charles didn't know what it would be, nor did he care much. It would probably be something silly and inconsequential. Anything for a bit of attention.

Rebecca stood by her father's left side, their mother on Alfred's right. Charles stood disjointed from the trio, painfully aware that he did not belong up there.

"Excuse me, everyone," Alfred projected. "I would like to make an announcement."

Charles looked out at the crowd. Some he recognized, but most were strangers. The only face he cared about was Thomas, who watched from the back beside Fiona. Charles offered him a smile, but the best Thomas could give in return was a brief nod.

"First of all, I would like to take a moment to wish a happy birthday to Charles." Alfred gestured to Charles, who was startled by the introduction. All eyes were on him, but he did not smile at the well wishes. "Happy birthday, Charles."

The party was silent except for a single "Woo!" from Fiona at the back of the crowd. Charles appreciated it, even though she was obviously intoxicated.

"It has been a difficult year for us," Alfred continued, not wasting another moment on Charles, "with the scandal and the disappearances, but we have made a decision that we believe will benefit the well-being of our family and our industry in the long-term."

Charles had no idea what Alfred was about to say. He watched the announcement as though he were just another member of the audience.

"We have decided to name our daughter, Rebecca Southworth, as our heir." Alfred placed a proud hand on her shoulder. She smiled at him, then at the crowd. His mother tried to smile, but the announcement clearly pained her. "Rebecca will take over the family business when my wife and I are no longer capable. We firmly believe Rebecca has the intelligence, maturity, and education to run the operations of our fleet with a sound mind and a heart of integrity. We are extremely proud of the woman she is becoming, and we are happy to bestow this honor upon her." Alfred smiled at Rebecca.

To Charles's disgust and horror, Alfred smiled at him next. Charles looked away, keeping his expression calm. He would not let Alfred see his pain. Even if Rebecca and his mother had already known this would happen. Even if the date of this gods-forsaken party was not a coincidence.

"Congratulations Rebecca," his father finished.

The crowd applauded in celebration of Charles's disgraceful loss. He scanned the crowd in search of the only person who could make this better. It was obvious now why his mother asked Thomas to join them. Charles couldn't survive this without him.

He finally found Thomas's face in the crowd, and their eyes met. Thomas wasn't angry anymore. His eyes held something softer and pitying, but it didn't make Charles feel pitiful. It made him feel loved. Thomas clearly cared about him more than anyone else. Even though Thomas was angry, he did not want to see Charles get hurt.

Charles was furious with himself. Why would he *ever* let the opinion of someone who found pleasure in publicly humiliating him affect the way he treated his favorite person? He had to do something.

The answer came to him as clear as the cloudless sky. Alfred had made a mistake inviting Charles to a platform to embarrass him. On his birthday.

Charles wasn't the same person Alfred thought he knew. He wouldn't take Alfred's abuse anymore.

"Yes, congratulations, Rebecca!" Charles spoke loudly and clearly, approaching the center of the platform and smiling at his sister like the world hadn't just been ripped from his hands and dropped into hers. "I know you'll take great care of this family and protect us all from *scandals.*" He paused, looking at his father. "I personally think the best way to handle a difficult situation is simply to tell the truth, so allow me to clear up any confusion that any of you may have over my *embarrassing* incident." Charles met the eyes of as many guests as possible, making sure they were listening. "I lied about Thomas Hambleton. Alfred Southworth told me to lie about him, and I did, because I am my father's son. A *liar.* I was in love with Thomas, and I still am." Charles found Thomas in the crowd again. Thomas's eyes now held surprise instead of pity. "He's here right now, as a matter of fact," Charles said, gesturing to the back of the crowd. "Thomas, will you please join me up here?"

Thomas whispered something to Fiona, who nodded encouragingly. Thomas pushed his way through the crowd until he stood beside Charles and slid his hand into Charles's. Charles held on tight, knowing better than to let go. Thomas was more important than anything or anyone else.

He took Thomas's other hand. "Thomas," Charles said, "I love you more than I ever thought possible. I know it hasn't been easy between us, but good things don't come easy. You're the best thing that has ever happened to me."

Thomas smiled, and it was brighter than all of the stars in the sky. "I love you too, Charles." Gods, he was perfect.

Charles dug in his coat pocket and pulled out the simple diamond ring his mother had given him, lifting it for Thomas to see. The diamond reflected dark starlight as brilliant glittering white and flashes of rainbow, a beautiful sign that it was real.

Thomas's eyes widened as he scanned the crowd. "What are you doing?" he asked quietly.

Charles kissed the back of Thomas's left hand. "I want the whole world to know how much I love you."

Thomas's jaw dropped, and Charles got a sinking feeling that this wasn't what he wanted. This was a bad idea, and Thomas would not respond well. Maybe Thomas was uncomfortable doing this in front of so many strangers, where he couldn't reasonably reject Charles without feeling like he was adding to the humiliation.

Thomas looked at the crowd again. His eyes locked on something in the distance and widened fearfully. He shut his mouth and glanced near Fiona before returning his attention to the garden entrance. Charles followed his gaze to where two new guests had joined them.

Edmund and Catherine Hambleton stood just within the gate, watching them.

Edmund's eyes were fixed on Thomas, his expression as unreadable as Thomas's always was. Catherine watched with hateful, narrowed eyes.

Charles couldn't have asked for a better audience.

He squeezed the hand he still held and smiled at Thomas, bringing Thomas's attention back to him. The fear did not leave Thomas's eyes, but a little bit of the love returned.

"Thomas Hambleton," Charles said, "will you marry me?"

TINERA

Felix waited in the dining hall until dinner to see Finnlay.

Finnlay was excited when he finally arrived. "I can't believe you found it!" he said as he sat down. "You got the potion *and* the recipe just by befriending the guards?"

Felix laughed and nodded before telling Finnlay all the details he couldn't share in the letter.

Finnlay shook his head slowly with a big smile. "I am amazed by you, Felix. Your mother would be so proud."

His breath caught in his throat at the mention of his mother. He hoped she would have been. "Thanks, Finnlay. I am amazed by *you*. You were able to figure out the recipe with my fragmented memories. It would have been basically correct if you had just used my blood."

Finnlay cringed. "I'm sorry."

"No, I'm saying you're a genius. You did it with almost no resources," Felix said. "I am so impressed."

A warm smile bloomed on Finnlay's face. "I had *you*. And the beautiful world that grows around us. I was not without resources."

"I can't believe we've come this far. We can *escape*, Finnlay. Right now if we wanted to."

Finnlay's eyes scanned the room. "We could . . . But what if we stayed a little longer and tried to save everyone else too?"

Felix also looked around the room full of fellow magi. His heart ached at the thought of leaving them behind. "I don't think we can. Catherine left in the middle of temple service today. I've never seen her do that before."

Finnlay tore his gaze away from his hall mates to fix his wide-eyed stare on Felix. "Really? Why?"

"I think she got the news that Thomas is home. I don't know how long they were intending to keep that from the Southworths, but how much longer *can* they hide it? Especially considering Thomas and Charles's history. I know for certain that if Charles finds out, it's over. Our cloaking grid won't work anymore."

"Charles?" Finnlay asked. "Thomas's . . . ex-boyfriend? Why would it matter if he found out?"

Felix panicked as he realized he hadn't told Finnlay who Charles and Rebecca really were. He hadn't wanted to share much with Aella, but Finnlay could know.

"Yeah. Thomas's ex-boyfriend, Charles Southworth," Felix said.

Finnlay raked his fingers through his curly hair. "Wow, so the girl who turned you in was . . . also a Southworth?"

Felix winced. "Yeah . . ."

"So they're not really our allies?" Finnlay asked.

"Not really."

Finnlay sighed as his eyes ran over the mess in front of them. They hadn't bothered to tidy up since it was their own hidden space, but there were extra bowls, dried flower stems, notes to each other, and pieces of charcoal lying around. These things on their own would get them in trouble, but the potion and the recipe Felix had stolen were damning.

"That means Fiona is here too," Finnlay said.

"Yeah. You need to find her before the Hambletons do."

Finnlay looked up, desperation in his eyes. "We need to do this right now. We can come back for the others."

Felix nodded urgently. "We can come back," he agreed.

"Okay, so . . . I'll have to drink it since you don't have magic. When I do, I'll cast a concealing spell on us both. It'll work on you if you hold my hand and don't let go. Then we can sneak out," Finnlay said.

"How will we get out?"

"That's easy. I'll create stairs from the earth and then flatten them again once we're on the other side," Finnlay said.

"Or not," Felix said.

Finnlay shrugged and nodded. "Or not. But if they know we've escaped, they'll come looking for us. Hiding the stairs will give us a head start."

Felix rubbed his chin. "That's true. How long do you think it'll take before they notice we're gone?"

"Hmm . . . Well, they may have already noticed you're gone since you waited for me here," Finnlay said. "I don't know about my hall. Maybe by tomorrow morning?"

Tomorrow morning. It was weird to think that by tomorrow morning neither of them would be here. They would probably be in Brenton, eating normal food in normal quantities. Felix's eyes wandered through the room again.

Something was off.

People spoke to one another with their heads together, their hushed whispers spreading through the room, and almost everyone was looking at Felix and Finnlay.

Felix whipped around to check on their boundary and found it was slowly shriveling. He quickly faced forward again. "*Finnlay!*" he hissed.

Finnlay chewed on his bread ration. "What?" he asked, unaware.

"People can see us," Felix said, nodding toward the shrinking braided stem around them.

Finnlay froze. He eyed the enchantment on the floor before his eyes skipped around the room at every guard and prisoner, then stopped at the potion on the table.

"What do we do?" Felix asked in a panic, gathering his mother's potion recipe up and stuffing it in his pocket.

Finnlay decisively popped open the vial, poured the potion in his mouth, and threw his hand across the table toward Felix. "Take my hand," he said. Felix took it without hesitation. Taking a deep breath, Finnlay whispered, "*Obsceal.*" A tattoo on his forearm glowed while he gestured toward himself and Felix.

All at once, the room erupted into chaos. Guards shouted, "Where did they go?" Finnlay's spell had worked. Other residents scrambled to get to the table while patrolling guards fought to hold them back.

"This is only going to last a few minutes, and if you let go of me, you won't be concealed anymore," Finnlay said. "We need to run." He squeezed Felix's hand so tight it hurt, then he pulled Felix after him as they left their seats. They weaved between residents and guards to get to the door.

"There he is!"

"Get him!"

The guards shouted at them, but it seemed they could only see Felix. Felix was not a magus anymore, and they weren't at their magical table. Spells cast on another person were similar to the magic done on an enchantment. Enchantments didn't work within range of a magic suppressant, and neither did this.

Felix struggled to keep up with Finnlay, forcing his tired feet to keep carrying him through the crowded, chaotic hall. Residents and guards alike searched the room, but their eyes skipped right over Finnlay. Only a few spotted Felix. He didn't seem to be visible behind Finnlay.

"Get the door!" someone shouted. Before they could reach the exit, two guards positioned themselves in front of it.

Finnlay swore under his breath, still clinging to Felix's hand with a death grip.

"Try the kitchen," Felix said.

Finnlay nodded and veered left toward the unguarded kitchen entrance.

Felix and Finnlay slipped into the kitchen area, where a few tired residents worked over the massive pot of stew. They eyed Felix warily until one of them said, "What are you doing in here?"

"Can they see us?" Finnlay asked.

Felix pushed him toward the exit until they were safely outside. "I think they can see me," Felix said.

"Then we have to hurry." Finnlay ran, pulling Felix close behind him. Moments later, two guards burst from the side door and chased after them.

Finnlay ran faster, and Felix couldn't match his pace. He was tired, he couldn't get enough air, his legs were too heavy, and the guards were gaining on them. They only knew where to run because they could see Felix. If Felix didn't let go of Finnlay now, neither of them would escape, and Finnlay would lose his magic too. Felix couldn't bear to let that happen.

"Finnlay, I'm slowing you down," Felix said. He dug in his pocket for the potion recipe and slapped it into Finnlay's palm, holding him by the wrist.

Finnlay looked back. "What are you doing?!"

"Take this and go on without me," Felix said through heavy breaths.

"What?! No!" Finnlay said. He watched Felix with horror, still running toward the distant fence. It was so far away. "This is your mother's—"

Felix shook his head urgently, eyeing the guards behind them. "Just go. I'll distract the guards. Get the recipe far away from Catherine and save Fiona."

"No, we can both make it," Finnlay said as he looked back again, but his eyes widened when he saw it wasn't true. Felix was significantly hindering their progress, and the guards were close.

"Please don't waste this opportunity, Finnlay. I trust you,"

Felix said. Then he let go and ran in the other direction, leading the guards away from Finnlay.

It worked. The guards followed Felix, not even acknowledging Finnlay's presence. Felix couldn't see Finnlay now that they weren't making physical contact, and he could only hope that Finnlay was smart enough to reserve his magic for surviving alone in the woods instead of saving Felix from something he had already lost to.

Felix ran toward the Oleander hall. It didn't matter where he ran at this point. He just wanted to get the guards away from Finnlay.

As he ran past Oleander, he caught sight of Rose leaning against the wall. She pushed herself up when she spotted him, her eyebrows high. "Felix?!"

Felix stumbled over his feet, and it was enough for the guards to catch him. A bigger man tackled him to the ground and pinned him against the cool, damp earth. Felix was forced to look Rose in the eyes as she approached.

"What is this?" Rose asked. "What did he do?"

"He stole a potion and tried to escape," the big guard said, forcing Felix's arms behind his back.

"You stole a potion?" Rose asked, defeated. "When?"

Felix didn't answer. He truly did not want to get Rose in trouble.

Rose's shoulders slumped. "I'm disappointed in you, Felix."

As the other guards surrounded Felix, the bigger guard lifted him onto his feet and faced him in the direction of the main courtyard. "Nice try, Warren. You're never getting out of here."

On the other side of the camp, in the darkness between the tree trunks, Felix spotted a solid column of earth rise from the ground and then lower as if the earth had never been disturbed.

"I know," Felix said, and he finally felt at peace with it. All he wanted was to prevent Finnlay from meeting his same fate, and now Finnlay was free.

Felix didn't have to fight anymore.

SOUTHWORTH MANSION

Thomas looked into Charles's bright, worried hazel eyes. The question Charles just asked collided with the sight of his parents lurking at the back of the garden.

They were so close to Fiona.

Charles wanted to *marry* him?

Thomas blinked hard and looked at his parents again with a furrowed brow. His father watched with an expression that Thomas could only assume was disappointment. His mother caught his eye and smiled, but it was fake. It was always fake.

Fiona watched them from the crowd with a big, beautiful smile. A *real* one. She was only twenty feet away from danger, and she didn't even know it. He wanted to warn her, but that would only give her away.

"Thomas?" Charles's voice was laced with concern.

Thomas looked at Charles again, nearly forgetting about the proposal. The entire situation was too much. Thomas opened his mouth to answer, not sure what he would say. Did he want to marry Charles? Did Charles want to marry *him?* Or was Charles just trying to make his father angry? Would that be Thomas's intention if he said yes?

He had no real reason to say no. He loved Charles. He wanted to spend the rest of his life with Charles, even though he would outlive Charles by centuries. So why was he unsure?

"Yes." The word left his mouth before he could give it any more thought. "Charles Southworth, I will marry you."

Relief washed the concern from Charles's face, and he showed off a perfect smile that Thomas could kiss forever.

Yes, he made the right choice.

Charles slid the ring onto Thomas's finger and pulled him close. Thomas kissed him, and all his doubt melted away. There was no crowd. No parents. In that moment, it was just Charles and him.

Charles pulled away from the kiss, holding Thomas's face in his hands. Thomas smiled dreamily up at him.

"Thomas," Charles whispered.

"Charles," he purred back.

Charles turned to look at his family, and Thomas followed his gaze. Alfred's jaw was clenched, his fists trembling at his sides. Rebecca frowned at a nearby hedge with crossed arms. Lucille was the only one smiling. She nodded her approval with her hands clasped together.

Charles looked at Thomas again. "We should go."

"My parents are here," Thomas whispered.

"I know," Charles said, glancing at the gate. His eyes widened, and Thomas looked to find his parents walking toward them.

Charles took Thomas's hand and pulled him away from the center platform. The crowd watched as they snuck between a break in the hedges to the edge of the garden. Charles dragged Thomas through the unlit space between the iron fence and the hedge as they made their way to the back of the garden to avoid Thomas's parents.

"Wait," Thomas said, stopping Charles. "We can't leave Fiona here."

Charles nodded. He eyed their surroundings, then brought Thomas to the end of the hedge. He whispered, "Stay here," and then he disappeared into the crowd.

Thomas could hear Alfred thanking his guests for their time, directing their attention away from the proposal. A few moments later, Charles emerged through the hedge again, Fiona close behind.

"Congratulations!" she whispered, lifting her wine glass in the air and splashing some of its contents onto the grass below. "I'm so happy for you! You're getting married!"

"Yes, thank you," Thomas said, taking her glass and setting it on the ground. "Fiona, listen. My parents are here. We need to get you out of here."

Fiona's cheerful expression quickly faded. Her rosy cheeks paled, and she whipped her head back and forth down the length of the garden in search of the threat.

"I don't think Edmund and Alfred would pass up this opportunity to argue," Charles said. "They love being angry with each other. If they engage in conversation, it'll be pretty easy to sneak out."

Thomas approached the hedge's edge and peered around it. The majority of guests appeared mildly perturbed. In the other corner of the garden, his father was engaged in a fierce argument with Alfred. Charles was right. Lucille stood behind Alfred, staring at Thomas's mother, who watched back with a blank intensity Thomas had never seen before.

Thomas ducked out of view and returned to Charles and Fiona. "They're arguing. Let's run."

"*Thomas?!*" his father's voice called across the garden.

"Shit. Oh gods. Uh . . ." Thomas grabbed Fiona and Charles and pushed them toward the gate. "Run!"

Charles did not move. "I'm not leaving you."

Fiona looked toward the back of the garden. "I think I'll be on my way," she said. She gave one last departing wave and disappeared behind the hedge toward the exit.

Thomas's father appeared around the hedge and grabbed

him by the shoulders. He turned Thomas so they were face-to-face and held Thomas in place, looking him in the eyes. People had always said Thomas looked like his father, but he didn't see it. His father was taller and held himself with more dignity. The only similarity Thomas could discern was the eyes. He got his green eyes from his father and, apparently, their intimidating nature. People sometimes said Thomas looked angry, but never when he was actually angry.

"Oh thank Dei. You really are alive," his father said, looking him over a few times before he stopped and frowned, letting go of Thomas. "You're not a shapeshifter, are you?"

Thomas glared at him. "What does it matter? You can't tell the difference."

His father hesitated, a flicker of surprise passing through his green eyes. "Thomas . . . I'm so sorry you felt like you had to leave."

"I did have to leave," Thomas said. "Neither you nor Mother ever wanted me here. Letting Felix take my place was the closest you ever came to having the version of me that you wish I could be."

His father's expression darkened at the mention of Felix. "Felix was nothing like you."

"That's exactly my point," Thomas said. He felt himself losing his temper again and forced himself to take a breath.

The gentle pressure of a hand on his back made him flinch until he realized it was Charles. His temper immediately cooled, and he leaned against Charles for the support he desperately needed.

His father narrowed his eyes. "Charles."

Charles nodded once and slid his arm around Thomas's waist. "Mr. Hambleton. Nice to see you again."

"Thomas, you are *not* marrying him," his father said.

"Yes I am. I love him," Thomas said. He took Charles's hand and squeezed it tight.

"Did you forget what he did to you?" his father demanded. "He lied about you and got you kicked out of Blackwater! He's a selfish, scheming lowlife just like his father. You can do much better than him. Any other man in the world would be lucky to have you, but *he* does not deserve you."

Thomas was shocked into silence. His father didn't care he was gay? It was just . . . *Charles* he didn't like?

Before Thomas could ask, Alfred interrupted their conversation. "Edmund, Thomas. Get off my property and take Charles with you. I want *nothing* to do with this engagement."

"Charles is not welcome in our home," Edmund said.

"If Charles can't come with me, then I'm not coming either," Thomas said.

"Don't be ridiculous, Thomas. You have nowhere else to go," his father said.

Before Thomas could argue, Charles said, "Consider this, Mr. Hambleton. I know all the Southworth trade secrets, and I'll share them with you." He shrugged and looked away. "If you want them."

Thomas's father raised his eyebrows and examined Charles for a moment.

"Charles," Alfred said. "If you dare to share any of our secrets with the Hambletons, I'll—"

"You'll what?" Charles's tone was firm, but Thomas could hear the shaky fear beneath it. "You told me yourself that you don't have a son. If Edmund takes me in and I marry his son, I suppose I'll be a Hambleton. Whatever knowledge I have will belong to them."

Now Alfred was speechless; his face contorted with disbelief.

"We'll talk," Edmund said to Charles. "Let's go home."

Thomas could not believe Charles had talked his father into letting him come home with them. Of course, it was only because of matters of *business,* but it was still unbelievable. Charles was a clever negotiator.

Thomas's father headed for the exit without another word. Thomas took Charles's hand and followed him. Charles did not bother to look behind him as he walked away.

The silence between the three of them was tense as they made the short walk to the main garden gate. Thomas felt his father's eyes on him but did not acknowledge him.

"Thomas, I want to—" his father began, but Thomas cut him off with a scathing look.

His father let out a short laugh. "There's no doubt about it. You're my son."

"Did you ever think I wasn't? I wouldn't be surprised, considering how much you've lied to me," Thomas said.

His father fell silent again.

"Can I ask you something?" Thomas asked.

"You just did, but you can ask something else," his father said.

Thomas rolled his eyes. "What happened to Felix?"

His father looked straight ahead, his expression suddenly severe. "He got what he deserved. I don't think I need to say anything more."

"I think you need to say *a lot* more," Thomas argued. "That doesn't answer my question at all."

"You know what that means," his father said, looking him in the eyes.

"I want you to say it." Thomas refused to break eye contact.

His father hesitated, but their conversation was cut short when they stepped through the garden gate and onto the street. Thomas's mother was out here, and she was with Fiona. Lucille stood on the other side of Fiona, arguing with Thomas's mother.

Fiona's eyes were glazed over, and she stared at nothing. Like she was in a trance.

Thomas gasped and ran to Fiona, taking her by the hand to pull her away. "What are you doing?!" Thomas said. "Don't touch her!"

"Oh, Thomas! Darling, it's so good to see you!" his mother said, ignoring his demands and instead pulling him into a hug. "I was so worried about you." Thomas didn't let go of Fiona as his mother squeezed him and kissed both his cheeks. When she stepped away, Thomas took another step back.

"You don't mean that," he said, pulling Fiona closer. He tried to breathe through the tightness in his chest, but it wasn't helping. Fiona was in danger. He had no idea how to get her out of this, and she didn't seem consciously present to help herself.

He shook Fiona's arm. "Fiona," he said. "Are you all right?"

"I'm great," Fiona said with a distant smile, looking past him.

Thomas's heart beat hard. He looked to Charles for assistance, but Charles looked just as helpless.

"Catherine, please," Lucille begged. "Fiona is a bright young woman with her entire future ahead of her. You can't take that from her."

Thomas's mother eyed Lucille with disdain. After a moment, the harshness in her eyes eased and she quickly looked away. "This doesn't concern you, *Mrs. Southworth*."

"Catherine . . . I—"

"Charles!" Alfred yelled, stepping through the gate. Charles flinched and moved closer to Thomas, but it didn't stop Alfred from getting in Charles's personal space. Alfred had Charles's sleeve in his grasp as he watched Charles with malice. "I'll make you a deal. You can be part of this family, and I will give you back the inheritance. I will not bring *this* up, and we can pretend it never happened. All you have to do is promise that you'll never speak to Thomas again." Alfred stared at Charles for an uncomfortable moment. "But you have to make your decision right now."

Charles didn't answer right away. He opened his mouth like he was going to speak, but he didn't say anything.

Thomas felt the same sinking dread he had when Alfred caught them at Blackwater. This was all so terrifyingly familiar. He wanted to believe Charles would choose him this time, but he had believed that last time too.

Charles clearly didn't know what to choose. He would have answered by now if he did. Being a Southworth had always been important to him. Even when they arrived back in Brenton, he had tried to figure out the best way to convince his parents to let him back into the family and had chosen to pretend he was with Fiona to achieve it. He had already shown Thomas once that he would sacrifice their relationship for his family.

No. Not just once. *Twice.*

Thunder rumbled in the distance, and Thomas scanned the sky. Storm clouds lurked on the edge of the horizon. He took a deep breath, but it didn't calm him. It felt more like he was hyperventilating than gaining control over his tempestuous feelings. As the clouds came closer, he rapidly lost control. His magic quickened through his body, tingling on his skin. He couldn't keep it back.

"Fiona, help me," Thomas pleaded.

Thomas's mother stared at him like she was seeing a ghost. She had clearly done magic on Fiona, which meant she was still a magus herself. She could probably feel his magic. His inability to control it.

Which was *her* fault.

Thomas took deep breaths and looked to Charles again, hoping to find refuge in him as he had for the last two weeks, but Charles was watching Thomas with tears in his eyes. The comfort was gone. Charles was going to leave him, and Fiona wasn't here to save him.

Thomas was on his own.

"Fiona, snap out of it," he pleaded in a wavering voice. "You don't want to go with her."

"I do," Fiona said dreamily. "I want to find Finnlay."

"No, you don't. We'll find him another way. Please!" Thomas said as much to Fiona as to his mother. A tear fell down his cheek at the same time that cold droplets of water hit his face.

It was raining.

"No!" he pleaded. Now he didn't know who he was talking to. The sky? Himself? Mariana? *Dei?*

All at once, the tidal wave of control overtook him. He was trapped underwater in his own skin. He couldn't move, but he was moving. Someone else was moving for him.

It's time, Thomas, Mariana said inside his head.

No! Please, Mariana! Give me five more minutes! Thomas begged.

We don't have five minutes. We're out of time. It's raining, and I told you what would happen next time you lost control. You're ready to fight Caldwell, and you're avoiding it. If you don't do it now, I will die.

Fiona is going to get sent away! Thomas said.

She said herself that she's fine with it.

That wasn't her!

Mariana walked Thomas toward Charles. Thomas watched it all happen outside of his control. Mariana twisted the diamond band off Thomas's finger and offered the ring to Charles. *I'll make this easy for you,* she said.

A tear spilled down Charles's cheek as he watched Thomas, and Thomas realized with horror that Mariana hadn't been speaking only to Thomas. She spoke the words aloud to Charles too.

No! Thomas begged. *Don't do this, Mariana!*

If he decides to be with you, he'll find you. It's better that he's not here for this.

Thomas wanted to scream. Even if Mariana was right, he didn't want to decide for Charles. If he made it easy for Charles to leave him, Charles would be more willing to let it happen than if he had to make the decision himself.

Charles reached for the ring, and Thomas's heart shattered.

Chapter Twenty-Seven

Brenton

Mariana wouldn't let Thomas look behind him as they walked away. He wanted to know what was happening. He needed to know Fiona was okay. He needed to see Charles follow him. But no matter how much he pleaded, Mariana would not budge.

The low light of oceanfront streetlamps offered little guidance as he stepped into the pressing darkness of the harbor. Ships sloshed in the gentle wake of the bay. Darkness lay heavy over the city, hiding in the cracks and obscuring everything while the haunted corpse of Mariana lurked on the horizon. The sky and the sea met somewhere beyond the reaches of his vision at a pitch-black rendezvous.

The sailors of the harbor were either sleeping or drinking, leaving the rickety docks to creak against the high waves in privacy. Not even the taverns lining the shorefront street were as lively as usual. Their light didn't seem to reach as far, and the muted sound of sailors shouting and singing was barely audible.

The muffled merrymaking felt so far from him. It was part of a world he couldn't belong to anymore.

Thomas approached the docks, stopping before he reached the wooden platforms that extended into the sea. Reaching into his pocket, he pulled out the hilt of the sword Mariana had gifted him.

Mariana swirled out of the diamond hanging from Thomas's neck and stood tall beside him with her arms crossed. "Look at what she's done to me," she muttered.

Thomas staggered forward, gasping as he regained control of his body. "Mariana—why?!"

"Don't argue with me, Thomas. You're my servant. This is your priority forever," Mariana said somberly. "I'm sorry it had to be this way, but everything you walked away from is fixable. If I die, I will not come back."

As angry as he was, she was right. He had agreed to do everything she asked of him for eternity, and he couldn't claim she hadn't warned him.

Thomas swallowed hard, suddenly very aware that the forces he was dealing with were much larger than anything he could comprehend. Tetra was darkness. She was everything, and she wanted more. Who was he to stop her? He was barely a man.

"Well, well, well . . ." a soft low voice purred from the shadows. A man's silhouette stepped out of the darkness hiding the docks, twirling a sword. "Hello, Hambleton."

The hair on Thomas's arms and neck rose at the familiar voice, and he clutched the hilt of his sword tight. "Caldwell," Thomas said.

Caldwell laughed and stepped into view. The darkness seemed to ease away from him, allowing Thomas to see the sinister smile corrupting his face. He was younger now. Despite what he had said at the Pantheon, Caldwell clearly opted for the age reduction.

"You look, um . . . *young,*" Thomas said.

"Likewise," Caldwell sneered. He ran his fingers through his jet-black hair, which fell over his forehead again.

He wondered if Tetra made Caldwell change his age to mess with Thomas. He and Tetra had the same taste in men, as she had kindly pointed out. But Thomas did not care for Caldwell.

"Where is Tetra?" Mariana demanded.

Caldwell looked her up and down with a sneer. "I thought you were already dead. I was going to kill Thomas just for the fun of it, because Tetra doesn't want him serving her. And neither do I."

"Where is Tetra?" Mariana asked again.

Caldwell lowered his eyebrows. "She's around."

A large black wave exploded up from beneath the docks, drenching the ground around them in inky sea water. When the water settled, a wet and unpleasantly familiar voice dragged itself through the dark air. "*Thomas . . .*" The wobbly shape of Mariana rose behind Caldwell. The darkness around her pressed in so closely that Thomas almost couldn't see her. Her shoulders were hunched, and she held her outstretched claws at her side as if preparing to use them. A wide smile waited on her face beneath a pair of dead, dark eyes.

This wasn't Mariana. This was a monster wearing her watery skin.

Thomas turned to look at the Mariana by his side to make sure she was still with him. She watched her corpse drag itself toward them with complete composure.

"Tetra," Mariana said.

"I'm not Tetra," the wobbly, dripping corpse said. "I'm *you.*" It was Tetra's cold intonation in Mariana's voice. Tetra strained the elegant ripple of Mariana's friendly tone into a darker persona. Her smile sharpened, and her eyes held a look of detached sanity. What was left of Mariana had lost the battle.

"Stop playing games, Tetra," the real Mariana said. "It's time. I challenge you to a duel."

Tetra threw her head back and cackled, her watery edges splashing out of her as she laughed into the pitch-black sky. She brought her gaze back down and grinned. "*You?* You're just a drop of water. You're barely even a god."

"I'm still a god, and I still have my servant," Mariana said.

Tetra's horrible smile landed on Thomas, and she scrutinized him slowly. "You won't make it through the night, Thomas Hambleton." Her eyes flicked back to Mariana. "What are the stakes?"

"If I win the duel, you have to get out of my body, the ocean, and leave me alone. Forever. That includes all of the mermaids and sirens inside and outside of the ocean. Take your siren sickness out of the mermaids and stop infecting them forever," Mariana said. Her words were specific enough that Tetra couldn't twist them.

"Very well," Tetra growled. She walked toward Thomas and slapped a cold, wet hand on his chest. Tetra couldn't hurt Thomas, but he wasn't sure how much of Mariana was left in there or if that affected his protection at all. He stayed still as she curled her fingers around the chain and ripped it off Thomas's neck with a painful tug.

"What are you doing?" Mariana demanded. "You can't—"

With one easy motion, Tetra threw the necklace into the black sea, and Mariana vanished from beside Thomas.

"Wh—That's not fair! You can't do that!" Thomas yelled.

Tetra shrugged, her horrible smile held up by the plague of twisted darkness on Mariana's face. "If you win, you'll get it back. If you lose, it won't matter."

Thomas stepped away from her. She was right. He didn't need Mariana here for this, but her presence was comforting. Now he was alone with Caldwell and Tetra and the pressing darkness.

Tetra's eyes darted over to her servant, who had been watching everything with a sick smile. "Alastair," Tetra said.

Caldwell looked at Tetra.

"Kill him," she said.

Caldwell drew his sword. His smile did not falter.

Thomas got into the proper fighting stance, struggling not to think about the person who taught him how to fight.

He took a deep breath. This was it. Thomas would either die tonight or kill again. Did he have it in him to kill Caldwell a second time? Even if it was for the fate of the world? He could barely face the memory.

If Thomas died tonight, the world would fall to darkness.

If Thomas killed tonight, the world would be saved.

It was all up to him.

Thomas glanced at Tetra, only to realize how foolish he had been to look away from his opponent when Caldwell took the opportunity to strike.

Thomas lifted his sword and narrowly blocked the first attack. He was off to a terrible start, losing ground as Caldwell's offense strengthened fast.

"Have you been training?" Caldwell asked in a steady voice.

"I have," Thomas answered only when he felt he had the capacity to do so.

Caldwell barked a laugh. "That's embarrassing. You haven't gotten any better," he said, striking harder than before.

Thomas focused on his form, choosing to ignore the evil man trying to take his life and destroy the world.

Caldwell seemed to be enjoying himself, while Thomas struggled to block every attack, feeling like he would lose his footing any second.

Their duel continued in a steady pattern of defense and offense, until Thomas became suspicious that Caldwell was toying with him.

The fight suddenly stopped when Caldwell stepped back. The change in pace surprised Thomas so much that he did not take the offensive.

"Enough of this. I'm bored," Caldwell said with a flat expression. "It's been nice knowing you, Hambleton. Very entertaining, if nothing else."

Caldwell raised his sword and lunged for Thomas. Thomas blocked just in time, and Caldwell's face twisted with anger. He swung again, and Thomas, miraculously, blocked the attack again. Caldwell was hitting much harder. It was clear he hadn't been trying before, and now he was taking the battle seriously.

But Thomas held his ground. Maybe he had a chance.

Caldwell gritted his teeth and quickened his attacks. Thomas kept his strength and agility, but Caldwell's offense became so powerful that Thomas started losing ground. Caldwell continued striking until Thomas stepped back right into an overturned barrel.

Thomas lost his balance, tripping backward over the barrel. Before he could catch his momentum to pick himself up, Caldwell grabbed him and threw him to the ground. Thomas's sword clattered away, out of reach.

Caldwell wasted no time, not even allowing Thomas a moment to breathe before driving his sword into Thomas's shoulder. The blade cut through his skin as hot as fire. Thomas gritted his teeth and tried not to cry out, but the pain was intense. Caldwell watched with a sadistic smile, knowing Thomas could not get out of this.

But he had to. The world would suffer if he died.

Thomas couldn't move. He was pinned beneath the sword like an animal ready for dissection. Caldwell took the hilt in both hands and twisted it, his smile growing.

Thomas had only experienced pain like this when Tetra killed him, but that was spread over his entire body. This pain was acute and intense, and Thomas was barely aware he was crying and pleading for it to stop.

Miraculously, Caldwell did stop. Thomas took ragged breaths as he tried to mentally recover from the pain, only just noticing it had started raining again. "Why are you doing this?" he coughed. "Have mercy."

"But this is just getting interesting. Why would I stop now?" Caldwell asked.

Caldwell wanted to see him suffer. This was not going to be an easy death. It would take a long time, and it would hurt.

Thomas did the only thing he could think to do and tried to grab the blade to remove it from his shoulder.

Caldwell twisted the sword again, and nothing existed but horrible, blinding pain.

"Are you stupid?" Caldwell asked. "You think you can pull the blade out of your shoulder?" He threw his head back and laughed, sounding dangerously similar to his god.

Thomas took heavy, shuddering breaths. "Please stop," he begged.

"Fine," Caldwell said, removing his sword from Thomas's shoulder. Crimson blood glistened against the dark steel of the blade, but Thomas felt little relief as the sword sliced its way out.

Caldwell's mercy only lasted a moment. He lifted his foot and stepped on the shoulder wound, sinking his heavy foot deep into it as Thomas cried out.

Caldwell eased up enough to let the pain plateau so Thomas could hear him say, "You've had it too good for too long, Hambleton."

Thomas had no words. He tried to push Caldwell's foot away, but Caldwell stepped harder again. Thomas clenched his jaw and groaned through his teeth, trying to suppress his cries.

He felt so pathetic and weak. How did he ever think he could win this battle? He couldn't do anything. His sword had fallen when Caldwell tripped him, and he was pinned to the ground. This was the end.

He had failed everyone. He was going to lose. There was no way out of this duel but to die. His parents would continue taking magic from innocent people, and Tetra would have complete control of the world.

Caldwell placed the tip of his sword at the base of Thomas's throat. "Say goodbye, Hambleton."

But before Thomas could say goodbye, the pain eased, and Caldwell's sword toppled over as he backed away. Through blurry tears, Thomas saw a familiar dark silhouette.

Charles.

Charles grabbed Caldwell by the front of his shirt and punched him in the face with enough force to send him stumbling backward. He ducked down to swipe Thomas's crystal sword off the ground and faced Caldwell again.

Caldwell held his jaw and snarled, "Stay out of this, *Southworth*. This is between me and Hambleton."

"I'll fucking kill you!" Charles yelled. His hair fell messy over his forehead and tears streamed down his face. He looked deranged.

Caldwell gazed seriously at Charles briefly before he lunged for his sword. Thomas reached for it, clutching the hilt clumsily and rolling over the weapon to keep it out of reach.

Charles intercepted Caldwell with a furious swing of his blade, barely missing Caldwell's hand. Caldwell stepped back, watching Charles with alarm.

"What's wrong?!" Charles asked. "Didn't think you would lose?" His voice shook with anger.

"This—this is against the rules!" Caldwell said, looking around for Tetra. "You can't fight me! You're not a servant!"

"I'm not going to fight you," Charles said. *"I'm going to kill you."*

With a perfect swordsman's stance, Charles slashed the blade diagonally across Caldwell's chest, slicing him open to an immediate downpour of blood. He kicked Caldwell to the ground.

Caldwell rolled toward the pier, leaving a dark trail of blood in his path. Charles watched a few moments to make sure he didn't get up. Caldwell remained a lifeless pile on the ground.

Charles fell to his knees beside Thomas and gently took Thomas's face in his hand. "Thomas," he said shakily. "Gods, look at you. Oh, Dei. Are you okay?"

Thomas nodded. "I'm okay," he grunted.

Charles wiped Thomas's tears away while his own continued running down his face. "Do I need to find help? A doctor? An apothecary?" he asked as he frantically looked Thomas over.

Thomas shook his head. "It'll heal when Caldwell dies."

Charles nodded urgently and continued looking at the wound like he hadn't heard Thomas's response.

"You saved my life," Thomas said. "Thank you."

Charles attempted a smile, forcing himself to look at Thomas's face instead of his profusely bleeding body. "It's about time, isn't it?"

Thomas gave a ragged laugh, but the stinging pain in his shoulder stopped him. "I didn't think you would follow me . . ."

Charles kissed Thomas's forehead and pulled him into a hug. "I made that mistake once already, and it was the worst mistake of my life. I'm never letting you go again."

Thomas lifted his good arm to hug Charles back, wincing against the pain in his shoulder. "I'm sorry about your inheritance," he said.

Charles held him close. "You're worth it all."

Charles gently lowered Thomas down again. Thomas tried to prop himself up on his right arm. His shoulder injury limited his movement, and he fell against Charles. "Sorry," Thomas said, cringing through the blinding pain.

"You're okay," Charles said, placing his arm around Thomas to hold him as he sat up.

"Why isn't it healing? Caldwell is dead, isn't he?" Thomas asked. He could barely keep his eyes open from the pain, but he had to keep his wits about him. Something wasn't right. He forced his eyes open and looked into the darkness. The sea was as dark and black as before. If Thomas had truly won the duel, it would have lightened by now.

"If he's not dead yet, he will be soon," Charles said. "Don't worry. Everything is going to be o—"

Charles didn't finish his sentence. He was interrupted by a steel blade through his body. His eyes widened as he looked down at the bloody metal jutting from the center of his torso. He winced when it retracted and groaned as he toppled over.

"Charles!" Thomas shouted. Caldwell had used the darkness to sneak up on them. Panic took over, and Thomas felt no pain as he clutched Caldwell's sword and stood up. Caldwell stood over Charles and laughed a ragged, bloody laugh, igniting a fury in Thomas fiercer than anything he'd ever felt.

Damn the pain. Caldwell would pay for this.

Holding the unfamiliar weight of Caldwell's sword in his hand, Thomas faced him in a proper stance. Hot blood dripped down his arm.

Caldwell's upper body was drenched with blood so dark it looked black. He grinned maniacally at Thomas. "You don't really think you'll win, do you? You're *nothing*. Your boyfriend is nothing. Or should I say, he *was* nothing."

Thomas swung his sword furiously and without thinking, letting his injured arm dangle uselessly at his other side. The pain in his shoulder did not compare to the pain of losing

Charles. Caldwell blocked his attack and laughed, kindling the angry fire burning in Thomas's heart. Thomas continued swinging but made little progress.

He stepped back, careful not to run into anything this time. His foot landed on something hard, and Thomas realized he was standing on his own sword.

If he had both swords, what was Caldwell using?

The sword in Caldwell's hands was a basic steel cutlass. He must have found it somewhere. Wherever it came from, it wasn't a servant's sword.

Thomas ducked down to pick up his own sword. He retracted the crystal blade and dropped the hilt into his coat pocket. He wouldn't take any chances.

Caldwell was a strong fighter, but Thomas was smarter. He tried to recall the memory he had worked so hard to forget. How had he killed Caldwell last time?

Oh. Right.

Magic.

Thomas had been afraid to use his magic since then. He didn't know how to. He was useless when it came to magic, but he had to figure it out. Caldwell was much better with a sword, and this was the only advantage Thomas had.

Thomas raised his hand and focused his intention on the water in Caldwell's body. Caldwell rattled a bloody laugh, but he still stepped toward Thomas.

"Nice try," Caldwell said, taking another step closer. Thomas braced himself. "Magic won't save you this time. It has to be a sword, but you're *terrible* with a sword."

A sword? Not just any sword. A servant's sword. Did Caldwell not know that? Thomas recalled him looking bored while Dei explained the rules. He clearly hadn't been listening.

Thomas didn't wait for Caldwell to reach him. He couldn't

waste any time. Charles was dying—or possibly, gods forbid, dead—and Thomas had to get this duel over with quickly. He took the offensive and struck at Caldwell. Caldwell blocked easily, looking bored as he did. Thomas gritted his teeth and tried again.

Caldwell was too good. Thomas would never get around their difference in skill, and he was running out of time. His shoulder throbbed with each painful beat of his heart, and his strength was dwindling. He couldn't win. He had to come up with a strategy Caldwell wouldn't expect.

So Thomas let his guard down. With his next strike, Caldwell drove the sword directly into his heart.

Thomas's heart stuttered against his lungs, and he coughed. He gasped for air and waited, until finally, Caldwell withdrew his sword.

Thomas continued coughing and staggered backward. His injured heart beat erratically for a few seconds but quickly evened itself out. He fell to his knees and clutched the center of his bloody chest, which was no longer bleeding. The wound had healed. He gave a few more pathetic coughs for show.

Caldwell scoffed. "You really thought you had a chance, didn't you?" he asked. "Say hello to Southworth in the afterlife."

Thomas gripped the hilt of his sword in his right hand, preparing for the surge of pain about to shock his left shoulder. He knew what he had to do. As much as he didn't want to, it had to happen. Caldwell had let his guard down, and the moment was here. It had to be now. He could not give into his fear.

Thomas raised his left arm and focused his intention on the water in Caldwell's body once again, but this time he spread his intention through Caldwell's limbs.

"What are you—Why aren't you dying?!" he asked. Caldwell's panic encouraged Thomas to keep going.

Thomas stood, wincing against the pain of holding his arm up. It was just pain. It would go away as soon as he won this duel, which was moments away. He pushed with his magic as hard as he could, shoving Caldwell to the ground.

Caldwell tumbled onto his back. Before he could regain his bearings, Thomas pinned him with his foot against the bloody gash across Caldwell's chest, just as Caldwell had done to him.

Caldwell watched with wide eyes from beneath Thomas's boot. He lurched forward in an attempt to get upright but grimaced against the pain of Thomas's foot sinking into his fresh wound.

Thomas bounced the weight of Caldwell's sword in his hand. "You can't kill me with a regular sword. You should know that," he said. "I suppose you weren't cut out for this after all." He placed the edge of the sword against Caldwell's neck.

Caldwell placed his hands in a position of surrender by his head. His eyes widened. "No! We can call off the duel. You win! I surrender. I swear, I won't hurt you! Show mercy!"

Thomas closed his eyes and slashed the blade across Caldwell's throat. It was the most merciful thing he could think to do.

The throbbing in his shoulder immediately eased to a dull sting, then to a tingle. The dark blade in Thomas's hand vanished. Thomas turned away from Caldwell without opening his eyes. He didn't want to see what he had done.

When he finally opened his eyes, the world had lightened. Gentle rain washed away the blood in the grass. Charles lay crumpled beside the barrel that had almost caused Thomas's demise. He wasn't moving. His skin was stark white against the dark shadows of the night.

Thomas ran to Charles, dropping down beside him. "Charles," Thomas said, gently squeezing his shoulder. No response. "Charles, wake up," Thomas cried, shaking Charles. Still no answer.

Thomas placed his ear against Charles's chest. He wasn't breathing. There was no heartbeat.

Charles was dead.

CHAPTER TWENTY-EIGHT

"Mariana!" Thomas screamed. He slid his hands under Charles's body and lifted him, frantically searching the beachfront.

Mariana wasn't responding, and he needed help. Where could he go? Maybe the people in the tavern could help.

As he looked toward the tavern, its door exploded open and two sailors tumbled to the ground, pummeling one another. They would obviously be no help.

He turned to face the ocean again and flinched when Mariana met him with a big smile. She was alive again and as bright as before. "Thomas! You did it!"

"Mariana, help! Charles is dead! Bring him back!"

Mariana's smile fell as she inspected Charles's pale corpse in Thomas's arms. She placed a glistening watery hand on Charles's cheek. "He's not dead," Mariana said. "But he's close."

Thomas let out a cry of relief, but it was short-lived. If he didn't hurry, Charles would not survive the night. "Save him," he begged. "Please, Mariana!"

Mariana shook her head. "I'm so sorry, Thomas. There is nothing I can do."

"I just saved your life!" Thomas yelled. Warm tears fell down his face. "I'm begging you!"

"It won't do you any good to argue with me. You better find a doctor or a witch," Mariana said.

"Yes, you better hurry," another cold, dead voice said from behind him. Thomas whipped his head around to find Tetra watching him with a hateful sneer. "I'll be seconds behind you, Thomas. You took someone from me, and I'll be there the moment he's gone. You'll *never* get him back."

"I don't have time for this!" Thomas said, running from the pier as fast as his legs would carry him. He had to find someone. Anyone.

He briefly considered bringing Charles back to the Southworth house, but he decided against it. Alfred would happily watch Charles die.

He didn't trust his own parents to help.

Where else could he go? Most places would be closed at this hour. Everyone was asleep, except the fighting sailors.

There were other taverns full of people. There had to be *someone* in one of these places that could help.

Thomas ran to the shorefront inns and shoved his way into the first tavern. It was bright and loud and full of cheerful drunk people. The room was stiflingly hot compared to the cool night air outside, and the smell of alcohol was strong.

The room quieted as Thomas carried Charles toward the bar. He laid Charles on the bar top and waved to get the barkeeper's attention.

The big, bearded man scowled first at Thomas, then at

Charles, then he stomped over. "What d'you think you're doing?" he grumbled.

"I need help," Thomas pleaded. "My—my friend needs a healer. Please, someone help me. Anyone."

"Why in the world would you come *here* for a healer?" the barkeep asked.

"Please!" Thomas begged.

The barkeeper shook his head and looked out at the crowd of drunk sailors. Some had stopped their noisy shenanigans to watch the spectacle. Most carried on as if a bloody almost-corpse on the bar was normal. Maybe it was.

"AY!" the barkeeper barked. The room quieted down. Most heads turned to look. "Anyone in here a healer? This kid needs help." He thrust his thumb in Thomas's direction.

A few patrons laughed and returned to their drinks or cards. Most stared on in quiet disbelief. Thomas wiped his face, smearing Charles's blood across his cheek. This was stupid. Why did he think anyone at a tavern, of all places, would help him? Charles would bleed out and die here because Thomas made a bad decision in a time of urgency.

Thomas turned to Charles's unconscious form spread across the bar. He took Charles's face in his hand. "I'm so sorry, Charles," he whispered. He rested his head against Charles's chest and cried.

Charles had been right. This was the worst feeling in the world. Charles was going to die, and it was all his fault.

"I can help you."

Thomas jolted and turned to face the new voice. A young man around his age waited behind him, watching patiently. His wavy ginger hair fell around his pale, freckled face. His eyes were dark brown and very familiar, but Thomas didn't have the mental space to figure out why.

"You can?!" Thomas asked desperately. "Please, I'll do anything. Please!"

The man opened his mouth to speak but quickly shut it. His face paled and his eyebrows rose above his wide eyes. "Wait a second, I know who you are. I'm sorry. I—" His eyes landed on Charles briefly before returning to Thomas with a pained look. "I —" He was going to back out, but he couldn't say it.

"Please," Thomas begged, smearing more blood across his face as he wiped his tears away. This person knew who he was, and he was going to let Charles die because of it. Thomas had spent so long running from his name. Maybe it was time to lean into it. "I'll compensate you. You know I can. I'll give you as much as you ask for, and I won't say of word of this to anyone. I swear on my life. Please, *please,* help him."

The man seemed uncertain, but after another look at Charles's almost-corpse, he nodded. "Can you bring him upstairs?" he asked, pointing to the narrow staircase behind them.

"Yes!" Thomas said, sliding his arms under Charles again and carefully lifting him from the dirty bar top. The barkeeper grabbed a wet rag and swabbed the bloody wooden surface while glaring at Thomas, but Thomas didn't care.

Thomas followed the stranger up to the narrow room of beds, and the man pointed at one near the end. "Put him here," he said. "What happened?"

Thomas set Charles on the bed gently. "We got into a fight."

"*You* did this to him?"

"Me?! No!" Thomas said.

"Right. Of course not. Sorry," the man said, shaking his head.

Thomas watched as he got to work on Charles, swiftly unbuttoning his waistcoat. "Are you a witch?" Thomas asked quietly. "I'm a magus too."

The man's eyebrows bounced up. "Really?" he asked. "I suppose that's not surprising, since your mother is a witch."

Thomas reeled back. "You know my mother?" He knew his mother was a magus, but he had no idea she was a witch. After what she did to Fiona, he should have known.

The man watched him for a moment. "Um . . . Can you help me get him out of his clothes?" he asked as he began pulling Charles's coat off his shoulders.

Thomas nodded and lifted Charles so he could get the coat off completely. "How do you know my mother is a witch?" he tried again.

The man hesitated as he unbuttoned Charles's shirt. "I, um . . . I guess I don't." He examined the wound on Charles's chest and closed his eyes. He held one hand over Charles and muttered, "*Exectify.*" A tattoo on his upper arm glowed white. Just like Fiona, Thomas hadn't noticed the tattoos.

Just like Fiona.

Thomas suddenly realized why the stranger looked so familiar.

"Are—are you—Is your name Finnlay?" Thomas stammered.

Finnlay's eyes opened and his tattoo stopped glowing. He stared wide-eyed at Thomas. "Yes. How—" He shook his head and furrowed his brow, looking down at Charles and back up at Thomas. "I'm very sorry, Thomas. I don't know if I can help him. He's almost gone."

Thomas's heart beat frantically. "Please, Finnlay. I'm begging you. Is there *anything* you can do? Anything at all? I know you know as much about magic as Fiona does. There has to be something."

Finnlay gawked at him. "Well—um . . ." He shook his head again. "My questions will have to wait. There is still one option, but it's incredibly dangerous. I don't know how much you know about magic, Mr. Hambleton, but it's all about the exchange of energy. In order to keep him alive, it would require giving him the same amount of life he's already lost. I don't know where we could get that without bringing someone else to death's door."

Thomas gasped. "Use me. I'll give him my life."

"What? I—no! I'm not going to kill you to save him!" Finnlay said.

Thomas shook his head. "I won't die. I'm immortal."

Finnlay gave a laugh of disbelief, but his face fell quickly back into shock. "What?"

"Just trust me. We can't waste any more time. What do you need from me?"

Finnlay gaped at him.

"Finnlay!" Thomas said.

"Prove to me you're immortal and I'll do it," Finnlay said. "Otherwise, I'm not going to risk killing you."

"Who cares? I'm just a Hambleton. Aren't I your worst enemy?"

"You're a human being," Finnlay said softly.

As refreshing as it was to hear, the timing was terrible. Thomas sighed and pulled off his own coat, pointing to the ratty, blood-soaked holes in his shirt from his duel with Caldwell. "Look here," he said, pulling open both holes. "I was stabbed twice earlier tonight. Do you see all this blood?" Thomas pulled his shirt over his head and threw it to the floor. He rubbed the spots on his chest where he had been stabbed. A splotchy ring of dark dried blood circled where both wounds had been, leaving a spot of clean skin where the blade had entered his body. "It's completely healed now."

Finnlay's eyes were wide as he watched. When Thomas finished speaking, Finnlay nodded thoughtfully, maintaining his shocked expression. "In that case, we need to hurry. This spell doesn't work on dead people. If he dies, he dies."

"*Yes,* you better hurry . . ." A cold voice spread through the room like a gust of winter wind. The tall, shadowy shape of Tetra loomed over Charles, watching Thomas with her violent smile. "Your time is almost up." She crouched beside Charles and slid her dark claws up his face. "I may as well take his soul now."

Thomas gaped at her, his heart beating so fast he thought he would pass out. He ignored Tetra, turning to Finnlay instead. "What can I do?" he asked quickly.

"Go find me some ink or something similar for me to draw on your skin. I'll get the water," Finnlay said, standing and crossing the room toward the communal bathroom as he spoke.

Thomas jumped up and frantically searched the belongings of the sailors who were downstairs drinking. Someone was bound to have ink. It only took searching three beds before he came across a half-empty bottle of dark red ink. By the time he found it, Finnlay was already wiping the blood off Charles's chest with a damp cloth across from Tetra, who kept her eyes fixed to Charles, only looking up to smile evilly at Thomas.

"I found ink," Thomas said, lifting the glass jar with trembling hands. Heavy rain battered the windows behind them.

Finnlay looked up as he threw the bloody rag into a bucket of clean water. He reached for the bottle of ink. "Great! Now, wash the blood off your chest and your back if you can, while I draw the sigils on, uh . . ." He squinted at Charles as if trying to remember the name he had never learned.

Thomas nodded and reached for the rag. The water in the bucket was pink with Charles's blood. Thomas tried not to think about it as he hurried to scrub the dried blood from his skin. He distracted himself by watching Finnlay. "His name is Charles," Thomas said.

"Charles . . ." Finnlay repeated as he worked kneeling beside Charles. He dipped his index finger into the bottle of ink and drew a line across Charles's clavicle from his right shoulder to the left, then he drew two more lines down his torso, creating a large triangle. He began filling in the triangle with circular marks and lines that probably had meaning Thomas would never understand, carefully tracing lines around Charles's still-bleeding wound. Tetra did not acknowledge Finnlay, keeping her eyes on Charles, watching for the moment she could take his life.

Thomas tossed the rag back into the bucket as Finnlay finished his drawing. Finnlay stood and approached Thomas with the bottle of ink in hand. "I need to do the same to you. May I—"

"Yes. Do whatever you have to do. Quickly, please." Thomas could hear the tremble in his own voice.

Finnlay gave a curt nod and began drawing a line on Thomas, but the moment he made contact with Thomas's skin, he pulled his hand away. "Whoa."

"What? What's the matter?" Thomas asked urgently.

Finnlay shook his head and resumed tracing the same pattern across Thomas's chest with the dark ink. He worked fast, but it did not feel fast enough. "Do you know how much magic you have coming out of you?" Finnlay asked.

"Yes," Thomas said glumly.

Finnlay looked up at him warily before getting back to work. "Turn around."

Thomas did as he was told. Finnlay connected the drawing on his chest by a line around his waist and drew more symbols on his back. Thomas watched Charles while Finnlay's finger moved swiftly across his skin. Charles was as still as a corpse, and Tetra had moved her hands to rest on his chest, where his soul would be. Her dark fingers slowly dipped below his skin as easily as if it were water. "Time's up, Thomas," she taunted.

"Finnlay, hurry," Thomas said. "Are you almost done?"

"Nearly. Just crossing the i's and dotting the t's," he said.

Thomas didn't bother correcting him.

"Okay," Finnlay said. "Stand over Charles." He guided

Thomas to the foot of the bed, then took his place behind Thomas. "I must warn you that this will take a lot of life and energy out of you. Are you okay with that?"

"Just do it!" Thomas said as Tetra's claws sank deeper beneath Charles's skin. She grinned up at Thomas.

Finnlay didn't say anything as his warm hands pressed against Thomas's upper back. He spoke low, using words Thomas didn't recognize. A shiver ran up Thomas's spine and didn't stop. Finnlay's hands cooled, spreading their frigidity through his torso, up his neck, down his legs, and through his arms. All of Thomas's warmth moved to the front of his body until it was pushed out completely.

Thomas struggled to stay standing. He was cold from the inside out. His eyelids felt heavy and his body weak. A deep sting at his center shocked him awake. He looked down to find dark blood dripping down his torso from the middle of the triangle. He stumbled backward in surprise, too weak to catch himself. Finnlay caught him by his arms and asked him something, but Thomas couldn't focus. The pain was too sudden and intense.

Everything faded away as Thomas drifted into unconsciousness.

"Thomas?"

Thomas opened his tired eyes to an unfamiliar ceiling above him and two faces looking down at him. Finnlay watched him from his right and Charles from his left.

The sight of Charles woke Thomas up immediately. "Charles!" he yelled, bolting upright to throw his arms around Charles's neck. "Oh, gods. I thought I lost you." He turned to kiss Charles's face three times in succession.

Charles held him tight, smiling as Thomas kissed him. "I'm okay," he murmured. "You're crazy, Thomas. I can't believe you risked your life for me."

"Death is only temporary," Thomas said, kissing him one more time. He sat back to look at Charles but did not let go. "Are you okay? Are you hurt? How do you feel?"

Charles shook his head with a smile, brushing a lock of hair away from Thomas's eyes. "I'm fine."

"Good," Thomas said, letting his relieved smile take hold of his face. "Thank you."

"For what?"

"For fighting for me. For coming back. For . . . choosing me," Thomas said.

Charles's smile disappeared. "I'm sorry you ever doubted I would." He slid his hand into his pocket and pulled out the diamond ring, slipping it back onto Thomas's left ring finger. He opened his mouth to speak but froze, seemingly remembering they were not alone.

Charles and Thomas looked at Finnlay, who watched with polite curiosity. When Finnlay caught their gaze, he smiled and said, "You had me worried for a minute, Hambleton. I was sure I would get sent back to that camp for killing you."

Thomas released Charles from the embrace and sat back to look at Finnlay. "*Back* to the camp? Did you escape?"

Finnlay rubbed his neck and looked from Thomas to Charles and back again. "How do you know my sister?"

Thomas hid his face in his hands and sighed. "Oh my gods, *Fiona*." He didn't know if Fiona had escaped his mother's clutches, and he didn't know how to break the news to Finnlay that she might have been taken away to the very same prison he had broken free from. "We're friends. We met at sea when I found her in the brig of an abandoned Hambleton ship."

"You're Fiona's brother?" Charles asked, eyeing Finnlay. "How did I not see that? You look just like her."

Finnlay did not seem to know how to respond to either of them. He smiled uncomfortably. "Where is she?"

Thomas and Charles exchanged an uneasy look. "Did you see what happened to her?" Thomas asked.

Charles's mouth fell open as he tried to find an answer. "I wanted to save her," he said, "but I recognized that look in your eyes. I knew something was wrong. I had a feeling Mariana was going to make you face Caldwell, and I didn't want you to go alone."

"So you just *let* her get taken away?!" Thomas asked.

Charles's eyebrows shot up. "Thomas, you would have died if I hadn't followed you."

Thomas pressed his palms to his eyes. Charles was right. Thomas couldn't blame anyone except his mother. "*Fuck.*" He lowered his hands to peer through the windows behind him that looked out at the city. It was still dark and rainy outside, but not nearly as dark as it had been.

Finnlay raked his fingers through his waves and stared at the floor with fear in his eyes. "Oh gods, Fiona. No . . ."

Thomas and Charles sat in uncomfortable silence as Finnlay wrangled with the news. Charles rested his hand on Thomas's leg. Thomas took his hand and squeezed it. "Finnlay," Thomas said. Finnlay looked up at Thomas with wild eyes. "I can't thank you enough for saving Charles. How can I repay you? Money? Do you need a place to stay?"

"Help me free Fiona," Finnlay said. "Can't you take back her arrest? You're a Hambleton."

Thomas shook his head. "I'm sorry, no. I didn't even know about the camp until very recently."

"You didn't know? How?" Finnlay asked, leaning closer.

Charles slid his hand around Thomas's waist and pulled him close. Finnlay leaned back but did not take his eyes off Thomas.

"Because they took my magic first. They didn't want me to know," Thomas said.

Finnlay looked like he would be sick. "That's awful," he said. His willingness to believe Thomas was a relief. Thomas had been sure he would have to fight to convince Finnlay to trust him, but Finnlay seemed to take everything Thomas said at face value. Thomas hadn't met another person willing to believe the truth as easily as Thomas himself did. It was nice.

"Well then, if you can't save Fiona, then I'll take money and a place to stay. Thanks," Finnlay said.

Thomas couldn't stop a laugh from escaping. "Okay," he said, and then he realized what that meant. He had to go home. "Is this where you want to stay?"

Finnlay looked at the blood-soaked bed and then at the rest of the room. "This is all I could afford with the services I've sold so far."

"What services?" Thomas asked.

"Um . . . Just magic stuff," he said quietly, throwing a cautious look at the door.

Thomas nodded. "It's not safe to do magic here. I wonder if there's a magic community in Brenton where you could stay."

"There is," Charles said.

"How do you know that?" Thomas asked.

"My mother used to take me to that part of town. It's in southern Brenton."

"Okay," Thomas said, trying to think of a plan. "We should take Finnlay there, but I'll have to come back to give him money for lodging because I don't have any on me. And I should pay the innkeeper for the bed we ruined."

Charles eyed the bloody bed. "They're just going to take your money and then put new sheets over the blood. They don't care."

"Still . . ." Thomas said, pushing himself off the floor. Charles jumped up and took Thomas's arm to help him stand.

Finnlay also stood and corked the bottle of ink, placing it back on the bed Thomas had swiped it from. He picked up Thomas's and Charles's clothes from the floor. "I appreciate your concern for me, but I can find my way around the city on my own," Finnlay said, handing Thomas his shirt. "I think you should just go home for now. I'll manage for the night."

Thomas pulled his ratty blood-stained shirt over his head. "Are you sure?"

Finnlay nodded and handed Charles his clothes. Charles muttered a "Thanks" as he turned away to dress himself too.

"I am good at seeking out magic, and I doubt you want to put your fiancé in any more danger in these dark streets after nearly losing him," Finnlay said. He had a good point.

Charles whirled around. "You told him we're engaged?"

"Uh . . ." Thomas scratched his head and eyed Finnlay. He didn't remember saying that.

Charles examined Finnlay with narrowed eyes. Finnlay smiled in return. "It was fairly obvious," he said.

Thomas and Charles shared a look, and Thomas laughed. "Yeah, I guess it was," he said, remembering the way he had kissed Charles just before Charles returned the ring to him. "Are you sure you'll be okay on your own?"

Finnlay took a deep breath and nodded. "Yes. We can meet at the southern pier at dawn tomorrow, but get some rest for tonight."

"I'll bring you a change of clothes too," Thomas said, eyeing his muddy shirt and pants that he just realized were probably prisoner clothes. "Stay away from the docks while you make your way over there. That's where they scan people."

"Noted," Finnlay said, clasping his hands in gratitude. "Not to sound too picky, but if you do bring me clothes, can you bring me darker colors? Preferably black if you can."

"I'll see what I can do," Thomas said.

Finnlay smiled warmly at Thomas and headed for the door. "See you soon," he said, and then he was gone.

Thomas turned to Charles, who was frowning at the door. "Are you ready to go?" he asked, sliding his hand into Charles's.

Charles faced Thomas, watching him for a moment before he leaned down to kiss him. "Yes, darling. I'd go anywhere with you."

Chapter Twenty-Nine

Hambleton Manor

The house was dark and quiet when Thomas and Charles arrived. The door creaked open as they stepped inside. Thomas peered around the gloomy interior. High arched windows lined the main hall to provide natural sunlight, but the dark crimson curtains were always drawn. Orange lantern light flickered over the dim paintings on the walls and the ruby rugs that stretched across the wooden floors. The rain had finally stopped, and moonlight glowed faintly through the cracks of the drawn curtains.

A lot had changed since Thomas last stepped foot in this house.

"Thomas."

Thomas jumped out of his skin at the sound of his father's voice. He whipped around to face the dark hallway where his father stood with his hands crossed behind his back. His father scanned him rapidly from head to toe.

"Dei, what happened to you? Are you all right?" he asked, striding toward Thomas.

"I'm fine. It's not my blood," he lied.

His father's gaze turned to Charles, who was equally bloody. "Did you two kill someone? Who do I need to pay?"

Thomas felt a sharp spike of nerves at the question. He *had* killed someone, and he would have to live with it forever. "No," he lied again. "Everything is fine."

"Are you *sure?*" his father asked. "Because if you did kill someone, we need to get on it before someone comes for you."

"*No,*" Thomas said again, feeling sick at the way his father worried more about staying out of trouble than about whomever Thomas had killed.

Thomas's father approached him. "You can't be going out and getting yourself into trouble like this. We just got you back." He squeezed Thomas's left shoulder, and Thomas flinched. His wound was healed, but the memory of it wasn't.

"I'm still here," Thomas said.

His father nodded. "Thank Dei."

Thomas almost laughed at the divine praise. Dei was the reason it happened.

"Listen, Thomas," his father said. He looked at Charles. "And Charles . . . We need to talk about your engagement."

Thomas squeezed Charles's hand. "I'm marrying him whether you want me to or not."

"I know," his father said, shaking his head. "I don't particularly like you, Charles, but I'd rather have two sons than zero." He considered Charles a moment longer before taking a deep breath and sighing heavily. "I have to admit, he is a smart negotiator. He can stay on one condition."

Thomas shared a discreet look of surprise with Charles. "What is it?" Thomas asked.

"I want to speak to him alone."

Thomas glared at his father. "No. I won't let you take him away just so you can berate him where I can't defend him. Do you have any idea what he's been through? It's not fair for you to—"

Thomas's father raised a hand in the air to stop his rant. Charles flinched and looked nervously around the room. "Do you hear yourself? Charles is asking to live under my roof and marry my son, and all I'm asking from him is a simple conversation without you or . . ." he said, clenching his jaw and narrowing his eyes, "*Alfred* there to control the conversation. I don't think I am asking very much of either of you compared to what you are asking of me."

Thomas glared at the wall. He knew his father was right, but there was no way he would be kind to Charles. "Fine," Thomas relented.

Charles brought his hand up to squeeze Thomas's shoulder. "It's just a conversation. I'll be okay," he said with a smile.

Thomas rested his hand on Charles's and decided letting his father speak to his fiancé was a small price to pay. "All right. I'll be waiting out here," Thomas said. Charles smiled and leaned down to kiss Thomas on the forehead.

Thomas felt sick as he watched them disappear down the narrow hallway.

The wide double door to the main hall creaked open, and his mother stepped between the slim crack in the doors. She looked harried and she was wet, like she had just walked through a hurricane. Her pale blonde hair was strewn in clumps across her narrow face, and the black skirt of her dress fell to the floor inelegantly. She stopped when she spotted Thomas, her gaze lowering to the blood on his shirt. "Good lord, Thomas. What in the world happened to you?" she asked, marching toward him.

Thomas stepped back. "I'm fine."

"You're clearly not!" she said, tugging at his bloodied shirt and looking him up and down.

"I'm *fine,*" he said again, losing his patience quickly. "Don't touch me."

She looked into his eyes, and her concern warped into intrusive examination. "Thomas, you—"

"What happened to Fiona?" Thomas interrupted her.

She placed a hand against her chest and watched him with practiced concern. "You say that like I would hurt your friend."

"What happened to her?" he asked again.

"She's better off, darling. Trust me."

Thomas clenched his fists tight. He forced himself to breathe, worrying he would summon another storm if he couldn't contain this feeling. "*Where is she?*"

His mother straightened her posture and tugged at the cuffs of her sleeves. "She's agreed to be taken somewhere that will change her life for the better. She's perfectly fine."

Thomas released a breath through clenched teeth. "You're out of your mind. It's disgusting that you think you can control the way people live."

"I'm not controlling anyone, dear. It's entirely voluntary."

Thomas shook his head. "No. It's not. Tell me something, *Mother.* If you hate magic so much, then why are you a witch?"

Her eyebrows arched and she reeled back. "Pardon?"

"Don't lie to me. I know it's true."

Her fake shock simmered to a serious frown. "If it were up to me, I would accept salvation as well. I'm sacrificing my own soul in order to better the lives of my fellow humans. I gave you the gift of a normal life, Thomas. You should be grateful."

"Grateful for what?!" Thomas was nearly yelling now. "My life has been nothing but pain because of your 'gift.' I never wanted it."

"You're too young to know what you want. Do you want to know how I *know* it worked?" she asked.

Thomas shook as he asked, "*How?*"

"As a child you were always crying at the slightest disturbance and laughing at nothing. It wasn't normal. When I saved your soul, it stopped. How could that be bad?"

Thomas's blood went cold. He unclenched his fists and took a step back. "What?" he asked in a small voice.

"You stopped crying. That was all the proof I needed," she repeated.

Thomas furrowed his eyebrows, and it hit him like a squall in a stormy sea. Fiona was right. Having emotions was never his problem. The problem was how long he *hadn't* had them. He had no idea how to cope with his big feelings because his mother made sure he would never have emotions at all. She thought she was helping him, but she had hurt him more than she would ever understand.

"You have to stop," Thomas said, shaking his head slowly. Tears stung his eyes, and he let them fall. He didn't try to fight it anymore. "I'm begging you."

Her lips flattened into a terse line. "You'll come around, darling," she said, patting him on the shoulder.

He pushed her hand away. "No. You hurt me when you broke my soul. Babies are *supposed* to cry and laugh. How do you not see that?! You're hurting *everyone* you 'save!'"

"No, Thomas," she said. "I'm helping them."

She wouldn't listen. Not even when he spoke about his own experience. It was impossible to get through to her. "You're a monster," he said quietly.

"Thomas—"

Thomas turned around and walked away.

Everything Fiona had told him about controlling magic made sense now. Magic was not optional, and it was not meant to be kept inside. It was part of him.

It always should have been.

"Come, Charles," Edmund said, retreating into the dark hallway. Charles followed silently.

Edmund opened a large door carved from dark wood and gestured to the dim interior of the room. This house was too creepy to simply be a victim of bad décor. It had to be intentional.

Charles stepped inside the cold room and looked around. The dim orange lamplight that haunted the interior of the mansion also lit the inside of this room. Two red sofas sat across from one another at the floor's center with a low table between them. Crystal glasses sat around a decanter of amber liquid atop the table. An unlit fireplace opposite the door radiated darkness from its charcoal pit. Bookshelves lined the room, meeting at the left wall where a wide desk lurked.

"Have a seat," Edmund said, gesturing at the sofa near the dark fireplace. Charles sat on the firm cushion. The darkness behind him put him on edge, as if Tetra herself would spring from the fireplace at any moment.

Speaking with Edmund Hambleton alone was almost more frightening than confronting Tetra.

Edmund took a seat across from Charles and eyed him for an uncomfortably long moment. He looked a lot like Thomas up close. Edmund's hair was darker, but his eyes held the same bored stare Charles had spent years trying to understand on Thomas, and he used the same quiet indifference on Charles now that Thomas had used on him in the past.

Finally, Edmund leaned toward the center table and poured the amber liquid from the decanter into two glasses, pushing one toward Charles and holding the other in his own hand while he continued his scrutiny. Charles picked up the glass out of obligation but did not drink from it.

"Charles Southworth," Edmund began, saying his name like it was a riddle he couldn't solve. Charles's heart beat hard. He didn't see how this conversation could go well. Not after what he had done to Edmund's only child. "How in Dei's name did you convince me to invite you in here?"

Charles cleared his throat. "Mutual hatred for Alfred, I assume."

Edmund exhaled slowly and narrowed his eyes as he watched Charles a moment longer. Only a few words had been exchanged, but this conversation was excruciating. "Why aren't you drinking?"

Charles swallowed nervously. As much as Edmund didn't trust Charles, Charles didn't trust him either. "Why aren't *you?*" Charles asked.

Edmund raised his eyebrows and glanced down at the decanter before looking at Charles again. He raised the glass to his mouth and took a sip. Charles decided it was safe and took a drink as well. The alcohol burned his throat, but the flavor was rich and smoky. It was much better than the watery grog that had comforted him at sea, and it was probably as expensive as it was delicious.

His reaction must have been apparent, because Edmund said, "It's good, isn't it? I had it imported. It's older than you are."

"Yes, thank you," Charles said.

After another uncomfortable silence, Edmund said, "Did you really believe I would poison you?" Edmund asked.

Charles looked into his glass before answering. "I'm not sure, Mr. Hambleton. All I know about you is that you despise me for what I did to your son. And honestly, we have that in common."

Edmund lowered his eyebrows and took another drink before answering. "Thomas is a smart boy," he said. "I don't think he knows or appreciates how smart he is. He has never done anything to make me think I should question his judgment, but I find myself questioning him for the first time in my life."

Charles kept his eyes down. He didn't know how he had managed to convince Thomas to trust him again either.

"Maybe I just don't understand," Edmund continued. "He clearly loves you, and as much as I hate to admit it . . . You clearly love him too."

"I do," Charles said, looking up again. "Very much."

Edmund watched him for a moment, then shook his head with furrowed eyebrows. "If you *really* do love Thomas and want to spend your life with him . . . Then why did you accuse him of assault? This is what I don't understand. How did that happen?"

Charles shook his head. His throat burned. He didn't have the words to explain it to Edmund. It had been hard enough to explain to Thomas, the person he trusted most in the world. "Alfred . . ." he whispered. Charles wanted to say Alfred made him do it, but that wasn't entirely true. He wanted to explain how scared he had felt, but that only made him a coward. He *was* a coward. Alfred gave him the easy way out, and he took it. He didn't deserve Thomas's forgiveness.

He rubbed his burning eyes. The last thing in the world he wanted to do was cry in front of Edmund Hambleton.

"Say no more."

Charles's eyebrows shot up. "What?" He nearly choked on the word.

"I know Alfred. I've worked in this industry with him for a long time, and I know how underhanded he can be. He's very talented in the game of convincing people to do things his way and then making them think it was their idea. I can only assume that's what happened here if Thomas still trusts you."

Charles sat up straight and forced his expression not to crack. "I don't want to pretend I am not responsible for my own actions, but I would be lying if I said he wasn't part of it. My f—*Alfred* is a monster."

Edmund nodded pensively. "He is." He set his glass on the table and looked away. "When I found out Thomas was presumed dead, I didn't know what to do with myself. I couldn't believe I had let him slip through my fingers as he did. To let a *shapeshifter* take his place . . ." Edmund said with narrowed eyes. Charles sipped his expensive drink during the tense pause. "That's beside the point. I regretted every single decision I had ever made that led to Thomas's death. I would have done anything to get him back. Meanwhile, Alfred purposefully sent his own son away." Edmund looked at Charles again. His bored stare was stained with hatred. "As much as I didn't like you, Charles, it was insulting that he threw away the very same thing I would have killed to get back."

"He does not value me," Charles said.

Edmund shook his head. "He never was very good at valuation." He leaned back in his seat and smiled, and Charles felt a similar surprise as when he first saw Thomas smile. It occurred to him he had never seen Edmund smile either. "This conversation has been very enlightening. I've always expected you to turn out like your father. I thought he didn't like you because you were worse than him, but I can see that's not the case. You chose to stay with Thomas when he offered to give you back the inheritance."

"Of course I did," Charles said.

Edmund rubbed his chin and observed Charles a moment longer. Finally, he stood and extended his hand. Charles rose and hesitantly gripped it while Edmund shook firmly. "You made the right choice, son. Welcome to the family."

The words had a strange effect on Charles. It felt good to finally be accepted for who he was, but something as dark as the empty fireplace lurked deep within him. He didn't want to be part of this family. He wanted to be with Thomas, but he did not want to be a Hambleton. The Hambletons were a different kind of terrible.

"Thank you, Mr. Hambleton," Charles said.

Edmund nodded. "You can call me Edmund."

"Right. Edmund," Charles said, letting go of his hand. They stood in silence for a moment as Charles realized he was part of the anti-magus movement now.

Three sharp knocks at the door loosened the tension in the room. The door swung open before Edmund had a chance to answer it.

Thomas stepped through. Tears streaked his still-bloody face, and he rubbed the sleeve of his ruined shirt across his eyes.

"Thomas! What happened?" Charles asked, setting his glass on the table and walking quickly toward him. He pulled Thomas into his arms, Thomas's tense muscles relaxing at the contact.

Thomas let Charles hold him briefly, but he was quick to push himself away and wipe his face again. He looked at Edmund. "I need to talk to you. Immediately."

Thomas reluctantly stepped away from Charles and faced his father. His father considered them both for a moment, and then gave a curt nod. "Of course. Charles, can you please give us some privacy?"

Charles took Thomas's hand, turning to him with concern in his eyes. His willingness to show affection in front of his father meant the conversation must have gone well. "Are you okay? Do you want me to go?"

Thomas nodded. "I'll be fine. I'll meet you in my room." He kissed Charles on the cheek and gave him directions.

"All right," Charles said, squeezing Thomas's waist gently. "I'll see you soon." He shot a brief glance at Thomas's father before he left the room.

"What can I do for you, Thomas?" his father asked, gesturing to the sofa in front of the fireplace.

Thomas took a seat. His father sat across from him. "I need you to know the severity of what Mother is doing to magi," Thomas said bluntly. He didn't care if his father didn't want to hear it, and he didn't care how clumsily it came out. It had to be said.

His father leaned against the backrest of the couch and sighed as he crossed his arms. "I know, Thomas."

Thomas didn't know what to say. That was not what he had expected. "What? Why are you letting it happen?"

"It's . . . complicated," he said. "She's my wife. She has access to the same money and resources as I do."

"You've known all this time? You have more influence than anyone else. You have to do something!" Thomas couldn't believe it.

His father shook his head. "I haven't known all this time. Truthfully, Catherine's people believe they are fighting for good. I believed that too until I—" He leaned forward and hung his head, letting out a sigh. When he lifted his head again, his eyes were tired. "Tell me what it's like."

"W-what?" Thomas asked.

"Tell me how it feels to not have magic. I always suspected it was a mistake to take it from you. You were never the same after it happened, but Catherine didn't listen. She always managed to convince me it was the right thing to do when I brought it up, so it wasn't until you were gone that I realized you never got to . . . *live.*" He shook his head.

Tears burned Thomas's eyes again. "You're right. It did change me," he said. "Magic is part of the soul. To remove my magic, she hollowed out my soul and left it in pieces. I've felt empty my entire life. I didn't know how to *feel* anything until—" Thomas glanced at the door. The first time he had really felt something was when he fell in love with Charles, but since recovering his soul, *everything* felt bigger.

"Until you got your magic back," his father said.

Despite the content of this conversation, Thomas froze. His heart beat harder. How did his father know? "I-I did," he admitted.

His father smiled. "Good."

"Good?" Thomas asked in a small voice.

His father nodded and stood, crossing the space to sit beside Thomas on the couch. To Thomas's surprise, his father pulled him into a hug. He did not know what to do. His arms dangled lifelessly as his father squeezed him. He had never shown Thomas affection like this before.

"I've always felt guilty that I let this happen to you, and to avoid the guilt, I avoided you. I should have helped you. I'm very sorry," his father said quietly.

"O-oh." This apology was even more unexpected than finding Charles getting along with his father. The hug was awkward. "Thank you."

His father released him. "It will be hard, but now that I know the truth, I will do whatever I can."

"You can't just cut funding?" Thomas asked.

His father shook his head. "No. Like I said, what's mine is hers. I can't just take everything from her."

"Can you at least get Fiona back?" Thomas asked.

His father considered it. "I'll see what I can do." He smiled. "Is there anything else I can do for you in the meantime?"

"Um—yes," Thomas said. "Can I have some money?"

"Money?" his father said. "It always comes back to money." He stood and walked to his desk before Thomas could respond.

He withdrew a small ring of keys from his pocket to unlock a drawer in his desk. Thomas couldn't see from where he sat, but he knew what was in that drawer. His father returned with a stack of cabills and handed it to Thomas. "I'll have a key made for you soon. It's all going to be yours someday anyway."

Thomas took the money, still reeling from his father's apology. He struggled to find something to say, but his father beat him to it.

"Goodnight, Thomas. Don't get into any more fights," he said, eyeing Thomas's bloody shirt.

"I won't. Thank you."

Thomas numbly left the room with the stack of cabills in hand. His father shut the door behind him, leaving him alone in the dark hallway.

As he walked through his house, he thought about everything that had happened over the last several months. In that short time, his whole life had been flipped upside down. He met new people who had grown to be like family to him and lost them just as fast. There would probably never be another time in his life where those same people lived so close to him.

A profound sense of sadness met the guilt of murder and loomed over him like a storm cloud. He missed his friends terribly. As hard as these last five months had been, he missed how it was at sea. It was a time of his life he would never get to experience again.

When he made it back to his bedroom, Charles was asleep face down on his bed. He had taken off his shirt and cleaned the rest of the blood away. The sight of his sleeping form in Thomas's bed was strikingly normal. Everything about it felt right.

Thomas watched the slow rise and fall of his back as he snoozed. This was how it was going to be for them now. This was what he had always wished he could have, and now, after months of turmoil, they had it.

Thomas quietly peeled off his bloody battle clothes and cleaned the blood off himself as best as he could before sliding into bed with his future husband. Charles immediately reached for him, holding him tight.

Thomas wrapped his arms around Charles. "Charles," he whispered. "Are you awake?"

Charles grumbled something Thomas couldn't understand, but it answered his question all the same.

"Can I ask you something?" Thomas whispered.

Charles hummed his assent.

Thomas didn't know what he wanted to say. He didn't know how to express this sadness to Charles. Finally, he asked, "Do you think things will ever be the same as they were?"

Charles was quiet for a short moment, then his sleepy voice said, "Gods, I hope not."

Thomas smiled. Maybe he was right. Thomas never imagined his life could be like this.

He finally had Charles. Mariana was well again. His father would help him. Faya and Fyavine had each other, and he knew they would be okay. Fiona was gone, but Thomas had at least found her brother.

Things were different now, but they were still okay.

Chapter Thirty

After Finnlay's escape, Felix was once again thrown into the maddening dark of the underground cell. He didn't know how long they would leave him here. He had come close to death last time, and his sentence this time would probably be extended when they realized Finnlay had escaped.

As the night continued, the cell grew warmer. He had no water, and there was nowhere to sleep that wasn't muddy and damp. He had tried to fall asleep against a wall but the moment he slipped away into rest, he fell into mud. Instead, he spent the night awake and exhausted.

It was impossible to tell day from night. He had been thrown in here at night, but day never seemed to come. It was a dark, lifeless hole Felix was starting to think he would never escape. And maybe he didn't want to.

What point was there in carrying on? Finnlay was gone. Aella, as nasty as she was, was gone too. He had no one left in the camp, and he was not interested in getting anyone else into similar trouble. Felix only hurt people. Not even the camp wanted him. He was the only prisoner and the only person they weren't trying to convert. Even the woman they had punished by removing her magic was released to work, but Felix would be here forever. He would be stuck here with no one and nothing to make his life worth living.

Maybe it was for the best that Finnlay was gone. Maybe the guards would forget Felix was in here and let him starve to death.

He bowed his head and prayed to the gods to help end his suffering. He prayed he would see his family again. It brought him peace to think that it might all be over soon.

Time passed slowly, and Felix could only think about all the ways he had failed. He failed at being a shapeshifter, a boyfriend, a friend, and a magus. Catherine was right to treat him this way. This was what he deserved.

A creak echoed from the other end of the room. Felix didn't move. Maybe if they thought he was dead, they wouldn't bother dragging him out.

"Felix, darling?" It was Catherine.

Felix didn't respond.

The gentle sound of her footsteps squishing through the mud came closer. She whispered the fire spell and ignited a flame in her palm, lighting her familiar visage with warm yellow light that somehow did not make her expression any less cold, even though she was smiling.

Felix watched her but still did not speak.

"It's time to go," Catherine said.

"Already?" Felix asked.

"Do you want to stay down here?"

"Yes," Felix said. "I'd rather die down here than have to spend another moment with you."

"Don't be silly," Catherine said, pulling him up by the arm.

He didn't have the energy to fight her. His legs were wobbly and tired as she pulled him through the dark room. He stumbled after her through the curving hallway and up the muddy stairs.

The sun was blinding. Felix squinted as he looked around. It was early morning, and the courtyard was packed with people; a sight he hadn't seen in weeks.

He turned to Catherine as if she would answer his questions.

She smiled softly. "Your friends are gone, Felix. You have no magic. You're not a threat anymore." She leaned closer to quietly murmur, "No matter how hard you fight to escape, you never will. Not even with the restrictions lifted. Not even with your mother's recipe, which I *will* get back." She narrowed her eyes. "There is nobody left in the world who loves you. You've been left behind, and we've made sure the *entire* area of the grounds is magic-proofed now. You'll never escape. You're going to die here, unloved and alone."

Her words should have made him angry, but he felt nothing. His heart was empty, his feelings dulled. She had tried to get a rise out of him, but none of it worked. It just felt true. "I know Thomas is alive," he said.

Her eyes widened. "How—" She glanced around the grounds at the residents and forced a fake smile as she looked at him again. "His survival was a matter of luck. It doesn't change what you did."

"And taking away my magic doesn't change that I'm a magus. It doesn't change that about Thomas either, and it's only a matter of time before he finds out what you did to him, and why he's been miserable his whole life. I don't think I'm the reason he almost died, Catherine. I think you are."

Her expression remained calm, but a wild anger burned in her eyes. "I'm doing the world a service."

"The world will remember you as a villain," Felix said.

Catherine scoffed in the restrained way of a deeply offended member of polite society. "Time will tell."

"Yes, it will," Felix said.

Catherine left for the main building without another word. Felix watched her go, but his eyes caught on someone else.

A woman was speaking to a young girl who was sitting on her butt, looking up with teary eyes and a trembling chin. The woman was smiling and talking as she rolled up the girl's pant sleeve and exposed a bloodied knee. She tore a strip from her own sleeve and wrapped the linen around the wound.

Her orange hair was tied up in a pile on her head with a string and her pale skin was covered in dark tattoos. There was something terribly familiar about her that made his heart ache.

The child wiped her face and stood up. The woman said something, and the child nodded with a smile before running away. Felix only realized he was staring when the woman's eyes found him.

He looked away quickly but saw her approaching from his peripheral vision.

"Hello," she said, crossing the grassy field to join him. Her accent was from Dufonn. "Why are you muddy?"

The recognition hit him like a sudden storm on a cloudless day. This had to be Finnlay's twin sister. She looked just like him. It couldn't be anyone else. "What?" he said, completely forgetting what she had asked.

She smiled at him. "You're covered in mud."

"Oh," Felix said, frowning at the brown clumps of wet dirt clinging to his pants. He tried to brush them away but quickly realized the futility. "Yeah."

She waited for him to explain himself for a few seconds but gave up and asked, "What's your name?"

"Felix."

Her eyes widened briefly before a mischievous smile found her freckled face. "Right. I've heard that before."

Felix furrowed his eyebrows. Nobody had ever responded to

his name that way. "What?" he asked, surprised to hear himself laugh.

She waved the question away. "Long story. Aren't you going to ask my name?"

"I bet I can guess it," Felix said.

"Oh really?" she asked with a playful smile.

Felix nodded. "Let me think . . ." He pretended to consider the question as he rubbed his chin. "You look like a Fiona."

Her jaw dropped, then she looked around the camp like she could find an explanation for him having this knowledge. "You clearly know that for a reason," she said. "Which leads me to my next question." She locked her brown eyes on Felix. "Do you know Finnlay?"

Felix smiled sadly. "Yes."

She gasped and grinned. "You *do?* Nobody else will talk about him. Nobody will even look at me except you. It's like his name is a bad word around here."

Felix's stomach twisted. He'd have to break the news. "So nobody has told you?" he asked quietly.

Fiona's face paled and her smile withered. "What happened? Is he okay?"

"He's fine," Felix said quickly, "but he's not here."

Fiona froze, staring at him with wide eyes and a slack jaw. "What do you mean?"

"He escaped. That's why I was down there." He pointed to the cavern beneath him. "I helped him get out."

Fiona glanced at the grim doorway by their feet and back at Felix. "He's not here?"

"No. I'm sorry."

Fiona rubbed her eyes with one hand and sighed heavily.

"He's all right, Fiona. He's tough. It's not great here, so really you should be happy that he's gone."

Fiona dropped her hand and frowned. After a moment, she

smiled. "Yes, you're right. I should be happy, but . . ." She paused. "Our timing is remarkably bad."

Felix found himself laughing again. "It's not a coincidence, actually."

"No?" Fiona asked, raising her eyebrows.

"It had to do with Thomas arriving home on the same ship as you and—well, that's a long story too."

"You know Thomas?" Fiona looked him over once and her eyes widened. "Wait a second, are you *the* Felix? Felix Warren?"

Suddenly the comment about his name made sense. Thomas had probably introduced himself as Felix. Nobody in their right mind would introduce themselves to a witch as a Hambleton. He smiled. "I am," he said with a short bow of his head. "*The* Felix Warren. I like the sound of that."

Fiona giggled. "Stop it, you're adorable. Gods, I can see why your plan worked."

Felix's smile grew into a grin. He already liked Fiona a lot. "Well, it worked for him. I'm not sure how well it worked for me."

"You're mad, Felix. I don't know a single magus who would willingly trade lives with a Hambleton and *live* in their house."

Felix shrugged. "You do now."

Fiona laughed and tucked a stray lock of hair behind her ear. "I guess this isn't all bad, is it? A camp full of magi? The conversations must be interesting, at least."

"No, it's not all bad," Felix said. "People don't really talk about magic. It's 'against the rules,' but I'll talk about it with you any time. It's not as though they can take my magic twice."

Fiona covered her mouth. "Oh no . . . You poor thing. Are you all right?"

Felix shrugged. "I'm doing better now that you're here," he deflected. "But I miss Finnlay."

"I know how you feel," she said with a sigh.

They stood in silence for a moment, watching the yellow grass sway in the wind.

"Why did Finnlay leave you here?" Fiona asked.

"I made him leave me behind. He didn't want to, but he only had one chance to escape, and I wasn't going to let him lose his magic," Felix said.

Fiona watched him for a long time, then she said, "I'll get you out of here, Felix. And then we'll find Finnlay so I can rub in his face that I broke you out and he didn't."

Felix laughed again. He hadn't laughed so much since his soul was broken. "This sucks, but to be selfishly honest with you, I'm glad you're here, Fiona."

"You know what? Me too," she said with a smile. "I'm glad I got to meet the *real* Felix."

Fiona's comment warmed his numb heart. He couldn't believe he had been so ready to die when he was just minutes away from meeting her.

Maybe the gods had answered his prayers after all.

BRENTON

Thomas woke before the sun rose to prepare for his meeting with Finnlay. He searched his wardrobe for black clothing and managed to find an old mourning outfit from a funeral he had attended for some old businessman, along with a few pieces of navy clothing.

Thomas found a canvas bag and threw in the clothing for Finnlay along with a blank journal, a bottle of ink, and a pen. He took a portion of the stack of cabills for the innkeeper and shoved the rest of the stack into the bag, pulling the loops of the bag tight to prevent the money from escaping.

Thomas slung the bag over his shoulder and quietly stepped toward the bed, leaning down to give Charles a quick kiss before leaving.

Thomas had some time to kill before meeting Finnlay at the pier. He decided to pay the innkeeper first, slipping into the quiet tavern and leaving the money in an envelope with a note explaining it was for the bed, grateful no one was awake to ask follow-up questions.

The walk to the south end of town was peaceful. Thomas hadn't realized how ill Mariana had been until seeing her free from Tetra's hold. The water was still dark, but it was the dark blue of the early morning sky instead of the ominous jet-black of Tetra's shadow.

Thomas stopped walking halfway across town to watch the horizon. The night before, he couldn't see where the sea met the sky. Now there was a clear division. The cool wind blew his hair across his face and brought the salty smell of the ocean with it. He took a deep breath and exhaled slowly. The ocean had always been a happy place for him. He was glad Mariana was still around.

Thomas kicked off his boots, dropped his bag, and rolled up his pants to walk through the cool sand. It was a beautiful morning, and these silent moments before the world awoke brought the heavy reminder of what he had done. Now that Charles was okay and Thomas had a moment to think, it weighed on him.

He had taken someone's life.

He stepped into the surf and watched a crystal clear wave wash over his feet. When it receded, it left behind the tall shape of Mariana. Even in the early morning darkness, she was brighter than ever. She smiled down at him with a big grin. This was how she was meant to look.

"Hi Thomas!" she said in the bubbly tone that brightened his mood in the way only Mariana could.

He smiled weakly. "Hi Mariana. How are you feeling?"

"Much better, thanks to you."

Thomas looked at his feet buried in the rough sand. Another wave washed over them, burying them further. "Good."

"Thank you. I owe you my life."

Thomas nodded. "I suppose we're even now."

After a short silence, Mariana said, "How are you?"

Thomas looked up. He opened his mouth but had nothing to say. He shut his mouth and frowned.

"Not well?"

Thomas shook his head.

"I'm sorry. Do you want to talk about it?"

Thomas thought for a long time. "I killed someone," he finally said. "It doesn't feel right, even if things are better now."

Mariana considered this. "Yeah, you did. I don't think it would do you any good to convince yourself that it was 'right,' because you're kind and you've never believed killing someone was a good solution. However, you should consider the other option. He would have killed you with no remorse, and then we would both be dead. Thousands of mermaids would lose their lives and autonomy. You've saved all of their souls because you found it in you to do something you consider bad. Some people will call you a hero for it, some people won't, but at the end of the day, are you happy with the outcome?"

"I'm happy you're okay, and I'm happy the mermaids are okay, but I'll never be happy that I took a life."

"That's okay," she said. "Maybe you don't need to justify his death. You don't need to think it was a good thing for the consequences to be good."

Thomas shook his head. "I'm not sure I'll ever forgive myself."

"And you shouldn't," a dark growl of a voice emerged from all around. The beach darkened as if a cloud had passed overhead, but the sun wasn't out yet. The tall wispy shape of Tetra twirled up from Thomas's shadow to frown angrily down at him. "You should be ashamed, Thomas. You're a murderer."

All his remorse dissolved the moment he looked into Tetra's eyes. What was he thinking? Caldwell was a disgusting person who was more than willing to torture Thomas to death. Thomas at least made Caldwell's death quick and relatively painless. "I'm not interested in talking to you, Tetra," he said.

"You killed my servant after you promised to find him for me!" Tetra snarled. "You're a horrible, miserable little boy and you deserve an eternity of loneliness."

Thomas looked at Mariana instead, forcing a calm expression onto his face. He would not acknowledge Tetra's insults. She was nothing. She was only the absence of light, life, goodness, and courage. He had never tolerated evil before, and he would not start now.

"Leave us alone, Tetra," Mariana demanded. "You are not welcome here."

Tetra stretched her claws out as she eyed Thomas and Mariana. "Fine. I think I can still do something with what's left of Caldwell, anyway," she said, pinning her sharp gaze on Thomas. It took all of his strength not to acknowledge her. "I'll be seeing you soon."

Thomas finally looked at her, fighting the urge to ask questions.

Tetra's scowl curled into a twisted smile briefly before she vanished into dark air.

"I'm sorry," Mariana said. "She's not supposed to harass you, but you know how she likes to bend the rules."

Thomas nodded. "What did she mean by that?"

Mariana shook her head. "I wouldn't waste another thought on it. She's probably just trying to scare you."

"Right . . ." Thomas decided to listen to Mariana. He wouldn't think about it again.

"Is Charles okay?" Mariana asked.

"He's alive."

"Good." She held out her hand, dangling the diamond necklace in front of him. "Here. Try not to lose it again."

Thomas smirked as he took the diamond from her and draped it around his neck. "I won't."

"Let me know if you need anything," Mariana said. "I'll always be here, thanks to you."

Thomas nodded once and gave her a small smile as she collapsed into an approaching wave. Thomas let the cold water wash over his feet as he stared out at the calm sea.

"Thomas?!"

In the distant water, a head bobbed in the waves. It took him a second to recognize her, but when he did, he smiled from ear to ear. "Fyavine!" he yelled, running into the cold water.

Fyavine ducked underwater and came up seconds later much closer to the shore. She sat herself waist deep in the surf and waited for Thomas to reach her. Her tail glistened gold beneath the shimmering waves.

Thomas fell to his knees beside her and pulled her into a hug. She flung her arms around him and squeezed tight. "Gods, I'm so happy to see you," he said. "What are you doing out here?"

"I'm happy to see you too," she said, backing away from the hug to beam at him. "I'm just taking a morning swim. It's lovely out."

"Did you and Faya find somewhere safe to go? I've been worried about you," Thomas said.

"We did," Fyavine said, still wearing her beautiful smile. Her eyes fell to his hand where his ring sparkled under the water.

"What's this?" she asked, lifting his hand to inspect the diamond on his finger.

"Charles proposed to me," Thomas said, struggling not to smile himself.

Fyavine gasped. "Oh my gods! Congratulations! Charles is a lucky man."

"Just Charles?"

Fyavine's smile turned sly, and she dropped Thomas's hand. "All right, he's growing on me. I *guess* I'm excited for you too."

Thomas laughed. "Thanks." He looked around at the dark water before admiring Fyavine for a moment. She had always been beautiful, but there was something about being in the ocean that made her glow. "Hey, so . . . Just so you know, the sirens are gone now. There were never any sirens here in Brenton, but now there are none at all."

"Are you serious?!" She whirled around to scan the horizon as if she could see the change. Seemingly satisfied, she turned and pulled him into another hug, holding him in a long, tight embrace. "Thank you for saving us," she finally said.

Thomas smiled against her shoulder. Her gratitude made the whole struggle worthwhile, but his heart ached as he prepared to say the next part. "You're welcome. You can finally go home."

Fyavine's surprise and glee crumbled into a frown. "Home?" She looked into the water for a long moment and looked up again. "My home is very close by."

"You found it?" Thomas asked.

Fyavine bit her lip and looked northward. "Yeah, I did. It's somewhere near that mountain, teaching her daughter how to make a fire the unmagic way."

Thomas grinned at Fyavine. "Faya," he said.

She nodded. "Yes. I've never felt more at home than I do with her. Thank you, Thomas. You should come visit us sometime. And Charles can come too I guess," she said with a shrug.

"We will," Thomas said. "You're living on the mountain?"

"In domestic bliss," she said dreamily.

"I think you need a house for domestic bliss," Thomas said.

Fyavine rolled her eyes. "Shut up," she said with a laugh. "We're fine."

"I'm glad to hear that." Thomas dug in his pockets and withdrew a small stack of soaking wet crumpled cabills. The bag of money he had packed for Finnlay was still on the beach, but his pants had some change in them. "Here, take this. It'll buy you some supplies if you need it."

Fyavine gawked at the money as she took it out of his hand. "This is a lot. Isn't it?"

Thomas shrugged. "I guess so."

She shook her head in disbelief. "You crazy rich people. I can't believe you'd just hand all your money to some weirdo in the water."

It wasn't all of his money by far. It was a forgettable amount. "Money is the only thing I have to offer, and you're my friend. You can have more if you want it."

"No, no. This is plenty," she said, glancing behind her. "I should probably get back to Faya now. I'm glad I got to see you."

"You too, Fyavine. Tell Faya and Ametta I say hello," Thomas said.

Fyavine gave him one last wet hug. "I will. Bye, Thomas," she said, then she slipped under the surface of the water and was gone.

Thomas stood up. Cold seawater ran down his body as he trudged through the sand, and waves pushed against his legs, trying to trip him as he exited the water. The cool morning air worsened the chill from his wet clothes.

He held his hands over his body, concentrating his intention on the drenched fabric clinging to his skin. The magic flowing through him was not very fast, but he had never let Fiona teach him how to control it. A few seconds passed, and his shirt began to steam, stinging his skin with sharp heat.

"Damn it," he muttered, shaking out his hands. He would just have to deal with being damp. He shoved his wet, sandy feet into his boots and lifted the bag back onto his shoulder.

The walk to the southern pier was soggy and unpleasant. Thomas tried to distract himself by planning what he would say to Finnlay. He had so many questions, but he didn't know where to begin.

Thomas stood at the pier entrance and waited. It was nearly time for their meetup, and Finnlay hadn't arrived yet. Thomas sat on the small stone ledge separating the beach from the shorefront street and looked up at the brightening sky as it slowly erased the twinkling morning stars.

"Hello, Thomas."

Thomas came back down to reality, where Finnlay stood in front of him with his hands behind his back.

Finnlay's smile reached every corner of his face, and it lifted something heavy from Thomas's heart. It was like seeing Fiona again, but he was meeting someone entirely new and just as wonderful.

Finnlay's presence here and now was a miracle. How did he trust Thomas enough to meet him alone at the docks after escaping the rehabilitation camp? It was refreshing that Finnlay would simply take him at his word.

"Hi Finnlay," Thomas said, standing to greet him.

Finnlay's eyes fell to Thomas's wet clothes. "Whoa, what happened to you?"

"I got in the water," Thomas said.

"Why?"

"My friend was in there. She's a mermaid."

"You're friends with a mermaid?" Finnlay asked, narrowing

his eyes as he looked Thomas up and down before he raised his eyebrows and nodded. "Would you like some help?"

Thomas hesitated to accept, but the sensation of wet clothes against his skin was very unpleasant. "That would be nice."

Finnlay nodded and stepped closer. He whispered the water spell and raised his hand to pull the water away. Thomas instantly felt better in warm, dry clothes.

Finnlay flung the cold seawater to the ground. "Better?"

"Yes, thank you."

"So . . . Any good news about Fiona?" Finnlay asked with a smile so hopeful Thomas wished he could turn back time to bring him a better answer.

Thomas's chest felt tight. "No. I'm so sorry."

Finnlay's shoulders slumped as he let out a sigh and examined the sea. "In that case, I can't stay here. I need to go back for her. And for . . . Felix."

"You—you know *Felix?*" Thomas asked.

Finnlay nodded somberly. "He told me about your trade."

"Is he okay? I had no idea about my family when I met him, and I never would have let him trade lives with me if I had known. He didn't lose his magic, did he?"

Finnlay hesitated before nodding again.

Thomas hid his face behind his hands and let out a heavy sigh. He hated that he had caused another person that kind of pain.

"Perhaps Fiona and Felix will find each other. *We* ran into each other, after all," Finnlay said.

"Yeah, that was lucky," Thomas said, muffled beneath his palms.

"Or maybe it was fate."

"Fate?" Thomas lowered his hands to look at Finnlay.

He nodded. "I don't think it's a coincidence that you know

Fiona and I know Felix. I think we were meant to find each other. Magic has a funny way of bringing people together, you know."

"I didn't know that," Thomas said.

"A lot of people don't."

Thomas considered this new information. "Don't go back to the camp, Finnlay. We can figure out a way to free them without putting ourselves at risk of being captured."

Finnlay paused to think. "You said your mother took your magic, but I felt a lot of magic coming out of you last night. Did you somehow get it back?"

"Yes," Thomas said.

"How?" Finnlay asked, leaning closer.

"You wouldn't believe me," Thomas said.

"Tell me anyway." Finnlay tilted his head with a smile.

Thomas smiled back, charmed by his familiar mannerisms. "All right. Mariana fixed my soul."

Finnlay's eyes darted out at the sea and landed on Thomas again. "Why?" Of course Finnlay knew who Mariana was.

Thomas hesitated. "You wouldn't believe me."

Finnlay arched an eyebrow.

Thomas smiled again. "I'm her eternal servant. When she made me immortal, she fixed my soul."

"Oh." An awkward silence passed. "I suppose that's not a solution that can be shared . . ." Finnlay said.

"No. It's not."

After another moment of silence, Finnlay said, "If your mother used witchcraft to take it away, maybe we can use witchcraft to restore it for others. What do you think?"

Thomas scratched his face, fighting against the memory of his mother's earlier confession. Finnlay seemed to know a lot about his mother, which meant she likely spent a lot of time at the rehabilitation camp. "If you think it's possible, I'll do whatever I can to help. I, however, know nothing about magic," Thomas said.

Finnlay laughed gently. "That's an easy fix. I can teach you while we figure out a way to save Fiona and Felix. Not to brag, but I know quite a lot."

"You would do that?" Thomas asked.

"Of course. I love magic, and I think you will too once you get to know it," Finnlay said, his smile growing into a grin.

"Wow, thank you," Thomas said. "I'm glad magic brought us together."

"Likewise."

After a pause, Thomas said, "I'm a little surprised you're willing to help me."

Finnlay nodded, still smiling. How could he smile through so much hardship? "Fiona trusts you enough to be your friend, so I trust you too. Also, you somehow befriended a mermaid, and you're a human man. That's pretty significant."

"It wasn't really that hard . . ." Thomas said, rubbing his neck as he looked back at the ocean. "I just treated her like a person. I mean, she *is* a person."

"You would be surprised how many men disagree with you," Finnlay said.

"Do you?" Thomas asked.

"Absolutely not."

Thomas nodded thoughtfully. "I brought you some clothes and some money," he said, slipping the bag off his shoulder and handing it to Finnlay.

Finnlay took it from him and pulled open the straps. He lifted the flap of the bag to peek inside and immediately let it fall again to look up at Thomas with wide eyes. "*Some* money? Did you mean to give me that much?"

"Yes," Thomas said. It was becoming painfully obvious exactly how wealthy his family was.

"Thank you very much," Finnlay said, looking inside the bag again.

"I think I owe you a lot more than that. You saved my fiancé's life, and you're going to teach me magic. Also my mother imprisoned you for being a witch. Sorry about that."

Finnlay looked up, wearing a smirk. "I'm happy to teach you magic. It'll be fun."

Thomas forced a smile. He knew he had to learn, but he still hadn't gotten over the mental block of doing magic. "Yeah. Fun."

Finnlay laughed. "I've never seen anyone look so tortured about having fun before. Don't worry, I'll help you unlearn the biases your upbringing has taught you. It won't be as scary as you probably think it is."

Thomas's smile turned genuine. How did Finnlay know just what to say to make him feel better? "I *am* scared, but I trust you. Fiona always spoke very highly of you."

Finnlay grinned. "Leave it to Fiona to give me the opportunity to underwhelm. I'm not as great as she might have made me seem. She's much better at magic than I am."

"That's funny. She always said the same thing about you."

Finnlay laughed again. He seemed to laugh a lot, and Thomas enjoyed his lighthearted nature. "Well then I'll let you be the judge," Finnlay said.

"*Me?* I don't know anything," Thomas said, laughing with him now.

"You will soon. Are you ready to get started?" Finnlay asked with a wink. Thomas couldn't compose himself for a moment but didn't know why. He decided he did not want to investigate the feeling and moved past it.

"Yes," he said, smiling easily as he looked out at the bright morning sun rising over the sparkling waves. Yesterday had been difficult in so many ways, but today was a new day. It was the first day of the rest of eternity.

And it was going to be great.

Acknowledgments

You keep denying it, but this book could not have happened without you, Chet. Thank you for reading it three or four times and telling me exactly how to make it better. You are cool and smart and funny and honestly should probably be listed as a co-author.

Dana, thank you for scaring me with your accurate predictions about what would happen in the next book during the beta read. You are a genius and I hope you will continue to read for me.

Yesenia, thank you for letting me bombard you with questions and thank you for being honest with your answers. You have an impressive ability to give helpful feedback while also cheering me on.

Lindsey, you are just the best. I am glad I found you to edit this book. Your changes made it much better, and I am impressed that you did it all with a broken arm. I hope you're healing well.

And last but definitely not least, thank you to everyone who read *Song of the Dark* and took the time to let me know how much you enjoyed it, whether it was a TikTok/Instagram comment, a direct message, or an entire video about how much you liked the book. I love you all and I hope you liked this book just as much as the last one.

About the Author

Bryn Suddarth lives in Arizona with their sister and their cat Rabie. They are dedicated to writing fantasy stories with queer representation and will always make sure their books are available for everyone. Sign up for their newsletter at https://www.brynsuddarth.com/ to stay informed about upcoming releases and other things.